END OF
STATE

END OF
STATE

BASED ON THE BEST-SELLING

LEFT BEHIND® SERIES

NEESA HART

TYNDALE HOUSE PUBLISHERS, INC.   WHEATON, ILLINOIS

Visit Tyndale's exciting Web site at www.tyndale.com

Discover the latest about the Left Behind series at www.leftbehind.com

Written and developed in association with Tekno Books, Green Bay, Wisconsin.

Designed by Julie Chen and Alyssa Force

Scripture quotations are taken from the *Holy Bible*, New Living Translation, copyright © 1996. Used by permission of Tyndale House Publishers, Inc., Wheaton, Illinois 60189. All rights reserved.

Published in association with the literary agency of Alive Communications, Inc., 7680 Goddard Street, Suite 200, Colorado Springs, CO 80920.

Published in association with the literary agency of Sterling Lord Literistic, New York, NY.

Library of Congress Cataloging-in-Publication Data

Hart, Neesa.
  End of state / Neesa Hart.
    p. cm.
  ISBN 0-8423-8419-7
    1. Rapture (Christian eschatology)—Fiction.   2. Church and state—Fiction.   I. Title.
PS3558.A68357E63 2004
813'.6—dc22   2003020003

Printed in the United States of America

07   06   05   04   03
5   4   3   2   1

What People Are Saying about the Left Behind Series

"This is the most successful Christian-fiction series ever."
—Publishers Weekly

"Tim LaHaye and Jerry B. Jenkins . . . are doing for Christian fiction what John Grisham did for courtroom thrillers."
—TIME

"The authors' style continues to be thoroughly captivating and keeps the reader glued to the book, wondering what will happen next. And it leaves the reader hungry for more."
—Christian Retailing

"Combines Tom Clancy–like suspense with touches of romance, high-tech flash and Biblical references."
—The New York Times

"It's not your mama's Christian fiction anymore."
—The Dallas Morning News

"Wildly popular—and highly controversial."
—USA Today

"Christian thriller. Prophecy-based fiction. Juiced-up morality tale. Call it what you like, the Left Behind series . . . now has a label its creators could never have predicted: blockbuster success."
—Entertainment Weekly

1

Alexandria, Virginia
Local Time 1:21 A.M.

Bradley Benton stared at the television for long seconds after the signal went out. His top-of-the-line satellite service had failed, leaving a snowy mess on his flat-screen TV. But that wasn't what was worrying him.

Before the set went blank, he'd been watching a basketball game. The live feed from the West Coast was just what he'd hoped for—a tough match between the Lakers and the Knicks. Then, with two seconds remaining, the score tied, and the ball in the air looking like it might just sail into the net for three points that would give the game to the Lakers, the unimaginable happened. Both Lakers forwards disappeared from the court.

Vanished.

Their uniforms and shoes fell to the floor in crumpled heaps. A couple of eerie seconds passed as the other players reacted, skidding to a stop in horrified disbelief. The unnatural, sudden silence in the capacity crowd allowed the squeak of a tennis shoe on the boards to be picked up by the broadcast mikes.

The camera zoomed in on the Lakers guard who stood staring at his teammates' uniforms where they lay on the floor in impossible silence. A slight movement near the guard's feet caught the cameraman's attention, and he zoomed to the floor where a single gold wedding ring, once worn by one of the forwards, rolled along the boards until it bumped into the guard's shoe and rattled to a stop. The noise seemed unnaturally loud in the huge arena, but it seemed to galvanize the stunned crowd.

The spectators began to murmur, then cried out in disbelief as their shock gave way to realization. As the camera had panned from the missing players to the sellout crowd in the Staples Center, Brad saw the panic level beginning to rise. The realization hit Brad that over a third of the crowd was missing as well. Empty seats in what had been a packed arena were everywhere—as clearly visible to the camera as to the crowd in the stands. Thousands of people had disappeared, leaving crumpled piles of clothing, dropped sodas and beers, spilled popcorn, and all sorts of other belongings behind.

As Brad watched, the spectators' disbelief became hysteria. What looked like a riot erupted in the stands as people began to search for their missing friends and relatives.

Then the broadcast cut off abruptly.

Brad sat and stared. Just stared. Stunned, disbelieving, shocked. He watched the static on his screen, waiting for the picture to return. After long seconds, he punched a few buttons on the remote. Nothing. Frowning, Brad punched the buttons harder. Something in his brain told him it would do no good, but an unknown reflex kept his fingers moving over the controls. He needed answers. Fast. What in the world was happening?

When the red phone on his living-room desk rang, Brad jumped. It wasn't that he was startled by the sound. The knowledge that what he had just witnessed on his now-defunct television wasn't a figment of his imagination was what jolted him. He wasn't dreaming. There could be only one reason that red phone was ringing right now. On the third ring, he lunged for the phone. As White House chief of staff, he was used to taking calls at all hours, but something told him that this summons would be worse than any he'd experienced in the two years he'd worked at the White House.

"Benton," he said into the receiver.

"Situation Room. Status Eagle," came the response.

"Understood." Too worried even to curse, Brad slammed down the receiver and reached for the cordless phone on his desk. He punched the speed dial for his home in California. The rapid busy signal indicated the phone system was too cluttered to allow his call to go through. He tried the number again. This time a tinny voice said, "Your call did not go through. Please try again later."

Nearly frantic now, Brad grabbed his jacket and his cell phone. He'd continue trying to reach his wife on his way to the White House. He prayed that whatever had happened in the Staples Center hadn't affected Christine and the kids. It couldn't have—it couldn't have happened at all, even in the arena. It was all an illusion. His family was safe. He had to believe that.

But Brad wouldn't feel better until he spoke with his wife.

And the gnawing fear in the pit of his stomach was getting worse.

★   ★   ★

Twenty minutes later, after a nightmare ride through the streets of D.C., dodging crashed cars and cabs and stunned tourists and wild-eyed government employees roving the streets, Brad was sitting in the Situation Room of the White House, located securely underground in the heart of the historic building. He rubbed the bridge of his nose with his thumb and forefinger and tried to ignore the agitated thumping of the secretary of agriculture's designer pen on her White House notepad. His eyes felt gritty and his chest hurt.

His irritation at the late hour and the command-performance meeting had given way to cold terror once he saw the streets of the city. Whatever happened out there in L.A. wasn't a dream or an isolated incident. D.C. clearly had been hit, too. Hit hard, if what Brad had seen on the way here was any indication.

Now, as reports poured into this top-level meeting from around the country, Brad was forced to accept that the phenomenon was nationwide. His assistant was still trying to reach Christine. She'd promised to send him word as soon as she got through to his wife. Brad was praying on a moment-by-moment basis, whenever he could take his attention off the meeting going on around him. *Please, Lord*, he prayed, *let them be safe*. Ruthlessly, he ignored the voice in his head that told him that since he hadn't spoken to the Almighty in years, the Almighty might not have time for him right now. Christine was a devout, loving, God-fearing woman. God would have time for Christine, Brad told himself.

Brad was jerked from his reverie when the president brought his fist down on the polished table and roared at his hastily assembled cabinet and staff. He swore as he looked sharply at Edward Leyton, the secretary of defense. "Why didn't we know this was coming, Ed?" President Gerald Fitzhugh said. "Just what has the CIA been doing for the past ten years that we didn't know this was coming?"

Leyton cleared his throat. "We don't know if we've been attacked yet, Mr. President," he said. "I think we should reserve judgment—"

"Of course we've been attacked," the president barked. "We're missing millions of people. The phone lines are down, airplanes are falling out of the sky, we can't determine who's minding the shop at 90 percent of our nuclear power facilities, and we can't get a definitive answer on who's watching our missile sites. Not to mention the collateral damage to civilians. Did you look out the windows on your way here? It's a nightmare out there. If we haven't been attacked, what in the blazes do *you* think has happened?"

No one around the large table spoke. The president surged from his chair with a dark curse and began to pace. Charley Swelder— chief policy advisor to the president and the man widely believed to have orchestrated Fitzhugh's rise to power—leaned back in his chair. The chair groaned, drawing the attention of the other occupants in the room. In his characteristically steely tone, Swelder told the secretary, "Someone dropped the ball, Ed. Whether it's your intel or the CIA, somebody dropped the ball."

Ed Leyton scowled. "I'm not taking the fall for this."

"Then find someone who is," Swelder said flatly.

The ultimatum unleashed the barely contained tension in the room. As the president looked out the window, staring at the blazing skyline, Brad glanced at the faces of the group around the table.

Three cabinet members were missing. Though the secretary of labor's and the secretary of education's absences were notable in light of the type of crisis they now faced, the absence of George Ramiro, the White House press secretary, bordered on disastrous. Already members of the White House press corps were assembling on the lawn demanding answers.

Without George, whose expert handling of the media and seemingly endless supply of patience and charm had defused several potential scandals for the Fitzhugh administration, this situation could easily become a political bloodbath. The American public was going to demand answers, and if the president couldn't give them decisively, swiftly, and coherently, every political hound in the country would go for his throat.

Brad liked George, had, in fact, discovered that George was one of the few members of the Fitzhugh staff he both trusted and respected. George had come to Washington believing Fitzhugh was a modern-day savior for the country's beleaguered social ills. Somehow, George had managed not to lose his effectiveness, his idealism, or his self-respect as his opinion of his boss had been slowly and severely battered in a storm of scandals and lackluster leadership. George had been largely instrumental in the president's decision to bring Brad to Washington as his new chief of staff. Brad knew that without George, handling the media would be tricky. The White House press corps had shown a decided distrust of President Fitzhugh, and at a time like this, they weren't going to be put off in their demand for answers.

Brad could hardly blame them.

The sight he had witnessed on the television at the Staples Center had been only the iceberg tip of a nightmare stream of impossible disappearances. From all over the country, seemingly endless reports were pouring into the White House. People were missing everywhere. Millions, maybe even hundreds of millions, of people had apparently vanished into thin air.

According to the radio news, media theories about the disappearances currently ranged from government experiments to alien invasions.

A few insiders and pundits were already floating the idea that the White House had been hiding information for some time about whatever weapon of mass destruction had caused the catastrophe.

Brad almost wished that were true. If the White House, the DOD, and U.S. intelligence had known this might happen, they'd have a plan for diffusing it or answering it.

Here at the White House, the theory most widely held seemed to be that terrorists had developed a new and shocking weapon—one that could vaporize victims at random. The United States had been engaged in a self-declared "war on terrorism" for some time now, and the stakes had continued to escalate as a handful of Middle Eastern governments had toppled. Though most of the world's leaders supported the position of the United States, they were hesitant to offer that support publicly. Difficult economic circumstances at home, sparked in large part by rapidly increasing oil prices from the OPEC nations affected most severely by the continuing conflict, made foreign involvement unpopular in most of the European and Asian nations. Even onetime close allies of the U.S. had been reserved in recent years.

It wasn't difficult to believe that one of the nations with access to billions in oil money, a vast array of weapons from the former Soviet Union, and the help of several former Soviet scientists and military strategists could have developed a weapon devastating enough to vaporize a large portion of the population.

Brad, however, had another theory, a theory that had him literally shivering as he waited, agonized, for some kind of word from his wife. Every call that came into the Sit Room announcing the disappearance of another world leader or major figure or personal friend of someone seated at the table twisted his gut into knots. His head throbbed, and he was gripping his pen so hard his fingertips were numb.

Had the disappearances been limited to the U.S., the terrorism theory might have been believable. The American people were certainly terrorized by what was going on. While the U.S. had experienced a greater number of disappearances than many other nations, there were reports of entire communities wiped out by the disaster. In China, nearly ten thousand suspected dissidents, all members of the rapidly growing evangelical movement, were missing. South America had experienced devastating losses, while many European and Middle Eastern nations remained relatively untouched.

As it became apparent that the disappearances were worldwide, Brad began to suspect that he knew what had really happened. The pieces of the puzzle were falling slowly together into a frightening image. In his mind, he could hear the echoes of Sunday mornings spent in his mother's church in his South Carolina hometown.

The Second Coming. The Rapture. End times. The prophecies of fire and brimstone the preacher had thundered from the pulpit week after week in the accent of the deep South had seemed angry and threatening to Brad's young ears. He'd learned to tune out the man's rhetoric and concentrate on flirting with the girls from his Sunday school class.

But his mother had never given up hope of persuading Brad that the end was at hand, even though he had come to believe that the end was much more likely to come in the form of a nuclear attack than a supernatural intervention by God. As Brad had risen to political prominence, his mother had urged him to remember his roots, to be a force for God in the political arena. She believed that God was preparing Brad to effect change. Brad had never made promises to his mother, but he'd allowed her to believe that his religious convictions were stronger than they were.

Certainly, on the surface, Brad looked like a textbook believer. He'd married Christine Leon, the daughter of a Baptist minister. He and his wife had three teenage children, all of whom were active in their church youth group. He was a trustee of his church in California. He'd been a deacon, a member of the pastoral search committee, and a frequent speaker at business meetings and important gatherings of the church.

Brad's only regret had been that his mother had not lived to see him become chief of staff for President Fitzhugh. She'd died the year before from a massive stroke.

Under fire from conservative religious groups after his then chief of staff had resigned at the height of a sex scandal, the president had tapped Brad for the job. Despite his personal feelings about Gerald Fitzhugh's ethics, politics, and agenda, Brad had recognized the opportunity as indispensable to his own political aspirations. His wife, his friends, and his colleagues had all encouraged him to make the move to Washington.

Now, sitting in the White House in a meeting about what was developing into the darkest hour in the history of the United States—perhaps even the world—Brad wished he could consult his mother for her wisdom. He knew precisely what she'd say. He knew what his wife, Christine, would say. Increasingly, as the evidence mounted, Brad began to believe that his conversation with Christine before the basketball game tonight might well have been his last with her.

If his suspicions were correct, no weapon had caused this disaster. This had not been an invasion, an alien abduction, a natural disaster, a hostile strike by a terrorist nation, a government experiment gone wrong, or any of the dozens of possible causes being offered around the table by the most powerful men and women in the United States.

No, this was the stuff that a small-town Southern preacher had prophesied and Brad had rejected.

God had raptured His church.

He had left the unbelievers behind in a world now ruled by evil.

The time of tribulation was at hand.

Brad broke out in a cold sweat as he considered the implications. Though he couldn't remember precisely what all the prophecies were, he did recall predictions of death, pestilence, famines, and a host of other horrors that were supposed to follow in the wake of the Rapture. He'd generally tuned out sermons on the topic, choosing instead to believe the prophecies were not to be taken literally.

Now, he wasn't so sure.

As the president paced the large room, he was demanding that someone develop a reasonable media response. No matter what had caused the disappearances, Fitzhugh wasn't going to take responsibility for it—especially not with a midterm election looming and control of both houses of Congress at stake.

Brad looked at the haggard and drawn faces of his colleagues and made a rapid decision: under no circumstances could he afford to express his belief that what had happened tonight was a supernatural event. Something done by the hand of God. At best, he'd be ridiculed. At worst, Fitzhugh would use the pretense of an immensely unpopular theory as an excuse to exclude Brad from the decision-making processes in the days to come.

And Brad had the unshakable belief that the events of this night were only the beginning of something much worse.

The Rapture had come, and Bradley Benton and everyone in this room had been left behind to face the Tribulation.

God help us all. . . .

2

Crystal City, Virginia
Local Time 2:30 A.M.

The Reverend Marcus Dumont stared out the plate-glass window of the conference room. Even in the darkness, the devastation in the nation's capital was obvious. Everywhere the dull glow of red and blue emergency lights cut through a haze of smoke and debris that hung in the air obscuring the thousands of architectural lights that illuminated the city's familiar landmarks. The din of sirens and evacuation horns carried across the Potomac to the relative quiet of Marcus's eleventh-story office suite where he stood, watching the scene unfold.

The debris of several airliners that had been en route to or from Washington's Reagan National Airport extended from the dark waters in a tangled mass of twisted metal. Marcus could make out the shapes of human corpses floating beside the fuselages.

Not since September 11, 2001, had so many fighter jets and military and civilian emergency aircraft cluttered Washington's pristine skyline. From the spires of the National Cathedral to the dome of the U.S. Capitol, Marcus had a panoramic view of the disaster's aftermath.

At the Pentagon, every office was lit despite the late hour, and all around him in the large Crystal City business complex, terror and confusion reigned. He could see the White House in the distance, and there the lights burned also. It was an anomaly these days, since the first lady had demanded that the outside lights be shut off and the press banished from the White House lawn at 10 P.M. each night. But the president and the staff were up—as they would be, Marcus knew, for the next few days. He'd escaped here to the conference room of New Covenant Evangelical Ministries to get away from the incessant ringing of the telephone, the sounds of weeping and horror that carried up and down the halls of the office building, and the guilt.

Mostly, the guilt.

Because Marcus had the answers. He'd had them since he'd received the call at 1:30 A.M. from his frantic media director.

The call had come as no surprise. Marcus had been summoned into the office in the small hours of the morning many times. Through the years, there had been any number of national and international crises that demanded prayer support. He'd gotten phone calls from U.S. presidents, asking for wisdom and counsel. He'd sat in emergency meetings with his staff to discuss a nonfavorable story about their organization that would break in the morning's papers. He'd held prayer vigils for faithful supporters whose lives were slowly ebbing away.

Then, Marcus had admitted to no one but himself, his heart hadn't been in the fervent prayers he'd led for the healing hand of God. The death of a wealthy saint usually meant financial health for New Covenant. Marcus had an excellent economic development team that worked regularly with high-dollar donors to ensure New Covenant's place in their estate planning.

Perhaps that's why the feeling of guilt he now felt seemed to overshadow any sense of shock at what he was seeing. Nearly everyone was asking the same questions: what had happened an hour ago when nearly a third of the world's population had mysteriously and suddenly vanished? Was it an attack? Had their enemies developed a new and devastating weapon? Who was left and who was missing and why? Where were the missing people? What could be done to get them back?

While everyone else was asking those questions, Marcus knew, *knew* without any doubt or hesitation, that as horrible as this all seemed right now, it was only the beginning.

God had gathered His faithful. Christians around the globe had vanished, swept up in a massive and dramatic fulfillment of the Lord's promised gathering of His people. Leaving behind all who had rejected the truth of Jesus Christ, the Christians had been taken to their heavenly reward, and the horrible events of the Tribulation had begun.

Marcus had known the prophecies by heart. He had preached them for years. He had a fistful of degrees from Bible colleges and seminaries to prove his expertise. He had a multimillion-dollar evangelical empire with daily broadcasts around the globe and financial supporters among the world's most rich and powerful. He was respected, even revered, in some circles. He'd received national and international awards for his humanitarian efforts.

But he was a fraud.

Marcus scrubbed a hand over his face and thought wearily of what the next few weeks would bring. He couldn't allow himself to think beyond that. Even now, he had the few of his employees and advisors he'd been able to reach trying to determine how many members of his staff were missing. Marcus figured the majority were gone. Though he himself had rejected the truth of Christ, he'd preached it faithfully for years. Most of his organization and supporters were genuine believers who would have been sorely disillusioned to discover that Marcus had turned his back on God.

The door to the conference room burst open. Reflected in the glass, Marcus saw his media director, Isack Moore, looking haggard and shaken, rush in. "We've reached a few people, Marcus, but not many. The phones are a mess. It takes fifteen or twenty tries to get an outside line. I have one of the interns downstairs working the switchboard, but we're not getting anywhere. When we do get through, we get answering machines."

"I suspected that," Marcus said, turning his back to the window to face the young man. "How many have we found?"

"I finally got through to Theo. He's on his way in."

That didn't surprise Marcus. He'd hired Theopolus Carter, a young legal genius out of Harvard, to keep New Covenant out of hot water. Theo's personal religious convictions had never been an issue in hiring him—only his credentials. Marcus nodded, thoughtful. "What about support staff?"

"No one." Isack had been Marcus's media director for eight years, and Marcus had never seen the man rattled—not even when they'd faced federal mail-fraud charges several years ago. Now, however, Isack looked close to a meltdown. "Reports are coming in from around the country. This is—" he choked—"this is at least nationwide. Maybe worldwide. I've got the television on downstairs, but the signal keeps going in and out. I haven't been able to get on the Internet."

"I'm not surprised."

"I think we've been attacked." Isack shuddered. "I never thought—" He shook his head. "Marcus, this is awful."

Isack, Marcus realized, had not yet begun to grasp the magnitude of the situation. If Marcus's suspicions were correct, soon they'd have reports of hundreds of millions of people missing from the face of the earth. The scope of the disaster unfolding before them was almost unfathomable. At any moment, Marcus expected failures in the power grid, the communications systems, and the utilities. Here on the East Coast, where the late hour meant that many had slept through the event, the scope of the disaster was only now becoming apparent. But on the West Coast and around the globe, only God knew what had happened as the people left behind witnessed the disappearances.

"What are we going to do?" Isack asked. "What do you want us to do?"

Wearily, Marcus realized the enormous burden he was about to shoulder. As they had in the past, frightened and desperate people would begin to turn to him for counsel. Most of his ministerial colleagues, he knew, were gone, leaving behind only a handful of nonbelieving clergy to guide the world through this devastation. At times like this, it was normal for people to turn to God and the church for answers. Only now God had taken the true church, leaving nothing but a broken facade in its place.

How was he supposed to tell the inevitable truth seekers that he had known the truth? that he'd chosen to reject it, even while he urged them to receive it themselves? Once respected and revered, he would soon be exposed as the deceiver and fraud that he really was. Sadly, he was past the point of caring. But with Isack standing in front of him, his eyes pleading for hope and promise that Marcus simply couldn't give him, Marcus drew on his private reserve of strength and dignity. "This is not the time to fall apart," he reminded Isack. "We've got a lot of rough days ahead."

Isack's eyes filled with tears. "I know. I know, but . . . " His voice trailed off, his gaze filled with silent condemnation. "My wife. My children—" He broke off with a sob.

"Gone?" Marcus guessed.

Isack nodded as he wiped his eyes with the back of his sleeve. "I was reading the press briefing for tomorrow. *The Tonight Show* had just gone off. Lori was in the bed next to me sleeping." Isack shook his head. "I heard the sheets rustle. I . . . I thought she'd rolled over." His eyes widened with remembered terror. "When I finally glanced at her, she was gone." Isack shuddered at the memory. "My kids, too, Marcus. Everyone."

"I'm sorry, Isack," Marcus said. Isack and his wife had three children. "Lori was a godly woman."

"I've lost everything. Everything that matters."

"I know. I can't imagine the pain you must be in."

Isack studied him for long moments. Finally, he pinned Marcus with a hard look. "You knew, didn't you?" he asked quietly.

Marcus folded his arms across his chest. "That you weren't a believer?"

Isack dropped his gaze and nodded. "Yes." His voice was raspy.

"I didn't hire you because of your faith, Isack," Marcus stated. "I hired you because you were the best man for the job."

A loud explosion sounded in the distance, causing the building to rumble and the glass to shake. The lights flickered, plunging the room into momentary darkness. Seconds passed before the building's emergency generator kicked on, powering a limited number of the overhead fixtures. Marcus glanced out the window. "We lost the power grid," he said unnecessarily.

Isack met his gaze in the window, his expression angry. "Did you know this was going to happen?"

Marcus sighed. "I know what the Bible says." He turned to face Isack. "You know it, too. I preached it."

"You didn't make it sound urgent," Isack pointed out. "You didn't believe it. Why should I?"

Marcus had no answer for that, only a dreadful feeling that whatever he'd believed or hadn't, it was now too late.

"All these years . . ." Isack's voice dipped to a whisper. "All those people. You didn't believe any of it."

Marcus thought that over. That wasn't precisely true, he supposed. He believed in God. He believed that God had allowed his father to walk out and leave his mother to raise Marcus and his sisters. He believed that God had allowed the fire that had killed everyone in his family, leaving only a young Marcus behind to survive in a fault-filled foster system. He believed that God had denied his wife the children she'd prayed for so fervently. He believed that God had allowed his wife, riddled with cancer and twisted in pain, to die a slow and horrible death, leaving Marcus utterly alone.

And he believed that God was capable of allowing the massive destruction and terror now unfolding in the world. Hadn't God threatened in the Scriptures to do just that? Hadn't He sent prophets to rain down fire and condemnation against the unholy? Hadn't those threats been the reason Marcus had shaken his fist in rebellion and anger at a God who allowed righteous men to suffer while wicked men prospered?

He wasn't about to discuss these things with Isack, who looked perilously close to falling to pieces. Marcus was adept at many things, and one of them was offering comfort in times of great strife.

He had a five-inch stack of letters from various heads of state to prove his prowess at bringing calm to the middle of chaos. He crossed the room and laid a hand on Isack's shoulder. "What's done is done," he told the younger man. "We can't always understand the ways of God. What matters now is what we do with it."

"Do you believe this is the judgment of God?" Isack demanded.

"I believe," Marcus said carefully, "that people are going to need answers. Some of them are going to turn to us to provide them."

"Did you know you are a fraud?" Isack shot back, his voice angry.

Marcus hesitated, then nodded. "Yes," he admitted. "I did."

Isack's short laugh was harsh. "I thought I was the only one." He flung the papers in his hand onto the conference table. In the dim lighting, the angles of his face made him look years older. "I used to think I just had doubts, that it was natural."

Marcus shook his head. "I don't think anyone can have a relationship with Christ and not be sure of it."

"That's how you knew?"

"Yes," Marcus said.

"All that praying. Those meetings where we talked about what God was doing in our lives. The rhetoric. The books. The sermons. You didn't mean any of it."

"I meant every word," Marcus assured him. "I meant that God is a terrible, just, and righteous judge who will condemn the wicked and punish the ungodly."

"Then why are you here?" Isack shot back.

" 'Do you still think it's enough just to believe that there is one God?' " Marcus quoted from the second chapter of James. " 'Well, even the demons believe this, and they tremble in terror!' " He shrugged. "How often did you hear me preach that?"

Isack's face was a mask of pain and disillusionment. Marcus wished he could offer him hope. "Too many times to count," Isack admitted.

"Then I'm sorry I wasn't more convincing."

Isack shook his head. "I can't reach my parents or my sisters or my in-laws. I can't get through on the phones."

Or, Marcus thought, there was no family to reach. Another explosion sent tremors through the building. Marcus drew a steadying breath and turned to survey the view from the window once more. "Keep trying," he told Isack. "And let me know when Theo gets here."

3

Mariette Arnold frowned at the clock on her bedside table as she reached for the ringing telephone. She'd called it a night a little after ten o'clock, exhausted after a week of organizing flood relief from a major storm system that had dumped twenty inches of rain on an already sodden Southeast.

The clock on her nightstand blinked midnight—a sure sign that the power had been off at least once tonight. "Yes," she said into the receiver.

"Mariette, it's David!"

David Liu, Mariette's assistant at FEMA, was probably the only person in this world more tired than she was. As the assistant director of the Federal Emergency Management Agency, Mariette was in charge of the agency's readiness, response, and recovery activities. She had chosen her personal assistant carefully. She'd wanted someone who shared her vision for bringing creative solutions to the sea of red tape that often limited the agency's effectiveness. Her boss, a recent presidential appointee, had shown limited effectiveness as a manager and a problem solver. Mariette had learned to rely heavily on David for assistance and insight. He'd been invaluable during the last week they'd spent sorting through the mess in North and South Carolina.

Mariette knew that David would not have called her had there not been an emergency of unimaginable proportions looming somewhere, ready to destroy the innocent and disturb her peace. "David," she said, "please don't tell me we've got another flood." Heavy rains in the Midwest and a major spring thaw up north were causing forecasters to speculate that the Mississippi River could flood. Despite the additional precautions the Corps of Engineers and state governments had taken following a memorable flood in 1993, many of the rural areas along the river still remained largely unprotected.

Flood cleanup and recovery was one of the most grueling tasks disaster agents faced, and Mariette wasn't emotionally or physically prepared to deal with another deluge so soon on the heels of her experience in the Carolinas.

Before she'd crawled into her bed, she had been told that, for the time being at least, the upstream levees were holding and that the flood damage might be considerably less dramatic than anticipated. When she'd gone to bed, it was with the comfortable conviction that the prospects for immediate disaster were limited.

"Not a flood. Worse," David told her. "You don't know, do you?"

Oh no . . . Mariette gathered the covers to her chest. This couldn't be good. "Know what?"

"Mariette, a third of the population has just disappeared."

"The population?" she asked, fighting her way through the last lingering layers of sleep. "What population?"

"The *U.S.* population," David replied. "Maybe the world population. We don't know yet. They just disappeared. Vanished into thin air."

Mariette frowned, struggling to make sense of David's explanation. A sense of disbelief rolled through her. "David, are you sure you're okay? I know you've been working long hours, but—"

"Listen to me, Mariette. I've been trying to reach you for nearly two hours, but most of the phone systems are down. Communications are a mess, and power grids are out all over the country. No one has a handle yet on what's going on, but apparently millions of people have disappeared into thin air. Really."

"David—"

"It's true," he insisted. "So far, nobody's got answers, but we're getting a few reports of people who actually saw their friends and families vanish."

Mariette shuddered as a sudden chill tripped down her spine. "Vanished? You're sure?"

"They disappeared right out of their clothes. The media's got lots of video of it happening—they're airing the tapes in super slow motion. All you see on the tapes is a person vanishing and leaving behind their clothes and jewelry and stuff."

Mariette rubbed her eyes. "You're kidding."

"I wish. It's the oddest thing to watch. In fact, it's the scariest thing I've ever seen."

"But, David—"

"You should take a look if your local station or cable channel's working. Most of them aren't. But the local channel was broadcasting earlier before the power grid went out. Somebody'd be standing there; then they'd disappear and whatever they were wearing would just flutter to the ground. It looks like some kind of movie special effect. But the disappearances are real enough. People are in a panic."

"I can see why." Though her sense that this couldn't be happening seemed to be keeping her emotions at bay right now.

"Yeah," David said. "It's creepy. And what's worse is the major-league havoc it's causing. There are planes down all over the world. The highways are one continuous pile of wrecked cars and trucks. Already we know about five major oil spills and two chemical tankers that are leaking thousands of tons of toxins off the Atlantic Coast. And I don't even want to talk about the train derailments. Since a lot of the communication grid is down, this is probably just the beginning of our problems."

Wide awake now, Mariette swung her feet off the bed and hurried to her window. Her suburban neighborhood seemed eerily quiet. But then in the distance she heard the wail of emergency sirens through the darkness. It sounded bad out there.

Her job—not to mention many people's lives—depended on her ability to think clearly in an emergency. She had to keep it together, even if it meant keeping her emotions under control until she had the leisure to deal with them. Putting a lid on her fears, she said, "Where's Musselman?" Bernie Musselman was the director of FEMA and a first-class jerk.

"At the White House. Emergency meeting in the Sit Room."

"Do they think it's an attack?"

"I don't know. They haven't issued a statement yet—or if they have, the communications system is such a wreck, no one knows," David told her. "But I'm sure it's a disaster, and we're going to have to handle it. You'd better get in here when you can. We've got a mess on our hands."

"I can be there in twenty minutes," she said.

"I wouldn't count on that," David said. "The Beltway looks like the leftovers from a demolition derby, the Metro's not running, and with all the signal outages the side roads are almost impassable."

Mariette was already reaching for her clothes. "I'll get there, David," she assured him. "Start putting together a team. We'll need rescue workers, claims agents, field-workers, surveyors, chemical specialists. . . . You know the drill. Now, what am I forgetting?" Propping the phone against her shoulder, she hopped on one foot as she pulled her jeans on.

"I've already started lining up the teams," David said, "but it's not pretty. I'm trying to get through to your contacts at Homeland Security, Interior, and Energy now. I've got calls out, but the phones are ridiculous. It's taking me twenty tries just to get an outside line. And even when I can get through, almost nobody's answering."

Mariette shrugged on a sweatshirt. "What about the emergency agency lines?" she probed. "Have you tried them? Times like this are what they're made for." Those dedicated lines were reserved for government use during epic disasters. In theory, the system had been built to withstand a nuclear attack. "Did you activate the emergency broadcast system?"

"I tried. Nothing," David told her. "The emergency lines are down, too. I've got Manny working now trying to figure out what's going on. It's like the entire communications grid is too overwhelmed to function."

Mariette pulled on her left tennis shoe and considered the implications of what David was telling her. How many employees, she wondered, would she find missing? And how difficult were relief efforts going to be if her agency was decimated and her people were gone?

Evidently, the worst disaster in history had just struck the United States. Since her boss couldn't be counted on for much more than panic and mayhem, Mariette was in charge of the cleanup. Okay—she would deal with it. She had to. She slipped on her other shoe. "All right. I'll get there when I can," she told her assistant. "Keep trying the phones. Do what you can to hold down the fort until I can get there."

"This is bad, Mariette. Better prepare yourself for the worst. You won't be disappointed."

"Thanks. I'll keep it in mind." Mariette ended the call.

She waited for a dial tone. Nothing. She put the useless chunk of plastic back in the cradle; then she retrieved her cell phone and hit speed dial. Though she knew she probably wouldn't be able to get through, she was worried about her son, Randal. He was a senior at Penn State, where he was completing his degree in media and digital communications. Mariette couldn't imagine that whatever had caused this nightmare would have reached the cloistered environs of State College, Pennsylvania, but she wanted to hear his voice, make sure he was all right.

While she was waiting for the call to go through, she reached for the remote for the television in her room. The cable must be out, she decided, when she found nothing but snow and lines on all channels.

"We can put a man on the moon, but we can't get the emergency broadcast system to function when we need it." She shut the TV off in disgust.

She flicked on the radio but again found nothing but static. Maybe it was better, she thought, if she didn't know the true extent of the problem just yet. When things were really bad, ignorance had its uses. What she didn't know wouldn't make her run back to her bed and hide under the covers.

Mariette headed downstairs and pulled a jacket from the hall closet. Despite the warmer spring temperatures Washington was enjoying these days, the nights still had a winter bite. While she was at it, she snagged a spare flashlight and put it in the jacket's pocket, along with her cell phone. From the kitchen she grabbed a bag and filled it with bottled water, fruit, and energy bars.

She worked for FEMA. She wasn't going to head out into an emergency unprepared. It looked bad if she did that. A bag of supplies was always a good idea in a disaster.

As she pulled open the door and headed for her car, she realized that the phone in her pocket still hadn't connected. She pulled it out after she settled the bag of groceries in the backseat. The "Wait for Service" message was still flashing on her cell phone's color screen.

Frustrated, Mariette tried dialing the number again. Nothing . . . Cursing, she set the phone to auto redial and put it back in her pocket. It would beep when her call connected.

As she opened the door of the government-issue sedan she'd left parked in her driveway the night before, she noticed that one of her neighbors' cars was wrapped around a tree near their driveway, its engine still steaming in the cold air. It looked like the kind of crash caused by somebody who'd had too much to drink, but she knew for a fact that her neighbor never drank anything alcoholic. He and his family were churchgoing Baptists who wouldn't touch anything stronger than root beer.

There were no emergency vehicles on the site. Hadn't anyone called in the wreck? Worse, was somebody still trapped in that car?

With a sense of dread, Mariette hurried across the street to check. The family was a nice middle-aged couple with two teenage daughters and a son in the navy. Prepared for the worst, she pressed her face to the window in the darkness, using her flashlight to peer into the vehicle. Three sets of clothing lay in crumpled piles on the leather seats. In the driver's seat she could make out a pair of khaki pants, a button-down white dress shirt, and a tweed sport coat. A pair of polished loafers sat on the floorboard, one propped on the brake pedal, trailing an empty argyle sock. The direction of the steering wheel and the front tires suggested that the car had been turning into the driveway when the driver somehow lost control. In the backseat, two smaller sets of jeans and sweatshirts indicated that the two girls had been there. The clothes were tangled with a fleece blanket, suggesting that the girls had been cuddled together asleep.

Three of her neighbors were clearly among the missing.

Mariette felt a sense of horror as she realized that she was seeing in microcosm what people were experiencing all around the globe.

Shuddering, she went back to her house and got a small digital camera, one she had taken with her to the disaster sites in North and South Carolina. She snapped hasty pictures of the crash scene and the car's interior, not quite sure why she felt the need, then headed for her car.

When she tried to call in the crash, her cell phone was again useless. *Priorities . . .* she reminded herself. *Find my son. Get to work.* She reset her cell phone to auto-dial Randal until somebody picked up, and got in her car.

Too worried to think straight, she backed out of the driveway and headed to work. The thought of what might await her there was giving her chills. If nothing else, the stark scene at her neighbor's driveway had given her a renewed sense of urgency.

She checked the cell phone. It had just dialed Randal's number again. Nothing. Her heart pounded, and she prayed that her baby was all right. Never mind that he was a resourceful young man who'd been living away from home since he started college. He was her child, and she needed to hear his voice like she'd never needed anything in her life.

As she headed out of her neighborhood and into the chaos of the main streets, she wondered if she should call her ex-husband. As quickly as the thought occurred to her, Mariette dismissed it. Whatever this disaster held in store for her, whatever had caused it, Senator Max Arnold, her philandering ex-husband and the chairman of the U.S. Senate Armed Services Committee, would already be in it up to his no-good, cheating neck.

She would save her energy for those she loved and for those who truly deserved her help.

4

Washington, D.C.
The White House
Local Time 3:20 A.M.

Brad rubbed the grittiness from his eyes with his thumb and forefinger. His gaze strayed to his watch for the countless time in the last few hours. It was midnight in California. Why hadn't his assistant been able to reach Christine and the kids yet? Even if they'd gone out, they'd surely be home by now.

"Benton ought to know," Charley Swelder was saying.

At the sound of his name, Brad tuned back in to the conversation. "Know what?"

Swelder gave him a chilling look. "You could at least pretend you're paying attention, Benton."

Why? Brad wanted to ask. It had been made quite clear to him from his first day on the job that he was here for window dressing. His opinions were neither solicited nor welcomed. He levelly met the other man's gaze. "Know what?" he asked again.

Robert Filstein, the secretary for Homeland Security, dropped his fountain pen on his legal pad. "If we should put together some kind of religious council on this." He looked around the room. "We're already getting reports of people claiming this was an act of God. I think it would be politically wise if we pulled several ministers together on a task force to advise us."

"Or," Swelder bit out, "it would look like we were pandering to the general hysteria of the public." His fingers curled into a tight fist. "I can't see that there are any other options that need exploring. We've been attacked."

The president turned from the window. "And all the American people want to know is what we're going to do about it."

A tense silence gripped the room. Brad gingerly rubbed the back of his neck, working the tension knot he'd had since the red telephone on his desk rang. "I think Bob is right," he said, shooting a quick look at the secretary for Homeland Security. Though Brad suspected that whatever spiritual leaders they could assemble would have little hope to offer. The Christians were gone. Whoever was left among clergy and religious scholars weren't going to be able to explain why the God they hadn't followed had just unleashed a plan they'd never believed. Nonetheless, he had no doubt that people who were now grieving, terrified, and in shock would want answers from the church. "We've got a panic situation on our hands. People are going to naturally look to the church for answers."

"That's just like you, Benton," Charley shot back. "Figures we could count on the extremist view from our representative for the religious right."

Brad didn't respond.

Bob Filstein leaped to his defense. He gave the president an angry look. "I'm getting a little weary," he told Fitzhugh, "of this administration being run out of the policy advisor's office." He quickly glanced at the other cabinet members in the room.

Many, Brad noted, had suddenly busied themselves making copious notes in order to avoid eye contact. Resentment, he knew, had been building about Charley Swelder's prominence in administration decisions. Several cabinet members and their deputies had complained to Brad. He'd recommended they take it up with Fitzhugh. Now, he probably would have told them, was probably not the best time.

President Fitzhugh looked slightly flustered. Charley Swelder appeared on the verge of a major meltdown.

Bob Filstein picked up his discarded pen and leaned back in his chair. "I was under the impression," he continued, his tone quiet but direct, "that the policy advisor was supposed to *advise* on policy—not *make* policy."

Charley came out of his chair. "Listen, you little—"

The president brought a hand down on Charley's shoulder, cutting off the counterattack. "Sit down, Charley."

For a moment, Brad thought Swelder was going to refuse. He gave the president an enraged look, then turned back to Filstein. He kept a contemptuous gaze trained on the secretary but sank back into his chair.

Fitzhugh gave his shoulder a slight squeeze before turning back to the group. He looked at Bob. "It's obvious you've got some frustrations with the way we've been doing some things. Once we get through this, I'd really like to sit down with you and see if we can come up with a plan to alleviate some of that."

Thus speaks the politician, Brad thought cynically.

"Right now, though," Fitzhugh continued as he looked around the group, "I think we can all agree that what we need is unity."

The tension level in the room seemed to drop several degrees. Fitzhugh glanced at Brad. "Benton—since you and Bob are in accord about this religious council thing, why don't you two have your people pursue it? We'll see if it's feasible or not." The president rubbed his hands together and took his seat at the head of the table. "Now, let's talk about how we're going to handle this." He glanced at the secretary of state. "Have we heard from Moscow yet?"

Crystal City, Virginia
Local Time 3:45 A.M.

Marcus pulled himself from his reverie and headed down the hall of his expansive suite of offices. Over the past two hours, several members of the ministry staff had made their way into the office. In their confusion and terror, they'd naturally turned to the office

as a haven. They'd turned, he thought grimly, to him, wanting answers and hope.

His gut twisted when he admitted that he could provide the former but not the latter—at least, not the kind of hope they wanted.
Their families and friends were not returning. There was no morning after for this crisis; no pat happy ending where the sun would
shine again and life would return to normal. No, he knew, life
would never return to normal. In fact, having studied the Scriptures,
he could emphatically say that what they'd faced tonight was only
the beginning of the horrors to come.

He heard the sounds of weeping, anger, and confusion traveling
along the art-lined hallways. He found the strength to set aside the
guilt that was gnawing at him and face the handful of people gathered there who had devoted their lives and careers to building his
ministry. Many of them had sacrificed better job opportunities and
higher salaries. Most had worked countless unpaid hours on his behalf. All had looked to him for spiritual guidance. Their presence
meant they'd busied themselves doing God's work but had never
trusted God's Son for their salvation.

Like Mary and Martha, he mused, recalling the passage from the
book of Luke. While Martha had toiled over the meal she was preparing to serve Jesus, her sister Mary sat at His feet and listened to
Him teach. Resentful, Martha had demanded that Jesus instruct
Mary to help her. He had responded by saying, "There is really only
one thing worth being concerned about. Mary has discovered it—
and I won't take it away from her."

How true that was, Marcus now thought. These people had busied themselves, like Martha, and missed that the only thing worth
worrying about was their relationship with the Lord. He sent up a
quick prayer for mercy as he braced himself to face them. Though he
sorely wanted to flee, to hide from the inquisition he was about to
face, he admitted that he'd failed them too many times in the past.
They'd come like sheep to the shepherd—hurting, lost, confused.
He owed them at least the comfort and leadership he'd given so
many others during their times of grief. Marcus had been called by

heads of state to attend funerals, had led the nation in prayer during countless memorial services during times of tragedy. But nothing had required the courage he now needed to face his staff.

He took a deep breath and pushed open the glass door that separated his executive suite from the large area that housed most of the offices. It struck him, suddenly, in the same way that a person can pass a certain landmark or look at a picture innumerable times before really noticing it, that his office, with its plush carpet and mahogany hand-built furniture, was roughly the same size as this cramped space where so many people toiled at his bequest. Tiny cubicles separated some desks, while others were pushed back-to-back and side-to-side throughout the tight space. The furniture looked worn and shabby, the computers cramped into the space.

Isack, along with six others, stood clustered around a young woman Marcus recognized as one of the bookkeepers. She was crying hysterically into a handkerchief while her colleagues stood numbly by, unable to respond when they, too, were in the grip of grief.

"It was my baby," she wailed. "I was nursing my baby and he vanished. He's just gone. Him and my husband. They're gone."

Isack seemed to sense Marcus's presence. He looked up, his face a mask of pain. "I lost my kids, too," he told the young woman, his gaze fixed on Marcus. Marcus saw the anger and resentment in the younger man's face. "We'll get through this, Velma."

Velma mopped at her eyes. "No, no. We waited so long. My husband and I—we've tried to get pregnant for years. When it finally happened . . ." Her voice broke and she buried her face in her hands.

A large woman Marcus didn't recognize placed her ample hand on Velma's shoulder. "God will sustain you, child. You've got to have faith in that."

Isack raised an eyebrow.

Marcus cringed but forced himself to approach the small group. As they sensed his presence, he felt the familiar quiet and reverence fall on them that he generally experienced in the presence of his staff. There was a natural deference they afforded him. He spoke first. He led the discussion. He always had the final word. No one seemed to expect or demand that it should be any different. Though he'd never demanded the treatment, he'd never had to. It came naturally, as if his presence and stature inspired the deferral. Until tonight, Marcus had considered the respectful admiration of his staff as his due and his right as their leader and their pastor. Now it made him painfully aware of his failures and deceit. The knife of guilt twisted again, forcing a grimace to his lips.

Only Velma, too consumed with her grief, failed to look at him. The other members of the group moved back from her huddled, sobbing figure, allowing Marcus to approach her. He placed both hands on her shoulders, turned his face to God, and prayed silently for several seconds. He remembered how his own beloved wife—perhaps the only person Marcus had ever loved more than himself—had wept bitter tears over her inability to conceive a child. Though Marcus had never confessed it to her, he'd been relieved. He had difficulty picturing himself as a father. But his wife had mourned, often in silence, often, he knew, thinking he was unaware or oblivious to the pain it caused her.

Now he could only imagine what Velma must feel. The horror of holding her long-awaited and cherished baby in her arms, cradling him for the intimacy of feeding, and then to have the weight and warmth simply disappear from the blanket. How many seconds, he wondered, had she clutched the empty cotton blanket in agony and disbelief before calling out in horror to a husband who could no longer answer? He could picture her running frantically through the house calling his name, clutching at her robe, clinging in desperation to the cotton blanket. The starkness of the image made him shudder.

He struggled with the tightness in his throat and chest as unshed tears threatened to overwhelm him. Though he knew from the prophecies and Scriptures that in the coming weeks and months of the Tribulation, Velma would rejoice that her husband and son were with the Lord and not here to experience the tragedy of it all, that would give her little comfort now.

Jesus Himself had said on the night of His death, "Don't weep for Me, but weep for yourselves and for your children. For the days are coming when they will say, 'Fortunate indeed are the women who are childless, the wombs that have not borne a child and the breasts that have never nursed.' People will beg the mountains to fall on them and the hills to bury them."

Velma, as if the burden suddenly became more than she could physically bear, doubled over in her chair, collapsing across her knees with a heavy sob. "Oh, dear God," she wailed. "Why? Why?"

Marcus remembered making the same demand, tearfully and angrily asking the same question when his wife had died. God had not answered then, and he didn't expect Him to answer now. Marcus placed one hand on Velma's head and raised his face to heaven. "Almighty God," he finally said, his voice a hushed whisper even as he wondered if the Almighty had turned His back on him. Would God listen to him now? "If ever You have heard the prayers of unworthy children, then please hear them tonight. Grant us strength as we grieve for our losses."

"Yes, Lord," an older woman whispered.

"Grant us wisdom," Marcus continued, his voice breaking slightly, "to see Your hand."

"Show us," another staff member declared.

"And grant us courage to seek Your truth." Marcus added a silent plea of his own that God would have mercy on this small flock that he'd failed to tend, that they should not suffer undue hardship because the man they'd followed had misled them. "Amen," he finally said. He didn't dare add his usual pious tag, saying that he was "asking all these things in the holy and precious name of Jesus that His will might be accomplished on earth." God might, he suspected, and very well should, strike him dumb for making that statement now.

Marcus raised his head and looked around the small group. Isack was looking at him angrily, accusingly, his expression filled with contempt. The young man who had previously never even dared call him anything but Reverend Dumont now watched him in suspicion. Marcus accepted it as his due. Isack needed a focus for his grief and despair, someone to blame for his suffering. Unwilling and unable to blame God, he turned to the man he saw as God's representative here

on earth. He was, Marcus supposed, as good a target as Isack was going to get. At least tonight.

Marcus drew a deep breath. "I have something to share with you
all. I'd appreciate it if you'd join me in the chapel in fifteen minutes."

"What's happening, Marcus?" one of the young men insisted.
"Do you think we've really been attacked?"

Marcus recognized him as a member of Theo Carter's legal team.
"No," he said, "I do not believe that we've been attacked."

"Marcus thinks we've missed the Rapture," Isack said shortly.

Marcus heard the stunned gasps and muttered disbelief of the
group. The older woman vigorously shook her head. "That's not
true. That can't be true. I've been in church my whole life."

"So have I," another man added. "My mother raised me in a decent Christian household."

"But it wasn't enough," Isack said, his gaze boring into Marcus.
"Was it?"

Marcus hesitated, then slowly shook his head. "If you'll join me
in the chapel. I'll explain what I believe to be true."

"But there's no hope," the legal assistant said. "If what you say is
true, there's no hope."

"There's always hope," Marcus assured him. "God has not de-
serted us."

Velma looked up, her eyes puffy and red. "I wouldn't be so sure. I
wouldn't be so sure at all."

★　★　★

Washington, D.C.
Capitol Beltway, Outer Loop
Local Time 4:00 A.M.

Mariette punched the buttons on her cell phone with mounting
frustration. She still had not been able to reach Randal. Fearing that
the auto redial was not working, she'd taken to dialing the call man-
ually. She continued to receive an error signal or a prerecorded an-

nouncement that the network was too busy to complete the call. Scared and anxious for the welfare of her only son, she angrily punched in the number again. Her fingers shook so much she misdialed it twice. Though the voice of reason told her that Randal was smart, self-sufficient, and, as her son, had better survival training than probably 99 percent of the kids his age, she knew the desperation in her soul wouldn't quiet until she spoke to him.

The driver in front of her slammed on his brakes, forcing Mariette to follow suit. She brought her palm down hard on the steering wheel. The resulting jolt that traveled up her arm and into her shoulder made her wince. "Come on," she muttered as the traffic crawled past yet another wreck, "come on." *Stay calm,* she told herself in a silent mantra. *Stay calm. Stay calm.* She needed her wits, of that she had no doubt.

As she negotiated her way through the crush of traffic, she finally got her phone to dial out. When she heard ringing, hope sprang into her heart. "Randal—," she said. Then the ringing stopped. Only silence greeted her desperate call. "Randal," she said louder.

A prerecorded voice, sounding painfully polite and harshly robotic, came on the line to apologize that the call had not gone through. "Due to heavier than normal call volume," the voice added, "your service provider is unable to complete your call at this time. Please try again later."

Mariette groaned. In fact, she barely resisted the urge to hurl the phone across the car in frustration.

"Stay calm," she reminded herself as she eased her car around a hubcap that had rolled from a wrecked vehicle into the center of the four-lane roadway. On both sides of the busy highway, traffic was nearly at a standstill. She'd tried the side streets but had found them mostly impassable. Wrecked and abandoned cars littered the roads. Where vehicles had run off the road and crashed into trees or concrete walls, the path through was blocked by debris, tree limbs, or still more chunks of concrete.

Though her mind told her that every person on the Beltway felt the same sense of urgency she did, she wanted to demand that they clear a path for her. If only she could get to the office, she could try reaching Randal on the emergency lines the agency maintained. The emergency lines were designed to remain free, open, and operable in all kinds of disasters, from hurricanes to nuclear fallout. Surely she could reach her son if she could get to an open line. He would be all right. He had to be all right.

When the car in front of her slammed to another stop, Mariette automatically laid on her horn. "Come on," she said between clenched teeth. She cast a quick glance at the clock on her dashboard. As morning rush hour crept closer, she knew the situation out here would only worsen. Washington's traffic was notoriously horrid. On a normal day, rush "hour" lasted from four-thirty to nine in the morning and from three to seven in the afternoons. Even the slightest traffic accident sent the already overcrowded system into a tailspin. A major blockage, like a single overturned tractor-trailer or a multicar pileup, could have motorists stranded for hours. She could only imagine what the roads would be like when the commuters, many unaware of what was happening until they awakened that morning, joined the mess.

She drew a calming breath and tried Randal's number again. An exit loomed ahead. She knew a back way to the office from there. She'd risk it and hope the road wasn't blocked ahead.

★   ★   ★

Washington, D.C.
The White House
Local Time 4:05 A.M.

Brad felt the color drain from his face as he sank into the leather chair in his office adjacent to the Oval Office. White House security hadn't wanted him to leave the more secure subterranean Sit Room, but Brad had needed a break from the endless rhetoric and posturing. As tension in the room mounted, tempers had risen in tandem. The venom in the Sit Room was now at a record level—even for this administration—so he'd slipped upstairs to find his assistant weeping into an embroidered handkerchief. Emma Pettit had worked for Brad for fifteen years. Prior to that, she'd worked for his father for nearly twenty-five years in the family trucking business. When Jonathan Benton died, Emma had grieved over his death as much as any Benton had. Brad had offered Emma a job in his consulting firm in California, and she had surprised him by taking it. She was sharp, experienced, a natural problem solver, and could outwork most of the support staff at the White House.

She'd ignored White House security that night in her determination to reach Brad's family. Brad had found her seated at her desk in his outer office. Her face was red, her eyes streaming with tears, and she was clutching the small handkerchief in her hands like a lifeline. "Brad," she'd said when he entered. Her voice had broken on his name, and he'd known his worst fear was about to be realized. Emma always called him Mr. Benton unless something was serious.

Brad had felt his heart twist. "What's wrong? Did you reach Christine?"

She shook her head with a choked sob. "I'm sorry."

Brad wasn't about to accept what his heart was telling him. He walked into his office with Emma on his heels. He reached for the phone to dial his mother-in-law's number. "Maybe they went out of town. Maybe she took the kids—"

Emma gave him a teary look. "No, Brad, I talked to your friend Mike Wellins. He went over to the house and checked on them. When he couldn't get an answer, he let himself in with the key you gave him."

Brad's fingers tightened on the receiver. "And?"

"Gone," Emma said, "just like all the reports. Mike found the girls' clothes on the sofa in front of the television. Christine's were on the floor in the kitchen, and Brad Jr.'s were at his desk upstairs. Your family has vanished."

Brad had stood perfectly still for a while. He felt like his heart had suddenly stopped beating. His body felt simultaneously cold and feverish. His head pounded, his palms felt clammy, and he had a strange feeling that the buzzing in his ears was never going to stop. For a moment the world went black, and he swayed slightly before Emma came back into focus. He stared at her as his stomach clenched into a tight fist. "No."

She pressed her handkerchief to her eyes. "I'm so sorry. I'm just so sorry."

Brad shook his head. "No," he said more forcefully. "It can't be."

Emma didn't respond.

"I want you to keep trying."

"Brad—"

"Keep trying," he said again. "You have to find them."

Emma stood in silence for several seconds. "I won't find them. I can't. They're gone, Brad. I'm sorry."

Brad's mind reeled with the thought that, despite his personal clout, despite his access to the most exclusive and powerful corridors in Washington, he could do nothing to change the thing that mattered most to him in the world.

The breath had left his body in a whoosh as he'd sunk into his leather chair. Emma had muttered something about getting him a cup of coffee as she'd fled the confines of his office.

Now Brad studied the family picture on his desk. Christine had insisted on having it taken a few weeks before Brad left for Washington. His kids had grumbled about having to dress up, and his son had almost boycotted the event, but Christine had conned them all into it. With her subtle ways and her maternal influence she had somehow managed to get them all to the studio at the same time—a minor miracle—for the sitting.

Brad picked up the picture, cradling it in his hands. Christine's smile, warm as ever, made his heart ache. How could he survive without seeing that smile? How was he supposed to go on living without Christine as his partner? She was by far the strongest part of the pair. Without her, he felt like he barely existed. Christine alone knew his vulnerabilities, his passions, his dreams, and his fears. Christine alone knew how to give him hope, how to inspire him, how to make him believe in himself.

Christine alone, he admitted as a wave of grief brought tears to his eyes, gave him a reason for goodness and honor. Without her, he had nothing.

Loneliness washed over him in a torrent as the hot tears scorched a path down his cheeks and landed, unheeded, on his hands and arms. A tear dropped onto the glass of the picture, and Brad rubbed it frantically, irrationally afraid that it would somehow dim the image behind the glass.

He couldn't afford that—not when this picture was all he had left. His heart told him that Emma was right. His family was gone.

And Brad knew exactly what had happened.

Both his mother and his wife had tried to tell him that this day was coming. Soon, they'd said, God would gather from the far corners of the earth everyone who had trusted Christ as their personal Savior. He'd sweep them to heaven in a dramatic exodus that would leave the world shaken and unsteady and wholly unprepared to face the disasters that would follow.

From there, Brad was sketchy on the details. He'd heard his mother talk about what she called "the time of tribulation." He remembered sermons about horsemen and plagues and something about seven seals and seven lampstands. It had all seemed vague and inapplicable to him—like something not meant to be taken literally.

So Brad had never paid much attention to the story. But he knew just enough to realize that his wife, his three children, and his mother had gone to heaven to be with the Lord, while he had been left behind. Did they know? he wondered. Were they searching the streets of heaven looking for him, or was Christine seated somewhere, weeping those quiet soft tears she tried to hide from him? Was she mourning his failure as much as he was mourning her loss? The idea threatened to fell him. Brad couldn't bear the thought of her disappointment in him.

Shuddering, Brad traced his finger over the outline of Christine's face. When people had asked him about his Christian beliefs, Brad had blithely and pompously responded that his faith was something between him and his God. He hadn't elaborated on that. He hadn't said that, in reality, he had very little faith. God was there, he had supposed, but He was not someone to be trusted and followed, not someone to believe in and sacrifice for.

Now Brad wondered despondently if Christine had known what he felt. Had she suspected that he was a sham?

As suddenly as the thought occurred to him, Brad rejected it. Instinctively he knew that whatever and wherever heaven was, it was *not* a place where people felt the pain of loneliness or the grief of loss. No, somehow he was sure, Christine wasn't missing him.

But he was here, trapped in a world launched into a nightmare, missing her. The thought made him feel so lonely that he clutched the picture to his chest with a muffled sob. Everything he'd ever heard about the hell that awaited unbelievers now dimmed in comparison to the pain that ripped a mile-wide path through his soul.

"Oh, Christine," he said, his throat aching. "Forgive me. Please forgive me."

The silence in his office was deafening, stifling.

Brad clung to the picture. Rocking slightly back and forth in his executive chair, he thought of each of his children. His son had been about to enter West Point. His daughters were blossoming into beautiful young women. He'd been so proud of them—had such dreams for them. Dreams of careers and marriage and children and long, healthy lives.

In some ways, he considered his kids to be among his best friends. They'd shared his hobbies, his disappointments, and his victories just as he'd shared theirs. Now he realized that he'd never play another game of one-on-one in the driveway with Emily where he could tease her about the way her ponytail bobbed and rotated when she ran; that he could never listen to another of the songs Megan wrote and played on her cello, which moved him to tears when he thought about how profound her artistic gifts were; that he and Brad Jr. would never again share those precious moments in the workshop in the basement where they talked about everything from basketball to the responsibilities of manhood.

He understood that there would be no more long walks with his wife, no more nights spent with her loving arms around him, no more heated debates about politics or child rearing or paint color, no more cracking open the doors in the wee hours to check on his sleeping children, no more family meals or celebrations.

Brad's soul went ice-cold. He'd never felt so lonely, so desolate in his life.

With a quiet sob, he sank to his knees in front of his chair, doubled over in his grief. Great wrenching sobs tore from his chest. His heart felt lacerated, his bones ached as he accepted the truth: he was a failure. Despite a wall full of certificates and awards, despite his position as one of the most powerful men in the country, he'd failed at the one thing that truly mattered. He'd failed to build a life that would last once the fires of judgment were released.

His life was shattered.

And nothing would ever be the same again.

★　★　★

Washington, D.C.
FEMA Headquarters
Local Time 5:00 A.M.

David Liu looked like death warmed over, Mariette thought when she finally arrived at her office. He glanced up from his computer console, gave Mariette a piercing look, then crumpled in an exhausted heap and dropped his head to his desk. "I'm so glad you're here," he told Mariette, his face buried on his crossed arms.

Mariette took a deep breath and crossed the room to his desk. "It's okay, David," she said, though she wasn't sure why she said it. She was becoming more and more certain that, whatever was going on, it most certainly was not okay. It might never be okay.

She handed her cell phone to an intern who hovered near David's desk looking lost and slightly panicked. "Keep trying to get through to that number," she instructed the college student. "It's my son's apartment in State College, Pennsylvania."

The intern nodded. "Sure."

"When you reach him, let me know." Mariette waved a hand in the general direction of the door, dismissing the young man. She glanced at David, who still had his face hidden against his arms. "All right," she said as she shucked off her jacket. "Give it to me."

David raised his head. The lines of fatigue and stress on his face made him appear years older than he had the day before. "You won't believe me," he said grimly. "I'm not sure I believe me."

She tossed her jacket onto an empty chair and approached the large LCD map of the U.S. on the east wall of the office. Here they traced the path of hurricanes and tornadoes. Here, they marked flood and earthquake damage, blizzards, storm systems, oil spills, and any other disaster that demanded a federal response. The map had computer controls that automatically lit affected areas with yellow and red lights, depending on the scope of the disaster. The main power switch was off, a feature that allowed them to power down the display without terminating the computer feed.

Mariette gave David a sharp look. "You've got the map off."

He nodded, his eyes weary and bloodshot.

"Why?" she pressed.

"Turn it on," he told her. "You'll know why."

Mariette punched the power button. The map flickered once, then blinked into focus. She watched in horror as a wave of red light spread from the East Coast to the West Coast, completely covering the continental United States, Hawaii, Alaska, and the U.S. territories. The computer's assimilated data had declared the entire United States, every acre of it, a federal emergency of epic proportions. "It can't be right," she said quietly.

"I don't even know where to start," David admitted.

Mariette switched off the power. For a moment, she shut her eyes and considered what she should do. On the way into the office, unable to get any news on her car radio, she'd thought through what David had told her. A chill had begun spreading through her as she'd considered the apparent disappearance of her churchgoing, Christian neighbors.

Before she'd been disillusioned by her ex-husband's betrayal, before she'd seen the level of corruption and moral ambivalence that dominated Washington politics, Mariette had been a good political wife with excellent credentials and connections. She'd frequented country club events. She'd played tennis, held teas for Senate wives, traveled widely with her husband. And she'd attended the same church as two former U.S. presidents. A significant number of senators and members of Congress sat among the congregation at the 150-year-old downtown church. On religious holidays or Sundays following events of national proportions, the pews were generally packed with high-ranking public officials.

And as far as Mariette could tell, few, if any of them, carried any of the teaching they heard in that church with them through the week.

But Mariette had been raised by a Christian mother who had instilled in her daughter several core beliefs. She believed in God. She believed there was a heaven where people like her mother spent eternity. She believed in the forces of good and evil. And though she'd never been able to accept that the good and loving God her mother had claimed to know could condemn anyone to hell, she believed that such a place existed for the wicked. Her mother had talked often about the importance of what she called a "personal relationship" with Jesus Christ. Mariette had never seen the need—or the point—of trying to have a relationship with someone she could neither see nor hear. She'd brushed aside her mother's teaching with a what's-right-for-you-doesn't-have-to-be-right-for-me attitude.

But now, as she considered what was unfolding before her, a memory stirred in her mind, like the quiet, soft voice of her mother instructing and teaching her. It floated across the periphery of her mind, teasing her, beckoning her to recall those lessons from Bible school all those years ago. Something about end times and tribulation. Seven letters. Seven seals. Judgments. Armageddon. The word *rapture* had been used, but Mariette had been too young and too disinterested to understand.

But she did recall seeing a postcard once in a Christian bookstore where her mother had taken her shopping. The painting on the card depicted a city scene where people were floating heavenward while the world below experienced unprecedented devastation. Cars lay mangled on the roadways. An airplane crashed into one of the buildings. Fires blazed through the streets where unattended gas lines had ruptured. Mariette had stared at the picture for a long time, fascinated by the detail and the concept of the scene. When she'd asked her mother about the card, the explanation had centered on that word: *rapture*. Mariette remembered thinking that a word associated with joy and excitement was a strange description for the devastation she'd seen in that picture.

Rapture. The believers taken to heaven before a time of tribulation. Mass confusion and disaster on the earth.

How familiar that sounded. Now Mariette turned the idea over in her head a couple of times and tried to ignore the way it made her palms go damp and her stomach clench. It couldn't be. It couldn't possibly be.

But what other explanation . . . ? Mariette shuddered. One thing she knew—any effective response her agency could make to this disaster relied on information, education, and truth. She couldn't possibly formulate a plan until she knew what she was dealing with. If, indeed, the disappearances were some type of supernatural phenomenon, then FEMA's response would have to be different than if a foreign government had launched a global attack.

She needed answers. Fast. And the best way to get them was to begin asking questions.

Resolute, Mariette gathered her determination and turned to her assistant. "All right, David. First things first. How are you?"

He gave her a blank stare. "Me?"

"Yes. You know the rules of relief work as well as anyone. You've got to take care of your own people before you can expect them to take care of others. How are you holding up?"

He slumped in his chair. "I'm okay, I guess."

"Have you heard from your family?" She thought a moment. "Aren't your parents out of the country right now?"

"In China," he affirmed. "Visiting my grandmother."

"Any news?"

"I talked to my sister in Detroit. She's trying to reach them, but the connections are almost impossible."

"I can imagine," she said. She was having enough difficulty reaching her son, and he was only a few hours away. "Have you lost anyone close to you?"

"Not that I know of," David assured her. "I'm just waiting to hear about my folks." He gave her a probing look. "I'm sure you're worried about Randal."

"Extremely."

"He'll be okay, Mariette. He's a sharp kid."

"I know." She drew a deep breath. "I know. I keep telling myself that."

"You have to keep it together, too, you know," he pointed out. "You're just as important as the rest of us."

"I'll make you a deal. I'll nag you and you nag me."

He managed a slight smile. "Deal."

"As soon as you start feeling fatigued, David, you have to promise me you'll take a break. I need you on top of your game."

"I promise. Right now, it's—" he shrugged—"just easier being here."

"I understand."

"So what do you need me to do?"

"I want you to gather whoever you can from the administrative offices and have them begin making phone calls to the Pentagon, the White House, Capitol Hill, and whoever else will talk to us. We've got to know what's going on before we can respond to it."

David gave her a grateful look. He appeared relieved to surrender the controls to her. "Got it. Anything else?"

"Not yet," Mariette assured him. "We can't move until we know what we're up against."

He nodded. "What if we can't get any answers?"

"Then we'll make a hot list of where this is having the greatest impact and start from there."

David stood and stretched his arms above his head with a low groan. "This is turning out to be the longest night of my life. I never imagined—"

"Who could have imagined it?" she said quietly.

"What are you going to do while we try to get through on the phone lines?"

Mariette walked across the room to the desk. She picked up the receiver on the phone and punched the outgoing-line button. "I've got some calls of my own to make."

"Personal connections?" David prompted. He knew her ex-husband was a man of significant political influence.

Mariette shook her head. "Church leaders." At his raised eyebrows, she added, "We're going to need shelters and emergency relief centers."

David thought that over. "That's probably true. We already know about several major chemical spills."

"If transportation is gridlocked," Mariette continued, "food goods and emergency supplies are going to be difficult to distribute. It's going to get ugly out there."

"I hadn't even thought of that."

Mariette reached for the agency emergency phone index on the desk. "Let's get to work." She flipped open the book. "I want those answers as soon as we can get them."

He nodded and headed for the door. As Mariette watched him go, she wondered why she'd been unwilling to tell him her true reason for the phone calls she was about to make. Probably, she thought grimly, because he'd think she was nuts. No one was going to believe this ridiculous theory she'd formulated—that God had taken away the believers and left the rest of the population behind. It sounded so outrageous, even to her, that Mariette wondered why she was unable to put it from her mind. Shaking her head, she dialed the first number in the book.

Whatever the reason, she knew she wouldn't be able to move forward until she verified or dismissed the theory—no matter how ludicrous it seemed. And the best way to get the answers she wanted was to go straight to the source. Since, in her experience, God wasn't

in the business of answering direct questions, Mariette figured her
best bet were the men and women who claimed to know Him.
Somewhere, somehow, there had to be a church leader she could
roust out of bed who could tell her what was going on.

★   ★   ★

Washington D.C.
The White House
Local Time 6:13 A.M.

Brad walked down the hall of the East Wing, his head pounding.
He'd finally spent himself in his office—he'd cried until he felt like
he'd emptied his soul onto the Oriental carpet. When he'd dragged
himself off the floor, he found a fresh cup of coffee on his desk.
Emma must have slipped in unnoticed and placed it there. Brad
didn't even have the energy to feel embarrassed that she'd witnessed
his mourning.

He'd taken the coffee, downed it, and wiped the tears off his face.
Then he'd braved the walk out of his office to Emma's desk and
found her already going about the day's business. It was as if the
routine of keeping his schedule, preparing his correspondence, and
generally managing his professional world made her more able to
cope with her own grief over the loss of Brad's family. She'd loved
them like her own for many years.

Brad had placed a hand on her shoulder and gave her a slight
squeeze. She put her hand on his, and a flow of silent sympathy
surged through their grip. Then she turned back to her work, barely
missing a beat as she typed. Even if neither had said anything, the silent communication that passed between them in that instant had
meant the world to Brad. They were in this together. Emma, who
knew better than anyone the kind of obstacles he faced here at the
White House, had his back.

Brad felt bolstered as he left his office to return to the tension-
charged meeting in the Sit Room. Though his head ached and his

heart felt lacerated, he felt compelled to attend as much of the high-level strategy session as he could endure. World-changing decisions were being made in that room—decisions that Christine had sent him to Washington to affect. He couldn't fail her again and still live with himself.

As he turned the corner, he saw Jane Lyons, one of the deputy press secretaries, come out of an office carrying a stack of reports. "Jane," he greeted her.

She looked up from the reports, visibly startled. Her face was flushed, her eyes teary. "Mr. Benton. I . . . I thought you were in the Sit Room."

"Taking a break." Brad looked at her closely. "Is everything all right?" He glanced at the door of the office she'd just exited. The Press Room was on the other side of the building with the rest of the policy team. On this side of the White House, administrative, security, and business-oriented offices were housed, as well as the first lady's office. There was nothing on the door to indicate who the office belonged to.

"Fine," Jane told him. "I was just getting some things ready that Mr. Swelder requested. Background stuff. You know."

Brad studied her a moment. He'd always liked Jane, thought she was one of the sharpest of Ramiro's team. "You seem upset. Have you . . ." He hesitated. "Lost someone?"

Jane's eyes teared. Brad wondered at his newfound patience for what he would have labeled hysteria a mere twelve hours ago. "It's Mr. Ramiro," she said. "I just can't believe . . ." She broke off on a muffled sob.

"George was a good man." Brad gave her a pointed look. "He had good people under him."

Jane shuffled the papers she was holding so she could free a hand to mop her eyes. "I'm just not sure—I mean, I don't really feel ready . . ."

"You are," Brad assured her, knowing that the young woman was under tremendous pressure. Without George to prepare the president's statement about the disappearances, the bulk of the responsibility, the media's questions, and, unfortunately, the fallout would land squarely on Jane. "Even George thought so."

She struggled a moment, then pulled herself under control. "I just can't believe he's gone. This whole thing—it's like a really bad dream that keeps getting worse."

"I know." Brad reached to take the stack of papers from her. "You going to the Sit Room with these?"

"Delivering them," she confirmed.

"I'll take them. I'm headed that way."

"That's okay—"

"No," he insisted. "I'm sure you've got your hands full."

Jane gave him a grateful look. "Thanks, Mr. Benton."

"Sure." He tucked the reports under his arm. "Reminds me of my days as a page in the California legislature." He managed to give her a slight smile. "Only I was forty pounds lighter and had more hair back then."

Jane answered with a muffled laugh. "Don't let me deprive you of the pleasure of reliving your youth," she said as he headed down the corridor.

5

Washington, D.C.
The White House
Local Time 7:00 A.M.

The president today issued the following statement:

December 7. September 11. These dates are emblazoned on the pages of American history and in the hearts of the American people because of the insidious events of foreign aggression that violated our fundamental rights to peace, freedom, and security.

Our government could not have imagined or anticipated that an attack of even more immense proportions awaited us. Now we, and many of our allies around the globe, are facing an unprecedented disaster. Like many of you, I am grieving over the loss of close friends and family members.

Rest assured, this attack will not go unanswered. Though we do not yet know the scope of what we face, nor do we know the identity of our enemies, we will not rest until the perpetrators of this terrible act are brought to justice.

Justice will be swift, severe, and certain.

I am confident that the same resilience that carried this great nation through the Great Depression, two World Wars, the horror of terrorism, and the greatest challenges of our history will, once again, sustain us in this time of national grief and challenge.

Brad Benton read the statement a second time before setting it aside on his desk. In less than ten minutes, the president planned to deliver that statement in the White House briefing room. The sun had risen on a world vastly different than it had set on the evening before. But for Brad at least, the sunrise had come as a welcome relief to the oppressive questions and emotional and physical exhaustion of the night before.

It had also brought the responsibility of a response to the American people from the White House. After endless verbal sparring in the Sit Room, the language for the president's statement had finally been drafted and a press briefing called for this morning. As Brad had suspected, the bulk of the responsibility for preparing the statement had fallen on Jane Lyons. In George's absence, Charley Swelder had dumped an enormous load on the young woman.

Brad had voiced his objections to the content of the statement, arguing along with the secretary of defense that it was both reckless and absurd to tell the public the United States had been attacked when they could not name an enemy or find the weapon responsible, but Charley Swelder had insisted on including the word *attacked*. In Charley's opinion, President Fitzhugh must come off looking strong and determined, no matter what. The best way to do that, according to Charley, was to rally the public with a display of national pride and patriotism. And the best way to do that was to invoke an enemy to unite against.

Which, Brad thought cynically, was just great for Charley, who wouldn't have to face the deluge of media questions that would follow the president's statement. In the absence of George Ramiro and given Jane Lyons's relative inexperience, Brad probably would have to answer those questions.

There was little he could say, he knew, that would stem the growing tide of public panic. Because of the timing of the disappearances, many people had actually slept through the night completely unaware of what was happening around them. Rural America had not felt the impact as severely as the urban areas in the first rush of time after the event. But with the sunrise came realization, shock, and terror—everywhere. All of America was now waiting to hear what the chief executive had to say.

And it wasn't going to be pretty. The news that the president had taken the nation to Defense Condition 2—the second highest security level and the level just short of actual war footing—would have severe consequences on every aspect of American life from transportation to the economy to education to industry. Fitzhugh had made the decision in the depths of the night, after consulting with the national security advisor and the Joint Chiefs of Staff . . . or, at least, those among the joint chiefs who weren't missing.

The nation had not been at DEFCON 2 since the terrorist attacks of September 11, 2001. For most Americans, those long fall days after the devastating attacks on the Pentagon and the World Trade Center were rife with memories of fear and the unaccustomed sound of military aircraft overhead. The subsequent wars on Afghanistan and Iraq, along with a generalized War on Terror, had lulled the nation into an uneasy calm. Despite intermittent terrorist acts, many of them serious, enough time had passed that America's citizens once again felt cushioned and isolated from the possibility of nationwide disaster.

But now Brad heard the steady drone of the planes that patrolled Washington's airspace, a reality he knew was made necessary by the worldwide terror sparked by the disappearances. Security at the White House had tightened to maximum, and they'd talked last night of evacuating the president to a secure facility. As all the world's nations sought answers to the horror of the disappearances, the level of distrust and tension between the major powers had steadily escalated through the early hours of the morning.

Now it seemed to Brad that the world was poised right on the edge of sudden and complete disaster. One false move, one diplomatic or military blunder, one more event like last night's, and it could easily set a match to the incendiary conditions, creating a geopolitical bonfire that could swallow the whole world.

And Brad was supposed to have answers.

Politically correct answers. Reassuring answers. Hope-giving, compassionate, confident answers.

What can I say? he thought grimly. *If I tell what I now suspect is the truth, it's potentially disastrous. A political nightmare, even.* He couldn't imagine the White House press corps responding favorably to his suspicions that this was no foreign attack or natural phenomenon. He didn't think that the American people still here to hear the message would like it much, either. Yet to say anything else made him acutely aware that he deserved to feel all the guilt that had been clawing at him for the past several hours.

Wearily, Brad turned to gaze out the window of his office across the Ellipse. The outline of the Washington Monument cast its towering shadow in the predawn sky. The large memorial, which to Brad had always seemed an indomitable symbol of power and hope, now offered him little comfort as it loomed over a city filled with terror, grief, and uncertainty. The D.C. air was hazy with lingering clouds of smoke and fumes from the events of the night. The murky air shrouded the monument in an eerie cloak of gloom and destruction.

Brad shuddered. If his suspicions were correct, he knew this was only the beginning of the living nightmare—a position that was certain to be unpopular with a president and a government that were desperate to turn the agenda toward talk of rebuilding and recovery. Perhaps, Brad thought grimly, this was what his mother had meant all those times she'd claimed to believe that God had set Brad apart for a unique mission—"to be a voice in the darkness," she had called it.

The last few hours certainly qualified as darkness—literally, physically, spiritually, and emotionally. Not that he'd done much yet to speak out through the gloom.

Besides, Brad didn't want to be a voice in the darkness.

What he wanted was to wake up in his Alexandria apartment and realize this had all been some terrible dream. What he wanted was to hop on a plane, fly to Los Angeles, and find his wife, his son, and his two daughters waiting for him. What he wanted was to turn back the clock and give himself a chance to make things right—to confess to his wife that he'd been a fraud. He wanted to stand in front of his church body and ask why he'd been able to serve as a deacon, an elder, a lay leader, and no one had known his heart. If he'd managed to fool them, hadn't others done it, too? How many people, he wondered, were in his shoes tonight? All around him were people grief stricken at the loss of their loved ones, but they didn't know the truth.

Brad knew it, had known it all along, and had chosen to live his life without taking it to heart.

Brad's guilt and shame and sorrow at all the chances to let Christ into his life that he'd squandered were like salt on the open wound of his misery.

What he wanted was to take his mother's hand and beg her to forgive him for all the times he'd scoffed at her ideas and privately ridiculed her beliefs.

A soft knock on his door demanded his attention. Brad turned from the window, glad for whatever intrusion had pulled him from his grim thoughts.

Colonel Grayson Wells, a military attaché to the White House, stood watching him, his expression intent and serious. "Excuse me, Mr. Benton, I need a minute of your time before the president issues his statement."

"Certainly." Brad indicated the seat across from his desk with a sweep of his hand.

The colonel closed the door after he entered the office. "I don't think you'll want anyone to hear this." He sank into the leather chair with a weary sigh. "I've checked into things the best I can. When you asked me earlier to see how many troops we'd lost—" he shrugged—"I guess I didn't anticipate it would be this bad."

"How bad is 'this bad'?" Brad picked up a letter opener and rolled it between his fingers. Late last night, he'd pulled the colonel aside during a break from the Sit Room meeting and asked him to begin gathering intelligence about the state of U.S. troops around the globe. "What are the numbers?"

Colonel Wells swallowed. His eyes were bleak. "I haven't been able to get through to every unit—"

"I understand."

He shook his head. "The best I can tell, we're down at least 20, maybe 25 percent. Much higher in some units, not as severe in others." He wiped a hand over his regulation military haircut. "Our commanders are doing what they can to stem the panic, but we've got a lot of soldiers out there who've never seen a war that wasn't fought with smart bombs and computer technology. Frankly, they just aren't psychologically prepared to take these kinds of losses in their units. That means you can't really count on all the troops we have left."

Brad nodded. "Which makes our military position precarious."

"Yeah. That's one way to put it. Especially in the Middle East, where we're already divided along several fronts." The colonel shook his head. "Preliminary reports indicate that none of the opposing forces in that area suffered losses like we did."

Brad managed a sardonic smile. "Preliminary reports from both Gulf Wars indicated that the Iraqis were winning."

The colonel shrugged. "I know, but this is what I'm getting from our intelligence officers, not Radio Baghdad. What's worse is that we had several trustworthy agents in place on hostile territory. We've sustained some fairly heavy casualties there, and our intelligence is now pretty severely compromised."

"What do your people think is going on?" Brad asked.

The colonel shot a nervous glance over his shoulder. "Well, sir, here's the thing. Nothing—" he swept his hands through the air for emphasis—"I mean *nothing* in any of our intelligence reports indicated that anyone was developing a weapon of this caliber. And, frankly, if anyone had been, we'd not only have known about it but we probably would have created it first and known how to counter it. There's not another nation in the world that has the ability or the resources to develop sophisticated weaponry like we do. As you can imagine, the top brass at the Pentagon have been scrambling to get Secretary Leyton every shred of intelligence we have from the past few years. It just doesn't seem possible that we could have missed this."

That, Brad acknowledged, was probably true. "So you don't believe we've been attacked."

"Not by a foreign government or terrorist organization," Colonel Wells said flatly. "I know the president is putting forth that theory, but frankly, I don't think it's true."

Brad took a steadying breath. "Then what's the Pentagon's position?"

"They don't have one yet." Colonel Wells paused. "Officially."

"And unofficially?"

The colonel met Brad's gaze with a serious look. "Mr. Benton, I think you can understand how delicate—"

Brad held up a hand. "What you tell me stays here in this room, Wells. I'm not interested in destroying your career."

The colonel nodded. "I appreciate that, sir."

"Tell me what you've heard."

"It seems that General Marsden, General Cranston, and General Mayweather are pushing the hardest for a first strike against the Russians."

Brad knew Dave Marsden and Hubert Mayweather. Both were four-star generals with long, illustrious careers. Brad knew that the men, after years of conditioning by world events, had experienced difficulty putting the Cold War behind them. "That doesn't surprise me," he said. "Let me guess. Marsden, especially, would like to use this as an excuse to pour billions back into new arms development."

"Yes, sir. He's not alone. Mayweather has been one of the chief critics of the president's foreign policy. Though they won't admit it in public, the two of them would like to see Fitzhugh roasted to death over a bonfire as the first act in a more aggressive use of the military."

"So I'd guessed. How about the third guy you mentioned—Todd Cranston? I'm not familiar with the man, but I've heard the name."

"He's the most political of the three. The youngest, too. He has the most to gain from playing this out to his own advantage. He's sharp and photogenic. A successful war would turn him into a national hero. No telling where he could go from there."

Brad thought that over. "What about the rest of the joint chiefs?"

"They pretty much *are* the joint chiefs. The rest are missing, as far as we can tell," the colonel admitted. "We're filling in from the remaining available ranks of officers. There are some dissenters in the group, but Marsden is the main voice. If he pushes hard enough for a first strike, it'll be difficult for the president to deny him."

"I'm sure that Dave Marsden would say that it isn't a first strike. It's a response."

"I'm aware of that, but I can only think of three possibilities, sir, for the hand that unleashed this weapon, and frankly only one doesn't seem completely absurd."

"Look, Colonel, the entire thing is absurd. We're missing nearly a quarter of our adult population. As far as we can tell, every child in this country who hasn't hit puberty is gone. But it happened. It's real. And I'd like to hear any theory you've got—no matter how absurd it is—about how we got into this situation. At this point, I don't think anything is beyond consideration."

"Okay. I'll lay it out for you. But it doesn't leave this room with my name on it. Understood?"

Brad nodded.

"Well, I spoke with one of my sharpest counterparts at the Pentagon just before I came up here. In addition to Marsden's theory of a Russian-based attack, there's a troika of theories floating around over there. First, there's the alien-attack hypothesis." The colonel shrugged. "I don't find that very likely."

"No?"

"No, sir. Our space exploration has been extensive. Not just manned missions—we've had a lot more success with our unmanned probes and surveillance installations. In particular, we've listened to every radio and electrical disturbance of the past thirty years, hoping to find signs of intelligent life. We've had nada. Zip. Despite what the conspiracy theorists say. It's a little hard to believe that if some alien population were planning to devastate us like this that we wouldn't have had some indication before now.

"Besides, this wasn't some random sampling of the population that we lost last night. I could maybe buy the alien thing if a third of the world's population had indiscriminately vanished, but some countries appear to have lost a far greater percentage of people than others. The disappearances were quite selective. All the kids are gone. From what I can tell, the adult populations in North, South, and Central America have been hardest hit, and there are indications from other places in the world that large and specific concentrations of people are missing."

"And you think an alien attack would have been more general?"

"If this were just some kind of global weapon, it seems to me that whatever blanketed the world and caused this mess wouldn't have been so discriminating. I mean, I can see the thing with the children—" The colonel's voice cracked.

"Did you lose someone?" Brad asked gently.

"My sister's family . . ." Tears welled in Wells's eyes as the man struggled for control. He clearly wasn't going to allow himself to lose it in front of Brad. After a moment, he got it back together and continued, his voice once again resolute. "She's got four kids. I really got a kick out of them. They're all gone."

"I'm sorry." Brad fought a wave of grief as he thought of his own missing family. "I lost my wife. And my three kids."

Colonel Wells shook his head. "I'm very sorry, sir."

Brad swallowed hard, past the lump in his throat. "I'm not entirely certain they're gone yet," he hedged, still clinging to an irrational thread of hope. "Just that I haven't been able to contact them. I've got to get home and see for myself."

"Of course." The colonel visibly collected himself again before he continued. "Like I said, the missing kid thing makes a certain sort of sense. Maybe, if this thing acted on molecular structure or something, it would be reasonable to think that the children were more vulnerable, or maybe, if this is an attack, that the attackers wanted to eliminate the future of the human race or something, but the thing with the uneven adult population loss—well, it just doesn't add up."

"Why not?"

"If it was going after military might, it should have taken out the Chinese and the Middle East and Russia as well as us. It didn't.

Statistically, in comparison to our losses, those areas are almost untouched, other than the kids. And it took out vast chunks of Central America's population. They were hit much harder than we were. There aren't a lot of serious, world-class military threats in Central America. So, as a weapon, it makes no sense."

"I can see that," Brad stated. "What are your other two theories?"

"Well, the one that seems the most palatable, the most believable to me, is that this is some natural phenomenon. Maybe we caused it by a combination of the nuclear disasters of the twentieth century. With episodes like Chernobyl, Nagasaki, and Hiroshima, and who knows what all was released into the air during and after the Gulf War, it could be that a cloud of toxin has been developing in the atmosphere, and it finally reached critical mass. That also could explain why the children are missing—their bodies and immune systems are less developed. It could also explain the concentration of disappearances in certain areas of the globe. Wind currents, tides, all the things that cause instabilities in the atmosphere. They could distribute whatever's causing this unevenly. But I'm afraid that's full of holes, too."

Brad thought it over. It could be spun into something the public would believe. It sounded rational, at least. People were probably more prepared to accept a scientific long shot than anything that might require a little faith on their part. "I could sell that. But you clearly don't think it's the case, even though you want to."

"It's definitely more palatable than anything else out there." The colonel leveled Brad with a narrow look. "But I'm afraid when we really study that line of reasoning, we're going to find out it's not true."

Brad was equally afraid of that. "Why?"

"We've been studying and sampling the atmosphere for decades," Colonel Wells explained. "We have spent billions investigating the hole in the ozone layer, ocean-pollution issues, the thawing of the polar ice cap. If a toxic cloud that could do this was forming in the atmosphere, I find it hard to believe that somebody, somewhere, wouldn't have noticed something before now. Somebody should have been yelling dire warnings of destruction. We might have ignored him or labeled him a nut, but at least we could look back now and see that he was telling the truth."

"We've had plenty of people screaming about air quality," Brad said. "The environment's not one of Fitz's stronger points as president."

"Yeah, well, even this president would have noticed an environmental screamer who said that toxic fumes would disintegrate a quarter of the world's human population. Nobody's tried that tactic. Not even the most radical environmental alarmist. I looked. And whatever this is, it doesn't appear to have touched nonhuman life-forms. I talked to some people over at the EPA, the Smithsonian, and the National Geographic Society. There are a number of indicator species that we monitor to see if the environment is in trouble. Butterflies, frogs, birds, delicate plant species—they all vanish long before we humans notice any serious environmental problems. They're like the caged canaries coal miners used to take down into the tunnels with them to be sure there was enough oxygen in the air. They just keel right over before we humans can tell there's a problem.

"We've seen problems in indicator species before. Lots of 'em. But they didn't get any worse overnight, as far as the scientists watching 'em can tell. And the areas with problems that we know about don't correlate with the areas where people were hardest hit. I think it's safe to say that in rural Central and South America the atmosphere is in better shape overall than in New York City. But we think that the proportion of the population missing down in, say, backwoods Costa Rica runs as high as 80 percent. New York only lost about 20 percent of its adult population. So the toxic cloud wrecking the ecology theory isn't workable. Unless you know something about air quality that I don't."

"No," Brad admitted.

"I've got people looking and putting out feelers on the issue. We've talked to several leading environmental lobbies and think tanks. Nobody's aware of any theories on the subject other than the usual ecological gloom and doom."

"So that leaves the third possibility," Brad said. He shot a quick glance at the clock. Two minutes to the president's press conference.

Colonel Wells looked visibly nervous. "Yes, sir."

"Don't worry, Colonel. Believe me, there's nothing you can say that's going to be any more outrageous than most of what I've already heard tonight in other meetings."

The colonel spread his palms on his thighs. "Well, sir, mind you, I have trouble really believing this myself, but there's got to be some explanation . . ."

"Go on."

"There are a few high-ranking leaders at the Pentagon who are insisting that this was an act of God," Colonel Wells said. "And the pity of it is, I'm beginning to think they're right. I don't have any other theory that makes as much sense. I've already talked to Senator Arnold over at Armed Services. He's going to call hearings in the morning. He made it painfully clear that if the Pentagon leaders come to the Hill with nothing more than a theory about God and some religious event, he's going to have somebody's head."

Brad felt a strange sense of relief and dread—relief that he wasn't alone in his theory about the Rapture and dread that of all the possible answers he'd considered tonight, the one with the worst future consequences for the human race seemed to be the most believable.

"That doesn't surprise me," Brad said. "I'm sure Max Arnold is trying to figure out how to use this disaster to further his presidential aspirations."

"Maybe so, but it looks to me like if somebody doesn't come up with something soon, he's gonna use it to take down anybody who is standing in his way. Including the president. That's what I think is going to happen in the next few days when the hearings start."

"Then let me put you out of your misery, Colonel," Brad said. "I'm assuming that some people over at the Pentagon have suggested that God has gathered up all the believers and left the rest of us behind. That every faithful Christian is now in heaven, and those of us still here on earth didn't make the cut?"

The colonel's eyes widened. "Yes, sir."

Brad saw the minute hand on the clock snap to twelve. He rose and reached for his coat. "That's what I needed to know." He shrugged into his jacket.

"But, sir, you don't think—"

Brad sighed wearily. "I think that I've got a press briefing to attend, and I'm going to be called on for answers. If that's the best answer I've got, then that's what they're getting from me."

"But, sir—"

Brad offered the man a grim smile. "It's fine, Colonel. This won't be the first time I've taken heat for having an unpopular idea." It happened nearly once a month in cabinet meetings.

"I can't believe—"

"I didn't want to believe it either," Brad confessed, "but I'm fresh out of better ideas."

"All I'm saying is that Marsden is going to come out this morning publicly calling for a strike on the Russians. If you announce at the briefing that the Pentagon is undecided, he won't like it."

"I'm not really concerned about what Dave Marsden likes. He works for us, Colonel. Not the other way around."

The colonel winced. "It's just that the president's relationship with the Pentagon is already strained. They don't like some of the decisions he's made."

"I'm sure they don't."

"And I feel that if you'd wait to discuss this until after the joint chiefs have reached a conclusion—"

"Marsden's not planning to wait, is he?"

"No, sir."

"Then he's made his choice," Brad said bluntly. "That's his problem."

A knock sounded on the office door before it swung open. Emma glanced at the colonel, then at Brad. "Press briefing," she prompted.

Brad nodded. "Tell them I'm on my way." He shot a quick look at the colonel. "And as soon as you can, Colonel, I've got to arrange a ride to California. Do we have anything in the air?"

"I just got news that the president is considering a trip to a few strategic spots around the country to check the extent of the devastation. He'll probably start on the West Coast. It'll give him a chance to check out the progress on the new *Air Force One*."

Brad was well-informed about the controversial new aircraft being built in Boeing's Seattle facility. Congress, and chiefly Max Arnold, had been decrying the expense, while the Pentagon insisted the new, more secure aircraft was necessary for the president's protection. The new 757 was supposedly a technological marvel, and Fitzhugh was as enthralled with it as a kid with a new bike on Christmas morning. Gray was right. No way was the president going to miss the opportunity to inspect the progress. With any luck, Fitzhugh would care enough about the midterm election to make a first stop in California. The voters needed to believe he cared more about their losses and grief than the status of his new airplane.

It didn't particularly surprise Brad, however, that the decision to make the trip had been made without his counsel. Fitzhugh's insiders made no secret of their dislike and distrust of Brad. Brad knew that he had been brought to Washington as a figurehead. As a sop to the religious right. Any attempts on his part to change that fact had been met with hostility. Especially now, when the stakes had never been higher, Brad was even more removed from key decisions and policy discussions than ever. Charley Swelder was calling the shots. At least when George Ramiro had been around, he'd been in Brad's corner. Now Brad was on his own. And he didn't think the president was going to like what he was thinking.

Brad looked at Colonel Wells and nodded. "Thanks for the tip. I'll try to catch a ride."

6

Marcus Dumont took the call from Mariette Arnold with mixed feelings. Her call was the first of the many he was expecting. She'd be only the first who wanted answers from him. But he'd thought he'd have until later in the day before he was hounded for an explanation. He'd planned on having most of the morning to prepare himself.

He should have known better.

"Hello, Ms. Arnold," he said softly into the receiver.

"Marcus!" She sounded genuinely relieved to talk to him. "I can't believe it."

"I'm here," he said flatly, wondering if she had any idea of all the implications buried in her simple admission.

"I've been going through our entire list of clergy trying to find someone who'll answer. I'm all the way to the end of the Ds and you're the first person I've been able to reach."

Marcus wasn't surprised, though the news depressed him. This was as bad as he'd thought. "These are difficult times. What can I do for you?"

"We've got a mess on our hands," she said quietly, "and I'm trying to see who I can reach to help us clean it up."

Marcus glanced at the window where wedges of light had just

broken the grip of darkness on the city. "I've been in the process of pulling together whoever I can find on my staff. We're here to help."

"Good. I don't have a game plan yet. I'm still building a resource list. I haven't been able to reach most of my usual contacts."

And wouldn't be able to, Marcus knew. Ever. "You know we'll do whatever we can. We've always made a point of giving as much as we could to this community."

"I know, and it's appreciated." Mariette sounded tired. "Believe me, it's appreciated."

"Do you have any idea yet what's going on?" Marcus probed, curious what the rest of the world was thinking.

"My boss has been in a meeting at the White House since this happened. I haven't heard from him yet, but I know the president is set to make a statement in a few minutes. We've finally got cable back on here at the office."

Marcus reached for the remote control on his desk. Tired of watching the static, he'd switched the set off earlier. A punch of the button found CNN, where the White House correspondent was discussing the developments of the story. "Us, too. I'll be curious to see what the president has to say."

"Me, too." Mariette paused. "Um . . . Reverend—"

"Yes?"

"Do you think—I mean, what do you . . . what do you think is going on?"

His fingers tightened on the receiver. "That's the question on everyone's mind. There could be a number of explanations."

"Yes, but . . ." Mariette trailed off again.

"Is there something specific you want to know, Ms. Arnold?"

She drew a deep breath, audible on his end of the line. "Yes."

"You want to know," he supplied, "if I believe this is an act of God. If the disappearances are the result of His judgment on the world."

"Yes," she admitted.

Marcus momentarily closed his eyes. Confessing to his own staff and inner circle that he'd been a fraud had been difficult, but now, here before him was the opportunity to finally assuage his conscience by admitting it to the world. He could salvage his pride by spinning the story in a more favorable direction, he knew, but the crushing weight of guilt had become too much to bear. Unbidden, the image of his wife in her dying days came to his mind. She'd been in such pain, such terrible agony from the cancer that had slowly eaten away at her resilience, yet there'd been a look of peace on her face that Marcus had envied. She'd seemed content, almost hopeful of what lay before her as she'd suffered through the final waning moments of her life.

Her last words to Marcus had been, "I'll save you a place at the table, dear." Then she'd slipped quietly away from him, leaving him bitterly alone and angry at a God who would allow that kind of suffering.

For perhaps the first time in his life, Marcus now truly believed in the awesome power of that God. He now knew what the Bible meant when it referred to the "fear" of the Lord as a blessed thing.

In the image of his wife he found a courage he'd never known, and when he opened his eyes, for the first time in years, his vision seemed clear, his focus steady, his goal defined. Marcus felt a strange sense of relief as he set aside his pride and prepared himself to tell the truth.

"Yes, Ms. Arnold," he said, his voice stronger than it had been in years, bolstered by a newfound conviction, "I believe this is the hand of God. I believe that God has gathered His faithful in the Rapture of the believers."

"But—" Mariette hesitated. "But you—"

"His faithful," Marcus said quietly. "The true believers." He paused, lowering his voice. "Not the frauds."

"Reverend—"

"Ms. Arnold, unfortunately not every man who preaches the Word of God *believes* the Word of God. Some believe but don't accept. Some know but don't listen. Some openly rebel against God's teaching. Preachers are fallible, too. Just like everyone else."

"Are you saying that you—?"

"That I was a fraud? Yes. That's what I'm saying." Marcus was surprised at how easily the confession rolled off his lips. For the first time in years, he felt the tremendous weight of pretense slipping away. "I've already discussed this with the few members of my staff who are left. You can expect to see a public statement from me later today."

"Reverend, I'm sorry, but I can't believe that a man like you, who has committed his life to helping people, can call himself a fraud. You're a great humanitarian."

"It's not enough, Ms. Arnold. What happened last night proved that. The only road to salvation lies in Jesus Christ."

Mariette didn't respond for a long time. Marcus studied the painting of Jesus kneeling in prayer in the Garden of Gethsemane in his office. The drops of blood on the Savior's forehead now had an entirely new meaning to Marcus. Christ hadn't been praying simply to be spared the pain of the coming crucifixion, he realized. He'd been praying for the souls like Marcus. Souls that were facing an eternity in hell.

Mariette finally responded. "If what you say is true, then what's going to happen now?"

"I'm not going to pretend I have all the answers. I just know that the proof is incontrovertible. Every God-fearing man and woman in my organization is gone. If you've done any digging at all, I'm sure you know that all the children are missing—they're gone worldwide. I've had my staff checking into reports from mental hospitals and organizations that treat the mentally disabled. Some facilities have lost all their patients. I don't have global reports yet, but I suspect we'll soon learn that pockets of Christian believers have vanished. The evidence is clear. God has swept up His children and left the rest of us behind."

"But I don't understand how good people—"

"It has nothing to do with good and evil. No one is good apart from God. The Bible clearly teaches that without Christ, all our good works are like rags in the eyes of a holy and righteous God."

"So you've been saying," Mariette pointed out, "for the last few years."

"I said it, but I didn't put my own words into practice." Marcus sighed. "As I said, it's not about good or bad; it's about *belief*. Those who believe and those who do not. Those who accepted God's gift of redemption through Jesus Christ—those people have been taken. Those of us who rejected it, either by word or action, are still here. It may sound crazy, but in the days ahead, I assure you, you'll find it's true."

"I'm sorry, Reverend. I just can't believe that," Mariette said. "I can't believe that a good God—"

"You can't condemn God's goodness because of evil in the world, Ms. Arnold. There's evil in the world because man chose to separate himself from God's grace."

"Sorry. I can't buy that."

"I understand," Marcus assured her. "Obviously, I had my own doubts about God."

"But not anymore?"

"No."

"So what are you saying? That there's no hope for the rest of us?"

How many times, he wondered, would he have to answer that question in the coming months? He'd already answered it for his devastated staff. Perhaps that was the mission God had called him to—responding to the plea for hope from a world shocked into new awareness of God's power. "There's always hope. God's grace is infinite."

She didn't respond immediately. When she spoke, her voice was hushed. "I'm glad that brings you comfort, Reverend."

But not you, Marcus mused. Normally he would have accepted her rejection, politely ended the conversation, and moved on, but he felt compelled now, almost desperate to reach people with the truth they had missed. He took a deep breath and forged ahead. "We're all going to need comfort in the weeks ahead. I've studied the biblical prophecies extensively over the years. I'm very familiar with what the Bible says about the end times. Believe me, what happened last night is only the beginning."

"Sorry, Reverend, but you aren't making any sense. If you're so knowledgeable about the Bible, why didn't you know this was coming? Why didn't you do something about it—or at least save yourself?"

"I preached the need for salvation for years, Ms. Arnold, just like most of my colleagues. We talked about the importance of having a relationship with Jesus Christ. We spoke the message of salvation and grace. We preached about the end times and the coming tribulation. See, I've been *telling* the truth for years."

"But you didn't believe it?"

"I believed it. I mean, I knew it was true. But I didn't accept it."

"I don't understand."

"I know," Marcus said gently. "Let me explain it like this. Has there ever been a time in your life when you cried out to God for help?"

"Sure."

"Most people answer that question the same way. There's something in each of us, something central in our soul that *knows* God created us, that knows we need Him. Many people spend a lot of time trying to meet that need artificially—with everything from drugs and alcohol to money. Some people try to fill it with good deeds and humanitarianism.

"But none of those things really works. For a while, they can keep the yearning satisfied, but the truth is, each of us reaches a point in our life where we must choose to accept God or reject Him. I believe God brings us to those circumstances. That instant you were talking about when you cried out to God for help—did you get the answer you wanted?"

"No," Mariette said bluntly. "I didn't."

"And because of that, you rejected God."

"A good God—"

"The Bible does not just say that God is good," Marcus told her. "The Bible says God is the Alpha and Omega, the beginning and the end. He is everywhere, knows everything. Like a parent, He knows that what we want isn't always what's best for us. He works to bring us into relationship with Himself, and because of the presence of evil in the world, we sometimes suffer inexplicable pain along the way."

"Look, Reverend," Mariette said, her tone exasperated, "I'm not really up to this right now. I've got a crisis—"

"I know," he said. Marcus had done what he could to reach her . . . for now. "And I won't take any more of your time. But if you have any questions in the future, please feel free to call me for anything you need. Even if you just need someone to talk to." He paused. "Have you lost anyone close to you?" He might not have believed everything he'd preached, but Marcus had mastered the skills of his trade.

Mariette sucked in a sharp breath. "I'm not sure. I have some distant relatives I haven't tried to reach yet, but—" Marcus heard the tension in her voice—"I haven't been able to reach my son, Randal."

"I'm sorry," he said, unwilling to offer hollow assurance that surely the young man was well. There had been too many disasters in the wake of the Rapture, too many lives cut short by car and plane crashes, fires, explosions, and other catastrophes to rule out the possibility that the young man was seriously injured or dead. "Where is he?"

"Penn State. I've got an employee trying to call him."

"I'll pray for you, Ms. Arnold," Marcus assured her.

Marcus glanced at the television, where the president was approaching the podium in the White House briefing room. "I know the next few weeks are going to be extremely difficult. Again, I just want you to know that I'm here for you. I'll do whatever I can to help."

"Thank you, Reverend. I may take you up on that."

"I hope so," he said. "I would like to ask one favor."

"Yes?"

"I'd like you to promise to think about what we've discussed and call me with any questions you have." Marcus had witnessed to thousands of people in his life. He'd led hundreds through the process of confessing their sins, repentance, and the prayer for salvation. He'd preached the message of God's saving grace from the pulpit and seen thousands walk down the aisles for counseling.

He'd lost count of how many people he'd baptized. But he'd never felt the sense of urgency he now felt to communicate God's truth with others. For the first time in his life, he accepted that lives hung in the balance, that the coming horrors would be worse than anyone could conceive, and that the only hope anyone had was the mercy of God.

Mariette hesitated before she responded. "I'll remember that. Thank you for the offer."

"Of course. And, Ms. Arnold? I hope you find what you're looking for," he told her as he hung up the phone. He couldn't tell her he hoped she reached her son soon. He knew that while her relief at finding her son alive would be enormous, once she realized what the future held, she'd soon experience a new level of fear for his safety and well-being.

Marcus had studied enough Scripture to know that the devastation of the past few hours was only the tip of the iceberg. Things were going to get far worse—quickly. People like Mariette Arnold, he feared, had only begun to experience pain and suffering. Marcus, at least, had no family, no intimate friends left here on earth to concern him. He was free to plunge into what he knew would be an unimaginable conflict between good and evil, and his only hope of looking himself in the mirror and feeling anything but disgust was to begin telling the truth. No matter what it cost him.

With an odd sense of hope, Marcus turned up the volume on the set and listened to the president's statement. It was short, and the president took no questions. An assistant press secretary informed the media that the president would begin a multistate tour later that day to inspect the extent of the damage. After his first few stops, he'd be more prepared to answer questions about the nature of the U.S. response.

Marcus switched off the television and sat in silence for several seconds. The world outside seemed to have stilled finally after the hours of chaos and mayhem. A blanket of quiet seemed to cover the city as horror had given way to shock.

Marcus looked again at the painting on his wall and felt his eyes well with tears. He'd seen it countless times. He'd seen every detail, every fine stroke the artist had used to portray a grief-stricken Jesus in His final hours of earthly life. But Marcus saw it now with new eyes. For the first time, he saw the pain on the Lord's face and realized it was not merely the anguish of knowing He would soon face the betrayal of His friends, the pain and horror of the beatings, and the agony of crucifixion. Jesus' suffering in the garden came from knowing what would eventually unfold in the world, and that despite His willingness to pour Himself out as a sacrifice for the salvation of man, there would be people—people like Marcus—who would not accept Him.

Marcus's throat tightened at the thought. For the first time since the night his wife died, he felt the genuine and uncontrollable rush of tears. Sobbing, Marcus slid from his leather chair to his knees on the plush carpet. As a harsh cry ripped through him, he felt crushed by the realization of how unworthy and undeserving of God's mercy he was. The weight seemed to bear down on his shoulders, forcing him lower until he lay prostrate on the floor and surrendered to the great, purging groans that came from some long-buried reservoir of grief. His body quaked with the sobs that tore from his chest, and he screamed into the carpet as he poured out the pride and arrogance that had driven him for so long.

"God," he cried as his weeping increased. "Oh, my God. Hear me. Please hear me."

As his spirit flailed for comfort, Marcus sought an anchor in the recesses of his mind. How many times had he quoted passages of Scripture to bring comfort to the hurting? How many times had he brought forth a theological truth to offer hope in an otherwise desperate situation?

Yet now, in his own hour of grief, he found nothing to cling to, nothing to quiet his anguish. There were no well-spoken or thoughtful passages from his sermons to ease his pain. Nothing in his vast library of reference books offered him solace. Nothing he had learned or known or taught eased the grief. He felt stripped bare before the piercing, all-knowing gaze of God. The emotional pain was so intense Marcus gasped for breath.

And then a voice, still and small, seemed to whisper quietly, "'And I, the Son of Man, have come to seek and save those like him who are lost.'"

Marcus had read that verse countless times, had used it in innumerable sermons, but only now, as he sought refuge in the unfathomable grace of God, did he see a facet of it that he'd always missed. Jesus not only saves lost souls; He pursues them. He had sought Marcus's soul, and Marcus had rejected Him. Could there be any grace left for him? He'd assured his staff and Mariette that there was always hope in God's mercy, but did that apply to even him—the vilest of sinners who had used God's Word as a launching pad for his own career? Would God now receive him, or was it too late for a man who had known the truth and refused to surrender himself? People like Mariette had not sinned so egregiously. Such was Marcus's rejection of Christ that he might as well have been the Roman soldier who drove the nails into the Savior's hands or Pontius Pilate who had ordered His death. Could anyone have sinned more surely and completely against God than a man who had used Jesus' sacrifice for his own personal gain?

"God?" Marcus pounded the carpet with his fist. "God, have You forsaken us? If You have withdrawn Your mercy from me, I understand, but is there nothing I can offer these people in their anguish?"

God did not answer, but Marcus's spirit began to quiet. As he thought through the events of the horrible night and realized that God had fulfilled all that He had promised, he came to the grim conclusion that God had every reason to withdraw His grace from the earth.

Marcus choked on another sob. "Forgive me. Oh, dear Lord, forgive me, please."

No sooner had he uttered the words than he felt a sense of peace begin to envelope him. The cleansing feeling of having poured out

his soul to God, of having set aside his pride and admitted his help-
lessness before God was both humbling and fortifying.

He felt stronger.

Purged.

Marcus rested for long moments on the floor, afraid to move lest
he disturb the pool of calm that had settled on him. This, he imagined, was what his wife had felt in those moments before she died.
This almost blissful relief that felt slightly euphoric and supernatural. Had Moses experienced this same sensation when he'd confronted the burning bush? Was this what it meant to find oneself in
the presence of God?

He wasn't sure, but he clung to the moment as long as he could.
Finally, when he found the strength, he levered off the floor to his
knees, where he turned and buried his face on his forearms in the
cushions of his leather chair. "Jesus, please save me," he whispered,
knowing in his heart that he meant not from the terrible events that
he knew would follow, not from the horror and suffering that the
Bible said were yet to come. That would have been his prayer, he
knew, only a few hours ago. But now, Marcus had seen the hand of
God, and he longed only to be saved from the terrible loneliness
and grief of facing whatever lay ahead without the presence of God's
grace in his life.

Even his soul didn't concern him now. The only thing that mattered to Marcus was the knowledge that in the days that lay ahead
God would help him be the man he'd never been. He yearned to be
a voice of truth and righteousness—to help those who had missed
the hand of God now find their way in the darkness.

"O Jesus, save me," he whispered again.

And in that instant, Marcus felt a rush of peace. He practically
felt the comfort of the Lord's arms wrapping around him, infusing
him with courage and strength, affirming that he did, indeed, still
have work to do, that there was still room for him in God's grace,
and that God had not turned His back on him, despite his transgressions.

Marcus rocked back and forth as he cried. These were softer tears of relief and thanksgiving in contrast to his desperate sobs of earlier. Somehow, in the stillness of his office, God assured him that He had not abandoned him. His mercy still stood, ready to reign down on a repentant heart, ready to set aside judgment and offer grace instead.

Like a burst of sunlight through a stormy sky, the thought sent joy streaking through Marcus's soul. Why, he wondered, had he allowed pride and bitterness to stand in the way of receiving this cleansing, purifying gift from God's hand? What a fool he'd been. What an arrogant, self-righteous fool to think that God was somehow not worthy of his attention. Marcus released a long sigh as his tears finally stopped. "Forgive me," he whispered. "Forgive me for my pride and my arrogance and my sin and my foolishness."

Humbled, feeling vaguely as though his soul had been literally scrubbed clean and his heart had been torn asunder, Marcus took a moment to bask in the feeling of relief that now cloaked him. Tonight, he mused, despite the chaos that reigned in the world and the uncertainty of the days that lay ahead, tonight might be the first time in years that he actually got a decent night's sleep.

7

The president stood at the lectern as he read his statement to a mostly bleary-eyed White House press corps. Brad looked around the room, and despite the early hour, he could tell that the media had showed up in record numbers. Though there were a few notable absences, making Brad wonder if those members of the press corps were now among the missing, every media outlet who could wrangle an invitation and credentials had sent at least one staff reporter. Brad was fairly certain he even saw two college kids he recognized from a local university paper.

Charley Swelder had grabbed his elbow moments before Brad entered the briefing room and told him to mind what he said to the gathered reporters. Charley had a piercing gaze that reminded Brad of a snake's—the look was both brazen and predatory. And as Charley spoke, that snakelike stare fixed on Brad like he was some kind of prey. "After the president speaks," Charley said, "we've decided to let you take questions."

"I wish George were here."

"He's not." Charley's expression hadn't changed.

"And what do I tell them about that?" Brad pressed. "The press corps respected George. They're going to want to know where he is."

Charley seemed to think that over. "Tell them he resigned."

Brad's gaze narrowed. "Did he?"

Charley had crossed his arms and given Brad a hard stare that dared him to question him. "George resigned late yesterday afternoon for personal reasons. He declined to come to the meeting in the Sit Room because he'd already given me his resignation letter."

"I'm the chief of staff," Brad pointed out, not buying the story. "He would have talked to me first."

Charley's shrug was nonchalant and unconvincing. "Maybe he couldn't reach you. I've known George for years."

The mounting tension between George and Charley had been obvious in recent weeks. Brad carefully weighed his options, fully aware that Charley would not back down from the explanation if pressed, though the man's motives intrigued him. It would have been easy to pass George's disappearance off as one of many in the events of last night. The White House had already issued a statement about cabinet members and upper-level administration officials they knew were among last night's missing. Why then did Charley seem determined to keep George's name off that list? "Did you speak to him after the disappearances?" Brad pressed.

"Of course not. You know what it was like. Phones down, e-mail out, cell-phone network crashed. I couldn't have reached George Ramiro if I'd tried."

Brad considered that statement and the ramifications that Charley evidently had not tried. Brad knew, however, that given the magnitude of the crisis, George was the kind of man who would have put aside whatever personal problems he might have with the administration and Charley Swelder and risen to the occasion. Something was definitely not right there.

Brad had hesitated a moment longer but on instinct made a decision to keep his suspicions to himself—at least for the moment. He squarely met Charley's gaze. "I'm willing to say that the only information I have is that George resigned, and I haven't had time to inquire about the circumstances. That's all."

Charley's grunt was scornful. "Whatever satisfies your principles, Benton. That's what really matters these days."

"I'm your last resort, Charley. Don't push your luck with me."

"Don't kid yourself." Charley had straightened his tie and looked over Brad's shoulder, surveying the roomful of reporters. "I could replace you in an instant. I picked you because we felt you'd put the best face on this for the administration."

Charley, Brad noted, no longer felt the need to pretend he was only acting on presidential authority. He now seemed perfectly comfortable admitting that he was in charge of the administration's key political decisions. "And now you think I won't spin it right? Is that it?"

"I got the impression in the meeting that you weren't entirely on board with this."

"I told you my opinion." Brad had shrugged. "You've always been able to count on me for an opinion."

"Just mind what you say," Charley had said flatly.

"If you're that concerned, why let me take questions?"

Charley's slight smile was unpleasant. "Because we can disavow anything you say."

"I'm the most dispensable one here—is that it?"

"Yes. And don't forget it, either."

Standing next to Charley in the Press Room now, Brad tried to ignore the persistent smell of cigar smoke and liquor that seemed to cling to the man. Something about Charley always gave Brad the feeling that he'd just left a clandestine meeting where all parties involved had plenty to hide and everything to lose. His first impression of the man had been of a political warhorse who hadn't possessed the looks, the charisma, or the personality to run for office. So Charley had settled for the next best thing. He'd risen to power as a brilliant campaign strategist and ruthless party leader.

The longer Brad worked at the White House, the more that impression of Charley changed. Charley Swelder wasn't merely a powerful political ally and chief advisor to the president. There was something sinister about the man.

As the president finished reading his statement, reporters leaped to their feet. Fitzhugh held up his hands. "I haven't got time to take questions. As you can imagine, things are a little busy around here today."

"Mr. President," pressed a reporter from *The Washington Post*, "Mr. President, is there any direct evidence that the U.S. has been attacked?"

"Do you know who did it?" yelled the *Associated Press* columnist.

"What kind of response are you planning?" someone shouted from the back of the room.

"Could it have been a nuclear attack?" asked a veteran White House correspondent.

Fitzhugh gathered his papers. "I'm going to leave your questions to the chief of staff." He glanced at Brad. "He'll take as many as he can. Brad?"

"Is George Ramiro among the missing?" someone asked.

Brad stepped up to the lectern. "I was informed this morning that George Ramiro resigned last night from the White House for personal reasons. That's all I currently know."

The room quieted slightly as the president swept out the door flanked by his personal aide and Charley Swelder. Brad braced both hands on the lectern and looked at the group. "Let me say at the outset that our information is still very sketchy. I can't give you details on who might be responsible for this or what kind of response we're planning. The joint chiefs are meeting on the matter, and the president has already been on the phone with General Marsden. We're in the process of conducting troop-loss analyses and crisis-response plans."

"Is it safe to say that the United States is at DEFCON 2," pressed the *Associated Press* reporter, "because we believe another attack is possible?"

"We're at DEFCON 2," Brad said, "because preparedness seems wise under the circumstances."

"But you don't think we're facing another assault?"

"We can't say."

A network correspondent stood near the center of the room.

"But the White House position *is* that the disappearances were the result of some form of aggressive act?"

"That's the White House position, yes."

"What about the theory that this was some kind of act of God?" the reporter queried.

Brad felt his pulse accelerate and his stomach begin to twist. "That theory was discussed. As were theories about aliens, natural phenomenon, and chemical and biological warfare. We're studying the matter, and information continues to pour in from around the globe. The White House position is that it is much too soon to reach a final conclusion. We'll make an official statement once we know more."

"How many other nations were hit as hard as the U.S.?" someone asked.

"Our early reports indicate that the U.S. and South and Central America were apparently hardest hit. Canada and Europe and Africa also sustained heavy losses. In the Middle East and Asia, the losses weren't as significant."

"But all the children are missing?"

"As far as we know, yes. That appears to be a global phenomenon."

"What plans have been made for disaster response in the U.S.?" the *New York Times* journalist asked.

"Director Musselman has already consulted with the president. FEMA will play a major role in helping the nation recover."

"Does the president plan to survey the damage personally?"

Brad couldn't see who asked the question. "He's planning a trip to the West Coast this afternoon. He'll start in Los Angeles, then stop in several strategic cities on his way back."

"Is the Secret Service concerned about his safety in the air?"

Brad managed a slight smile. "The Service is always concerned about his safety." A bubble of quiet laughter broke some of the tension in the room. Brad welcomed it. It would be a very long time, he suspected, before any of them found something to really laugh about. "The DOD has assured us that they can protect the president on this trip. I'm confident they can."

A reporter he didn't recognize stood in the back of the room. "Just so we're clear, Mr. Benton, does the administration believe that these disappearances were the direct result of a global terrorist attack or the work of a particular nation or individual?"

"As I said, the administration is considering a number of possibilities." Exhausted, Brad picked up the remaining papers on the lectern and held up a hand. "I'm sorry. That's all I've got time for."

"Mr. Benton, has the president spoken to the Russian president?" someone yelled.

"But do we think this was a terrorist act?" came another question.

Brad shook his head and turned to go. "Nothing more for now. We'll have another briefing as soon as we have more answers."

He ignored the barrage of questions and strode from the room. He had no idea what time Fitzhugh was planning to leave for California, and Brad wasn't going to let anything keep him from boarding that plane.

★   ★   ★

Washington, D.C.
FEMA Headquarters
Local Time 8:00 A.M.

Mariette studied her staff and wondered if she looked as exhausted and wrung out as they did. Many had eyes reddened from crying; most were disheveled. She'd seen that look before. It generally came at the end of the third day of a major relief effort when few survivors had been found and the initial adrenaline rush of emergency response had waned.

At times like that, even the rescue dogs showed signs of fatigue and depression. She knew rescue workers who routinely asked volunteers to hide among the rubble so their dogs could find someone alive. The discovery gave the dogs renewed energy and purpose.

Soon, she knew from looking at her staff, they were going to have to find a live body. Even if she had to provide one herself.

"Okay, I think we have a decent idea what we're looking at here." She turned on the electronic map.

Gasps and mutters of distress filled the room.

Mariette forged ahead. "We all heard the president's statement this morning. And I've spoken to Mr. Musselman. I'm confident we'll have all the resources we need to tackle this."

"What we need," David Liu muttered, "is a miracle."

Mariette ignored him. "The largest problem that we face right now is transportation. The airlines are grounded. We don't know yet how many planes were lost."

"The interstates are almost impassable," David added.

Mariette nodded. "And several major derailments make relying on train cargo unrealistic." She tapped the map. "But we've got waterways."

David stood and began passing out hastily assembled packets to the other nine people in the room. "The secretary of the navy and the Transportation secretary have promised us full access to whatever facilities and staff they can spare. We're in the process of building contact lists for the navy, the coast guard, and the merchant marine."

"Our first priority," Mariette said, "has got to be to get goods and supplies into the major urban areas. We're planning a convoy of supply barges up the East Coast—" she pointed to the Atlantic coastline and then the California coast on the map—"the West Coast, and along the Gulf states. From there, goods can be moved inland along the rivers for distribution."

David dropped into his chair. "We're also coordinating with the Red Cross. We can tap into their resources and stockpiles."

"Volunteer efforts?" someone asked.

Mariette nodded. "I've been contacting our usual list of shelters and local relief agencies." As she studied the faces around the table, she remembered her conversation with Marcus Dumont. Determined to concentrate on the job at hand, she pushed it from her mind. Even the president said the country had been attacked. And after her conversation with Marcus, she'd been able to find a number of

Catholic officials, priests, rabbis, and Protestant ministers who had all disagreed with Reverend Dumont's theory. Had it not been for the haunting voice of her mother's preacher ringing in her mind, she might have felt relieved.

"Whatever we're facing," Mariette said now, "whatever lies ahead, it's important for us to depend on one another. I know that many of you have lost family members." One of the interns began to quietly cry into her hands. "People are depending on us, and the only thing that could make this an even greater tragedy is if we fail each other. We're very short staffed, but if anyone needs some time to deal with some family issues—" She paused. No one spoke. Mariette said, "Good. Then we've got a real mess on our hands. Let's get to work."

★   ★   ★

Aboard *Air Force One*
Local Time 11:01 A.M.

Brad ducked his head into the president's office. "You wanted me, Mr. President?"

Gerald Fitzhugh looked up from his desk. Charley Swelder and Forrest Tetherton, one of George Ramiro's deputy press secretaries, were seated across from him. "Uh, yeah, Brad. Come on in." He summoned Brad into the space with a sweep of his hand.

Brad glanced at the other two men, then took a seat across from the president.

Fitzhugh leaned back in his chair to prop his feet on the wide cherry desk. "We've been discussing George Ramiro."

Brad nodded grimly. "He was a good man. A great press secretary, too." From the corner of his eye, he noted Forrest shifting uncomfortably.

"Not everyone shared that opinion," Charley said.

"I'm sure they didn't." Brad gave Charley a shrewd look. "George didn't always agree with you, I know, but no one can deny that he had real skill in handling the media that would be a great asset right now."

Charley inclined his head to the side. "Maybe. But we've got to move on. We need someone in that office. With George gone . . ."

Brad frowned. "About that—," he said, glancing at the president. "Were you aware George intended to resign?"

The president flushed. Since coming to the White House, Brad had come to recognize the sign as an indication of the president's mounting anger. "No, we did not." Fitzhugh looked at Charley. "Charley told me about it just before we entered the Sit Room last night."

Brad nodded. "I see."

Forrest Tetherton cleared his throat. "The issue at hand is not the timing of George's resignation. The issue is what we're going to do now that he's left us in the lurch. We've got to have someone serving as front man."

"My recommendation," Brad said, "is Jane Lyons. George trusted her."

Charley cursed. "You've got to be kidding."

"Not at all," Brad assured him. "Jane is extremely competent."

"And female," Charley said. "The public and the press would respond better to a man in that office."

Brad's eyebrows lifted. "What decade are you living in?"

Charley gave him a chilling look. "One where I'm more concerned about what I know is true than in being politically correct. I don't care if NOW and the feminist movement want to burn me in effigy. The American people are scared out of their minds, and they don't want some farmer's daughter speaking for the president." He looked at Fitzhugh. "And I think you feel the same way."

The president looked uncomfortable. "Keep it down, Charley. We've got an airplane full of reporters. I'd rather not have to answer questions that would offend more than half the voting population."

Charley rose from his chair with a dissatisfied grunt. He strode to the small wet bar in the corner of the office and poured himself a liberal glass of scotch. "It doesn't matter," he stated, then downed half the liquid. "We've already made a decision."

Brad wasn't surprised. Tetherton's presence on *Air Force One*—and his presence in this meeting—told the story.

Charley gave Brad a cold look that defied objection. "We've tapped Forrest."

Brad didn't respond.

Forrest began to fidget in his chair. "I was very surprised. I wasn't sure that I—"

"Shut up," Charley said flatly. He looked at Brad again. "We just wanted to give you a heads up in case you get asked. Forrest is our man. He'll be handling media inquiries from now on."

Brad held Charley's gaze for a few seconds, then glanced at the president. "And when asked about George?"

"Refer them to me," Forrest said. "I'll handle it."

A tense silence gripped the room. Fitzhugh, Brad noted, eyed Charley Swelder as if he, too, had his doubts about George's alleged resignation.

Forrest Tetherton immediately leaped to fill the silence with an unnecessary and tedious recap of the administration's position on the disappearances. Brad tuned him out and studied Charley, who was finishing off his glass of scotch. *Probably not his first*, Brad thought.

Charley's face looked florid and tense, grooved with deep lines of bitterness and strain. Something about George's apparent disappearance was wearing on the man, and Brad decided he'd better find out why. Though George had not been present at last night's emergency meeting, Brad could not make himself believe that the press secretary was among the raptured believers. He had known George Ramiro for years, and the man had never given Brad a reason to believe he was a Christian—devout or otherwise. As far as Brad knew, George was what his kids would have called a "C and E churchgoer," meaning he went to church on Christmas and Easter only. His religion, or lack of it, had little or no influence on the rest of his life.

"Until we're sure," Forrest was saying, "that George—"

Charley gave him a sharp look. "What do you mean, until we're sure?"

Forrest seemed to cower under the unexpected onslaught.

"Take it easy," the president told Charley. "I think Forrest means that we can't tell the press anything else until we've heard from George. It's possible he disappeared with everyone else—resignation or not." The president looked carefully at each of the three men in the room. When his gaze rested on Brad, he left it there. "For obvious reasons, gentlemen, we've got to remain united on this. With or without George Ramiro, we're in the middle of a midterm election. I have to know that the public and the press are going to see us all on the same team. Does everyone understand that?"

"Yes," Forrest assured him. "Absolutely."

Charley's only answer was a slight shrug.

Fitzhugh kept his gaze trained on Brad. "What about you, Benton? Are you on board with us or not?"

Brad hesitated for a moment, then nodded. "I told you I'd be loyal to your administration when I came to work in Washington. If my position changes, you'll be the first to know."

★   ★   ★

Long Beach, California
Local Time 11:22 A.M.

Brad ignored the pop of the cameras and the clamor of reporters as he shouldered his way through the heavy crowd at the Long Beach Airport. The Joint Chiefs of Staff and the Secret Service had decided to land *Air Force One* at Long Beach rather than face the reported destruction at LAX. The previous night's disappearances had caused havoc in most major cities, especially at airports. The parking decks at LAX were a crush of abandoned cars and wrecked vehicles. Downed planes had left gaping craters in two of the runways.

Brad glanced at his watch and acknowledged that one of the benefits of flying *Air Force One* to the West Coast was that you arrived at roughly the same time you departed D.C.

"Mr. Benton? Mr. Benton?" said an insistent female voice to his left.

Brad ducked his head and tried to edge his way clear of the crowd. He had one thing on his mind, and it didn't entail fielding questions for the president.

"Mr. Benton?" The voice was more insistent. "Mr. Benton, wait—"

With a heavy sigh, Brad turned to face the woman calling his name. He recognized Liza Cannley, a reporter for the *Los Angeles Times*. She'd covered the gubernatorial campaign Brad had managed before his move to Washington. He wiped a hand over his face, exhausted. "Yes?"

"Mr. Benton, I'm covering the story of the disappearances. I caught your statement at the press briefing this morning. I thought maybe—"

"If you heard my statement," he said, "then I don't have anything to add. We haven't had any additional information."

Liza raised an eyebrow. "I just thought—"

Brad shook his head. "I'm actually here on personal business. If you want answers from the White House—" he waved his hand in the direction of the crowd surrounding the president—"he's got people for that."

She snapped her notebook shut. "I guess the move to Washington has changed your priorities. You were so helpful during the governor's race. I thought . . ."

Brad felt a twinge of guilt. The young woman had done him a significant favor during the campaign season. He owed her his civility at least. "I'm sorry. As you can imagine, it's been a stressful night." After his meeting with Tetherton, Swelder, and the president, he'd managed to fall into a fitful sleep on board the plane, but even that had been short-lived. Charley Swelder had shaken him awake shortly after he'd closed his eyes. The president had wanted Brad's opinion on how the disappearances were playing in his home state of California.

Brad continued. "And I'm in a hurry to get home right now. Maybe if you call me tomorrow."

Her eyes widened. "Home? Your family. They stayed here when you went to Washington, didn't they?"

Brad didn't respond.

Liza shoved her notebook into her back pocket. "I'm really sorry, Mr. Benton. That was thoughtless."

"None of us are at our best right now."

"Have you heard from them yet?"

"No."

She let out a long breath, and her eyes filled with tears. "I lost my dad. He was in a nursing home near San Diego where my brother lives. I finally got confirmation this morning."

"I'm sorry."

Liza studied him for a minute, then tipped her head in the direction of the parking lot. "My car is here. Do you need a lift?"

He'd planned to rent a car, but suddenly the thought of a solitary drive to his home in East L.A. felt repugnant. The lift from Liza would give him at least forty more minutes before he would be forced to think about what he was going to face at home. "That would be great."

Beyond Liza's shoulder, he caught the watchful and suspicious eye of Forrest Tetherton. After the meeting on board the plane, Tetherton had cornered him near the galley as Brad had headed for his seat and a much needed rest. Gone were the deference and self-deprecation Forrest had shown in the presence of Charley and the president. He'd faced Brad and told him belligerently that while Brad had handled himself well that morning at the briefing, henceforth he was to keep his mouth shut regarding the disappearances. Any and all information coming out of the White House was to come from Swelder or Tetherton.

Brad had just nodded and stepped around the man. He had more important things to worry about than dealing with some kind of dominance display.

Now, standing on the tarmac, Brad shot a quick look at Swelder. A gaggle of reporters surrounded him, and he was pontificating about the seriousness of the attack and the necessity of support for the president's planned response. "The American people," he could almost hear Swelder saying, "need reassurance and recovery." That statement had been drafted minutes before *Air Force One* touched down at the Long Beach Airport.

"Mr. Benton?" Liza prompted, pulling him from his reverie.

"Sorry," Brad muttered, thinking cynically that Swelder was far more concerned about Gerald Fitzhugh's trailing approval ratings than the needs of the American people or even the global concerns triggered by the recent events. Forrest Tetherton was still watching Brad with an icy glare and an unspoken warning. Brad shook his head slightly and looked at Liza. "I'd love a lift. Thanks for the offer."

★   ★   ★

Washington, D.C.
FEMA Headquarters
Local Time 2:45 P.M.

Mariette looked up from her desk at the intern who had rushed into her office. "My son?" she said. "Did you reach him?" She was just beginning to put together the structure of a relief effort for the havoc caused by last night's events, but her thoughts had never been far from Randal.

The intern shook his head. "Got his roommate. Line two."

Mariette reached for the phone. "Don? Don, is that you?"

"Hi, Mrs. Arnold." The twenty-year-old sounded exhausted and frightened.

"Are you all right? Is Randal all right? Where is he?"

"We're okay," Don assured her. "We didn't even know what was going on until we started hearing all the sirens. Things are really crazy here."

"Where's Randal?" she asked again.

"On his way to you. They've canceled classes for at least a week. Randal couldn't get through to you, so he decided just to drive down to D.C."

Mariette's mind reeled with the possibilities. Gas stations closed.

Roads blocked with wreckage from last night, spotty phone service, and unpredictable radio transmissions would make the trip difficult at best and potentially extremely hazardous. "Oh no."

"He'll be okay," Don said. "Randal knows what he's doing. He took blankets, a flashlight, some extra gas, food—all that kind of stuff. Really . . . all the stuff he could need. You know, he's your kid."

Mariette found small comfort in that. "The roads are bad. He has no idea how bad—"

"He was an Eagle Scout, Mrs. Arnold. He'll be fine."

Mariette thought how little prepared Don was to judge that. She wasn't sure that *she* was prepared to judge how bad it was out there. And it was her job, one she had years of experience doing. "He took his cell phone?"

"Of course. It's just not working right now."

She rubbed her eyes with her thumb and forefinger. "What time did he leave?"

"About two hours ago. I'm sure he'll call you as soon as he can."

"I'm sure he will," she said. "What about you, Don? What are your plans?"

"I haven't been able to reach my folks yet," he said softly. "I'm going to stay here for a bit."

Mariette remembered that the young man's parents lived in Kansas. "I'm sorry. I know you're worried."

"Yeah. I figured the best thing I could do was stay put until I can get a line out and maybe talk to somebody at home. I'll have to work out what to do from there."

"Are you by yourself?"

"I was, but I ventured out of the dorm about a half hour ago. I found some guys I know, and we've decided to pool our resources and just sort of tough this out together. You know—like a blizzard or something. A disaster party . . ."

"Yes," Mariette told him. "It's almost a college tradition. I'm glad you've found friends. You need to be with other people." She took a minute to give Don her direct-dial number and to assure him that he could call if he needed anything.

"Thanks, Mrs. Arnold. I'm sure you'll hear from Randal soon."
"I hope so," she said. "I sure hope so."

★   ★   ★

Los Angeles, California
Local Time 11:45 A.M.

Brad stared out the window as Liza drove up the Pacific Coast Highway toward the home he'd shared with his wife for the past ten
years. He'd driven this road many times. He'd seen this part of the
world after earthquakes had ripped through Los Angeles, after riots
had trashed parts of the city, after mud slides and wildfires had torn
through and left broad paths of destruction in their wake. He'd
driven this road to think, to celebrate, to remember, to find himself.
It had always reflected the ever-changing dynamic that had drawn
him to the West Coast. Even in the wake of the city's greatest disasters, there had been signs of hope, of renewal, of community—signs
that gave the area its character and depth.

None of that prepared him for what he saw now.

It looked like a bomb had been dropped here. Wrecked and abandoned cars littered the roadways. Looting had left many businesses
ransacked. The shells of their burned buildings dotted the highway's
edge. The ecosystem of the area appeared to be in shock as well. Trees
were down. Entire expanses of the delicate sea grasses that lined the
highways were reduced to muddy pits where motorists, in fear, impatience, and desperation, had left the road and driven around the
snarled traffic that had resulted from the disappearances.

When Brad caught an occasional glimpse of the shoreline beyond the heavy development, he saw garbage and debris littering
the beaches and floating in the Pacific surf. Piles of garbage smol-
dered along the shore, where sanitation workers, in desperation,
had resorted to simply burning the refuse that had begun to accu-
mulate in the city. Lack of workers, wrecked and destroyed vehicles,
and the virtual destruction of much of the city's infrastructure

would have even the most basic of services nearly impossible to render. Unable to truck the garbage out to the landfills, the city had authorized beachside burning. A few weeks ago, the action would have sent the environmental lobby into overdrive, but now, only a few lone protestors lined the beachfront. Everywhere, people appeared shocked and adrift.

"It's worse than you thought," Liza prompted him, "isn't it?"

"Maybe. I'm not sure," he confessed. "I'm still exhausted and a bit numb from the onslaught of the past several hours." He glanced at her. "To be honest, I hadn't given California a whole lot of thought. My focus has been so . . . myopic."

"I understand. It's hard to look past what you're already dealing with."

"I've been in meetings all night talking about national security and defense strategy. We had Apache helicopters circling the White House and the sound of emergency sirens all over the city. I hadn't given much thought to what things were going to be like in the rest of the country."

"I'm sure." Liza nodded. "The president said this morning that the administration believes we've been attacked. Do you think it's going to happen again?"

Brad drew a weary breath. "On or off the record?"

"Off."

He shook his head. "Then, no. I don't."

"What does the administration believe—" she shot him a close look—"on the record?"

"That would be a question for Forrest Tetherton."

"Who?"

"Tetherton. He's the new press guy."

"What happened to Ramiro?"

"Resigned," Brad said, stifling a yawn. "At least, that's what I'm told."

Liza pulled her gaze from the road briefly to give him a confused look. "Resigned? When?"

"Last night."

"Before or after the disappearances?"

"Before. Yesterday afternoon."

"Did you see his resignation?"

"Nope. Charley Swelder says George gave it to him."

"Aren't you the chief of staff?"

"That was my question, too."

"Hmm." Liza took a minute to think that over. "Would it do me any good to ask you more questions about this?"

"Not right now," Brad told her. "I don't have the answers. You know everything I do on the issue."

She nodded, apparently taking that at face value. "Okay. So keep talking about what things were like on the East Coast when this happened."

"You know, I thought I was through being shocked." He frowned as they passed an overturned tractor-trailer. A group of teenagers were painting the side with obscene graffiti. "I guess not. This one took me totally by surprise."

"I imagine things were pretty bad in D.C. Maybe even worse than here. Everyone and everything are closer together."

"I don't know. The devastation was—" Brad struggled for the right words—"human in scale. The timing helped. It hit while nearly everybody was home and asleep. We didn't get the kind of damage you got to the environment and the infrastructure because people weren't out and about when it happened. At least we haven't got it yet, not when I left and not that I saw. You guys seem to have been hit harder because it struck earlier, not in the dead of night like it did on the East Coast."

Liza seemed to think that over. "That makes sense. A lot of the damage you're seeing occurred in those first few minutes after it happened. People just went nuts. And the fact that Los Angeles is really a desert trapped between the ocean and the mountains doesn't help. We're dependent on technology to keep the city going. Everything is so fragile here. We're always right on the verge of an environmental catastrophe anyway. It doesn't take much to push us over the edge. It's going to take months, maybe years, to repair the damage to some of the vegetation."

"It's dry out here. It's more spread out," Brad agreed. "And that makes the landscape more vulnerable."

"What happened last night—" Liza shrugged—"was like a chain reaction that set off a whole series of events. Once it started, the trouble seemed endless."

"Yeah. That pretty much describes what it was like in D.C., too. Though the visible damage isn't as bad there as it is here."

"It's just like you said. It was prime time here. Things could only have been worse if it had happened during rush hour."

"Where were you at the time?" Brad asked.

"Lakers game," she said. "It was scary being in that huge crowd. You?"

"At my apartment. Watching the Lakers game. It was amazing. I couldn't believe what I was seeing."

"Oh." Liza pursed her lips. "I've talked to several friends here who were watching it, too. Was the coverage the same on the East Coast?"

"The wedding ring?" Brad asked, still unable to shake the dramatic image of the ring rolling across the boards in the near silence of the packed arena.

"Yeah." Her voice was hushed. "It was bad seeing it in person. I imagine it must have been nearly as bad on television."

"Probably not," he assured her. "At least I didn't have to worry about getting caught up in the crush when people in the stands began to realize they had missing loved ones."

"Yeah. It was probably more confusing in person," she said. "It was hard to tell what was going on at first. The crowd got real quiet—you know, scary quiet. The same way crowds here get when an earthquake starts."

Brad remembered the feeling. A huge crowd of people would suddenly fall silent as they waited in anticipation. The silence always preceded the screaming. "Hushed. Like the air going still before a big storm."

"That's it. Everything went perfectly still for a couple of heartbeats.

I swear I heard that ring plink onto the boards. And then it was just chaos."

"My cable went out a few seconds after it happened; then I was called in to the White House. I never saw the aftermath at the arena. And I can only imagine what it was like trying to get home afterward." He pointed up the road. "Speaking of which, you need to take the next exit to get to my house."

Liza acknowledged his instructions with a slight nod. "It was bad at the Staples Center that night. Screaming and panic. Way worse than earthquakes, because we're used to earthquakes. The disappearances—well, nobody knew what was going on. It took hours to get out of the place. People started looking around for their friends and family who had disappeared. The parking lot was a madhouse. Some people who were watching the game on TV rushed to the arena from all over the city to find out what was going on. People jammed the streets trying to get to their loved ones."

"How long did it take you to get home?"

"I was there with a friend who's a sportswriter. We decided to wait it out. The cellular phone system crashed—"

"In D.C., too."

"So we just sat and talked about what was happening until around four in the morning. When it finally seemed like everything had settled down a little out there, we decided to try getting to the office."

"Story of the century," he mused.

"You bet."

"How bad were things outside the arena?"

"It took us hours just to make it in to the *Times* building." Liza shook her head. "It was crazy. Looting, riots, fires, you name it. The worst in a long time, maybe the worst ever."

"And your editor put you on the story," Brad guessed.

"We're covering a lot of sides to this story, as you can imagine." Liza took the exit Brad had indicated. "I'm still on the political desk, so that's how I got the assignment at the airport today."

"Wouldn't you be better off sticking with the president's entourage? Tetherton's going to be making all the official statements, you know."

"Maybe." Liza gave him a speculative look. "But I'm not sure. You always shot straight with me, Mr. Benton. I have a feeling I might get some entirely different answers from you than I would from Tetherton."

Probably true, Brad mused as he recognized the familiar landmarks near his home. He pointed the direction for Liza to turn. His stomach was beginning to twist into knots as he thought of what might await him at home. "I'm not authorized to give you a statement."

"Maybe not," Liza said, turning into his neighborhood, "but I'm pretty confident I'll get more from you than just the party line. Like this business with Ramiro. I bet there's a story in that. Even if it's off the record."

He wondered what she'd say if he told her that his off-the-record opinion was that God had moved across the face of the earth and that those left standing were about to endure unforeseen horrors in the little time left before the end of the world came. It probably wasn't what she'd want to hear. He put the thought aside as his tree-lined street came into view. "It's this street," he told Liza, pointing to the right. His voice, he noted, had turned slightly raspy. Brad's throat tightened. "Fifth house on the left."

Liza turned slowly into the driveway of the contemporary brick home where Brad had seen his children grow up and his dreams come true. He stared at the cracked sidewalk, wondering why he'd never gotten around to fixing it like Christine had asked. It had never seemed like a priority. Just like his faith had never seemed like a priority—until now. The house looked untouched, pristine, and impossibly still. The hedges were perfectly trimmed. Christine wouldn't have had it any other way. Even the geraniums were blooming, a fact that seemed incongruous to him when he considered the devastation he'd witnessed on the way to the house.

But, as perfect as it looked, it wasn't the home he remembered. It was too quiet. Too lonely. No one came to the door to greet him.

Emily wasn't shooting baskets in the driveway, ready to meet him with her beautiful smile and a flip of her ponytail. Brad Jr.'s feet weren't sticking out from beneath the old Mustang he'd been working on for the past nine months. There was no stereo blaring from an upstairs window. Inside, he wouldn't find Megan practicing her cello or Christine curled up at one end of the sofa with a novel.

He'd find nothing but a dark, cold reminder of what he'd lost and how much of a fool he'd been.

For a moment he considered asking Liza to turn around, to take him away from this place and the horror he knew lay inside. He was beginning to understand how victims felt when asked to view a crime scene. The fear clawing at his gut was tearing at him relentlessly, making his breath short and his pulse quicken. He felt light-headed and slightly nauseous.

"Mr. Benton?" Liza laid a hand on his sleeve. "Are you . . . okay?"

Brad took a fortifying breath and reached for the door handle. He had to flee the vehicle before he embarrassed himself by breaking down. "Fine. I'm fine."

"Do you want me to go with you?"

He shook his head. No. *No.* The last thing he wanted was to let someone witness the horrible grief he was about to experience. It would be harsh and stark, angry and frightening and consuming. For a while, he needed nothing but silence to listen to the accusing voices in his head. "No," he said, his voice raw. "I'll be fine."

"Mr. Benton—"

"Really."

Liza seemed to hesitate but finally took him at his word. He had no doubt that she'd experienced this kind of situation several times already. She was bound to have friends who'd lost loved ones. She'd lost a loved one herself. Why did his grief seem so much more tragic and real to him? he wondered. Was it because he knew he had no one to blame but himself and his own failure to heed God's call?

Liza shifted the car into gear and gave him a sympathetic look. "Okay, I understand."

Brad forced himself to step onto the driveway. The concrete felt unforgiving and unwelcoming. Reaching into the pocket of his jacket, he pulled out a business card, then turned to Liza. "If you'll call me tomorrow, I'll tell you what I can about what you're looking for."

She looked at him curiously. "Mr. Benton—"

"I have a lot to say," Brad said. "I'll have more to say, I think, after I've spent some time here."

With a slight nod, she tucked the card into her sun visor. "Any particular time?"

Brad shook his head. "It doesn't matter. My cell number is on the card." He stepped away from the vehicle and pushed the door shut.

He gripped the handle of his briefcase and headed for the front door. Behind him, he heard Liza's car back out of the driveway. He began to feel that same distant feeling he'd experienced in the Situation Room the night before.

Was it only last night? He felt like he'd lived a hundred lifetimes since then. For most of the tedious hours in that room, he'd felt a sense of detachment and preoccupation. In his mind he'd turned over every sermon he'd ever heard, replayed his mother's frequent lectures and the soft voice of Christine's quiet prayers and persuasive debates. He'd felt himself sinking slowly and irrevocably into a dark, cold sea of guilt, and he knew his darkest days lay ahead.

With trembling fingers, Brad reached in his pocket and found his keys. He still had the key chain with the map of California that Emily had given him when he'd gone to Washington.

"Don't forget the way home, Dad," she'd teased.

He'd assured her he couldn't. Now, chest tight and palms damp, he slid the key into the lock and gave it a firm turn. The door swung open with a groan of protest—another problem Christine had asked him to fix. Another way he'd failed her.

The silence hit him in the face with the chilling effect of a blast of arctic air. With three teenagers living at home, his house was *never* silent. Christine had worked hard to make the large space homey and welcoming. All of his children frequently invited friends over. Brad was used to having at least one dinner guest a night when he was in town.

Not now. Now the silence gripped him like a glove of fear and grief.

He took in the view from the foyer. The living room to his left had the familiar soft blue walls. Christine had sent him back to the paint store four times until the color suited her. The dining-room table held a fresh bowl of flowers, as it usually did. His wife was a fan of fresh flowers and customarily had several small arrangements throughout the house. The oak stairs to the second level were polished and clean. As usual. Christine left nothing out of place, nothing untidy, nothing undone. She managed his home and his life with an efficiency that Brad had both appreciated and envied.

Everything was as he remembered. Fresh, welcoming, clean, but silent. Eerily, hauntingly silent. His gaze traveled through the cathedral-ceilinged foyer, through the living room, where the edge of the kitchen counter formed the breakfast bar. He and Christine had sat there many mornings and discussed some story they'd read in the paper or what the kids were up to. His heart seemed to stand still when he finally saw the first evidence of the night's tragedy in his life. Christine's cotton pajama bottoms and the fleecy cardigan she normally wore around the house lay on the floor in a crumpled heap, a wooden spoon abandoned next to them.

The bowl on the counter told him that Christine had been in the middle of mixing up a batch of cookie dough when she'd disappeared. Christine always used the green glass bowl for cookies. It had been a wedding present from Brad's mother, who had also used it for baking. Legacy and heritage were important to Christine.

Brad looked again at the pile of clothing, so out of place in the otherwise tidy house. The invisible fist of grief squeezing his heart and cutting off air to his lungs tightened relentlessly. Tears scalded his eyes. His head began to spin. And before he could catch himself, his knees buckled, sending him to the Oriental carpet, where he buried his face in his hands and gave free rein to the agony of a broken heart.

8

Marcus fought his way through layers of sleep as he groped for the ringing phone on his nightstand. It was hard to believe it had been less than twenty-four hours since the Rapture and the chaos that had ensued. Marcus had spent a grueling day trying to piece his organization back together, to give comfort to the hurting members of his staff, and to help everyone, including himself, face the realities and failures of their immortal souls.

By all rights, he should be up late worrying about what the future held. His staff was decimated, with most of his key executives gone and only a few of his upper-level staff and some support staff remaining. Even they couldn't be counted on. Those people who had been left behind after God raptured His church were reeling in a sea of grief over their missing family and friends.

Marcus had gathered his skeleton crew together at the end of the day for prayer and a call to repentance. He'd given them a scriptural perspective on what he thought the weeks and months ahead would bring and a humble apology for all the ways he felt he'd failed them with his own duplicity and doubts. He'd wept before the small group as he'd told them of his encounter with the Lord in his office and pleaded that all of them consider their own soul and their need for grace as they faced the future.

Exhausted and emotionally depleted, he'd finally left the office and made his way to his Georgetown home for some desperately needed rest. He'd fallen asleep before the sun had set. For the first time in years, his mind had surrendered to dreamless peace the moment he'd crawled into bed. Had it not been for the insistent ringing of the phone, he had no idea how long he might have slept.

Marcus finally found the receiver and pressed it to his ear. "Hello?" He twisted to look at the digital clock on his nightstand. The darkness in the room told him it was not yet dawn, but he was surprised to find it was only a little after ten. The harsh weight of fatigue had fooled his body into thinking it was much later.

"Marcus? I'm sorry if I woke you." Theopolus Carter, the young lawyer for Marcus's extensive organization, sounded grave and far older than his twenty-nine years.

"No problem," Marcus assured him. "I told you earlier this evening. I'm always available to any of you."

"I was calling about business," Theo said.

That statement needed no clarification. Theo Carter was not interested in discussing his soul, immortal or otherwise. Marcus sighed. "What's the problem?"

"We just got word that Senator Max Arnold is calling for hearings on the disappearances tomorrow."

"That's not surprising."

"The Judiciary Committee is in the process of putting together witness lists. I have a source near the committee who tells me Arnold is going for a broad sweep, from the White House to the Pentagon to a couple of think tanks."

Marcus didn't doubt that Max Arnold was looking for a way to turn the events of the Rapture to his political advantage. With midterm elections looming, Arnold probably hoped to shore up his party's slim majority in the Senate and bolster his own presidential hopes. A series of senatorial hearings at a time when people were desperate for answers would have Arnold's image in front of voters for several weeks. Not that Marcus was being cynical . . . in a political town, even something as dramatic as the Rapture was merely a tool to be spun by the image makers. "I can see why Senator Arnold would want to do that," Marcus told Theo.

"We have an opportunity to put you on a panel."

Marcus considered that information. Forty-eight hours ago, he'd have not only leaped at the opportunity, but he'd have had his extensive public-relations staff securing the invitation for him. Keeping his image in the public eye had been crucial to keeping donations flowing into his organization's coffers. Now he considered the opportunity from another perspective. Chances were slim that Arnold would have many witnesses willing or able to tell the truth about what had happened. "I'll do it," Marcus said.

"Marcus—" Theo's voice held a note of warning.

"What's the problem?"

Theo drew an audible breath. "I'm just not sure. . . . I don't think that's wise."

"Because of what I have to say?"

"Because I think that we're going to face an enormous fiscal crisis in the near future. We still don't have a feel for how much of our donor base is gone. And I don't think it's wise for you to be too public with an opinion that many people are going to find unpopular."

"It's the truth, Theo."

"It's your version of the truth," Theo said, his tone frustrated. "It's not politically smart. And it opens you up to lawsuits."

"Lawsuits? Because people aren't going to like my opinion?"

"Because arguably, if you are right, you've been taking donations under false pretenses. You could be sued by donors and their families if you go public now with what you told the staff this afternoon."

"Only a lawyer could think that way, Theo."

"I *am* a lawyer. You pay me to think that way."

Marcus sighed. He had hired Theo for his professional credentials and his instincts. Together, they'd devised a strategy of public appearances, political favors, and high-visibility humanitarian efforts that had moved Marcus's reputation into a tight leadership circle recognized and respected by presidents and world leaders. Less than a year ago, Marcus would have had to lobby hard for a spot on Max Arnold's high-profile witness list. Now the invitation came naturally, obviously, and largely due to the efforts of Theo Carter. "I understand," Marcus said, "and I'm sure it's sound advice."

"I'm glad you realize that." Theo sounded relieved.

"But I can't take it."

"Marcus—"

Marcus swung his feet over the side of the bed and rubbed a hand over his face. "I meant what I said this evening. I'm through telling the truth and not living the truth. I'm through with worrying more about my reputation than my self-respect and the Lord I represent here on earth." He took a deep breath. "I've failed that Lord too many times. I'm not going to do it this time."

"I just think that some time—"

"I know," Marcus assured him. "I know you think I should consider this, and if we'd been having this conversation at eleven o'clock last night, I'd have agreed with you." He paused. "But these are extreme times. They demand men and women who are willing to take an extreme stand. They demand men and women who are willing to come down on the side of good. God demands it. And for the first time in my life, I'm going to rise to the occasion."

There was a tense silence on the line, and when Theo spoke, his voice sounded tight. "Then I don't think I can work for you anymore, Marcus."

"I'm sorry to hear that. I had hoped—"

"To save my soul?" Theo's laugh was harsh. "I've been listening to your sermons for over a year. Don't you think I've heard whatever you have to say about eternal damnation and treasures in heaven?"

The accusation brought a stinging reminder of Marcus's failures. "You listened to my words. But not to my conviction. I had hoped that you'd give me some time."

"So I could listen to you tell me that this . . . mess . . . was the work of God?" Theo laughed again. "My eighty-year-old grandmother is missing from her nursing home. My six-year-old niece and my five-year-old nephew have vanished. My sister is frantic with grief. My mother, who took in laundry every day of my life to have enough money for me and my sister to make it through school, was on a church choir trip in New York, and I still haven't been able to reach her. Sorry, Marcus. I'm having a little trouble believing God's hand is in this—and if it is, why would I want anything to do with Him anyway?"

Marcus heard the raw note in the young man's voice and recognized it as the same bitter tone he'd used for years to excuse his flight from the hand of God. He'd railed in that same tone when his mother died, done it again when he'd lost his wife. The wounds had been so deep, so raw, that nothing had been able to stem the tide of grief. "Theo, I wish I could tell you I had an answer for that question."

"There is no answer."

"I know. I've been there."

"Yeah, sure. And now you've seen the light, and you're ready to accept a God who metes out justice like some cosmic toddler, who decides on a whim who's worthy and who's not? Sorry. I'm not interested."

"I understand," Marcus admitted. "I've been there." Theo didn't respond. Marcus could almost feel the young man's anger burning through the phone line. "Theo, I'm not asking you to agree with me."

"Good thing."

"I just want you to give me some time. I need you. I'd like you to stay on with us, at least for the next couple of months."

"I can't do that. I'm leaving tomorrow to help my sister in New York. She needs me right now."

"Take a leave of absence," Marcus urged.

"No, Marcus. It's over. I just wanted to let you know about the Senate hearings before I resigned. I would have made the same decision regardless of whether you decided to testify or not."

"I see."

"You gave me a start. I owe you for that."

"You gave me everything I asked for and more, Theo. You don't owe me anything."

"Take care of yourself, Marcus."

"Let me know if I can ever do anything for you, will you?"

"Sure. Good-bye."

Marcus waited until he heard the line go dead before he replaced the receiver. His stomach twisted with the realization that Theo Carter, at least, was one young man God had sent into his circle whom Marcus had allowed to slip through the cracks. He shuddered and reached for the Bible on his nightstand. It had been his wife's— it was the only copy Marcus had in the house. His extensive library of translations, commentaries, and reference materials in his Crystal City offices served as an excellent backdrop for photos and press conferences. And he'd read them, knew them all well. But like his home, his heart had been empty of their truth.

He flipped open the book to a passage he'd quoted a thousand times:

> I am telling you this so that no one will be able to deceive you with persuasive arguments. For though I am far away from you, my heart is with you. And I am very happy because you are living as you should and because of your strong faith in Christ.
>
> And now, just as you accepted Christ Jesus as your Lord, you must continue to live in obedience to Him. Let your roots grow down into Him and draw up nourishment from Him, so you will grow in faith, strong and vigorous in the truth you were taught. Let your lives overflow with thanksgiving for all He has done.
>
> Don't let anyone lead you astray with empty philosophy and high-sounding nonsense that come from human thinking and from the evil powers of this world, and not from Christ.

Marcus closed the Bible with a heavy sigh and dropped his head to rest against the smooth leather cover. "Lord God," he prayed, "please forgive me. O God, forgive me."

The familiar sense of disquiet that had kept him awake many

sleepless nights in the past now returned to settle on his soul. Marcus recognized the feeling and knew he stood no chance of going back to sleep. Wearily, he tossed the covers aside, gripped the Bible, and headed for his study. He'd use the next several hours to work on his Senate testimony. God had handed him this opportunity to use his knowledge and his training for something other than duplicity and fraud.

He was determined not to squander it.

★   ★   ★

Los Angeles, California
Local Time 7:12 P.M.

Brad had no idea how long he stayed on the floor in his foyer. His knees ached, his head throbbed, his throat felt raw, his eyes were swollen from weeping, and the light streaming through the front windows had waned. Weary and exhausted, he pushed himself off the floor. He wiped his eyes and face with his shirtsleeve even as he stumbled toward the kitchen.

He found he couldn't bear the thought of leaving Christine's clothes in a heap on the floor for another moment. She wouldn't have liked that. Yet as he approached the pile, he realized he didn't want to touch them, felt vaguely as though he was trespassing on something sacred, but he couldn't simply leave them there as if no one cared enough to see to them.

He'd always wondered when he'd heard victims' families crying for closure after disasters like plane crashes and building fires. Their relentless demands for a body—even a portion of a body—had confused him. If someone was dead, why did people feel the need to lay eyes on the corpse?

He understood now. There was something haunting about having nothing left of Christine but his memories and a pile of her clothing.

When he reached the kitchen, he found the dry ingredients were mixed in the green glass bowl. Brad wiped his eyes with the back of his hand again and dumped the contents of the bowl in the trash while he reached for his courage. Finally he bent down to gently touch the fleece cardigan. It was cold, empty. How many times had he touched that sweater to feel Christine's warmth seeping through the fabric? He had taken it for granted, he realized, all her warmth and tenderness that had seen him through so much.

Now the cardigan was nothing but an empty piece of clothing. His fingers trembled as he raised it slowly to his face. He heard something plink on the tile floor, then saw his wife's wedding ring bounce twice before rattling to a rest. He remembered the scene at the Lakers game when the forward's ring had dramatically rolled across the boards.

Brad reached for the gold ring he'd placed on Christine's finger twenty years ago. It looked so small in his palm. Christine had always had elegant fingers—slim and long. He'd thought of them as a lady's hands, despite her practical short nails and the calluses from her beloved gardening. His fingers closed around the ring in a tight fist until his palm ached from the pressure. Finally, he slipped the ring into his shirt pocket. He looked again at the floor and saw the gold-and-diamond triple locket that held a baby picture of each of their children. He'd given it to her on their fifteenth wedding anniversary. Brad lifted the pendant and put it in his pocket with the ring.

He pulled the cardigan to his face and inhaled a great breath. The soft fabric still held her sweet scent. That same fascinating mix of a gentle floral perfume, combined with cinnamon and nutmeg and lemons that had captured Brad's attention the first time he met her. He took a deep breath and pressed the cardigan to his lips. "Oh, God." He wept into the fabric. "Oh, Christine. No, please, no."

Silence filled the house. Brad's body trembled as a fresh surge of tears had him weeping into the sweater. "I'm sorry," he called to his wife. "I'm so sorry." The words broke on a sob as he realized the enormity of what he now faced. Though he'd paid little attention to his mother's lectures about the events of the Rapture, he'd heard them often enough to remember mentions of the Tribulation, Ar-

mageddon, and a host of other horrors that were supposed to follow. Now he would face them alone, without his wife or his family.
Though a part of him was grateful that Christine, Emily, Megan, and
Brad weren't here to experience what the future held, he couldn't
imagine going through these things without them.

Christine had been his rock, his counsel, his anchor for so long,
the idea of even existing apart from her made him feel barren. He
rubbed the fleece against his face and continued to weep into it as a
thousand memories floated across his mind. The first time he'd met
her at that college dance. She'd worn a green dress. He'd seen her all
the way across the room, her lips curved into an ever-present smile,
her blonde hair pulled back off her face. His friends had urged him to
talk to her. He remembered feeling afraid for the first time in his life.

But Christine had not rebuffed him. She'd given him a dance.
Which had led to a date the following weekend. Which, in turn, had
developed into a summer romance and then stretched into a two-
year engagement. He'd married her three weeks after their college
graduation. She'd spent their honeymoon and the first six months
of their marriage on the campaign trail with him, working to elect
him as some now-forgotten state legislator.

Christine had never complained about his long hours or the grueling pace of campaign work. She'd seemed, instead, to thrive on the
energy of it. He'd been in New Hampshire for the presidential pri-
maries when she'd gone into premature labor with Brad Jr. He'd
made it home minutes after the tricky delivery, just in time to hold
his newborn son.

His wife had graciously encouraged him to accept the next opportunity that came his way—a gubernatorial campaign that had re-
located them all to California. Through everything, through every
valley and peak in their lives, she had been the foundation that kept
their family life stable and secure. Brad had missed too much of that
family life in pursuit of his own dreams and ambitions.

Only now, as he cradled her sweater, did he wonder how many
of her dreams had been sacrificed along the way. Only now did he
finally hear her quiet prayers and insistence that all she desired was

for her family to know and follow God's will for their lives. Only now did he hear the thread of pleading in her voice when she spoke to him about eternity.

Only now did he see how much he must have disappointed her.

The bitter thought had him doubled over the counter, his grief so acute it roared like a physical pain through him. He struggled for breath even as he flailed emotionally for something—anything—to hold on to.

For what seemed like hours, he stood, hunched over the counter, emptying himself until finally a sort of numbness seemed to seep through his limbs and into his brain.

Brad sank to the floor, where he braced his back against the pickled oak cabinets. Knees bent, he dangled the now-sodden sweater between his legs and stared vacantly at the ticking clock over the sink.

He might have sat there for hours had the sound of his cell phone ringing not startled him. Brad slowly wiped his eyes again and plunged his hand into his pocket to retrieve the phone. The display flashed a coded number he recognized. Brad contemplated not taking the call but dismissed the thought. He'd wasted too many years being a coward, he realized, too many years fleeing from the call of God and the demands of commitment and faith. He was through with all of that. He owed Christine all the things he'd failed to give her in life. "Benton," he said, his voice raspy and tired.

"This is Forrest Tetherton. Where are you?"

"On my own time," Brad told him. "I told the president I was taking a leave of absence as soon as we touched down in California. He approved it."

"We're on your turf here. Your contacts could be useful to us."

"I'm sure you and Swelder have things covered," Brad said. He rubbed his thumb over the soft fabric of Christine's cardigan. "I have some personal business to take care of."

"Business that involves a reporter from the *Los Angeles Times*?"

"An old friend. She gave me a lift home."

"Well, we have a problem."

Brad wondered if Forrest had any clue of the extent of that

understatement. A problem indeed. With the end of the world at hand and untold horrors about to sweep across the globe, the problems were only beginning. "Problem?"

"Max Arnold is calling hearings on the Hill."

"I heard that."

"When did you hear it?" Tetherton demanded.

"This morning. Colonel Wells told me."

"You discussed this with Colonel Wells? Why weren't we involved in that discussion?"

Brad sighed. "I *am* the chief of staff, Tetherton, no matter how much you and Charley wish I weren't."

"This isn't personal, Benton. And this isn't the time to make it that way. It's just as the president said—we've all got to stick together."

"Sure. None of it's personal." Brad wiped a hand over his face and realized how terribly weary he was. "I had a discussion with Wells just before the president's press conference. I wanted to be up to speed on what the Pentagon was thinking before we walked into the briefing room."

"What did he tell you?"

Brad frowned. "That Marsden and the rest of the Pentagon brass are considering the same theories we are. That they've got some strange reports coming out of their units in the field, including some massive manpower losses in some divisions. That they're looking into several possibilities and trying to ensure that our national defense, despite any evidence to the contrary, is still secure." Brad paused. "I found it comforting that they believe it is, considering that they believe we've been attacked and have no idea who did it or why. I'm not precisely sure how they can claim we're secure when they can't do better than that."

If Tetherton sensed his sarcasm, he ignored it. "Anything else?"

Brad considered the discussion he and the colonel had had about Brad's Rapture theory. Charley, no doubt, would have brought Tetherton up to speed on Brad's objections to the president's statement. No need to get into that again. "Only that Arnold was planning to order hearings. Which you clearly know already. Those are the high spots. Why?"

"I don't suppose you've been watching the news?"

Brad knew most of his Washington colleagues would find the notion shocking, but turning on the news was generally not his first priority outside of work hours. He'd learned soon after his arrival in Washington that the news saturation in the area tended to blur the edges of reality. Broadcast news began at 4:30 P.M. and ran straight through until 8:00 P.M. It picked up again at 10:00 and didn't end until midnight. With the addition of CNN and the other cable news networks, it was painfully easy to feel inundated. So Brad had made a point of limiting his news exposure to two hours a day. Today he hadn't even felt the desire to know what was happening in the rest of the world. Nothing much mattered to him beyond the tragedy in his own house. "No," he said quietly. "I haven't."

"About four hours ago, one of our fighter planes was shot down by a Russian MiG outside Gdansk, Poland. The jet was an escort for one of the B-52s."

Brad closed his eyes. "The pilot?"

"Dead on impact. No eject. Which is probably a good thing."

Brad hoped he never reached a point in his life when he felt that the death of a young man was a good thing. "We wouldn't want any prisoners," he said bleakly, certain that had been the president's position.

"Exactly. It could compromise the entire mission."

The mission, Brad knew, was a potential disaster. Against his advice, the president and the national security advisor had met with the joint chiefs and decided to put B-52s in the air near the Russian border in case the U.S. needed first-strike capabilities. Brad had felt the action was unnecessarily inflammatory, that it escalated the crisis in an area of the world that had been tense even before the disappearances. But the president and Charley Swelder had reiterated their need for Fitzhugh to appear fearless and strong to the American people. Now a young pilot was dead, and the Russians knew the U.S. had bombers in the airspace near their borders. Fitzhugh had gotten more than he bargained for. "The Russians are blaming us?" Brad guessed.

"Our proximity to their border gave them the excuse they needed to claim we're poised to attack."

"We *are* poised to attack, Forrest."

"This isn't a secure line," Tetherton told him curtly.

Brad didn't bother to point out that the president had virtually told the media that morning that he was planning a strike. "What do the Russians want?"

"They want us to give their people back."

"Back?"

"Yeah. Back. They fired up a propaganda campaign that says that we kidnapped nearly 20 percent of their total population and all their children—that we have a new and unknown weapon of mass destruction and that we're ready to strike again."

"You're kidding."

"No. 'fraid not."

"Did anybody mention to the Russian government that the Cold War has ended and that when the Soviet Empire collapsed, their propaganda campaigns stopped working? They get CNN in Moscow now, you know."

"Maybe so, but a few hard-liners in the Russian parliament seem to be calling the shots. We haven't been able to determine whether they've had a coup over there or if they're all that's left of the government. Kolsokev and the rest of the leadership may be among the missing."

Brad doubted that. "Looks like their casualty rate wasn't as high as ours." A fact that didn't surprise him. After years of religious persecution and oppression by the Communist Party, the church in the former Soviet Empire was still recovering. "Did anyone point that out to them?"

"Of course. But you can see why the Russians are trying to turn the catastrophe to their political advantage."

"Like we are?" Brad asked sourly.

Forrest's tone turned disapproving. "I don't think I need to remind you—"

"I know. I know." He closed his eyes as a wave of fatigue washed over him. "We're a united front."

"To the Russians and anyone else who might ask," Forrest said grimly.

"So we've been unable to reach Kolsokev?" Brad asked. Though the peace-oriented new Russian president had made great strides toward religious and civil liberties in recent years, Brad doubted that Kolsokev had been a closet Christian who'd been swept away in the Rapture. More likely, the Russian military and its old-school allies had seen the opportunity to retake control of the beleaguered country. Since Kolsokev's election, they'd sorely missed their large share of the country's budget, their political power, and their international prestige. "You know, we could easily be facing a civil war in Russia," Brad said. "Especially if Kolsokev is still alive."

"And Max Arnold? What's your take on that?"

"He's using Senate hearings as a platform to claim that the president's foreign policy isn't sufficient to deal with a Russian threat. It advances his political agenda and puts him in front of the American people, advocating a strong defense at a time when people are scared out of their minds."

"That's what we suspect, too," Forrest said.

"We should have seen it coming. Since when has Max Arnold wasted an opportunity to campaign against the president? It's practically a foregone conclusion that he's going to get his party's nomination next cycle."

"No one is surprised by the hearings," Forrest said, his voice pained, as if the effort of explaining this to Brad was more than he should have to endure. "But we just got word that Arnold wants you to go before the committee."

That did surprise Brad. Max Arnold would be much better served with Secretary of Defense Ed Leyton or Stan Palatino, the national security advisor, than with Brad. Brad wasn't nearly as good political fodder as either of them. As White House chief of staff, he was generally briefed and aware of high-level strategy and defense decisions, but he was rarely, if ever, tapped to represent those decisions to Congress or to the American people. "Why me?"

"That's what we'd all like to know." Tetherton made a small clucking noise with his tongue. "I talked to my contact on the committee. I suggested Leyton or Palatino to represent the administration's position—these are issues, after all, that pertain to the Armed Services Committee. If Arnold were chairman of Labor and Human Resources, that would be one thing, but there's only one possible thing the Armed Services Committee might want to know."

"Are we going to attack or wait to be attacked?"

"Exactly."

"And Arnold has no reason to think I'd be in a position to answer that question—so he must want me there for a different reason. Is that what you think?"

"Yeah. I think he's looking for cracks in the president's armor. It's not the best kept secret in Washington why you're in that office, Brad."

"I'm aware of that."

Tetherton sighed. "I was told quite firmly that Arnold wants you. Just you. He's not particularly interested in hearing what the president's defense advisors have to say."

Brad thought that over. Unless Colonel Wells had revealed something to his contacts at the Pentagon, he had no idea why Max Arnold would be interested in his take on the events of the previous night. Brad had managed to keep his differences with the president out of the news so far, so it made no sense that Arnold would be fishing in that pond. "I don't know what to tell you. I can refuse his invitation to testify."

"He'll subpoena you if you refuse," Tetherton assured him. "My source told me that, too."

"What grounds does he have for a subpoena?"

"Another excellent question, isn't it?" Brad could hear Tetherton's impatience. "What have you gotten us into, Benton?"

Brad was silent for a minute. "Nothing that I know of."

"That had better be the case. You'd better believe I'm going to monitor everything you say to that committee. If you embarrass this administration—"

"I understand my responsibilities," Brad said. Besides, the administration was doing a decent enough job of embarrassing itself without his help.

"I hope so," Tetherton said. "You'll have to take the red-eye back to Washington tonight. Arnold's starting in the morning."

"On Saturday?"

"He's eager, it seems."

Brad didn't doubt it. It *was* an election year. Arnold had a lot riding on his party's showing in the midterm. Every day counted in his race to secure his party's nomination to challenge Fitzhugh. "I need a few more days at home," Brad hedged.

"Sorry. Can't give you that. Arnold won't budge." Tetherton paused. "Neither will we."

Brad's fingers tightened on the phone. "I lost my family, Tetherton. I have to set things right here."

"Then you'll have to do it after you testify."

"I'm not—"

"Look, Brad. I'm sorry for your loss. Honestly. But I'm sure you've made family sacrifices because the job came first in the past. Everyone in this business does."

Too many times, Brad thought grimly. "I just need a few days."

"I'm sorry. Arnold's not going to take no for an answer and neither is the president. There's no way around this."

"Are you threatening me?"

"Just letting you know where we stand. You're a part of this administration because you're politically expedient. If you quit being an asset and become a liability, I don't have to tell you that there are a significant number of people—including the president—who won't especially miss you when you're gone."

Brad managed a bitter laugh. "I won't miss them either, Forrest. I've done a good job for the president, but I'm not in love with Washington politics or the White House."

"Just remember, Brad, there are some enemies that follow you long after you're gone. You ruin us with the committee, and you'll make some."

"Thanks for the tip. Are there any commercial flights in the air yet?"

"There's one flight to Reagan National out of Long Beach tonight. Your assistant's booked you on it."

"What time?"

"Ten. Be on it, Brad. Do yourself a favor and be on it."

"I'll consider it." Brad ended the call before Forrest could say anything else. Everything in him wanted to rebel. He didn't care if he never saw the West Wing or any of the people he worked with again. Working at the White House had quickly lost its appeal when Brad had begun to experience the political backlash of his appointment.

He had no doubt that the president and Charley Swelder had both known about the previous chief of staff's transgressions and had both participated in the cover-up. These days, though he couldn't prove it, he was sure that wasn't the half of what the two were involved in. Fitzhugh was up to his neck in bad business deals and crooked political allies who had begun dropping like flies in SEC and FTC investigations.

The idea of representing the president's position at Max Arnold's hearings was repugnant, particularly when Brad felt sure that the administration's claims of a foreign attack were unfounded, unjustified, and untrue. But Forrest had made it painfully clear that if Brad didn't support the president's position to the committee, he could kiss his job good-bye—and maybe any hope of future employment. And that wasn't all.

A part of him screamed that the worst they could do to him was fire him. In light of what he'd already lost, it seemed a small price to pay. But another part still remembered Christine the night they'd discussed the job offer in Washington. He'd taken her to dinner at one of their favorite restaurants on the beach. They'd discussed the kids, their vacation plans, her progress on a Bible study group she was organizing. Brad had not broached the subject of the job offer until they'd gone for a walk on the beach.

Christine had been ecstatic at the opportunity, if disappointed at his suggestion that she stay in California. He'd pointed out that he expected the move to be temporary. He wasn't liked by many high-level administration officials. He'd known, even then, that Fitzhugh was bringing him to Washington as a purely political decision. He'd known before he even accepted the job that it was probably only a matter of time before he was sacrificed to further Fitzhugh's ambition.

Christine had been the one to point out that often God had called men and women in the Bible to extraordinary circumstances. Daniel had served Nebuchadnezzar, Esther had married Xerxes, and Joseph had risen to power as Pharaoh's number-two man. Though God had placed them all in circumstances where they confronted persecution, injustice, and immorality, each had accepted God's call and risen to the occasion. Brad, she had insisted, should view the opportunity to serve at the White House the same way. He could be an extraordinary man of God amidst difficult circumstances.

She couldn't possibly have known, he thought, how dismally unprepared he was for that task. And now? Now that he knew that he wasn't God's man at all—that most of his life had remained woefully unsurrendered—was he supposed to believe that God was calling him to be a voice of truth? He'd virtually ignored the Almighty up until now. Why would God want anything to do with him?

The question depressed him. He closed his eyes and dropped his head back against the cabinets, too weary to contemplate anything so weighty. Right now he wanted only to set his house straight, to take care of his family's belongings, to see that their memories were properly honored, to crawl into the bed he'd shared with his wife, and to somehow pretend the situation wasn't as hopeless as it seemed.

Once he'd accomplished all that, maybe then he'd think about Max Arnold's hearings, his responsibilities, and what he was going to do about them.

Brad carefully folded Christine's clothes and set them in a neat pile on the counter. He took an excruciatingly long time folding the cardigan. He did up the buttons, carefully folded the sleeves back, then creased it in the middle. She'd folded his shirts that way every time he packed for a business trip. Brad had always said that Christine was the only woman he knew who could pack a dress shirt so it would arrive unwrinkled.

He found a strange solace in the simple task of folding her clothes, as if he were taking care of details for Christine—details he'd too often neglected in his own drive for success and acclaim.

"I'm not going to let you down again," he told his wife. "I promise, Christine. I'm not going to fail you again."

9

"You've got to be kidding." Mariette stared at David Liu in disbelief. She was in the middle of arranging an emergency convoy of barges to deliver food and necessities to East Coast cities via the major waterways when her assistant came into her office to inform her that she had to prepare testimony for her ex-husband's Senate committee.

David shook his head. "Nope. Just took the call."

"We're a little busy, David. Did you happen to tell him that?"

"It wasn't Senator Arnold's office that called," David told her. "It was Musselman."

At the mention of her very politically connected boss, Mariette groaned. "Why can't he go?"

"He's on the West Coast with the president, surveying the damage. Told me he wanted you to cover it."

"Great," she muttered. "Just great. We're up to our necks here while Musselman gallivants across the country, and now he wants me to drop everything and protect him on the Hill."

"Basically," David agreed.

She exhaled a weary sigh. "When am I supposed to be there?"

"The hearings start tomorrow."

Mariette frowned. "Tomorrow? Isn't tomorrow Saturday?"

David blinked. "Um," he said as he looked around for a calendar, "to tell you the truth, I'm not sure what today is."

"It is," she said, mentally counting the days in her head. Time was beginning to meld together. "I think."

David walked to her desk and flipped a couple of pages on her planner. "We came back from South Carolina on Wednesday, yes?"

"Yes."

"Then tomorrow's Saturday."

"So why is my illustrious ex-husband starting hearings on a Saturday?"

"He's in a hurry, I guess. Or maybe he's just as confused about the date as everyone else."

"Or maybe," Mariette said dryly, "the senator wants to maximize his free airtime before the midterm elections heat up."

David acknowledged that with a slight tilt of his head. "Whatever. You're on the agenda. Want me to call and get you a time?"

"Are you sure I can't get out of this?"

"I'm sure. Musselman was insistent."

She stifled a groan. "All right. Get me a time slot. Something not dreadfully early but early or late enough not to be prime-time TV. Okay? I really don't want to shoot a whole day down there listening to Max pontificate."

David winced. "I'll do the best I can, but you know—"

"I do," she assured him, waving her hand in absent dismissal. "Did you happen to tell Musselman that the hearings would be televised? He likes being on television."

"Tried that. No dice. He's getting better coverage flying all over the country in *Air Force One.*"

Mariette scrubbed a hand over her face. She had two lights blinking on her phone indicating holding calls. Though she felt better having talked to Randal's roommate, she was still hoping to hear from her son.

"Any word from Randal?"

"Not yet. I have to assume he's still on his way."

"I'm sure he's fine," David said. "We know how bad the highways are. It'll take him a while to get here if he's traveling local roads."

"I know. I keep telling myself that."

"He's your kid. He knows what he's doing."

Mariette nodded. "I keep telling myself that, too." Her gaze flicked to the insistently blinking lights on her phone. "But I'd still feel better if I talked to him. And much better if I could just see him."

"No doubt."

She noticed the lines of tension on her assistant's face and suppressed a twinge of guilt for not having noticed them earlier. Too late, she realized that she had not taken time to notice that David's stress level was mounting. "Are you still doing okay, David? Have you heard from your parents yet? They're overseas, right?"

"Yeah. I finally talked to my dad about an hour ago. Everyone's okay as far as we know. A few friends of the family are missing, and my mom lost some teachers at her school. Things weren't too bad in China overall, they said. They really didn't even know what was happening until they caught the reports on CNN."

"I'm glad. You should probably take a break and get some rest."

David shrugged. "I guess I'm too busy to be tired. Adrenaline is still carrying me. As soon as I think of something I should be doing, something else comes along to demand my attention."

"Have you had any rest?" she prompted.

"I took a nap in the med center a little while ago." He managed a weak smile. "I'm raring to go."

"David—"

He held up a hand. "I know—I'm no good to anybody if I'm too tired to think. I appreciate your concern." He glanced down and studied his shoes. "But the truth is, I don't *want* to go home. I haven't been out since this started, you know." When he looked up, his expression was boyish and raw. "I was here wrapping up from South Carolina when the thing hit. I can't really explain it. I just don't want to see what it's like out there."

Mariette avoided the urge to press him for details. His tone was edgy, very unlike the confident, competent young man she knew. She made a mental note to add stress counselors to her list of contacts. It was obvious that her staff was going to need them. No doubt plenty of other people would need their help as well. "I understand. Just make sure you're taking care of yourself. You know you're only as good as you are strong."

"I feel better when I'm working."

She couldn't fault him for that. For most of her life she'd buried herself in work to erase the harsher realities of the outside world. Here, she felt in control. Contained. Empowered. All the things she'd never felt during her disastrous marriage to Max Arnold.

Mariette nodded. "I'll trust you to tell me when you've reached your limit, okay?"

"Sure, boss."

"Why don't you call and get me that appointment with the committee? When you're done, we'll meet and see where we are on putting our contacts together. Peter told me we've got clearance at most of the major ports for barge deliveries. I'm waiting on the New York Port Authority—" she checked the paperwork on her desk—"and Portland." She glanced at David. "New York, I understand. But what do you think is tying up Portland?"

"Who knows?" He tapped the doorframe of her office with his knuckles. "I'll have Peter chase it down, and I'll see what I can do for you with the committee."

"The best thing you can do is get me out of it."

His smile was rueful. "I wouldn't count on that. According to Musselman, Arnold wants to know how many troops we think we're going to need in disaster areas. He's assessing U.S. readiness for a counterattack."

Mariette frowned, thinking that Max had no idea what he was getting into. In her heart, she didn't believe this was an act of terrorism. If Max wanted to attack the enemy this time, then he'd finally met his match. "Counterattack on whom?"

David's eyebrows rose. "You heard the president's statement. The White House believes this was an act of terrorism."

"I know," she said.

He looked at her narrowly. "But? Do you know something, Mariette?"

"David, even when I was married to Max Arnold, I was the last to know what was happening. I certainly don't know anything now. I just think we might be getting a little ahead of ourselves. It doesn't seem wise to start launching attacks on enemies we haven't even identified yet."

"I think they know more than they're letting on. I mean, the alien theory is just ridiculous, and I find it hard to believe this was just some natural phenomenon. There's no way something this catastrophic could be lingering out there without our having some warning signs." He shook his head. "I think it's terrorists, all right, and we're probably going to blow them off the face of the planet."

Mariette winced but didn't argue. She wasn't prepared to tell David, or anyone else for that matter, just what she was thinking. Not until she had some proof of some sort. "You might be right," she said vaguely. "Whatever the case, I'm sure the Senate committee isn't interested in my opinion. They just want the facts on reserves and National Guard placement."

"I've got an intern pulling that together for you."

"Thanks. Efficient as usual."

David grinned at her. "I learned it from you. Can I get you anything? You need a soda or something?"

She reached for the receiver of her phone. One of the blinking lights had gone out—the caller evidently got weary of holding. "I'm doing okay. Just make sure everyone knows that Randal's call gets through no matter who I'm on the phone with at the time."

"Got it, boss."

★   ★   ★

Los Angeles, California
Local Time 8:30 P.M.

Brad leaned back on the small bench and watched the tumble of the ocean surf. There was a full moon out this evening. It felt better to be here, away from his home.

Soon after he arrived, the confines of the house had become stifling. Unable to face the unbearable silence, he'd tried making several
phone calls. He'd been unable to reach most of his wife's friends. A
call to their local church had yielded a message stating that the church
was temporarily closed but that someone would be in the office tomorrow morning to take calls and questions. Brad wondered who
had changed the message and how well they were facing the same reality he was: that church membership and a good reputation had
meant nothing when God had sifted through humanity and separated the believers from the frauds, heretics, and skeptics. He had
made a mental note to call the church tomorrow morning, then
headed out of the house for some fresh air and perspective.

On his way to the beach, he'd decided to call Liza Cannley on
her cell phone. Brad had explained that Senator Arnold's hearings
meant he'd have to leave for Washington on a red-eye flight tonight.
She'd assured him that she was eager to talk to him and would be
glad to do so now instead of Saturday morning. Brad had set the
time and place here at the pier, where he and Christine had often
come in the evenings to walk and reconnect.

He'd arrived before Liza, which gave him time to think about
what he was going to tell her. Forrest Tetherton had made it clear
that any statements Brad might make outside the administration's
position that the U.S. had been attacked would be unwelcome. That
made him wonder again why Arnold had singled him out for testimony. Brad seriously weighed the option of resigning his position
at the White House. But while he'd been carefully tending to the
clothes his family had left behind, he'd remembered again the discussion he'd had with Christine when he'd been offered the job.
They'd come here that night, to this bench, to discuss it before
they'd told anyone about the offer.

Though Brad had wanted the prestige that came with the title,
he'd been uncertain about working for Fitzhugh. Christine had listened intently to his concerns, allowing him to talk through
everything from the separation for the family to the realities of
working in a White House with a man he didn't trust. When he fin-

ished, she'd taken his hand and told him in her quiet, charming voice that she'd known the minute she met him he was destined for greatness . . . and that sometimes greatness came in unexpected ways. He remembered her telling him that Pharaoh had his Joseph and perhaps Gerald Fitzhugh would have his Brad Benton.

The advice still rang true. He had the unshakable feeling that several key decisions were going to be made over the next several weeks, and if his theory on the disappearances was correct, many of those decisions would have global and potentially disastrous circumstances. Still ringing in his ears were his mother's consistent statements that Brad's rise to power in politics had happened because God had a job for him to do—much the same way God had sent Esther into the court of the Persian King Xerxes. Her cousin Mordecai told Esther that she had been placed in the court of the enemy "for just such a time as this." Brad's mother had often said she felt the same way about him. That somehow, someway, God was preparing him for a moment of great risk, great challenge, and urgent need.

If she was right, then his connections to the Oval Office would perhaps be invaluable to God in the days to come. But how, he wondered, could he compromise between what he suspected to be true and the administration's position? How could he possibly be the man God had chosen when he obviously had failed to be the man God wanted him to be before all this happened?

"Mr. Benton?"

He turned to find Liza watching him curiously. Brad indicated the empty seat next to him on the bench. "Sorry to drag you away from home at this hour."

She shrugged and joined him on the bench. "No problem." Her smile was the same lopsided grin he remembered from the gubernatorial campaign. "I'm a journalist. By definition, it means I have no life. It also means that whatever's claiming my attention gets dropped when the White House chief of staff calls."

Brad had felt that way about his job once, he thought sadly. And those same mixed-up priorities had cost him his family, and now potentially his life. If things were about to get as bad as he thought, they were all living on borrowed time.

"Priorities are important," he remarked. "I should have taken better stock of mine."

She gave him a curious look but didn't respond. Instead, she turned to watch the surf for several seconds as clouds drifted across the moon. Though the beach was littered with debris, it was cleaner than the stretches he'd seen on the way to his house. Brad enjoyed the companionable silence. Christine had been like that. She could sit for hours in silence, liberated by some inner peace that gave her the freedom of not filling the gaps in conversation with chatter.

Eventually, Liza looked at him. "How did you . . . um . . . find things at home?"

"As I suspected," he answered, the wounds still fresh. "My family is gone."

"I'm very sorry. I lost my dad, but we hadn't been close in years. And I didn't have a spouse or kids to lose. I can't imagine what you must be going through."

Brad drew a fortifying breath. "It's devastating. I see the world differently now."

"I-I know several people who lost their kids. I don't think there's an answer for that kind of pain. I wish I had something more adequate to say."

He studied her intelligent brown eyes. "It's difficult to offer empathy when the events are so overwhelming, isn't it?"

Liza nodded. "Yes. At least let me assure you that all this is off the record. I'd never capitalize on your personal grief just for a story."

"I appreciate that."

"I have colleagues who would, but I find that kind of thing repugnant. That's not why I went into journalism."

Brad sighed. It was time to get to the heart of this meeting. "Then why did you want to talk to me? Besides my obvious connection to the administration."

"It's no secret that you and the president aren't on the best of terms. Insiders know that Fitzhugh brought you to Washington to smooth out his reputation with the voters. You're squeaky-clean, and you represent a faction of the party that the president has alienated. The scandals before you got there—"

"I know all that," Brad assured her.

"So I've been watching the news coming out of the White House. The president and his staff seem very . . ."

"Unified?"

Liza smiled. "It's a little hard to believe there are no 'sources close to the president,' or 'upper-level members of the administration' with a dissenting opinion." She gave him a narrow look. "I thought you might have one."

"A dissenting opinion?"

"Or at least one outside the official line. I've always been able to count on your candor, Mr. Benton."

Brad carefully weighed his next words. Fresh in his mind were Forrest Tetherton's implied ramifications should he do anything to compromise the White House's position. "You can understand how the gravity of the situation has led to extreme measures by the White House."

"Yes."

"Generally, in any matter of national defense, it's important for every member of the administration to be on board with the president's policy. Especially when the country is in this kind of turmoil." He thought about it for a moment. "After a tragedy like this the national good demands unity. There are times when personal opinions have no place in the public forum."

"I would agree," Liza said. "That's generally true."

Brad glanced at the surf again. He found a certain courage in the sure knowledge that the same tides that came and went yesterday had come and gone again today. The universe still had its order, no matter how disturbed it might be right now, and tomorrow its order would remain . . . or so he hoped. "On top of the question of national security and the common well-being of the American people, we're headed into a midterm election. You can understand why the president is concerned about how this is going to affect him politically."

"Of course."

"I'm not precisely certain how George Ramiro would have handled this—"

"Tetherton's statement claims that Ramiro resigned for personal reasons," Liza interrupted. "Doesn't that seem a little odd? I mean, right before all this happened."

"It is odd."

"It has people speculating."

"Speculating what?"

"Well, most of my colleagues believe he was either involved in some scandal that was about to break or he just couldn't buy into the administration's agenda anymore."

Brad frowned. "George never arrived in the Situation Room. So he never even heard the administration's agenda. I can vouch for that. And I can assure you there weren't any scandals closing in on George. I would have known."

"You and Ramiro were tight?"

"Not exactly," Brad told her. "But we were allies. Ramiro is the one who persuaded the president to bring me to Washington."

"I remember that."

"If he'd been in trouble, I would have known. I'm sure of it."

"So you think he resigned and just had really lousy timing?"

Brad hesitated, then shook his head. "Had George resigned yesterday afternoon, he would have come in last night anyway. He would have known the country and the president were in trouble. George was not the kind of man to walk away from that type of responsibility. I don't care what the circumstances were."

"You're referring to him in the past tense," Liza pointed out.

Brad gave her a searching look. "That's because, even though I may not be able to prove it, I believe he's gone."

That made Liza's eyebrows draw together. "Gone? Like disappeared? But why wouldn't the White House simply say that?"

"Because I think George didn't disappear. I think he's dead."

"Dead?" Liza's eyes widened. "Dead," she said again, more quietly. "Dead like murdered or dead like accidentally?"

"I don't know, but it's the only explanation I can come up with for why the White House keeps insisting he resigned. If they weren't afraid someone was going to find out the truth, it would have been far easier to claim that George had disappeared along with everyone else."

"But surely Forrest Tetherton—"

"Wouldn't lie about George Ramiro?" Brad asked cynically. "Isn't that why you're meeting with me? Because you think Tetherton might be lying?"

"I think he's probably not being entirely forthcoming. I don't think—"

"Then you're in serious danger of underestimating him. I assure you, Forrest Tetherton will do whatever it takes to keep Fitzhugh in the White House." He paused. "Including covering up the disappearance of George Ramiro."

"I can see that."

"They had already announced to the staff that George had resigned before we had a firm picture of what was happening. I think had they been able to wait a little longer, they would have passed him off as among the missing, but Charley Swelder had to give an explanation of why George wasn't in the Sit Room last night."

Liza tapped her pencil on her notebook. "How long have you suspected this?"

"Since the instant I arrived at the Sit Room and George wasn't there."

"And you're really convinced that he wasn't just another casualty of the event? Couldn't his resignation have preceded the disappearances? If he were among the missing—"

"I don't think the disappearances were indiscriminate," Brad said. "I think there's a reason that the people who are gone are gone and the rest of us aren't."

Liza gave him a narrow look. "You have a pretty strong church background. I'm assuming that you're talking about the God-and-the-end-of-the-world theory."

"On the record," Brad told her, "I support the administration."

"And off the record?"

"Off the record, yes, I think the explanation that God has set the end of the world in motion is the truth behind what's happening."

"You're kidding, right?"

Brad shook his head. "I wish I were."

"But how do you explain why people like you are still here? You were very active in your church, if I recall. Weren't you a leader or something?"

"A deacon," he confirmed. He felt like he was walking through a verbal minefield. "And I'm not going to pretend that I have all the answers."

"But surely you don't believe—"

"That the biblical prophecies are true? Yes, I do. Why shouldn't I?"

She let out a low whistle. "I have to admit, I'm a little surprised. I never took you for one of those religious extremists."

"Me either," Brad said sadly. "Which probably explains why I'm here and my family isn't."

"I think you're being a little hard on yourself," Liza insisted. "There are plenty of other more plausible explanations, you know."

"I'm aware of that. I think you'll hear most of them coming out of the Senate testimony."

"My source at our Washington bureau says Arnold is trying to get Chaim Rosenzweig to testify."

Brad recognized the name of the prominent Israeli scientist whose recent innovations in desert agriculture had given the once impoverished nation unforeseen prosperity. Rosenzweig was quickly emerging as an international figure and a frequent spokesman for the Israeli government. "Do you wonder why?"

"He'll have a scientific perspective," Liza said. "I assume Arnold wants to look at the issue from several angles—and for publicity's sake, it can't hurt to have one of the world's most talked about scientists on one of his panels."

"Have you considered that Arnold may want Rosenzweig for another reason?"

"The Israel connection?" Liza asked. "I doubt that Max Arnold is particularly interested in a lesson on the judgment of the Jewish God."

"Max Arnold is interested in winning votes," Brad concurred. "But I suspect he wants Rosenzweig there to counter whatever biblical theories anyone may put forth. I'm sure if you check your source, you'll find that Arnold's got several other high-level church officials on the agenda as well."

Liza nodded. "Cardinal Peter Mathews is on the witness list. He probably would have subpoenaed the pope, but word has it His Holiness is among the missing."

"I'm sure the senator's staff has briefed him on every available theory. He's looking for the one that best suits his needs."

"That we've been attacked?"

"War is always good for the economy and politics."

"So then, why do you think he wants you? You're not exactly known as the administration's yes-man."

"I've thought of that, and maybe that's exactly *why* Arnold wants me there. If he can force me to admit that the White House is divided about this, he can make the president look weak."

"So are you going to tell the committee that you think this might have been some supernatural event where God picked over the world population and took away anybody who was worthy?"

"It's a little more complicated than that," Brad said.

Liza hesitated. "It's nuts is what it is." She frowned at him. "I can't believe you would even consider it."

"My wife was a Christian."

"So are you."

Brad shook his head. "I was a churchgoer. It's not the same thing."

"Don't you think you're taking all this a little too literally?"

"No, Liza, I don't. A lot of people believe that if you live a pretty good life and go to church, that's all God requires of you. You're covered. Maybe, for a while, I believed it myself. But there's more to being a Christian than serving as a deacon, sitting on the board of trustees at a church, and living a decent life. I never crossed the bridge between lip service and self-sacrifice. I wanted to hold on to my pride and reputation more than I wanted to surrender myself."

"Mr. Benton—"

He held up a hand. "I told you I don't have all the answers. Officially, I shouldn't even be having this conversation with you."

"Then why are you having it?"

"Because I made a promise to my wife back in my house today," Brad said sadly. "I wasn't as diligent as I should have been about keeping promises to her. This time I won't let her down. Such as I understand the truth, I will tell it. As I find answers, I'll reveal them." He paused. "No matter how unpopular those answers might be."

Liza pursed her lips. "This could cost you politically. And probably personally."

"I know."

"I can't just sit on this forever. Sooner or later—"

"I understand," Brad interjected. "I know you'll be responsible with what I've told you, but I don't expect you to keep it entirely under wraps."

"Do you plan to stay on at the White House?"

"For now." He gave her a rueful look. "They might fire me after I give my testimony at the hearings."

She shook her head. "I don't think so. You're valuable to them right now. As long as Arnold is interested in you, the president needs you at the White House."

"Tetherton said the same thing."

"He's right."

Brad stood and slipped his hands in his back pockets. "I have no idea what the future holds, but I know this. If my suspicions are right and the hand of God was in this, then this is only the beginning. A time is coming when all of us will have to choose which side we'll be on." He heard himself speak the words and wondered at his newfound confidence. A month ago—a *week* ago—he'd have heard those words and thought they sounded like the ravings of one of his mother's preachers. Now they rang with a certain truth that gave him strength.

Liza was looking at him curiously. "Look, even if you think this was an act of God, you're not telling me that you honestly believe all that stuff about the coming battle between good and evil, are you? I mean, there's a guy at the bureau who keeps talking about what the Bible says about all this. I mean, horses of the apocalypse, one global religion, all of that. Come on—you know that's just too far out there to be real."

"I know this much," Brad said. "No matter what you and I believe or don't believe, we can't begin to imagine what's going to happen." He shook his head. "I know I probably haven't been much help to you, but I've always been able to trust you professionally."

"You've been good to me. I appreciate any politician who gives me straight answers."

"And I appreciate any reporter who keeps her word."

Liza laughed. "If I were in your shoes, I'd probably feel the same way."

"You asked me for my perspective," Brad said. "And this is it: the president is using this as part of a political strategy. Soon, I think it'll become obvious that he's building an international alliance that isn't necessarily in the best interest of the United States. I don't know it for sure, but I think that Charley Swelder is giving him some very bad advice. Keep looking for answers, Liza. This country desperately needs people willing to find and tell the truth."

"Can I call you if I have questions?"

"You have my cell phone number. Call me anytime."

"And what about this thing with Ramiro?"

"Keep asking questions," he urged. "See where it takes you. I think there's a story there that's about to be largely ignored because of everything else that's going on."

"Can I count on you to keep me informed?"

"Anything I find out, I'll send your way," Brad promised. "You can depend on it."

10

Green tablecloths, Mariette thought cynically as she entered the Indian Treaty Room on Capitol Hill. The ornate reception room in the U.S. Capitol had served as the backdrop for some of the country's most publicized hearings: the McCarthy hearings, Watergate, Iran-Contra, the Clinton impeachment hearings, and now, Max Arnold's unofficial launch of his presidential campaign. Every major scandal in America's recent history had been aired before the American people from this room—and they always used the green tablecloths. Max possessed a flair for the dramatic.

"Mariette?"

She turned to find her ex-husband's press secretary studying her closely. "Hello, Helen."

"The . . . um . . . senator was under the impression that Mr. Musselman would be here for FEMA."

"Mr. Musselman is in California with the president," Mariette explained. "Max is stuck with me."

Helen gave her the same cold glare Mariette had seen many times during her marriage to Max. Helen had never felt that Mariette took Max's greatness seriously enough. Helen was right about that, Mariette conceded. The younger woman clutched her notebook to her chest. "This is very serious business, Mrs. Arnold."

"And I'm very seriously here to testify on behalf of the agency. If the senator doesn't want me . . . ," she said hopefully.

"Someone from FEMA is necessary," Helen insisted. "We need answers to key questions from your agency."

Mariette wondered if she should point out to Helen that Max didn't actually have any oversight at FEMA, that whether or not the agency presented testimony was strictly her decision to make, and that if all of Max's questions went unanswered, the sun would still rise tomorrow. With a shake of her head, she shot a quick glance at her watch. "I'm on at ten?"

"I'll have to check with Stacey. He did the scheduling. Now that we have you instead of Mr. Musselman, I'm not sure if he'll want to do some shifting in the witness order."

"Gotta maximize the TV coverage, I guess."

Helen's expression turned even more glacial. "I'll let you know when I can. Don't wander off."

Mariette gritted her teeth at the command and passed Helen a copy of her statement. "I have a lot to do today. In case it didn't occur to you or to Max, FEMA is a little preoccupied right now cleaning up all this mess."

"The American people—"

"I know, I know. But, Helen, I don't think the American people are as concerned about Max's opinion on this as they are about getting their water turned back on." She considered that for a moment. "Has it entered his mind that a lot of rural and suburban power grids are still shut down? Probably half the country doesn't have access to C-SPAN right now."

"We're being carried on the networks," Helen pointed out.

"And in most of the country, the network affiliates aren't consistently broadcasting. What a shame it would be if Max goes to all this trouble and doesn't get very good exposure out of it."

"Despite what you might think," Helen shot back, her tone hard, "this isn't about publicity."

Mariette's eyebrows rose as she scanned the room. The gaggle of reporters clustered around Chaim Rosenzweig told a different story. "Then what's Rosenzweig doing here?"

"We felt he'd offer an interesting opinion on how this may affect the world's food production. He's a respected scientist and a spokesman for Israel. We hope to gain both a scientific and religious perspective from him."

"I'm sure you do." Mariette drew a breath. "But the facts Max wanted about the National Guard and reserve troops I think we'll need for the relief effort are in that statement. If it's all the same to you—I'd like to get back to work. While Rosenzweig is discussing global impact economics on world hunger, I've got a few million lunches to deliver to New York City."

Helen tucked the statement into her notebook. "I'll see what I can do. Given the circumstances, Stacey may prefer that we simply enter your statement into the record. If that's the case, you're free to go."

The circumstances, Mariette knew, were that her presence in the hearings wouldn't tantalize the press as much as Bernie Musselman's. She could only hope that Max's ego would let her off the hook. She'd left David and her staff up to their eyeballs organizing the three convoys of supply barges she planned to launch tomorrow.

Mariette sank into one of the battered leather chairs and used the time to make a few notes on her Pocket PC. She'd forgotten to tell David to arrange extra stevedores at each port to cut down on the time needed for off-load. If she hoped to make it all the way to New York by nightfall, she'd need efficiency, speed, and luck on her side.

She was mentally calculating manpower hours when she saw Helen approaching, her expression grim. "The senator would like to see you," she said tartly.

Mariette raised an eyebrow. "You're kidding, right?"

"I only wish." Helen glanced at her watch. "We're supposed to drop gavel in ten minutes. We're on a very tight schedule."

Mariette stood and stretched a little, easing her tense muscles. Maybe this wasn't as bad as it could be. Maybe Max wasn't about to pull a fast one. Whether it was intuition or sheer maternal instinct that alerted her, something told her she knew what Max wanted. Though her own relationship with her ex-husband had soured long ago, he was a decent enough human being to inquire about the well-being of their only son during this crisis. Her more cynical side insisted that Max would need answers for reporters who wanted to know if he'd been personally affected by the disappearances. But the only way to find out what was going on was to give Max a free shot at her.

Randal, she suspected, who still held his father responsible for the mess of the divorce, had probably not bothered to try contacting him. She doubted that Max knew how to contact Randal at school, so he likely hadn't had the benefit of speaking with Randal's roommate. She had a slight twinge of guilt when she realized that the phone message from Max her assistant had handed her yesterday might not have been merely another in the many congressional inquiries she'd received. She'd assumed Max was following suit with his other colleagues on the Hill. The disappearances had caused major disasters in every state—and especially in their densely populated urban areas. Congressmen and senators were lining up for FEMA assistance, and when they found the FEMA director either unable or unavailable to answer their questions, they had begun applying pressure on Mariette.

When she'd seen Max's message in the pile, she'd assumed he was another in the long line of elected officials who wanted to assure his constituents that he was doing all he could to ease their pain.

It had never occurred to her last night that he might be concerned about Randal. Max was rarely concerned about anyone but himself. Well, she'd find out soon enough what was going on with the man. Wordlessly, she followed Helen through the crowded reception area of the Indian Treaty Room and into the private conference room the senators used for strategy and policy meetings.

Helen indicated a chair with a wave of her hand. "He'll be right in."

"Thanks."

The other woman watched Mariette through narrowed eyes. "This is a very big opportunity for the senator," she said needlessly.

"I don't think I have to tell you what this kind of publicity will mean to his political aspirations."

"Nope."

"I trust you'll put whatever personal feelings you have aside and bear that in mind then."

Mariette crossed her arms and gave Helen a shrewd look. "I've been putting aside my personal feelings about Max for the past twenty years, Helen. What makes you think I'm going to air them now?"

Helen seemed slightly taken aback. "I just meant—"

"I know." Mariette held up a hand. "You meant that with Max eyeing a presidential bid, the last thing you want to see on TV is a petty exchange with his best-forgotten ex-wife. This might surprise you, but I'm not really keen on that idea myself."

"I wasn't insinuating—"

"Sure you were. And it's okay. I know you can't possibly conceive why I can't stand the man when you think he walks on water."

Visibly stung, Helen bristled. "I think Senator Arnold has done a lot of beneficial things for this country and for his party."

"I'm sure you do."

"All I'm saying is that a little tact on your part might be in order here."

"I guess you've forgotten that I wasn't the one sleeping around on my spouse. Max wasn't terribly concerned about tact then, was he?"

"Mrs. Arnold—"

The door to the conference room swung open, and Max rushed in with the subtlety of a hurricane. "Mariette," he said by way of greeting. Not even a pretense of courtesy. He glanced at Helen. "Give us a minute alone."

"We're supposed to drop gavel—"

"I've seen the clock, Helen. Give me a minute."

The aide glanced at Mariette, then strode from the room. Max wiped a hand over his face. He looked old, she noted, more so than usual. But then, she couldn't remember the last time she'd actually seen him in person. Perhaps the cameras took the edge off his hollow-looking eyes and sagging jawline. "I suppose Musselman's in California with Fitzhugh."

"Yes. You're stuck with me. Sorry you didn't get the word."

"It's not optimal," he conceded.

"I'm not exactly thrilled about it, either."

Max exhaled a long breath. "Stacey told me you were here. I . . . uh . . . I wanted to ask about Randal."

She nodded. "I'm sorry I didn't return your phone call last night. I spoke to Randal's roommate. Randal is fine and making his way home. He decided to drive—"

"Drive? What is he thinking? Does he have any idea what the roads are like?"

"Better than the airports and railroads," she pointed out. "I wasn't thrilled about his decision either, but I want him home."

"When do you expect him?"

"I'm not sure. I'm hoping he'll make it today."

Max nodded, thoughtful. "He's resourceful. He should be okay."

"Randal knows how to take care of himself," Mariette agreed. "And if he runs into trouble, he'll find a way to call."

"Will you let me know when you hear from him?"

"Of course. It didn't occur to me until just now that you were trying to reach me to ask about Randal."

"He *is* my child, Mariette."

"You have the luxury of being sure of that."

Max had the grace to look slightly uncomfortable. After their divorce, the evidence of his infidelity had made tabloid headlines. "Look—"

She shook her head. "Sorry. It's been a long day. I already told your minion that I wouldn't make a scene this morning. Sorry my boss ruined your show by sending me."

Max shrugged. "You'll be more informative, I'm sure."

She arched an eyebrow. "Wow, Max, that's almost a compliment."

"I never doubted your abilities," he said. "You should know that."

The door opened and Helen stuck her head in. "Senator—"

Max held up a hand. "Yeah. Coming." He looked at Mariette. "You'll call me?"

"As soon as I hear," she promised.

Max turned to go, then looked at her again and reached for her hand. "I'm glad you're all right." He gave her hand a brief squeeze, then left before she had a chance to respond.

As Mariette entered the hearing room again, a flurry of activity to her left caught her attention. Brad Benton had arrived to testify on behalf of the White House. A gaggle of reporters flocked in his direction. Mariette let out a low whistle as she gingerly made her way through the crowd to her seat. Max had pulled out all the stops this time. It was no secret in Washington that Benton's politics weren't in line with the president's. The administration wouldn't have sent their controversial chief of staff unless Max had required it. And Max wouldn't have required it unless he planned to use Benton to make Fitzhugh look like he was losing control at the White House.

She shook her head and settled into her leather chair to watch Benton negotiate his way through the heavy crowd. One of Max's minions was already descending on him. Soon they'd have him ensconced in the rear reception room, where he could wait in peace until his testimony was required. Max wouldn't want anything to dim the impact of Benton's testimony, especially not any prehearing statements.

The heavy bang of the gavel drew her attention. Max was calling the committee to order. With a weary sigh, Mariette wondered how long Stacey would make her endure this.

Marcus entered the Indian Treaty Room as Brad Benton was beginning his testimony. The soft-spoken White House chief of staff seemed composed and at ease as he took questions from the committee. Scanning the room, Marcus noticed several people he knew, a veritable armada of reporters, and, to his surprise, Mariette Arnold.

Given the highly publicized and apparently bitter details of her divorce from Max Arnold, he couldn't believe she was here for any reason other than official business. Marcus knew from the morning news that her new boss at FEMA was in California with the president. Musselman must have sent Mariette to cover his testimony for him.

What fun for Max . . . and probably not the exchange wanted on national television. Grilling his wronged ex-wife wouldn't go over well with the American people.

Marcus eased farther into the room and into the seat next to her. "Good morning," he whispered.

She shot him a surprised look. Marcus noted the wariness in her gaze. Apparently she was unsure how to respond to him after their conversation. "I didn't expect to see you here," she said.

He grinned. "I didn't expect to see you either."

That won a slight smile. "I guess that's probably true."

From the corner of his eye, Marcus caught the disapproving look of one of Senator Arnold's staff members. He shifted in his seat. "Are you testifying?"

"At ten, I think. You?"

"Eleven o'clock panel."

Mariette looked at him. "What are you going to tell them?"

"The same thing I told you."

She shook her head, though her eyes held a look of admiration. "You're a brave man, Marcus."

"If I were brave," he countered, "I wouldn't still be here."

It took a moment for that to register, but Mariette's expression turned wary again. She looked at Benton. "I'd like to hear this," she said carefully. "We can talk at the break."

Marcus settled in to hear the chief of staff. In his years of ministry, he'd mastered the art of timing. "Of course."

Max Arnold leaned back in his massive leather chair and studied Brad Benton from his elevated perch atop the second tier of the committee's bank of chairs. "So," he said carefully, "you found things in California to be more or less catastrophic than here?"

Brad took a sip of water. *So far, so good,* he mused. The committee had thus far limited their questions to the White House's response to disaster recovery. "Different," Brad said. "Greater loss of human life and greater environmental consequences, but not as much damage to infrastructure."

"When I spoke to the president yesterday about your testimony, he told me that you were tending to some family matters. I'd like to offer the committee's condolences on the loss of your wife and children," the senator said.

Brad acknowledged that with a tilt of his head. "Thank you."

"I appreciate your willingness to return and testify today. I'm sure you had many other things you could have been dealing with at home."

"I'm glad to be of assistance," Brad said. "The White House understands the importance of providing the American people with whatever information and policy we have available, Mr. Senator." He didn't bother to point out that Arnold had made it abundantly clear that Brad had no choice in the matter.

After his conversation with Liza, he'd hurried home to pack a few things, secured the house, and headed for the airport. On impulse, he'd placed the clothes his wife and children had been wearing in a carry-on bag. They'd given him comfort when he'd stopped by his apartment this morning to shower and shave. He'd left the bag on his bed.

Max seemed to consider that. "I would agree. And that's why I'd like to ask you a question about a statement you made yesterday morning at the president's press conference."

Brad tensed but didn't respond. He watched Arnold sift through the stack of papers on his desk, ostensibly looking for the information he wanted. He made a great show of discovering what he sought. "According to this transcript from the press briefing, you were asked, 'Does the administration believe that these disappearances were the direct result of a global terrorist attack or the work of a particular nation or individual?'" Arnold leaned forward. "Do you recall that question?"

"I was asked a lot of questions, Senator. It had been a long night."

"It was for all of us, Mr. Benton. Do you recall the question?"

"It sounds familiar," Brad conceded.

"And do you remember how you responded to that question?"

"Not precisely, no."

Arnold cleared his throat and perched his glasses on the end of his nose. "According to the transcript, you answered, 'The administration is considering a number of possibilities.' " He looked up from the paper. "Does that sound accurate?"

Brad felt the hair on the back of his neck stand up. "I suppose so, yes."

"The president's statement that morning said conclusively that the administration's position is that the U.S. has been attacked. Isn't that correct?"

"That was the content of the statement, yes." A sudden silence settled on the room. Brad felt the scrutiny of a hundred sets of eyes.

"So," the senator pressed, "I'm curious why you stated that the administration was considering a number of possibilities when the president's statement seemed to identify only one possibility."

Brad took a deep breath. "Perhaps I misspoke. I can emphatically state that as far as the administration is concerned, what happened the other night was definitely and certainly an attack on the United States."

"As far as the administration is concerned?" Arnold repeated. "What about you, Mr. Benton? Do you have a different opinion?"

"I don't get paid for my opinion," Brad quipped. That won a laugh from a good number of people in the room.

Max Arnold frowned. "I don't find this a laughing matter, Mr. Benton."

"Neither do I, Senator, I assure you. But surely you can understand why, no matter what opinions and theories may have been discussed that night, the only one that matters now is the White House's official position."

"Then in your opinion, is the White House position correct?"

Brad carefully considered his next words. "It would depend on whether you're asking my opinion as the White House chief of staff or as a private citizen."

"Both," Arnold said.

Brad nodded. "Then as chief of staff I would say that I support the president's position and believe the administration is working diligently to identify the enemy. Once we have ascertained the source of the disaster, we will not hesitate to respond with due force. The president has stated repeatedly that justice will be 'swift, certain, and severe.'"

"The president is putting together an international coalition—is that true?"

"All our reports suggest that several other nations were hit as hard as the United States. This wasn't an isolated incident."

"And in addition to the traditional European bloc, the president is also including several Eastern European nations among his allies. Is that true as well?"

Where in the world, Brad wondered, was Arnold going with this? "I believe so, yes."

"You believe so?"

"Senator, the president has military and national security advisors he relies on for matters of national defense. I'm not generally someone whose advice he solicits in those matters." That was unusual for a White House chief of staff, Brad knew, but then, his was a unique situation. Charley Swelder made sure Brad's influence and presence were as limited as possible.

Arnold reached for a report, flipped it open to a bookmarked page, and scanned it briefly before looking at Brad again. "According to this report from the National Security Council dated last month, the president feels it is especially important to strengthen our ties with the Eastern European countries at this time. Do you remember seeing that report, Mr. Benton?"

"Yes." At the time, there had been significant unrest and turmoil in the former Soviet bloc countries. Romania, especially, had just undergone a particularly bizarre coup that had resulted in the voluntary secession of the sitting president and his enthusiastic endorsement of his successor, Nicolae Carpathia. Carpathia had been a low-level elected official with little clout and even less name recognition. But apparently the Romanian president had found Carpathia's vision and charisma attractive and had handed over his office to him.

Distrustful of the report, U.S. intelligence had tried to see if Carpathia had somehow manipulated the situation, but they'd found no evidence to indicate that he had. The National Security Council found the situation and instability particularly alarming given Romania's strong position as a nuclear presence in the former Soviet bloc. Though Carpathia claimed he sought only global peace, the U.S. wasn't ready to believe he didn't have greater aspirations.

"If I recall," Brad told Arnold now, "that report was issued not long after Nicolae Carpathia's unusual rise to power in Romania. The administration was—and continues to be—very concerned about the apparent instability in the Eastern bloc. As you know, our intelligence sources have not yet been able to give us a firm idea of where the nuclear capabilities of the former Soviet bloc now rest. Political unrest in those regions raises significant concern when we're uncertain which nations may or may not have access to weapons of mass destruction."

"And the White House is particularly concerned about Carpathia?" the senator asked.

Brad nodded. "His situation is unique. I understand that he's taken a keen interest in the UN and is scheduled to address the General Assembly on Monday." Brad thought about it a minute. "I have no idea if President Carpathia is still planning to come to the U.S. in light of this crisis."

"Our sources indicate that he is," Arnold assured him.

Brad tipped his head. "It's my understanding that this committee has called Chaim Rosenzweig to testify later today." He'd seen the renowned Israeli scientist when he'd entered the room. Rosenzweig had been the one person on the committee's witness list that took media attention away from Brad. For that, he was eternally grateful.

"That's right."

"Then he might be able to answer any additional questions you have about Carpathia. I believe Carpathia has called on Dr. Rosenzweig for advice regarding his country's ties with several Middle Eastern nations."

Arnold seemed to consider that. "I'd like to know how the White House feels about those diplomatic ties in light of the current crisis."

"Senator, we've been conducting a war on terrorism for a number of years. You can understand why we're wary of any nation that has continued its relations with countries who harbor and support international terrorist organizations."

"Has the president considered Romania's possible role in the Russians' failed attack on Israel?"

Brad nodded. "Certainly the White House is considering any number of possibilities. I assure you we're closely monitoring the situation in Russia, and the president has been in touch with Carpathia a number of times. He's hoping to arrange an official diplomatic reception when Carpathia comes to New York next week."

The senator studied Brad closely. "Does the White House believe that if the Russian attack on Israel is tied to the disappearances in any way, we are in a position to form an adequate response?"

Brad finally understood where Max Arnold was trying to go with his line of questions. The fact that a U.S. fighter plane had been shot down in Poland had played big in the media and with the public. Arnold was trying to capitalize on national fears that war with the Russians might be imminent, and the U.S. might not be as lucky as the Israelis had been.

"The president, the secretary of defense, the Joint Chiefs of Staff, and the national security advisor are probably in a better position to answer that question, Senator," Brad said evasively. "I'm the chief of staff. I handle personnel."

A murmur rippled through the crowd. Max Arnold scowled at Brad. "I remind you, Mr. Benton, that this is a very serious matter."

"And again, I'm taking it seriously, Senator," Brad assured him. "That's why I think you should have someone with more knowledge of the president's foreign policy here to answer these questions."

The senator leaned back in his chair and studied Brad with probing speculation. Short of admitting that he'd requested Brad's appearance with hopes of embarrassing the president through the remarks of his somewhat estranged chief of staff, he had no rejoinder to that. "I appreciate that advice, Mr. Benton," Arnold finally said, "but I have to assume that as chief of staff you're fully briefed on the president's policy decisions and directives."

"Yes."

"Are you aware, then, whether or not the president has spoken with Russian President Kolsokev?"

"I haven't seen the president since we deplaned at the Long Beach Airport yesterday morning," Brad said. "Between 1:30 A.M. yesterday and my last conversation with the president, no, he had not spoken with President Kolsokev."

"Given the skirmish on the Russian border yesterday, do you know if he plans to?"

"I am not aware of any plans to speak with President Kolsokev at this time, no."

Arnold frowned. "Then can you at least assure the committee, Mr. Benton, that the White House has considered the potential implications if civil war breaks out in Russia?"

Brad knew precisely why the senator was so determined to force him to respond to the issue about the Russians. Nothing would help Arnold's presidential aspirations like the reemergence of a solid, identifiable enemy in Russia and the former Soviet bloc. Voter fears about foreign aggression had historically favored challengers over incumbents in presidential politics. He drummed his fingers lightly on the table. "I'd say that I believe the White House is looking after the best interests of the United States and considering every possible scenario we might now face, including the possibility of political unrest in Russia and around the globe."

"What about the best interests of the president?" Arnold shot back, his tone cynical.

Brad remembered why he disliked Max Arnold so much. Gerald Fitzhugh might be self-serving and morally weak, but he didn't possess Arnold's raw appetite for power. "Begging your pardon, Senator, but many people would argue that the president's best interest is indistinguishable from the best interest of the country."

At the crowd's light laughter, the senator's face reddened. He sifted through the papers again until he found what he wanted. "I also have here a copy of an e-mail message you sent a Colonel Wells after the press briefing. In it—" he glanced at the paper—"you mention that you are giving the colonel's information serious thought and that you'll get back to him after your trip to California." The senator picked up a second piece of paper. "But I'm looking at a roster of attendees at the president's emergency meeting in the Sit Room that night. I don't see Colonel Wells on the list."

"Colonel Wells, as you know, Senator, is the Pentagon's attaché to the White House. He was kind enough to meet with me for several minutes before the press briefing to discuss the Pentagon's position."

"Which is?" Arnold pressed.

Brad took a deliberate sip of his water. "That's something you'll have to ask the Pentagon, I suppose."

Another laugh from the crowd made Arnold's face flush again, but he banged the gavel hard to regain order in the room. "Order, order." As the crowd quieted, he gave Brad a steely look. "Thank you for your time, Mr. Benton. If we have additional questions, we may recall you." He addressed the crowd. "We'll take a brief recess, then return in ten minutes."

Brad exhaled deeply as he reached for his notes and rose from his chair. He had the feeling of having narrowly escaped a disaster. If the senator had pressed him much harder, he'd have had little choice but to admit that, in his opinion, Fitzhugh's theory was politically self-serving, that the time and effort the administration was exerting in seeking a foreign enemy were a waste of both.

He'd have had no choice but to say that Max Arnold could hold all the hearings he wanted, but when he found the answers to his questions, he probably wouldn't accept them.

Brad fought an overwhelming moment of fatigue.

"Mr. Benton?"

Brad turned to find Marcus Dumont studying him intently. He'd met the charismatic minister at a rally for the president's civil rights legislation the previous year. Brad frowned as he considered the ramifications of Dumont's presence. "Reverend Dumont, good to see you again."

A subtle smile played on the man's mouth. "Not to mention surprising, I suppose."

Brad didn't respond.

Marcus reached into his pocket and produced a business card. "I caught your testimony. If you have some time, there's something I'd like to discuss with you."

"Oh?" Brad accepted the card.

Marcus leaned closer. "Yes. I think you and I may have something in common."

"What's that, Reverend?"

Marcus paused. "I think you and I may both know why we're still here. I think we both know why we were left behind."

Brad's heart rate accelerated. He glanced over his shoulder. Though he'd all but accepted the idea himself, there was something almost shocking in hearing it put before him by another man—a man who was a respected member of the clergy and a widely published and televised evangelist. "You believe we were left behind?" he asked carefully.

"Don't you?" Marcus pressed.

Brad hesitated. He'd suspected it, thought about it, considered it, but wasn't sure he was ready to admit to Marcus that he believed it. "I don't know for certain."

"But you haven't ruled it out?"

"No, I haven't ruled it out."

"Then that's what I'd like to discuss with you."

Wearily, Brad remembered his futile phone call to his church in

California. He'd intended to call back this morning, but his plans had been interrupted by Arnold's hearings. Marcus Dumont could probably answer many of his questions. "When?" Brad asked.

"I like to run in Rock Creek Park in the mornings," Marcus said. "I start at the Calvert Street entrance around 6:30."

"I'll meet you there tomorrow." Brad looked around again, saw the crush of reporters around Chaim Rosenzweig, and decided to use the opportunity to escape. He shook Marcus Dumont's hand. "Now, if you don't mind, I'm going to head home and get some rest. I'll see you in the morning."

11

This was the hardest part—this crushing silence and the weight of loneliness. Brad had let himself into his apartment with a sense of dread. Except for the few hours he'd spent in his house in California, this was the first time since the Rapture that he'd been alone.

He was used to walking into the nearly empty apartment, had done so nearly every night since he'd moved to Washington. The space in the short-term lease building had come furnished, and Brad had seen little point in adding many personal touches. Christine had bullied him into bringing a few pictures, some books, his grandfather's antique writing desk. She'd insisted the items would knock the edge off the sterility of the apartment.

Brad had refused. But when he'd unpacked his suitcase the first night here, he'd found the items tucked beside his perfectly folded shirts. Now he glanced at the family portrait on the desk, and his soul felt hollow. It was a bleak reminder of what his future held. He was left with nothing but memories and mementos to ward off the lonely hours and the gnawing fear that he would never feel at peace again.

He was bone-tired, having slept little on the plane from California. The TV remote, he noted, was still on the couch where he'd dropped it when the Rapture had interrupted the Lakers game. He'd stopped there earlier that morning to shower and shave before heading for Capitol Hill but had not had the time to really look at the place.

This is what his life had become. An empty, lonely, sterile world where he had no one to turn to, no one to trust, no one to lean on or to rely on. He thrust his hands into his pockets, and his fingers brushed the business card Marcus Dumont had given him.

How many times had he heard his kids use the term *divine appointment* to describe a coincidental meeting? Was that what Marcus Dumont's sudden appearance at the hearing today had been? A divine appointment? Surely the minister would be able to answer some of the questions that had been nagging steadily at Brad since the disappearances.

Marcus would be able to tell him if there was any hope, or if it was too late for those who had denied God before the Rapture. The thought made Brad shudder. He wasn't certain he wanted to know the answer to that question, and yet he couldn't put it from his mind. The idea that this was all there was, that the future held nothing but this lonely, desperate existence nearly choked him. Surely the God that his children had talked about in such eloquent terms, that his daughter had sung to and his son had prayed to and his wife had followed, that God would not simply pull the plug on the earth and leave everyone who had missed their chance with no hope. Surely.

But why not? he wondered. Hadn't he had his chance? Hadn't God given him every opportunity to surrender? Why, then, should someone like him deserve anything but God's judgment and condemnation?

Brad closed his eyes briefly and pictured Christine's face. Had he told her lately how beautiful she still looked to him? Had he told her that he still had moments where he couldn't believe she had put up with him for the past twenty-plus years?

Christine's face always looked so serene, her eyes peaceful and knowing, as if she possessed a peace and confidence that were far beyond his grasp. Now, during what was turning out to be the greatest storm of his life, he missed her strength.

He opened his eyes and his gaze fell on the suitcase full of his family's clothes. Gingerly, he picked it up and headed for the bedroom. He would unpack them and place them in a drawer for safekeeping. He had a feeling that in the days ahead, he would need the tangible reminder that someone . . . sometime . . . somewhere . . . had loved him.

★   ★   ★

Washington, D.C.
Rock Creek Park
Local Time 6:32 A.M.

Despite the signs that spring was in bloom in Washington, Brad could see his breath as he made the short walk from his parking space to the Calvert Street entrance to Rock Creek Park. He'd passed the tidal basin that morning on his way into the city. Somehow, the festive site of the blooming cherry trees had seemed in stark contrast to the feeling of gloom that still hung over the nation's capital. Crater-sized holes littered the open spaces where planes had fallen from the sky when their pilots went missing. Though no aircraft had been inbound or outbound for Reagan National at that hour—the city's long-standing 11 P.M. curfew still in effect for takeoffs and landings at the urban airport—Washington was in the flight path for international flights to and from Dulles International Airport twenty miles outside the District.

Fires had broken out across the city when pilotless vehicles had crashed into power lines. The D.C. fire department had been overwhelmed by the sheer enormity of the crisis. In some areas of the city, the fires still burned. A cloud of gray smoke and the smell of charred earth and steel hung over the city.

Yet the cherry blossoms bloomed in apparent defiance of the devastation. Brad had found comfort in the sight of the cheerful pink flowers, just as he had in watching the tide roll in two nights ago on the California beach. The order of the world remained, despite the chaos of its human occupants.

When he saw Marcus Dumont leaning against a tree, waiting for him, Brad hastened his step. He had questions for Marcus, lots of them.

After unpacking his family's clothing last night, Brad had tried to sleep. Exhaustion and fatigue were biting at his heels, but too many questions had plagued his mind. When sleep had failed him, he'd gotten up. Restless, he'd pulled his wife's Bible from the suitcase and searched it for answers.

He'd listened to enough sermons to know that the book of Revelation—*one* Revelation, his mother always said, not Revelations—held the majority of the prophecies people had referred to as the "end times."

But Brad found the text confusing and difficult to follow. The Bible talked about seven seals and seven trumpets, lampstands, horsemen, and a great tribulation. Brad had once dismissed the writing as allegorical and symbolic, not worthy of his time or consideration, but now he felt frustrated at his lack of understanding.

The truth was there. He just couldn't see it.

He'd prayed hard that God would somehow reveal the truth to him through what he was reading, but nothing happened. Finally, exhaustion had claimed him and he'd fallen into a fitful slumber.

Now he figured that Marcus Dumont possessed the answers he sought, and Brad didn't intend to wait any longer to get them. "Good morning," he told the minister.

Marcus extended a hand to him. The preacher's eyes were warm and, unless Brad missed his guess, surprised. "Thank you for coming, Mr. Benton."

Brad shook the younger man's hand. "Please, call me Brad." He studied Marcus closely. "You didn't think I'd come, did you?"

"I wasn't sure," Marcus admitted. "I just know that something you said yesterday—something in the way you answered the senator's questions—made me feel the need to speak to you."

Brad nodded. "I'm glad you reached out to me. I have some questions, too."

"I'm sure you do." Marcus tilted his head in the direction of the paved pathway. "Let's run. I think we should keep moving. It'll give us some privacy."

Brad's eyebrows rose. "Privacy?"

"There's a difficult climate here in Washington these days," Marcus said. "I think we can both agree that caution is prudent."

Brad pursed his lips. "Do you think we're being watched?"

"I think that we can't afford not to be careful."

Brad considered that for a moment, remembering his phone call from Liza Cannley late last night. She'd watched the hearings, caught his testimony and Rosenzweig's. According to Liza, her political sources thought that Brad's answers about Carpathia had raised more than a few administration eyebrows. She also mentioned George Ramiro. She'd been unable to locate anyone at the White House who would acknowledge that they'd spoken to the former press secretary since hours before the disappearances.

"I have to admit," Liza had told Brad, "that you're right. Everything about Ramiro's precipitous departure seems suspicious."

Brad thought the irony was that if Charley Swelder really were behind the press secretary's demise, if he'd merely sat on the information for a few more hours, he could easily have passed it off as part of the global tragedy. With millions missing, who was going to miss one more person? But in his effort to squelch suspicion, Swelder had created a quagmire. He'd told people about Ramiro's resignation before the Rapture. Now he was stuck with the consequences.

"Not to mention," Liza continued, "why the White House was so adamant not to include him in the statement about who was lost."

"We had no problem admitting that the secretary of labor and the secretary of education were gone. But Ramiro wasn't on that list. The only thing I can think is that Swelder knew if he claimed Ramiro disappeared, it wouldn't stand up to press scrutiny. Which means that there's something there to find out."

Liza had agreed to keep digging.

Now Brad considered the potential ramifications of that conversation and of Liza Cannley's investigation. Marcus was right. The political climate *was* difficult and potentially volatile. The Rapture only made it more treacherous. Brad knew it would be prudent to keep a low profile, to not appear to be holding clandestine meetings with anyone—even an apparently harmless activist preacher who'd been left behind. But he'd had enough of that kind of thinking. It was past time to live his life like God wanted him to. He looked at Marcus and nodded. "Let's go."

The two men set off at a leisurely pace through the picturesque beauty of the park, which was largely untouched by the events of the Rapture. Brad had come here many times since his move to Washington—to think, to walk, to enjoy the lush foliage and rolling hills so unlike his California home. He loved the feel of the place, its tranquility amid the clamor of the city. This was as close as he got to his walks on the beach with Christine. Today it was even more poignant—he could almost pretend nothing had happened if he just kept his eyes and his mind on the beauty of the landscape.

As they made their way along the path, the sounds of traffic became more distant, melding with the lighter, more organic sounds of the woods. After they'd settled into a rhythm, Brad glanced at Marcus. "You mentioned yesterday that you thought I'd be surprised to see you," he said. "I'm curious to know why you said that."

Marcus looked at him. "I'm going to take a big risk here, and if I'm way off base, then we can just finish our run, and all I ask is that you hear me out. But if I'm right, I think you'll understand exactly where I'm coming from."

"All right."

Marcus's jaw set in a determined line. "It was something you said yesterday. . . . I can't quite put my finger on it. I just knew, somehow, that you had a deeper understanding of what's going on here."

Brad probed, "Deeper understanding?"

"Yes. Unless I'm wrong, I think that you are among the people who believe there's a spiritual explanation for what happened the other night. You might not have believed that God could work His miracles in the world before, but now you're ready to consider that this might have been the hand of God."

Brad wondered, had he really been that transparent? And, if

so, who else had noticed? Was Charley Swelder already gunning for him? Brad was not yet ready to be labeled a religious zealot. He was sure that God had shown him the truth because he was in a position to act, and he didn't want to jeopardize that position just yet. He wasn't ready to compromise his position at the White House because he was beginning to believe something he'd heard in sermons.

But Marcus Dumont was a preacher—an active, vocal Christian pastor. Which brought up an interesting point. Was it possible he could have been a fraud just like Brad? Either way, it was time to get the truth out.

"Maybe. You know my background. I was widely connected in the evangelical movement in California."

"Yes."

"That was one of the reasons the president asked me to be his chief of staff. He was trying to build bridges after the scandals of the past couple of years."

"There were many people who were glad to see you come to Washington," Marcus assured him.

"And just as many who weren't."

"I'm sure that's true," Marcus concurred. "It generally *is* true in Washington. This is a town that's built on alliances."

"And political types are always at each other's throats?"

"Always on one side or the other, and not necessarily predictably. Wasn't it Nixon who said 'politics makes for strange bedfellows'?"

"Yeah. But he stole the line." A trickle of sweat slipped down Brad's spine, and the cool air began to burn his lungs. "Nixon swiped it from Charles Warner. It's not exactly the first thing he swiped."

Marcus laughed and a plume of mist formed in the air. "That comes as no surprise. But the point is well-taken. In Washington, our economy is built on arguing and maneuvering. We have little to bind us together."

"The town—and the job—is tougher than I expected," Brad

admitted. "I thought my years in the California political system would prepare me for it, but it's more brutal here. There's less honor."

"You haven't enjoyed your stay in D.C., have you?"

"I haven't enjoyed being apart from my family, and I haven't enjoyed working in a mostly hostile environment."

"Hostile?"

Brad carefully considered how much he should reveal to this virtual stranger, a man who, for all intents and purposes, had appeared to be a great supporter of Fitzhugh in the past. "Suffice it to say, I don't agree with a lot of what goes on in the administration."

"I can understand that." Marcus glanced at Brad. "You're a moral man. I imagine you see things that bother you."

Brad nodded. "Yes."

"But you stay."

Brad wasn't certain if he heard an accusation in the statement. "Sometimes a man can effect change better from the inside than from the outside. When I came here, my wife pointed out the biblical precedents for that."

"She sounds wise."

"She was."

"I heard you say at the hearing yesterday that you'd lost your family. I know you must be hurting."

"What about you?" Brad pressed. His breathing was more labored now, but a rush of endorphins had given him a renewed energy. "Did you lose anyone?"

"My wife died years ago," Marcus said. "We had no children, and until the other night, I had made my work my life." He paused as they navigated a tricky set of bends in the path. "And, I'm ashamed to admit, I'd also made it my god."

Brad gave him a surprised look.

"Idols," Marcus said, "come in all shapes and sizes."

"You must have lost a significant number of your organization," Brad prompted.

"Several colleagues and a good portion of my staff. I had made a point of not having any close friends. Easier to keep up appearances."

They ran in silence for several minutes. Brad felt the initial stiff-
ness flood from his limbs and the pace became easier. He sensed in
Marcus the same desperate need for someone to understand, to listen, to unburden, that Brad had since Emma told him his family
was gone. There was a sadness in Marcus that Brad recognized, but
there was also hope. Brad found himself longing to discover the
source of that hope, because now everything in his world looked
terribly bleak.

Carefully, Brad chose his next words. "I've heard sermons for
years about the Rapture, about the end times. My mother was a devout Christian."

"She's gone now," Marcus said. It wasn't a question. Marcus
knew the answer.

"Yes. But not in the Rapture. She died several years ago. I miss her."

"How old were you when she died?"

"Twenty-six."

"I lost my mother at a young age, too," Marcus told him. "I don't
think you ever really get over that."

"I think I remember hearing that about you. You were just a
child."

"A young man. She died trying to take care of our family."
Marcus's expression was grim. "I lost my sisters, too."

"I'm sorry," Brad said quietly.

"I resented it for a long time. I stayed angry at God. When my
wife died, that pushed me to the edge." Marcus looked at him. "But I
can't say I'm sorry they're not here now. I think that in light of what's
coming, you and I are both going to be glad we don't have family on
this earth to witness it."

"What's coming?" Brad prompted, thinking of his readings last
night and of the confusing language about horsemen and seals and
judgments.

Marcus looked at him again. "How much do you know about
the Rapture, Brad?"

Brad shrugged. They turned a corner near a copse of trees. A bench sat at the foot of a large oak inviting them to rest. Brad indicated it to Marcus. "I think we're probably out of eyesight and earshot now."

Marcus agreed. The pair moved in silence to the bench.

Brad sat down and stretched his arms across the back. "I don't know enough. What I know about the Rapture is that the Bible teaches that at an unnamed but predetermined time God will sweep all His followers from the earth and leave the unbelievers behind. During the time that follows, there's a time of tribulation. I'm not precisely sure what that means, but I remember hearing about plagues and famine and the Antichrist. I tried reading the Bible last night, but I got bogged down in all the language about seals and lampstands and the beast. It didn't exactly track well with Washington politics."

"I can just imagine." Marcus's breathing was rapid after the exertion of the run. The sound reminded Brad of the preacher in his mother's church who would get wound up on those hot summer mornings and begin mopping his brow with a linen handkerchief. "The words that you're referring to are the teachings of the book of Revelation as well as the books of Daniel and Ezekiel. The Bible teaches that after the Rapture of the faithful, the judgments of God will begin to rain down on the earth. There have been many interpretations of those judgments, just as there have been many interpretations of the concept of the Rapture. Some men rejected it."

Brad saw the sorrow on the preacher's face. He sensed that this conversation was extraordinarily difficult for him. Men like Marcus had come by their pride and dignity the hard way. It was difficult to admit now that they'd erred. "Men like you?" Brad asked.

Marcus hesitated, then shook his head. "No. I was different."

Brad frowned. "How?"

"I didn't believe in the Rapture, that's true, but that's not why I was left behind."

Brad's mouth had gone dry. Here, he knew, were the answers he was seeking. He sensed that in the next few minutes, he was about to hear whether or not there was any hope for him or his soul. "Then why?" he managed to ask.

"Believing in the Rapture wasn't a prerequisite to participating in it," Marcus explained. "I don't believe that any God-fearing, Christ-believing man or woman who simply chose not to believe in the Rapture and the literal interpretation of the prophecies paid the price of being left behind simply for that disbelief. I believe that God's only requirement for salvation is that we acknowledge Christ as Lord—not that we have every interpretation of Scripture exactly right." He gave Brad a look. "We're supposed to *seek* God, not understand Him."

Brad wiped a hand over his face. "Then pardon me for asking, Reverend, but if what you say is true, why are you here?"

"For exactly that reason. God *requires* that we accept Jesus as Lord of our life. What we know about God doesn't really matter if we've never taken that step."

Something in Brad rebelled. Perhaps it was the same stubborn resistance that had kept him from accepting this truth before, but something kept him from simply swallowing that a man who had done as much good as Marcus Dumont had been left behind by the God he'd claimed to serve. "But you're a preacher."

"So? It's not enough, Brad." Marcus looked at him closely. "If I'm not mistaken, you were a trustee in your church. You're still here, too."

Brad felt the familiar rush of shame he'd been fighting for days. "I was. And I am."

"So in the end, it didn't matter, did it?"

Brad didn't know how to answer that. He waged an internal struggle for several seconds. Was this what Brad Jr. had meant when he'd talked about surrender? When Christine had prayed for the hearts of unbelieving friends to be broken, had this been what she was seeking? Setting aside years of pride and resistance seemed ab-horrent to him. It almost felt as though something—*someone*—was holding him back, preventing him from breaking through the fog of doubt and uncertainty that gripped him.

"Brad?" Marcus prompted.

He didn't answer.

Marcus laid a hand on his arm. "Are you all right?"

"It doesn't make sense," Brad choked out.

"It doesn't have to," Marcus insisted. "In fact, I would have to say it's not even supposed to. That's why it's called faith."

"But how could God . . . ?"

"Keep His promises? Fulfill His prophecies? Find men like you and me who rejected His word and His truth wanting? You tell me."

"I don't know," Brad admitted. "But I can't believe . . ." He trailed off, uncertain how to explain to Marcus the feeling that he simply couldn't actually say the words Marcus was looking for.

Marcus turned on the bench so he could focus completely on Brad. "Brad, before all this happened, I was never a believer in one-on-one evangelism. I preached the gospel, and people responded. I prayed publicly for the salvation of souls, and my ministry seemed to prosper. But I never put God on the throne of my own life. I never surrendered myself to Jesus. I never trusted God to be in control of my life, and I never confessed my need for Him. That's why I got left here."

"Then there's no hope," Brad said. This was exactly what he had most feared.

"No, I don't think that's true. Not exactly. I said that's why I got left here, but what I choose to do and accomplish now is up to me. I can keep living the life I had before—worrying about the future, looking out for myself, deceiving everyone about who I am and what I believe, or I can give God control. The way I see it, I made a big enough mess of things when I was in charge. It's past time I turned things over to God."

Brad saw a fervor, a strength of purpose in the other man's eyes that reminded him of his son.

Marcus leaned forward slightly and braced his hands on his thighs. "The morning after the Rapture, I fell on my face before God and surrendered my pride and my self-serving nature. I begged Him to forgive me for having deceived so many people . . . and most of all, for having rejected Him all these years."

Marcus paused, then looked Brad straight in the eyes. "I believe that He did that, Brad, and that He accepted me as one of His children."

Brad's skin felt clammy and cold. His chest ached and his throat felt tight. "I can't," he managed to say.

"Brad, this isn't the time to let pride—"

Brad shook his head. "You don't understand. I *can't.*"

Marcus's eyes widened. He placed one hand on Brad's shoulder and began whispering a nearly silent prayer. Brad caught snippets of words like *bind* and *flee* and *cast out*. He felt simultaneously strange and relieved as the preacher's grip tightened on his shoulder.

As quickly and as surely as it had come over him, the oppressive feeling began to flee. Brad exhaled a low groan as breath filled his lungs, and his heart rate began to slow to normal. "Marcus?"

Marcus opened his eyes. "Are you all right?"

Brad wasn't sure. He'd never experienced anything like the spine-tingling sensation that now had him feeling chilled. "I don't know."

Marcus drew a steadying breath. "Do you want to know what that feeling was, Brad?"

"I don't know."

Marcus nodded. "I can understand that." He looked around the copse of trees, down the path they'd jogged, and over the slight rise to their left. "I'm not sure I'd want to know either if I were you."

They sat in silence for a few seconds while Brad waited for his equilibrium to return. "Christine," he finally said, "used to talk a lot about spiritual warfare."

Marcus's gaze was both warm and open. "The presence, both physical and spiritual, of the forces of darkness and the forces of good upon the earth."

Brad swallowed deeply. "She believed we were always at risk of attack from the devil's forces." He lowered his gaze, slightly ashamed. "I thought she was being melodramatic."

"It stands to reason," Marcus said quietly, "that with the Christians all gone from the earth, the forces of darkness are slightly less restricted in their movements these days."

"And you think that's what that was?" It seemed impossible, and yet . . . it fit what he had just felt. Exactly.

"I think that the devil's full-time job before the Rapture was keeping Christians from being all that God intended them to be. His only hope was to limit their effectiveness on earth. He didn't have to worry too much about unbelievers. He already had them in his grip."

"I never thought of it that way," Brad acknowledged.

"But now that God has set the events of the end of the world in motion, the prophecies clearly state that Satan's days of power are limited. He will be defeated in the final battle."

"Armageddon," Brad supplied. "I've heard the sermons."

"Right now, I can see why the best the devil can hope for is to keep as many of us under his control as possible. I don't find it hard to believe that he wanted to prevent you from accepting what I think you already know is true."

"Maybe."

"And believe me, there are plenty of reasons not to accept it. To be perfectly honest, what I know from the Scriptures is that those of us who accept God's grace during this time of tribulation are facing a very uncertain future on this earth."

"I can remember sermons about plagues and famines and war and devastation," Brad told him. "I always dismissed it as allegorical."

"I know," Marcus said. "It's frightening and overwhelming. But the central truth is that those things *are* coming. I believe the Antichrist will begin his rise to power very soon. In fact, I think he may have begun it already." Marcus looked over his shoulder, then back at Brad. In a low voice, he asked, "How much do you really know about this Carpathia fellow?"

"Nicolae Carpathia?" It was the second time in two days that Brad had been quizzed about the obscure politician from Romania. Max Arnold had wanted to know about him, too. "Not much. The senator was looking for answers about him yesterday."

"I know. That's what got me thinking," Marcus admitted. "The way he took over in Romania, the location, his interest in the UN— it all fits. If I remember correctly, isn't there a conference regarding a global currency and a concurrent meeting of religious leaders seeking unification getting under way at the UN soon?"

"Yes," Brad concurred. "The secretary of the treasury and the president's economic advisor are scheduled to speak at the currency conference."

"What's the administration's position?"

Brad's smile was rueful. "The same position we always have. We don't like the idea unless it favors us."

"The merging of the global economy is one of the signs of the Antichrist's consolidation of power, Brad. It's one of the prophecies that precedes the coming of the judgments. So is the formation of one world religion."

"I've seen the UN in action on these issues before. There's a lot of noise, but not much gets done. Are you telling me that this time it will be different?"

"Yes. I think it will."

"Doesn't this seem a little unbelievable to you?"

"Doesn't the disappearance of a third of the world's population seem unbelievable?"

"Yes," Brad admitted.

"And because it was unbelievable, you never accepted it as a possibility."

Brad sighed. "No, I didn't. Not until it happened right before my eyes."

"I believed it would, and still I didn't let God into my heart." Marcus pinned him with a shrewd look. "I don't have all the answers, Brad. I wish I did. If I'd acted on the answers I did know, I wouldn't be here right now, facing a terrible future. So I intend to spend whatever time I have left on this earth speaking the truth and knowing that in His infinite mercy, God has agreed to save me, despite everything I've done to prove I don't deserve His grace. Justice demanded my soul, but mercy refused to surrender it. Jesus gave His life for me. I can do no less for Him." He paused. "I *want* to do no less."

Brad considered that, thought about what he'd seen at home, about how much he longed to see and talk to Christine again. He thought of the laughter of his children, the reassuring prayers of his mother, of all the men and women he'd known in his life who claimed to know the Lord and love Christ.

He'd been too proud to see his own need for God's mercy. He'd been too proud to admit that his sin was as unworthy of grace as everyone else's. He'd thought his reputation, his good life, his church membership, his solid marriage—all those things that had earned him the esteem of man made him somehow more worthy of God's blessings than the people around him. What a fool he'd been.

"Brad?" Marcus prompted.

Brad buried his face in his hands. This, he realized, was what Christine had talked about. This is why she had told him she prayed fervently for him every day. She'd known his heart wasn't right. She'd known him better than any person on the face of the planet, and she'd known he wasn't what he claimed to be. "I promised my wife when I found her clothes in my home in California. I promised her I wouldn't run from God anymore. I promised her I'd make a difference with my life."

"What did you mean by that?" Marcus asked.

Brad raised his head and met the younger man's gaze. "I can't keep that promise unless I give my life to Christ. I see that now."

Marcus briefly closed his eyes as his lips moved in a silent prayer. When he opened them again, tears dampened his dark lashes. "I'm glad to hear that. You have no idea how glad."

"I'm not sure I know what to do," Brad confessed. "I know it sounds pathetic, but I've been to church my entire life, and I don't really know how I'm supposed to make this happen."

"You can't make it happen. Only God makes it happen. All you have to do is accept His gift of grace."

Brad knew he'd heard sermons on this topic a hundred times. Once, when a prominent evangelist had visited his city, he'd even served as a counselor for seekers who'd responded to the preacher's invitation. He knew all the spiel, remembered the Scripture, but now, when it was up to him, he had no idea where to start. "I don't know how."

Marcus gave him a knowing smile. "Lucky for you I do. Brad, do you recognize that you have sin in your life?"

"Of course."

"The Bible says, 'For all have sinned; all fall short of God's glorious standard.' Do you know what the consequences of your sin are?"

Brad remembered a verse from childhood. "'For the wages of sin is death,'" he quoted.

Marcus continued, "'But the free gift of God is eternal life through Christ Jesus our Lord.'"

Brad was beginning to feel better as he realized that somehow, impossibly, God still had a place for him and a job for him to do. It truly wasn't too late. "Yes, yes. I remember that," he said, his voice warming to the topic.

"The Bible also says, 'If we confess our sins to Him'—that's God, of course—'He is faithful and just to forgive us and to cleanse us from every wrong.' That's the next step, Brad. You know you're a sinner; you recognize that only God can cleanse you from that sin. Are you willing to admit your need for His forgiveness and repent of your pride and your selfish nature?"

"Yes," Brad assured him, "I am."

"Then what you must do is tell God exactly that. 'For if you confess with your mouth that Jesus is Lord and believe in your heart that God raised Him from the dead, you will be saved. For it is by believing in your heart that you are made right with God, and it is by confessing with your mouth that you are saved. As the Scriptures tell us, '"Anyone who believes in Him will not be disappointed."'"

Brad held up a hand. "You lost me."

"If you confess your sin, Brad, God will forgive you, but if you wish to be saved, you'll have to surrender to His will for your life. He wants all of you, not just bits and pieces. Are you willing to follow Him no matter what it might cost you?"

The cost, Brad knew, could be high. His job, his reputation, and, if Marcus were to be believed, his well-being and perhaps even his life. What he had experienced a few moments ago could easily be only the beginning of the onslaught that would ensue if he chose to surrender his life to God. But none of that compared with being apart through eternity from God and the wife and family he'd already lost.

What had his mother always said? *"When God sacrificed the life of His own Son for us, was He really asking too much in return for His gift?"* The answer now seemed so clear to Brad that he wondered and shuddered at his own arrogance. How could he have missed it? How could he possibly have thought that he was too good, too righteous, to need God's salvation?

He looked at Marcus. "I am," he said, his voice surprisingly strong and sure.

"Then pray with me," Marcus urged as he bowed his head. "Lord, I know that You alone can save us. I know that You alone can make us whole."

Brad acknowledged the truth in his own spirit. Marcus continued. "Forgive us, Lord, for failing You, for doubting You. Strengthen us for the days ahead. Save us with Your mercy and grace. Lord, all that we have, all that we are, we commit now to You. Thank You for the gift of Your Son, for His death on the cross, for His sacrifice and His resurrection. Thank You for sending Him to reign in our hearts. We look forward to the day that we are united with You. Amen."

"Amen," Brad responded, his heart pounding. He felt a kinship with Marcus he'd never known with anyone, as if their souls, having yielded to the same Lord, now knew an irrevocable bond. He looked at his new friend with earnest intent. "Thank you, Marcus."

"Thank you," Marcus said. "I have hope now. I'm not sure I did before."

"Me, either," Brad admitted.

"God answered my prayer when He sent you to those hearings yesterday."

Brad exhaled a long sigh. "I was so angry when I had to leave California. I had to leave so much undone. I had no idea that God had arranged a divine appointment for me. What a fool I've been."

"I think that recognizing the extent of our own arrogance is one of the most pleasing confessions we make to God," Marcus said. "It's easy to confess individual sins when we have a clear picture of right and wrong, but being broken—" he shrugged—"that takes guts."

"That's the word Christine always used. *Broken*. I get it now."

"Me, too. Funny how I resisted it for so long, only to find out what a relief it is."

That made Brad laugh. "I know how you feel. So what do we do now? If things are going to get as bad as you say, surely we don't just sit and wait."

"We study," Marcus assured him, "and learn. I've been reading the Scriptures, trying to understand. I think we have to be prepared for whatever may come our way."

"I agree."

"And then I think we wait and see what God tells us. I believe He will lead us if we listen to Him. I'd like—" He paused.

"What were you going to say?" Brad asked.

"I know you're a busy man."

"So are you." Brad made a slight gesture with his hand. "Especially now, I imagine. There are a lot of hurting people out there. Confused people. I'm sure you're being called on to answer a lot of questions."

"I am," he admitted. "And I think we could both benefit from each other's perspective. If you will, I'd like you to meet me here every morning. We can jog, we can talk, we can pray, and we can learn from each other. I'll continue to study the Bible and tell you what God reveals to me if you'll do the same."

Brad thought that over and found the idea appealing. His wife and friends had urged him before to form that kind of relationship with other Christian men. Christine had referred to it as an "accountability partnership." Brad hadn't been interested in anything that smacked of what he considered pseudopsychology. At the time, he'd found nothing more loathsome than the idea of meeting with other men so they could talk about their struggles.

In his world, a successful man hid his struggles; he didn't flaunt them.

But now he felt a longing for more of the connection he'd formed with Marcus that morning. Here in the most unusual place, under the most unusual circumstances, Brad finally began to understand what his family had meant by the word *fellowship*. He couldn't feel closer to Marcus Dumont—a man he really barely knew, a man with whom he had little in common—than if he were his own brother.

Brothers, Brad mused. *Brothers in Christ*—another term he'd heard bandied about at his church over the years. Another term he was just beginning to understand.

He exhaled a long breath and looked at Marcus. "I'd like to. Very much."

A smile played at the corner of Marcus's mouth. "I almost wish my wife were alive so I could tell her my new jogging partner is the chief of staff at the White House."

Brad grinned. "Christine would never have believed that mine is an evangelical minister."

"God is in the business of bringing together odd friends," Marcus said. "The original twelve disciples were all very different men who came together for a common cause."

Brad liked the idea of being a disciple. It had a ring of courage and purpose to it.

"What bound them together," Marcus said, "was their love of Jesus and their public commitment to follow Him. In many ways, the risk they took with that commitment was much like the one you and I are taking. They had no idea what they were getting themselves into."

"I'm not afraid," Brad said.

"Neither am I."

"Maybe I should be, but the way I see it, I've lost everything that matters," Brad said. "Anything I have left is just window dressing."

"I know what you mean."

"When this is over," Brad asked carefully, "do you believe we'll be with our families again?"

"Yes, I do. And we'll be with them soon. The Bible says the time of the Tribulation is seven years. I'm not sure if the events that trigger it will start immediately or not. I'll have to study some more. But the end is near. Very near."

"And at the end of those seven years?"

"Jesus will return—the Bible calls it the Glorious Appearing. Those of us who have given our lives to Christ during this time—if we survive the seven-year Tribulation—will be gathered to Him."

Brad thought that over. "You know, I'd have done it anyway, even if it meant there was no hope in the end. I still would have chosen to spend whatever future I have left here serving God."

"So would I."

"It was miserable the other way."

Marcus laughed. "But we were both too proud to do anything about it."

"God's grace must be amazing," Brad admitted. He felt a strange sense of euphoria, as though the weight that had been bearing down on him for the last few days had finally lifted. The strange sense of oppression that had come over him just moments before had now departed completely. His spirit felt as buoyant as the waters of Rock Creek as they gurgled through the park. The sound of the water drew his attention. Brad glanced through the foliage and could just make out the rocky bank that sloped toward the fast-flowing creek. Recent rains had swollen the waters to higher-than-usual levels, and the creek, which normally bubbled almost silently, today rushed by as it washed the creek banks clean.

Washed clean. Brad was struck by the thought that for the first time in his life he understood the reason for the ordinance of baptism and why Christians referred to it as symbolic of Christ's death and resurrection. He'd never considered being baptized important enough to subject himself to the public display. Even his wife had believed that baptism was merely a symbol, not a prerequisite for salvation, so Brad had always managed to avoid walking through the baptismal waters. Though all three of his children had been baptized as young people, Brad had never revealed, even to Christine, that he had not. Now a thought so absurd that it would have made him scoff days ago had him looking at Marcus hopefully. "Marcus—"

Marcus glanced toward the creek, then back at Brad. His eyes widened. "Do you have any idea how cold that water is?"

A smile tipped the corner of Brad's mouth. "I don't mind if you don't."

"Brad, I'd be delighted to baptize you, but wouldn't you rather do it in my church? The baptistery is heated."

"No." Brad looked at the creek again. "I don't want to put it off any longer. I've waited too long as it is."

"Part of the importance of the ordinance of baptism is the public profession of your faith in Jesus that it makes to the congregation. It's a public way of saying you're not ashamed to be counted among His children."

"And I'll do it again, anywhere you say, anytime you want. You can baptize me in front of whoever will watch. I just—" He broke off, at a loss for words for an instant. "It feels like now is the time."

Marcus studied him a moment, then stood to pull his sweatshirt over his head. "This is crazy, Benton," he said. "But I have a feeling this is how Philip must have felt when he baptized the eunuch on the road to Gaza."

Brad grinned and rose. He walked toward the foliage along the creek bank. "Probably."

"If we both get pneumonia," Marcus said as Brad began picking his way through the shrubbery, "I'm holding you responsible."

"Deal." Brad stepped onto the rocky creek bank. The water looked clear and clean, and though it was moving fairly quickly, the current didn't look dangerous. "Looks okay to me."

"Looks cold to me," Marcus said from behind his shoulder.

Brad shot him a look. "How bad can it be?"

"This time of year? Forty or fifty degrees bad," Marcus told him. "That's how bad. Are you forgetting that we had snow on the ground less than a month ago?"

"That stream's shallow. It's got to have warmed up since then."

"Yeah, well, don't whine to me when you're in it. And be prepared to freeze in your wet clothes."

Brad pulled his sweatshirt over his head. "My running shorts will do. The rest of my clothes will be waiting for me, nice and dry, when we get out."

Marcus rolled his eyes, shook his head, and began untying his shoes. "I should have known better than to pick a guy from California for my spiritual partner. This is exactly the kind of dumb stunt you flakes and nuts from the West Coast are known for."

That made Brad laugh. He shucked off all his clothes except his running shorts and waited while Marcus followed suit. Suddenly, the scene took on a sense of seriousness. Marcus gave Brad a look that spoke volumes as he waded into the frigid water. Brad eased into the creek behind him. The river was even colder than Marcus had promised, but Brad didn't care. He was profoundly aware that no matter how many award ceremonies or swearing-in ceremonies or public recognitions he'd attended, this was, quite possibly, the single most awesome and inspiring moment of his life.

Marcus turned Brad to his side, took both his hands, and arranged them in one of his. Then he held one hand to heaven and said, "Brad Benton, because of your faith in the Lord Jesus Christ and because you have chosen to follow Him in obedience to His commands, I baptize you, my brother, in the name of the Father, the Son, and the Holy Ghost." He placed his hand between Brad's shoulder blades.

Brad bent his knees and leaned backward. Marcus continued, "Buried with Christ in the likeness of His death." He dipped Brad beneath the clear cold water, then raised him back to a standing position. "Raised to walk in newness of life."

Brad knew that he had tears in his eyes as the icy water streamed from his hair and ran down his face. Marcus embraced him, and despite the cold, the two stood there in that stream for long seconds. It was as if both of them wanted to preserve the fragile and holy moment. But when Brad's teeth started chattering, he eased away from his new friend. What Marcus had said was true. They were brothers now, bound together by the blood of Christ. "Thank you," he managed to whisper.

"Thank you," Marcus said. They both stood still a moment longer. Brad's body began to shake. "By the way," Marcus said, "your lips are turning blue." He nudged Brad toward the bank. "It's time to thaw out."

Brad laughed and followed Marcus out of the water. They dressed in silence. As Brad was tying his shoes, Marcus stood to pull his sweatshirt back over his head. "Brad, I really hate to cut this short. If we had time, I'd like to spend the morning talking with you, but I've got to preach in—" he glanced at his watch—"two hours. For some reason, I think I may need a shower first."

"Preach?" Brad asked, surprised. "You've got a congregation?"

Marcus shook his head. "To be honest, right now I don't know if I do. But I preach every Sunday morning at ten in a church in North West. I figured today, of all days, I'd better be there. Whoever shows up this morning is going to be in real need of comfort and truth. I'm finally prepared to honestly offer it to them."

For the first time in his life, Brad knew what his Christian family and friends had meant when they talked about "thirsting" for knowledge and a word from the Lord. There was a song his daughter Megan liked. It compared a deer panting after water to a soul longing for God. Brad remembered a verse in Psalms that used the same analogy. "Marcus," he said abruptly. "Would it be okay if I—?"

"Came along?" Marcus asked. "Absolutely. Although, I have to warn you, you might feel a little out of place. Even on a typical Sunday morning, we don't have a lot of White House chiefs of staff in my congregation."

Brad laughed, feeling amazingly renewed and restored despite all he'd been through in the last three days. "That's all right. I haven't fit in anywhere since I've been in this town."

"Then you're welcome," Marcus assured him. "I can't think of anyone I'd rather have there today." He held out his hand and helped Brad stand. "I'm planning on having a testimony time at the end of the service. That's just a time for people to share what they've been through in the last few days. I have a feeling that it might be a bit more interesting than usual this Sunday. If you'd be comfortable, I'd like you to speak."

Brad nodded. "I'd be glad to. Maybe my teeth will stop chattering by then."

12

Mariette stared at her own image on her television screen. At just this instant in her life, she had nothing to do but wait for her son to arrive, so she'd turned on the tube to pass the time and had been surprised to find her own face looking out at her on C-SPAN. Max had managed to get his hearings broadcast. But Mariette took a small, secret delight in the fact that the proceedings weren't creating a feeding frenzy on the major news shows. Max's grandstanding hadn't paid off in the way he'd hoped, at least not this time.

"Ms. Arnold," Max said. Any hint of warmth Mariette had heard in her ex-husband's voice when he met with her privately yesterday was long gone.

Which was fine with her. After he'd made her wait around most of the day Saturday to give her testimony, wasting her time during the biggest emergency the country had ever faced, she hadn't been particularly pleased with him, either. She'd had her temper under tight rein when she had finally been called to speak at the hearing.

"Can you explain why your agency suddenly needs twice as many troops as usual to serve meals and pass out blankets?" Max asked. "I think that at a time like this, our military might have better things to do than serve as America's wait staff. Isn't that a job better done by relief workers?"

Like she could find relief workers to use. Most of them were among the missing. And Max knew it. She'd given him the figures herself. She watched her image on the TV screen take a deep breath. She remembered how hard it had been to hold back what she'd really wanted to say as she replied to Max's question. But she hadn't lost it—it wasn't her style. She hadn't realized that her effort to suppress her irritation was so obvious, though.

The phone rang.

Randal . . .

Forgetting all about the hearings, she sprinted for the receiver and said a breathless, "Hello."

But it wasn't Randal.

"Mariette?" David Liu's voiced sounded practically unhinged. "Mariette, where are you?"

"Home, obviously. Waiting for Randal, just like we agreed. What's wrong?"

"Everything! You need to get in here," David said.

"Are you having trouble with the food convoys?" Mariette was surprised. "I thought we had that all straightened out."

"You did. I mean, we did. I mean, everything's going fine. They're getting the goods together right now." David paused, evidently needing the time to collect himself. Mariette's nerves, already stretched tight, kicked up another notch. David didn't sound good. Not good at all. "No, it's not the food convoy," David went on. "It's Musselman. He's having trouble with the press."

"Tell me about it. He kept calling me all night long for answers."

"It's not just that. He's on a tear about wanting you here. In case reporters call."

"He knows where I am. I'm happy to answer any press inquiries—just forward the calls here. I've done everything I can at the office for right now, and you know it."

"Of course I do, but Musselman doesn't. He wants all his worker bees in the office. I think it's an image thing. And I think your job depends on it."

"I'm not going anywhere until I lay eyes on my son. If Musselman wants to call me on it, he can just fire me."

"Mariette, don't say that. I don't want your job. I couldn't do your job."

"Sure you could—but it won't be necessary. I'll be in as soon as Randal gets here. He shouldn't be much longer. You can cover for me that long, can't you?"

"I'll try," David said. He sounded a little more together, Mariette was glad to note. But she'd feel better once she made it back into work. David clearly needed some downtime—and once she got to the office she was going to make him take it if she had to lock him in a closet.

"Thanks," Mariette said. "I'll make it up to you once we get through this mess."

"If we make it through this mess . . . ," he said softly.

"We're going to," Mariette said. "I promise."

"I'm going to hold you to that," David replied. "Get in when you can. I don't need your job. Bye."

"Bye. See you soon."

She hung up the phone and started fuming. So Musselman had decided to rear his ugly head again. Didn't he understand that she needed to make sure her son was all right? Didn't he understand that normal humans had lives? After a second, she shook her head at her own foolishness. Of course he didn't. Mariette had never seen him give a moment's thought to his own family unless he needed them for a photo op.

So Musselman wanted her in the office. Never mind that she and her staff had busted their guts to handle the unimaginable crisis facing the country. Never mind that her boss was off on a presidential junket to "survey the damage," instead of actually trying to do something useful about it. He wanted to *look* busy, not *be* busy. The actual work he left up to her.

And he wanted to sound competent. That was tough for him. He was a political appointee with only a vague notion of what his agency *could* do, much less any kind of grasp on what it *should* do. Especially in times like these.

He relied on his staff, especially Mariette, to provide the answers he claimed as his own. She'd taken three calls in the last twelve hours from the man: two at the office late the night before and one at home at three this morning, all asking for sound bites to give the press and the president.

It never occurred to him that she was going to need a clear head and some sleep and to see her son if he wanted her to function. Between him and Max, she'd already wasted enough time the last two days. So now she was sleep starved, mad at her boss and her ex, and worried desperately about her son. And she was starting to go stir-crazy.

It was no wonder. Between the crisis, Randal, Max, and now David and Musselman, she hadn't really stopped worrying since the disappearances. After she had finally finished her testimony yesterday, she'd returned to the office to nail down plans for the supply convoys. It had been very late last night before she'd finally heeded David's advice to get some sleep and made her way home.

She'd walked in the door well after midnight and found a message on her answering machine from Randal. He'd crossed the Maryland state line. He was going to find a place to crash for the night and then make his way home first thing in the morning.

Disappointed that she'd missed the call, Mariette had replayed the message four or five times. She was glad she'd changed her outgoing message to assure him that she was all right. Her son sounded fine. Tired but well and emotionally okay. Her job being what it was, she was fairly adept at recognizing stress when she heard it. Unlike David, Randal was coping. And he was coming home today. She was going to wait right here for him.

A significant number of major roads were still impassable, and she had no way of knowing how long it would take him to travel the rest of the way. Normally, she could have forwarded any calls from him to her cell phone and gone on into the office, but the phone companies were still running limited services, and at the best of times her cell phone coverage had a tendency to be sporadic. No telling how many towers were down or disabled.

Back at her office, David said that he had everything under control. After listening to the tone in his voice just now, Mariette was beginning to wonder. Her assistant was showing signs of serious stress and trauma. As far as Mariette knew, he hadn't left the FEMA building since the night of the disappearances.

So she could hardly blame David for sounding bad. To hold her own meltdown at bay, she'd tried to get a little shut-eye last night, not that it had done her much good. After dawn, to stem her growing anxiousness, she'd flipped on the television. The Capitol Hill network was rebroadcasting Max's hearings. Trying to keep her mind off her troubles, Mariette had watched both Brad Benton and Chaim Rosenzweig testify.

While Benton had seemed to her to be evading many of Max's questions, he'd also seemed genuine on the answers he did give and determined to do his best for both the administration and the country. She sensed that his position as White House chief of staff kept him from saying all that he wished to the committee. Her heart went out to him when he talked about his wife and three children. She knew what agony she'd suffered in the few hours she'd been unable to reach Randal. She couldn't imagine how she would have coped had she found her own son missing.

Rosenzweig, on the other hand, had seemed unreserved and flattered by Max's invitation to speak. He'd spoken at length about his concerns regarding the disappearances and about his country's very real fear that if the religious right succeeded in persuading the public that this had been a biblically predicted event, the Israelis would find themselves right in the middle of an epic conflict. His own theory about what had happened was that the disappearances were quantum events triggered by long-term environmental abuse, exacerbated by the recent nuclear attack on Israel.

Mariette, who had heard every theory by now—from alien invasion to mass hypnosis—had listened intently to the renowned scientist, looking for something—anything—that would allow her to

put from her mind the nagging memory of her conversation with
Marcus Dumont. But Rosenzweig's explanation sounded like so
much smoke and mirrors to her.

What Marcus had said was beginning to sound more like the real
truth to her than she cared to admit. Marcus's theories had been unwelcome, but his words had triggered too many memories for her to
ignore. As awful as Rosenzweig's ideas seemed, when she considered the consequences, Marcus's forecast seemed worse.

Didn't the Bible speak of plagues and famine and natural disasters that were supposed to follow the so-called Rapture? She remembered sermons on war and pestilence, violence, and the presence of
evil in the world. At the time, she'd tuned them out as the trumped-
up scare tactics of an overzealous preacher.

But now . . . after what she'd seen happen, she couldn't discount
anything as impossible. Shuddering, Mariette wrapped her arms
around her legs and stared out the front window. Her neighbor's car
was where she'd found it—still wrapped around the tree, as if no
one had cared enough to see to it. Or, she thought grimly, as if anyone who had cared enough to deal with it was no longer here to re-
move the vehicle. Frustrated and slowly going crazy as she waited
for Randal, Mariette reached for the phone. She might be about to
lose her job, but she wanted to be here for her son. In the meantime,
the least she could do was call a wrecker.

"Mom?" Mariette fought her way through layers of sleep as she felt
something tapping on her shoulder. "Mom? Are you okay?"

Suddenly she realized where she was and who the voice belonged to. Mariette sat bolt upright on her couch, her body in motion long before her mind was ready to catch up. As her brain fought
its way to consciousness, she focused on the concerned expression
on her son's face. He was watching her carefully, almost as if he
couldn't believe she was alive.

For an instant, she thought this was another of the dreams that had plagued her all during the night. But he was here, flesh and blood, and more importantly, safe and sound. The three-day-old growth of beard on his handsome young face sold her on the reality of what she was seeing. Even if he *was* looking at her just now as if she were some kind of pod-person from a monster movie.

"Oh, Randal." She reached for him as she scrambled from the sofa. "Randal. Oh, I'm so glad you're all right." Mariette hugged her son fiercely, not even bothering to fight the tears that sprang to her eyes.

"Mom," he said. He wrapped his strong arms around her. "It's okay. I'm okay."

"I've been so worried." She touched his face, his shoulders, quickly skimming her hands over him the way she used to when he'd fallen off his bike or tumbled from a tree. Though he stood before her whole and well, her mother's instinct had her looking for trouble.

Randal caught her hands in his. "I'm all right," he assured her. "No structural damage."

His slight grin was disarming. She exhaled slowly and hugged him close again. "I've been worried sick, honey. When your roommate told me . . . well, I imagined every horrible scenario I could think of involving your trip, and I've got enough experience to imagine some real disasters."

"I got here as quickly as I could."

Mariette struggled to gain control of her emotions. She couldn't seem to make herself let go of him. "I couldn't get through to you on your phone," she told him needlessly.

"Mom." He tugged gently at her arms. "Mom, come on. I'm okay. I promise I'm okay. I can't breathe."

A shudder ran through her. *Let go,* she told herself. *He's okay.* A few more internal lectures and she managed to unclench her hands from his shirt. Still, she found herself unwilling to turn him completely loose. The effects of three long, tortuous days of worrying about her only child didn't just vanish instantly. Randal wrapped one arm around Mariette's shoulders and guided her back to the sofa. He sat her down on it and then sat next to her.

"Are you all right?" he asked. "You don't look like it. You look exhausted."

"I know. It's inescapable. Between you and work . . . let's just say that it hasn't been the best week of my life and leave it at that." Mariette shook her head. "It doesn't matter now."

"I caught part of your testimony last night on C-SPAN. It was good to hear your voice."

"I can imagine," she said. "I'd have mortgaged the house just to talk to you."

"I'm glad you didn't." He grinned. "I'm glad I'm home. Things were . . . tough . . . out there."

"Have you spoken to your father?" she asked.

Randal looked away. "Not yet."

That didn't surprise her. Randal still hadn't forgiven his father for being unfaithful to Mariette. Max didn't understand Randal's feelings and blamed Mariette for Randal's distance. Despite her differences with her ex-husband, Mariette would never attempt to keep his son from him. But Max seemed incapable of believing that she'd never do such a damaging thing to her son—probably because he'd tried the tactic himself. It hadn't worked because Randal didn't give much credence to anything Max said since he'd learned about his father's philandering. Randal's deliberate disassociation from Max had been his own choice.

"Your father wants to talk to you," Mariette said. "I know he's worried. He asked me when I saw him at the hearings if you were all right."

Randal shrugged. "I'll call him sooner or later. I wanted to see you first."

"Thank you. I love you, too." She hugged him again, kissed his cheek, and smoothed a hand through his tousled hair. "Max has a right to know that you're here, Randal."

He gave her a piercing look. "It didn't seem to matter to him how I felt before—"

"You don't have to call him right now," Mariette cut him off, unwilling to dig up an old argument, not now, when she was so relieved to have him safe under her roof again. "For the moment, just give me permission to let him know you're all right."

Randal hesitated but then collapsed against the back of the couch. "Sure. Whatever."

She knew better than to push the point. Randal would talk to his father when he was ready and not one moment before. She'd learned from experience that pushing her son on the issue would do more harm than good. It was time for a change of subject.

"Are you completely worn out?" she asked. "When I talked to your roommate, he said you left shortly after everything happened."

"I'm beat," he admitted. "I slept in some motel last night, but not very well." He rubbed his eyes with his thumb and forefinger. "Before that, I pulled over at rest stops and slept in the car until I felt like I could get moving again. Mom, the roads are horrible."

"I know."

"It's just wrecks all over the place. I lost count of the jackknifed tractor-trailers. Part of what took me so long was that some truck hauling gunpowder had overturned on I-99. It looked like the end of the world—they said you could see the flames for miles when it first blew. They had the road shut down for hours, and the side roads were jammed."

"I can imagine. I haven't been out of D.C., but I've been monitoring the road conditions. It's one of the reasons I was so worried about you. It's been bad here, too. The Beltway has been almost impassable."

Randal shook his head. "I gotta say, I'm really glad I'm your kid and that I listened to most of the stuff you taught me. I was prepared for the worst out there. Hardly anyone is taking credit cards, and most of the ATMs are still down. I guess the banks don't have their networks up yet."

Mariette nodded. "Absolutely. People are running out of supplies simply because they can't access their cash. On top of that, the price gouging is getting ridiculous. I've pointed the problem out to the president's people. I hope they do something about it fast." She frowned. "So what did *you* do for money?"

"Are you kidding? How many times did you tell me to make sure I have four to five days' cash reserve in a safe place in case of an emergency? I've been waiting tables for three years in State College. I put most of my tip money in a safe-deposit box on campus." He shook the front pouch of his backpack. "It's a lot of small bills and coins, but it spends the same."

Mariette exhaled a long sigh of relief as she felt the knot of anxiety in her stomach begin to slowly uncoil. She'd spent too many moments worrying about him sleeping on the side of the road, short on food, and low on cash. "Then you've eaten?"

"Not well," he confessed. "I didn't want to stop much, and a lot of places still aren't open. I grabbed a couple of burgers, and I took what I had from the apartment—"

Mariette cringed. "Let me guess. Chips, junk food, and snack cakes?"

"Hey, at least I left the beer."

"Randal—"

"Kidding. I bought some supplies along the way, but mostly I tried to keep driving. I was afraid that if I pulled off the road for too long, it'd be too hard to get back on. It sort of reminded me of that time we drove through the blizzard on the way to see Gram. You remember—I kept whining about stopping and you kept telling me to chew more gum and let you drive."

That made her laugh. "I'm not surprised you remember that. You were only seven, but we didn't eat for twelve hours."

"That made a real impression on a growing boy." Randal patted his stomach. "Gum only goes so far, Mom. You know, I'm still a growing boy . . ."

"Hint taken. Come on." She stood. "Keep telling me about your trip and I'll get you some food."

Randal followed her to the kitchen. "I was actually surprised to find you home. I thought for sure you'd be at the office, managing a massive relief effort."

"I got your message last night, and I didn't want to miss you," she told him as she pulled a can of soup from the pantry. "I did everything I could, considering the circumstances, yesterday, and David's covering for me this morning."

Randal eased onto the stool at the breakfast bar and watched her pop open the can. "But you *should* be at work?"

"Yes. David's about to fall apart, and Musselman's losing it. Now that I know you're safe, I've got to get back to the job pretty fast. And there's plenty to do," she admitted. "I've got a convoy of supply barges going up the coast to drop food and necessities in several major cities tomorrow morning. The roads and railways are virtually impassable in too many places—and the airlines are struggling just to get back on a normal schedule. We need to get some basic supplies into the urban areas or people are going to keep looting and start starving." She gently touched his unshaven cheek. "But there's enough time to make sure you're okay. You can stay here and rest, if you want, or you can come in with me. It's up to you."

"I'll go with you," he said. "If you don't mind waiting until I've eaten. I'm sure you can use all the help you can get."

"We are short staffed." Mariette had dumped the soup into a pan and was reaching for a loaf of bread on top of the refrigerator when she felt Randal's hand close over hers.

"I'll get it," he said. "You don't have to take care of me, you know."

"I don't mind," she told him.

"I do." He gave her a gentle shove toward the stove. "So David is covering for you now?" he asked.

Mariette nodded, handing him a crock of butter. "David hasn't taken a break since the crisis hit. I've talked to him about it, but he says he needs the relief of working. That's normal, you know. Takes the edge off thinking about what happened." Something in her son's expression made Mariette pause. "What's wrong?"

He looked slightly uncomfortable. "I was thinking about what happened. What *did* happen, Mom?"

"I don't have any answers, honey," she said.

He seemed to think that over for a minute as he spread butter on thick slices of bread. "Do you have any hunches?"

"You said you caught the hearings on C-SPAN. I assume you know that the president has declared that we've been attacked and that he has elevated our defense position to DEFCON 2."

"Yeah." He shot her a probing look. "Is that what *you* think happened? You think we got hit by somebody's top secret weapon out of the blue?"

Mariette paused, then shook her head. "No. There are too many people missing around the globe. It doesn't make sense."

"What, then?"

She shrugged slightly. The soup had begun to boil, so she ladled it into a bowl for him. "I don't know. A natural disaster. Some kind of nuclear accident. Aliens. There are a hundred possibilities."

"There are some other theories, you know." He handed her a plateful of buttered bread. "Like the God thing."

Mariette frowned as she placed his bowl and a spoon on the table. "The Rapture, you mean?"

"That's what Gram called it."

At the mention of her mother, Mariette lifted her eyebrows. Randal had always been close to his grandmother. When he was a young child, Max and Mariette had often sent him to stay with Estelle during the summers of campaign seasons. They'd found that the pace on the road was too much for him. So he'd spent several months at a time on the family farm in Iowa. But since her mother's death several years ago, Randal had rarely mentioned his grandmother. Mariette had no idea that he'd absorbed some of her mother's fundamentalist ideas. "I know that."

He began wolfing down the soup and bread. "This is really good, Mom."

"Sure. Right now you're so hungry you'd probably say that about school cafeteria meat loaf," she pointed out. "It's not my best gourmet recipe."

"Who cares?" he muttered around a large mouthful. "Don't you want any?"

"I've eaten," she said. Though, come to think of it, she couldn't precisely remember when.

Randal merely nodded and continued to wolf down his meal like it might be his last one. "So, about Gram," he finally said, once he'd polished off all the food in front of him.

Mariette propped one hip against the counter. "Yes?"

"There are things I'd like to talk to you about. You know, about some stuff she told me."

She recalled her conversation with Marcus Dumont and wondered if she was really the best person to answer her son's questions. What could she say? That she'd heard everything her mother had to say? That she'd never bothered to believe it? At least, not until now, when she was terrified that it might actually be true?

She reminded herself that she and Randal had always had this arrangement. Any question, anyplace, anytime. He was allowed to ask, and she'd do the best she could to give him an answer or to find one for him. It made their relationship work as mother and son and as friends and confidants. With a brief nod at his now finished meal, she reached for her jacket. "Then grab your stuff. We can talk in the car on the way to the office. In fact, Musselman's already threatened to fire me if I don't get in there."

"Why didn't you say something? Come on, Mom, let's move!"

Mariette glanced at Randal as she drove onto the George Washington Parkway. She was going as fast as she dared, given the current conditions on the road. "So tell me how things were at school. What was it like when the big event went down?"

He whistled. "You wouldn't believe me if I told you. It was chaos. Really bizarre. People were so scared."

"I can imagine." She steered around a crater-sized pothole. "Where were you when it happened?"

"In my apartment studying. Don and I heard screaming from down the hall. I didn't really think much of it at first. I mean, it's a college complex. Parties and stuff can get out of hand. But then the noise got really intense. So I got up to check it out. This girl three doors down from us ran out into the hall and started yelling about how her boyfriend just vanished. I figured she'd gotten way too chemically altered for her own good, and I tried to calm her down. Then all the phones started ringing, and people started pouring out of their apartments. It was like, I don't know, we were ants and somebody had poked the nest or something. Everyone was still trying to figure out what had happened when there was this loud boom and the power went off."

"Someone hit a generator," she guessed. "Car crash, probably."

"Yeah, I figured. But the darkness just freaked everyone out. Big time. There were sirens going off and people were crying. Don managed to get out a couple of calls on his cell phone before the network crashed. I tried to reach you, but the system here must have already been down." He gave her a speculative look. "Nobody could get through. You know, I thought they said they fixed that."

"I imagine they didn't plan on a third of their human backup force disappearing right before something like that happened again."

"Hmmm." He rubbed his hands on the legs of his worn jeans. "Well, anyway, we were still getting radio, so we all sort of huddled around that battery-operated transistor radio you gave me last year. As best we could tell, the campus cops were saying that a bunch of professors and a lot of students were missing. The entire ACF house and the BCM were wiped out."

"ACF?"

"Alliance Christian Fellowship. BCM is the Baptist Campus Ministry."

"Ah, that one," she said. "We called it the Baptist Student Union when I was in school."

"Oh. Well, they were having some all-night prayer thing there or something, and like 90 percent of them vanished. The couple of guys that were left went ballistic. I saw several students just sobbing by the phones because they couldn't get in touch with their parents." He frowned. "One kid I knew was at the library when his girlfriend disappeared. He was so weirded out by everything that he walked back to our dorm and hung himself. That really bothered me. That was when I decided that I was getting in the car as soon as I could get my stuff together and coming home."

"Oh, Randal." Mariette didn't like the idea of him being exposed to that level of trauma, despite the rational side of her brain telling her he was no longer a child.

"It was the scariest thing I've ever seen," he admitted. "Except for maybe the disappearances . . . I was glad I didn't see anybody vanish."

"I can't imagine," she said, "what it must have been like for people who actually saw it happen."

"You weren't up?" Randal asked.

"I was recovering from disaster relief in South Carolina. I'd been asleep for a couple of hours."

"That explains it. Anyway, Don and I tried reaching a few people. One of the calls he got out was to a friend he has who works in the campus security office. She said the foreign students were really going nuts—nobody has a clue how all this is going to affect visas and stuff. Not that it matters much right now—getting a ticket out of the country's near impossible."

"The whole air-transport system's a mess," she said.

"Yeah. She also told us that the college had already decided to cancel Monday classes. I was on my way out of town to find you when I heard on the radio that they'd canceled everything through the end of the semester. So I kept driving, and here I am."

Mariette slowed to navigate around a mound of debris where a plane had crashed into the Potomac.

"Whoa," Randal muttered.

"Landscape looks a little different, doesn't it?" she asked.

"I avoided the cities on the way home," Randal replied, staring at the wreckage. "I haven't seen much except the truck crashes and that train derailment in southern Pennsylvania." He glanced at her. "I couldn't believe how many roads were closed."

"For good reason," Mariette said. "They're a mess."

"So did anything productive come out of Dad's hearings?" he prompted. "Any answers?"

"Several theories," she said, hoping he wasn't trying to engage her in another conversation about her mother's religious beliefs. She wasn't ready to talk about that.

"How come you had to testify?"

She hit her blinker when they reached the Roosevelt Bridge. "My boss was supposed to go, but he's in California with the president. They're due back tomorrow. Your father didn't want to wait that long."

Randal's expression was thoughtful. "That had to be a pain for you. I mean, putting up with Dad and the ego parade and stuff."

"I needed to be at the office. The timing could have been better."

"Is there ever a good time to deal with Dad?" he said cynically.

"I don't mind facing your father, Randal," she said. "I have nothing to be embarrassed about."

"Unlike him." His tone had turned bitter.

She laid her hand on his leg. "Let's change the subject, okay?"

Randal fell silent for several seconds, then made a disgusted noise in the back of his throat. "How do you stand it, Mom?"

"Stand what?"

"Living right here where he is. He's on the news all the time. It's like, every time I turn on the television he's blabbing about something. Doesn't he drive you crazy?"

"He used to," she told him, "but I decided I didn't want to give your father that much control over my life anymore. For the most part, I ignore him."

"It's kind of hard to do that when he's running for president. He's everywhere all of a sudden."

"This is an election year."

"I know, but it's only midterm. What's it going to be like when we hit primary season?"

"Worse," she said.

"You don't think he'll win, do you?"

"I don't know."

"I don't think I could take that. I'd have to defect or something." He grinned. "Can Americans defect?"

"I don't know," she said. "If you do, though, would you go some place I'd like to visit? I hear Lichtenstein is good. Nice climate, fine schools—"

"I'm serious, Mom. He disgusts me."

She shot him a concerned look. "Randal—"

"I know," he interrupted, having heard her lecture on the topic many times. "It doesn't do me any good to stay mad at him. That's what you keep saying."

"You're the only one who gets hurt. You have to keep feeding it if you want to stay angry."

"Actually, I'm not finding that to be true," Randal countered. "Dad does plenty of stuff to keep me thinking he's a two-faced jerk. I don't have to work hard at it at all."

"It's time to let it go, honey."

"But what he did . . ."

"I'm not going to lie and tell you it didn't hurt me. It was terrible and humiliating. For a while, I was devastated, but I won't let it *keep* hurting me. You ought to try it, too."

"Yeah, I guess," he said, looking away.

She merged into the light traffic on the bridge before she looked at him again. "All I ask is that you find five minutes today to call your father and let him know you're all right. Deal?"

Randal laughed. "Mom, since when has anyone been able to reach Dad on the phone in five minutes?"

"Point taken. Okay, you can leave a message with Helen—"

Randal groaned. "Helen?" He held up his hands as though warding off an attack. "That's like a fate worse than death."

"What have you got against Helen?"

"Haven't you noticed the way she thinks Dad walks on water?" His eyes twinkled in the late-morning sunlight. "You think I should tell her about that thing with his—?"

"*No!*" Mariette said.

"Well, you know, there's the way his—"

"Stop it, Randal." She suspected Helen knew just about everything there was to know about Max Arnold, but she wasn't going to say that to Randal. He was already angry enough at his father.

He shrugged. "Suit yourself. I'd pretty much guarantee, though, that we wouldn't have to watch him run a presidential race if I started talking. Americans are not ready to vote for a man who's got a—"

"Randal, that's enough," she said. "He *is* your father."

He leaned back in his seat. "You're a good person, Mom. I don't know very many people who could keep from slamming the guy after what he did to you."

She thought that over. Her conversation with Marcus Dumont came to mind again. Good person or not, it didn't matter to God if Marcus was right. "I've tried to be a good person . . . a decent person," she told Randal as she turned into the parking garage. "And I've tried to teach you to be one as well."

Randal shifted in his seat. "Um, Mom? About that . . . about what I was telling you about Gram and what she used to say about . . . you know . . . the Rapture and the end of the world?"

"I told you at the house, honey—I don't have any more answers than you do." Mariette pulled into her parking space and switched off the ignition. "I'm happy to talk to you about it, though. You know you can always talk to me."

"Yeah." He reached for his backpack. "The thing is, when it happened, I kept remembering all that stuff Gram used to tell me."

Though she and Randal had rarely spoken of her mother or his memories of her, she knew how close they'd been. Randal had retreated into a deep grief after Mariette's mother died. She'd worried, but she knew her son would talk to her if he thought she could help him. He wasn't alone in grieving. She'd missed her mother terribly, especially these past few days. There was something, she had learned, inherent in herself, that at times of great crisis, she desperately wished she could turn to her mother for comfort. Perhaps it was because nothing had cured childhood woes and hurts better than her mother's empathy and love. She wished life's problems all had so simple a solution.

Randal found what he was looking for in his backpack. "This was Gram's." He produced a battered leather-bound Bible that

Mariette recognized. "I . . . um . . . took it after the funeral. Nobody else seemed to want it."

Mariette vividly remembered what had happened after her mother's death. An only child, she'd had the responsibility of settling the large estate. Cousins, nieces, nephews, and a host of distant relatives had come out of the woodwork. What Mariette—and apparently no one else—had known was that she and Estelle had made an agreement that the land and the house of the large, fertile farm would go to Tom and Alyssa Madison—the young couple whom Mariette had hired several years before to manage the farm. Though Estelle left Mariette and Randal a sizeable financial settlement, the farm was a multimillion-dollar estate. Mariette had never regretted the decision to give it to Tom and Alyssa.

Her mother had suffered two strokes during the last five years of her life, and as her health had waned, the young couple had made her a part of their family. When Mariette finally had to place Estelle in a nursing home, Estelle had begged her not to move her from Iowa. She wanted to be near her friends, near familiar surroundings. Estelle had insisted that she couldn't leave her church or her community. Mariette had pleaded with her to move to Washington, where she could see her often, but Estelle would have none of it. Though she'd reached the point where she could no longer care for herself physically, she maintained her mental acuity to the end.

What had made the transition bearable for Mariette was Alyssa Madison's devotion to Estelle. She'd visited her regularly, sent Mariette reports about her health, had made every effort to ensure Estelle's comfort. When Estelle's health took a serious downturn, Alyssa had cried with Mariette as they'd spent long hours by her bedside. Alyssa, Mariette remembered, would read long passages from the Bible to Estelle and sometimes sing hymns while holding her hand.

That had seemed to calm Estelle's easily agitated nerves in the days before her death. Though Estelle and Mariette had discussed the issue of the farm long before that time, Mariette had finally found closure on the matter after a conversation with Tom outside her mother's hospital room. He'd explained that Alyssa's parents were foreign missionaries, and as a child she'd often been sent to live with distant relatives in the States. She was a born nurturer and had a way of making people part of her family.

At her mother's funeral, Alyssa, looking pale but composed, had stood next to Mariette and offered both strength and comfort.

The firestorm hadn't hit until after the funeral, when word began to circulate among the family that Tom and Alyssa were to inherit the farm. Tom had tried hard to refuse, but Mariette had insisted that both she and Estelle had wanted it that way.

Randal, who had been fifteen at the time, had wandered through the house looking at the things he remembered from childhood, while his distant cousins and relatives bickered over who should get the family china. Evidently, he'd picked up his grandmother's Bible.

Mariette looked at the tattered cover with a feeling of nostalgia and grief. "I had no idea you had that," she told him now.

"Yeah, well, I just picked it up. I didn't think to ask you—"

"It's okay. I'm sure Gram would have been delighted for you to have it."

"I haven't read it or anything, it's just . . . well . . . I remember her reading it to me, you know, as a kid. I remember the way her hands looked holding it." He gave Mariette a slight smile. "I remember thinking the skin on her hands looked just as grainy as the cover on the Bible."

"Too true." Mariette laughed softly. Her mother had been a good farmwife, had worked hard all her life, and though the mechanization of the farm had made it profitable long after her husband's death, Estelle had maintained many of her old habits. Many mornings she was up before sunrise feeding chickens and milking the dairy cow she kept in the small barn by the house.

Randal turned the Bible over in his hands. "I just remember that everyone was fighting that day. You were totally stressed. Tom and Alyssa were there, and everyone was bickering about Gram's stuff. I don't think Gram would have really cared who had her stuff, you know. She wasn't like that."

"I know. She wanted the farm to go to Tom and Alyssa because they'd made it possible for her to live there as long as she did."

"That was the right thing to do," Randal agreed. "I know it was hard for you, though. The whole family was carping on you to get a piece of the pie."

"Not that hard." She smiled. "I never really liked most of those people anyway."

He laughed. "Yeah, they were ghouls, all right. But you were under a lot of pressure."

"Sure," she admitted. "But remember what Gram used to say? 'Women are like tea bags; you never know how strong they are until you put 'em in hot water.'"

"She was sharp like that, you know. She was always saying something kind of pithy. She always could make me laugh. But I don't think everybody got her sense of humor."

"Your father certainly didn't," Mariette conceded. She glanced at the Bible. "So you brought that all this way with you from Penn State."

"Um, yeah." He looked uncomfortable again. "Mom, did you ever hear Gram talk about something like this happening? I mean, the Rapture?"

"Yes. I remember," Mariette said. "Honey, anyone who knew your grandmother heard her talk about the Rapture. She was a very devout woman."

"Did you ever believe it?"

"No," Mariette said, "but I've thought about it in the last few days."

"Do you think she could have been right?"

She released a long breath. "Maybe. I don't know. I suppose nothing is beyond the realm of possibility right now."

Randal seemed to consider that. "So if this was really God, I mean, if He just sort of wiped out all His followers from the earth, then what's going to happen to the rest of us?"

Her baby, she noted with a mother's ears and intuition, sounded scared. He was trying hard not to be, but he sounded confused and frightened. Mariette resisted the urge to reach across the console and hug him close. He'd pull away, she knew. At home, he was willing to let her embrace him, but public displays of maternal affection were taboo in his twenty-something world. "I don't know," she confessed. "I'm looking for answers, just like you."

"I think she might have been right, Mom."

Mariette's heart went momentarily still. "You do?"

"Yes." He clutched the Bible in both hands. "I hadn't even looked at this until the other night, but I've been kind of checking it out some since. You know, when I had a moment. It's kind of confusing, but I think I'm going to read this for a while and see if I can figure it out."

"That sounds like a good idea," she assured him, thinking again of Marcus Dumont. If Randal had questions, she wondered if she should refer him to the minister. Marcus would be better equipped to answer them than she would, but then Marcus also seemed to have the same agenda as every preacher she'd ever met. He wanted converts. Although, she admitted, he certainly had a more compelling argument to get them than most.

Shaking her head, she pulled the keys from the ignition and dropped them into her jacket pocket. "I'm going to be up to my eyeballs in work today, so you can start right now. In fact, there's a research library on the second floor just down the hall from my office." She covered his hand where it still clutched the Bible. "Take all the time you need."

13

Monday morning Brad walked into his office with a sense of determination and purpose he hadn't felt since coming to Washington. He stopped at Emma Pettit's desk and placed a hand on her shoulder.

He hadn't talked to her since he'd returned from California and that made him feel guilty. Emma was one of the few close friends he had in Washington, and Brad hadn't even bothered to find out if she'd lost anyone close to her besides his own family. Maybe she hadn't. She had a sister somewhere in the Midwest, he knew, but Emma had never married and had no kids. Brad and Christine had filled that role in Emma's life for as long as he'd known her.

"How are you doing, Emma? Have you heard from your sister?"

Emma nodded. "Yes. Everyone's all right, thank goodness."

He wished he could tell her he was glad they were still here, but given what he was learning from the Bible and from Marcus, he knew an uncertain future faced them all. It seemed that the missing people were the lucky ones. "I'm glad you're doing okay. I should have asked before."

She glanced at him in surprise, as if the idea of his caring enough about her to inquire after her personal life seemed alien. "You were a little preoccupied. How . . . how were things at home?"

He closed his eyes for a moment, this time in a prayer of

thanksgiving that God had revealed so much to him in the past twenty-four hours. Knowing his wife and children were safe and happy and well and in the presence of the Lord took some of the edge off his grief. As much as he missed them, as much as he longed to hold them again, he had the comfort of knowing he would see them again in eternity. "As I expected." He opened his eyes again. Emma's eyes were moist. He gave her shoulder an encouraging squeeze. "They're in a better place, Emma."

She reached for a tissue. "I keep telling myself that. I keep trying to believe it. It's just so hard."

"I know, but it's true. They're with the Lord."

Her eyes widened slightly. "Mr. Benton—"

Brad shook his head. "I'm sure of it. Absolutely sure. And one day I'll see them again. That gives me hope."

She dabbed her eyes. "I don't know how you do it. If I'd been through what you had these past few days, I don't think I could see any hope in sight. I just don't have your faith, I guess."

Sadly, Brad realized that he wished she did. A feeling of urgency he'd never had before now came over him when he thought of all the people lost and searching for the Lord. Emma was another person in his life he'd failed. If he'd been a Christian and not a fraud, perhaps he could have reached her with the truth of the gospel. What was it Marcus had said this morning? Something about 144,000 witnesses God would raise up to preach the gospel in the period after the Rapture. Brad made a mental note to call him this afternoon and ask for clarification. He wanted to drop into the chair by Emma's desk and immediately tell her what he now knew to be true, but something—Marcus called it discernment—told him this was not the time or place. He'd have to pray for the opportunity to witness to Emma, the teachable moment, and wait on God's timing.

Instead of witnessing, he collected a stack of messages from Emma. "Anything pressing here?" he asked as he flipped through the papers.

"Mostly the usual," she said. "Except for that one from Liza Cannley. She's called three times since yesterday."

Brad frowned. "I wonder why she didn't use my cell phone."

"She said she couldn't get through. I guess the cell networks are still sporadic."

"Must be."

"I know I had a hard time reaching my sister and her family. In the rural areas of the country, communications are still awful. I feel like we've been spared here in D.C. Things are getting back to normal."

No, Brad thought sadly, that couldn't be further from the truth. He recalled Marcus's sermon yesterday, which had been from the book of Revelation. He'd made a commitment to his nearly packed house of confused, frightened, and hurting congregants that every sermon he preached from now until his death would be on the saving grace of Christ, the hope for believers, and the prophecies of the end times. Nothing else seemed relevant.

Marcus had preached for an hour, beginning his sermon with a confession and apology to his congregation for his own lack of faith in the past. The stunned crowd had listened with rapt attention as Marcus told of his conversion the night of the Rapture, how God had literally brought him prostrate with a broken spirit and a repentant heart. At the end of his message, he'd allowed time for people who had similar testimonies to share them.

Though he'd promised Marcus he would speak, Brad had sat, almost unmoving, for the next two hours while person after person walked down the aisle and told their story. After years of pretending, years of fooling even family and friends, they'd finally realized that they'd turned their back on God.

Moved to tears by one woman's testimony of losing her four children, Brad had found himself unable to stay in his pew any longer. He—who had spoken with kings and presidents, who had testified before the United States Senate, who had given graduation addresses at Ivy League universities—stood before that congregation in that hot, crowded sanctuary, not as the White House chief of staff but as another sinner washed clean by the cleansing blood of Jesus Christ.

He'd never been more honored in his life.

As he left Emma to her work, he sent up a prayer that God would allow him to reach her before it was too.late. He couldn't bear the thought of failing her now.

Before he reached his office, Emma took a deep breath and picked up the calendar. "Are you ready to go over this? Or do you want to call that reporter first?"

"Let's do the calendar. I'll call Liza later." He slipped the phone messages into his suit pocket. "Come with me."

Ten minutes later, Emma was settled in the chair across from his desk. Brad had poured them each a cup of coffee, just as he usually did on Monday mornings, from the pot she'd made when she'd arrived at the office—no doubt, he thought, well before seven o'clock. Emma knew he would nag her if she stayed too late, so she had begun coming in earlier and earlier, thinking he didn't know.

He knew. He just hadn't figured out how to broach the subject yet.

Brad sat in his large leather chair. It welcomed him like an old friend. The chair had been the one piece of furniture he'd replaced when he arrived at the White House. He'd been unwilling to use his predecessor's chair after the details of the sex scandal that had driven him from his position were made public. Only Emma had found Brad's demand reasonable, and she'd fought hard to have his request fulfilled before his first day at the office.

It all felt so normal. But Brad knew that nothing would ever be normal again. But that didn't mean that normal things shouldn't be done. "Okay," he said. "What have we got?"

Emma perched her notebook on her knees. "The president's back in D.C., of course, so we're on the usual Monday schedule when he's in residence."

"No noise in the West Wing until after ten o'clock?" It was an insider's joke—Gerald Fitzhugh was not a morning person.

She gave him a chiding look. "Cabinet meeting at eleven. Press briefing, if necessary, at one."

"Got it. What else?"

"Another one of those messages in your suit pocket is from Bernie Musselman. He got your message about the supply crisis in the urban areas and the media interest. He says you can tell anyone who's interested that FEMA's got a few airlifts going into some rural areas starting this morning, but the urban areas are still a problem. Most of the airports are closed, and the railways aren't restored yet, either."

"I know. The president had to fly into Richmond," Brad told her. "Reagan National is still shut down."

"So, according to Musselman, Mariette Arnold . . ." Emma paused and looked up. "Do you know who she is?"

Brad nodded. "Musselman's deputy and the brains of the operation. I think she's Max Arnold's ex-wife."

"That's the one." Emma looked at the notebook again. "Anyway, she's organized convoys of supply barges. She's personally traveling with the one on the East Coast, and regional directors are overseeing the Gulf states and the West Coast. She plans to use major waterways, including the harbors, to distribute food and necessities to the larger urban areas."

"Good." Brad jotted a note on his pad. "Great idea. It'll do the job and play well with the press, not to mention being efficient, cost-effective, and creative. Remind me to call Mariette and assure her she can have whatever resources she needs from the White House."

"Will do. The only other major things on the calendar for today are Senator Arnold's hearing on the Hill and Nicolae Carpathia's speech at the UN this afternoon."

Brad steepled his hands beneath his chin. "Is that today? Max Arnold brought it up at the hearings on Saturday. That Carpathia guy's attracting a lot of attention lately. I wonder—" He broke off when his intercom buzzed. "Yes?" he asked, punching the button.

"Good, you're in." It was Forrest Tetherton. "Are you watching CNN?"

"I try not to do that before ten," Brad said. "White House noise protocols, you know."

Forrest didn't get the joke. "Well, turn it on. Carpathia's holding a press conference. You won't believe this guy." The intercom clicked when Forrest hung up.

Raising his eyebrows, Brad found the remote control on his desk and hit the button. He and Emma turned to watch the new Romanian president's first major media appearance since taking office under such unusual circumstances.

The man was younger than Brad had thought he'd be. Tall, with golden blond hair, he was attractive and very dignified. He wore a perfectly tailored suit. Brad wondered cynically how he'd procured it in economically ravaged Bucharest.

"He's impressive," Emma said with a glint in her eye that amused Brad. Carpathia clearly had a little something extra that the women liked. "Isn't he?"

But Brad didn't respond. As he watched the Romanian talk, something about the man bothered him. He couldn't put his finger on it, but there was something too polished, too perfect, just plain too good to be true, that nagged at him. Then he finally understood what was worrying him. He remembered Marcus's insights about Carpathia's similarities to the Antichrist prophesied in the Bible. Brad listened with renewed interest as the speech continued.

Carpathia made a great show of thanking his supporters, especially international financier Jonathan Stonagal and his investment in Romania. Chaim Rosenzweig stood to Carpathia's left in the outer periphery of the camera. He'd obviously made the trip from Washington in order to attend Carpathia's speech to the UN.

Carpathia then thanked the UN General Assembly for giving him the opportunity to speak later that day, and in a show of brilliant political one-upmanship—or unprecedented humility and grace—he proceeded to issue the same statement in eight more languages: Arabic, Chinese, French, German, Hungarian, Romanian, Russian, and Spanish.

Though his French was a little rusty, Brad spoke excellent Spanish, had a working knowledge of German he'd gleaned from his grandparents, and had learned Chinese and Russian in college.

Carpathia's accent and command of those languages was flawless. It was difficult to tell he wasn't a native speaker.

Drumming his fingers on the desk, Brad shot a quick glance at Emma. She was watching the press conference with rapt attention, despite the fact that the words were in a foreign language, as if she found Carpathia's mere presence enough to hold her attention.

As the Romanian president switched effortlessly between languages, Brad began to notice a pattern. The CNN reporter would break momentarily into the broadcast to announce the language Carpathia was using. When Carpathia began his address in Hungarian, Brad realized that the Romanian was using the six official languages of the United Nations and the three languages of Romania to communicate his message.

A brilliant piece of politics, Brad thought.

When the press conference ended, even the media seemed to sit in stunned silence as Carpathia exited the room. For probably the first time in history, none of the reporters could find the energy to ask a question.

Brad switched off the television with a feeling of unease.

Emma turned to him, her eyes alight with enthusiasm. "Well, that was certainly interesting."

He looked at her. "Oh?"

"For the first time in more years than I care to remember, there seems to be something going on at the UN besides bickering and nationalistic power brokering. It's no secret that the UN has been mostly useless lately."

Brad couldn't fault her for that opinion. Except for the obligatory statements the U.S. would present to the Security Council and the General Assembly on the advent of a major policy initiative, President Fitzhugh and his people largely ignored the international organization. Theirs wasn't the first administration to do this. Years had passed where Congress had either refused to pay or deliberately delayed paying America's dues to the UN until the organization had yielded on key points. That had created resistance and resentment among the permanent members of the Security Council and a general cooling of U.S. relations with the UN. Matters had gotten worse several years ago during America's self-declared war on terror and had escalated to a deep freeze during the presidential campaign when Fitzhugh had stumped for American withdrawal from the organization. As yet, he'd been unable to get the policy off the ground in Congress, but it wasn't for lack of trying.

Emma said, "I understand Mr. Carpathia has some very unusual ideas about global peace."

"Unusual isn't the half of it, if the White House's preliminary reports can be trusted," Brad said. Though he'd not yet made his agenda public, Carpathia had already floated the idea of voluntary nuclear disarmament, with the UN as the international watchdog for the world's antiproliferation treaty. He'd suggested relocating the UN to a more central location, specifically to Babylon, the ancient capital of the Persian Empire. The city, which was just fifty-six miles south of Baghdad, had been under renovation for years. Carpathia liked it, he claimed, for its central location and what he called its "ancient-future" appeal. Most world leaders had scoffed at his idea, saying that he had as much chance of relocating the UN to Iraq as he had of starting a blizzard in Saudi Arabia.

"Carpathia's radical," Brad said. "I'll give him that."

"These are radical times," Emma said. "I'm not so sure the idea of voluntary disarmament is as far-fetched today as it was a week ago. Maybe the world's finally ready to listen."

Before he could respond, his intercom buzzed again. He hit the button. "Yes?"

It was Forrest Tetherton again. "The president wants us in the Oval. He says we've got to figure out a way to get Carpathia to Washington."

14

The Atlantic Ocean
Off the Coast of New York
Local Time 11:04 A.M.

Mariette glanced over her shoulder to where Randal sat, deep in study, on the bridge of the tugboat. The skipper had assured her they were right on schedule to reach New York Harbor shortly after noon. Their transfers of goods at Baltimore Harbor and at the mouth of the Delaware River had been successful. With food supplies now headed for Philadelphia and New Jersey, the mission had been rapid and efficient.

From New York, she'd arranged a transfer of several sea containers up the Hudson to the freight rail depot, where they'd be forwarded to the Ohio River. Her reports indicated that the rail line there remained open. She'd then send the convoy from New York to Boston Harbor. From Boston, the convoy would go on to Connecticut, Rhode Island, and Maine, where it would round the upper tip of the U.S. and enter the St. Lawrence Seaway to the Great Lakes for distribution throughout upstate New York, Michigan, Minnesota, Wisconsin, and river distribution through the eastern U.S. She had a similar operation using the coastal waterways of California to reach the West Coast and the western cities of the United States.

David Liu had done a phenomenal job coordinating the logistics of the massive operation, and Mariette had already put in a call to the White House to ensure his commendation for the relief effort.

Now she crossed the bridge to sit next to her son. "Finding anything?"

He raised his bright, intelligent eyes to hers. "I think so. Mom, we really have to talk about this."

It was hardly the first time she'd heard him make that plea today. There was an urgency about her son she'd never seen before. Twice he'd tried to push her into a conversation about her religious convictions. Mariette had managed to evade him with protests of the demands on her time. She sensed he wouldn't be put off much longer.

"I know," she said. She wasn't quite ready for that discussion. She still wasn't sure what she believed. And she didn't want to be distracted while she tried to explain that to her son. "Can it wait until we're home tonight?" They were taking a military aircraft flight from New York to Andrews Air Force Base as soon as the transfer of goods was complete.

Randal hesitated, then nodded. "Sure. Tonight will be fine." He grinned. "I'll buy you dinner. I've still got tip money."

Mariette laughed and patted him on the shoulder. "That'll be wonderful."

The phone on the bridge rang, and the barge skipper picked it up. "Yes?"

Mariette watched him closely. The man frowned as he listened. "What do you mean blocked?" He nodded, then swore. "Well, clear it then. This is federal business." The voice on the other end grew louder. The skipper shook his head. "Look, I don't care if it's the king of England. We're coming in. Twenty minutes." He slammed down the phone.

Mariette met the man's gaze across the bridge. "Problems?"

"Some bigwig is in town at the United Nations. His presence is stirring up a lot of traffic in the city and on the waterfront. There are all kinds of security closures on the surface streets and the mass transit systems. People who couldn't get into the city by subway used the ferries and private watercraft, so water access is blocked." He shook his head. "Politicians . . . they think they're God. They've got no idea what's really important in this world. Don't worry. The Port Authority is taking care of it."

"I heard about this," Randal said. "It was all over the news. It's that guy from Romania. He's speaking at the General Assembly today."

"Great," Mariette muttered. "Nothing gets in the way of an emergency like a politician with an agenda."

"Well, the water is one place political hacks haven't got right-of-way." The skipper laughed. "Don't sweat it, Ms. Arnold. We've got precedence. There may be a lot of private yacht owners ticked off with the Port Authority by the end of the day, but that's not my problem." He leaned on the ship's air horn for emphasis as his ship cut through the waves. "We're on a schedule here."

★   ★   ★

Washington, D.C.
The White House
Local Time 11:05 A.M.

Brad strode into the cabinet meeting knowing he was the bearer of unhappy news. He saw Bernie Musselman and crossed the room to greet him. Bernie, he'd noted, was in his element, thrilled to be included in both the upper-level meetings and the president's U.S. tour. Generally, the FEMA director wasn't privy to these higher-level conferences, but the current situation had made for strange bedfellows.

"Bernie," Brad said, "I understand you've got quite an operation under way today."

Bernie gave him a blank look. "Operation?"

Brad resisted the urge to tell the director that he really should check with his staff on occasion. "The supply convoy," Brad clarified. "I believe Mariette Arnold is heading that up."

"Oh yes," Bernie said. "Mariette. She's outstanding."

"That's what I hear. Anyway, I got a message from her this morning. Something about putting David Liu, her assistant, in line for a commendation. I think he helped organize all the transportation logistics for the convoy. In record time, too."

The director beamed. "Well, you know, I've told them a number of times that they need to take initiative. Just because I can't always be on hand doesn't mean things should stop progressing."

Brad resisted the temptation to roll his eyes. "Well, just let Mariette know if you talk to her that I've already put in the request. Mr. Liu will be recognized for his efforts."

"Very good. Very good. I'll be sure to tell her."

Brad bit his lip and turned away before his expression gave his opinion of the man away. He was therefore the first to see Gerald Fitzhugh stride through the door flanked by Charley Swelder and Forrest Tetherton. The fun just never stopped at the White House.

"Ladies. Gentlemen." Fitz waved his greetings to the room's occupants. "I trust everyone's seen the news this morning."

The secretary of commerce nodded vigorously. "That Carpathia fellow is impressive. I'm headed up there tomorrow to speak at the currency conference. I hope I'll have the chance to hear him in person."

Fitzhugh dropped the stack of papers he was carrying on the table with an impressive thud. "This is all e-mail my secretary tells me has come in since Carpathia's press conference this morning. It seems every member of Congress and every voter left in America wants to know why we're not bringing this guy to Washington." He pinned Brad with a hard look. "So how are we going to answer that?"

Brad took his seat at the table. "Until this morning, meeting Carpathia wasn't high on your list of priorities."

Fitz dropped into his chair. "How was I supposed to know that the president of Romania was going to be an international media superstar?"

Brad shrugged. "I've contacted his people. They told me that this time, Carpathia's not available for a trip to Washington, not even to meet with the president."

The president swore. "What do you mean he's not available?"

"According to Mr. Carpathia, his country has limited resources and is already sacrificing too much for him to be in New York. Without the transportation advantages of an aircraft like *Air Force One*, traveling to Washington would be too time-consuming." Brad checked his notes. "Though he says he's grateful and humbled by the invitation, he regrets that he cannot make it at this time."

Charley Swelder frowned. "So what does he want? A first-class ticket? A ride on *Air Force One*?"

Brad shook his head. "I have the impression that he wants us to go to him."

The president's face turned red with fury. No one in the room could have missed the implications of that diplomatic slight. The president of the United States did *not* travel to visit leaders of minor countries. Fitz slammed his hand down on the table. "If the man can't figure out that he's got to have us on his side if he hopes to accomplish one blasted thing, then who needs him?"

The secretary of commerce coughed. "Mr. President, need I remind you that Carpathia is heading the people pushing for one global currency?"

"Which means squat without the backing of the U.S. dollar," Swelder shot back. "The whole thing will collapse if we don't buy into it."

"Still," the secretary responded, "I don't think we can simply ignore the man."

Forrest Tetherton nodded. "You may be right. We'll know more after Carpathia's speech this afternoon to the General Assembly."

"Fine," the president grumbled. He looked at Brad. "At least arrange a phone call. Find out where he's staying and get the room number. Maybe I'll call and shoot the breeze with him."

"Good idea. That way," Swelder added, "we can say we initiated contact."

★   ★   ★

New York City, New York
New York Harbor
Local Time 12:07 P.M.

"This is worse than it was after 9/11." Mariette looked out across the pier to midtown Manhattan. New York City was a disaster. She had expected wreckage and burned-out buildings, knowing that plane crashes, subway derailments, abandoned and crashed automobiles and buses, looting, power outages, and a host of other problems had left the city paralyzed after the disappearances. What she had not expected was the general hysteria surrounding the visit of the Romanian president. "You'd think Elvis was in town," she told Randal.

"Pretty close," he said as he followed her down the gangway. "The guy is really stirring folks up. Have you heard what he wants to do?"

Mariette accepted a clipboard full of paperwork from the Port Authority official who'd met their convoy. She looked it over as she absently responded to Randal. "I've been too busy to pay much attention. Something about one currency. Nuclear disarmament. I think he wants to relocate the UN to another country. That, at least, would be wildly popular in D.C."

"One of my professors has been talking about Carpathia a lot. He likes the guy for the next secretary-general of the UN."

"I wonder how the current secretary-general feels about that," Mariette said as she signed off on the stack of papers. "He likes his job. He doesn't seem to have plans to leave office, far as I can tell."

"He may not have much choice." Randal pointed to an LCD billboard that towered high above the city, where the World Trade Center had once stood. A larger-than-life picture of the Romanian president loomed over the city. The caption read "Bold New Leadership for Bold Times." A tiny logo in the lower-left corner indicated that the ad had been purchased by America's leading software giant.

"Impressive. I wonder what the computer geeks plan to get out of that." Mariette shook her head. "But right now we need to concentrate on our own affairs. They're going to separate the barges now. Our military escort should be here soon to take us to our MAC flight."

"Are we flying out of LaGuardia?" he probed.

"Who knows? We're flying out of whatever airport has an open runway. Could be LaGuardia, JFK, or maybe even Hoboken. I don't plan to be choosy. Let's go home."

★ ★ ★

Washington, D.C.
Local Time 3:08 P.M.

"Thanks for meeting me on such short notice," Marcus told Brad later that afternoon in front of the Lincoln Memorial. "I'm sorry I had to ask you to leave the office."

"No problem," Brad assured him. "You said you didn't want to talk on the phone."

"I think the topic might get you in trouble if anybody's listening," Marcus said. "It's Nicolae Carpathia. I've been watching the news from New York."

Brad wasn't surprised. If Carpathia's press conference that morning had made waves, then his speech before the General Assembly earlier this afternoon had unleashed a global flood. To say he'd taken the organization by storm was like saying a category-five hurricane was messy weather. After a glowing introduction by Chaim Rosenzweig, Carpathia had electrified the audience with an apparently memorized speech about the history and glories of the UN. He'd then proceeded to list, from memory and in alphabetical order, every nation represented in the assembly. By the time he'd reached the end of the list, delegates, representatives, and media from each respective nation had risen and cheered for their country. In an amazing display of unity, nation after nation, perhaps bound together by the collective trauma they'd suffered in the past several days, responded to Carpathia's impassioned speech with unforeseen fervor, patriotism, and global brotherhood.

Carpathia, showing an incredibly intimate knowledge of the UN, had gone on to talk broadly about all the former secretaries-general, the six principal organs of the assembly, and its eighteen agencies and directors.

By the time he was done, the general consensus among the White House staff had been that current UN Secretary-General Mwangati Ngumo should fear for his job. The General Assembly and the press had been so enraptured with Carpathia that it seemed it would be merely a matter of time before they demanded his installation as secretary-general.

Fitzhugh's mounting anger at Carpathia's continuing snub had ruled the day at the White House. Even now, Brad had his assistant on the phone trying to arrange a diplomatic call or meeting between Gerald Fitzhugh and the Romanian politician. It had been a long day—capped by the mysterious phone call from Marcus.

"I'm here now. So what did you want to discuss?" Brad looked closely at his new friend. In the late-afternoon light, Marcus looked weary and concerned. "What's worrying you about Carpathia?"

Marcus hesitated, then said, "Brad, I know this might sound a little crazy, but I really think . . ."

"What?" Brad prompted, relieved to discover he wasn't the only person in America who'd had a queasy feeling about Carpathia.

Marcus glanced over his shoulder, then met Brad's gaze again. "I really think Carpathia might be the Antichrist, Brad. I've studied the description of the white horseman again, and I think this is the guy."

Brad's heart began to race. After Marcus had planted the seed in his mind yesterday morning, Brad had found himself acutely attuned to Carpathia's language, personal charisma, and message of international peace. Though Marcus was right about the similarities to biblical prophecy, it seemed inconceivable that the long-predicted Antichrist would have such humble beginnings. "Marcus, he's the president of Romania."

"Romania *is* Eastern Europe," Marcus pointed out, "and I understand that the man was born in Italy. Carpathia's Roman by birth."

"It's a stretch."

"Maybe. But then there's the connection to Babylon. And he's pushing for one world currency. How coincidental is it that the world's religious leaders are meeting in New York right now while all this is happening? It's all there."

Brad considered that. Marcus's sermon on Sunday had included a description of the first four Seal Judgments—the four horsemen. The first of the four horsemen was the Antichrist, the one who would try to consolidate power in the world under his leadership. Though the Bible prophesied that the Antichrist would bring death and destruction, it also depicted him wearing a crown. Marcus had said it was symbolic of world leadership. The horseman also carried a bow, a symbol of war, but the bow had no arrow. Could that mean that the Antichrist would conquer through diplomacy and not through traditional warfare? And then there was all this media hoopla over an obscure Romanian diplomat rising out of no-where—it wasn't natural. Something unnatural *had* to be driving it.

Brad shuddered. "Okay, it fits. Back at my job, we've been tracking Carpathia since his rise to power. I'll never believe that the former Romanian president simply hands over control of the country to Carpathia as Carpathia claims. We don't have any conclusive evidence to prove that, but we've been suspicious from the start. It looks shady. But we can't get our usual sources to talk to us. The man has some pretty powerful backers."

"What is the White House position right now?" Marcus asked.

"The president is wary of the guy but for political reasons. Carpathia's UN speech today lit a fire under the world community. Fitzhugh doesn't like anyone who steals his spotlight."

Marcus stroked his chin. "I think you and I should find a time and place to talk about some strategy."

Brad raised an eyebrow. "Strategy?"

"I wasn't certain how long we'd have before all this started," Marcus said. "But the Bible is clear about the events of the Tribulation. It talks about the plagues and the famine, earthquakes, fires, all sorts of natural and human disasters. I don't know what the future holds for us, but I think we need to have a plan to face these things."

"But, Marcus, what can you and I possibly do if the die is already cast?"

"The Scripture says, 'Look, I am sending you out as sheep among wolves. Be as wary as snakes and harmless as doves.' I think our mission now is to reach the lost souls and help the faithful face whatever lies ahead."

Brad considered that for a moment. "I see. To show the world that there's still hope for the children of God. That it's not too late."

"Exactly."

"That makes sense," Brad agreed. "If Carpathia is really the Antichrist, then that means events are going to move fairly quickly, doesn't it?"

"It will depend on how fast his rise to power is, but based on what I saw today—"

"Our intelligence sources tell us to expect him to be installed as the new secretary-general of the UN by the end of the week," Brad confirmed.

"That fast, huh?" Marcus whistled softly. "Even I'm surprised."

"But I have to tell you this, Marcus," Brad said. "Being secretary-general of the UN is a far way off from being a world leader. Scholars and political groups harp about the UN a lot, but in reality, the organization doesn't really have that much power. The U.S. and most of the world leaders pretty much do what they want, regardless of what the UN says."

"But if Carpathia's plan to consolidate the world's nuclear weapons under the UN's authority succeeds—," Marcus said.

"Then everything changes." Brad finished the sentence. "I find it hard to believe that the members of the Security Council are going to go for that. Several of them are nuclear powers and won't want to give up that advantage. China, for example, is sure to veto. Not to mention France. France vetoes everything. I don't really see the Russians leaping at it either, not after what happened in Israel. Russia launched a nuclear attack on the Holy Land. It didn't work. In fact, it backfired on them horribly. But you can't tell me they'll want to give up the power to try it again."

"Maybe not." Marcus shook his head. "But I think the world is desperate enough right now to take desperate measures."

"That's certainly true."

"And with everything so tense, isn't there a general feeling that if something doesn't give soon, we're headed for another world war?"

"Sure, there are people who feel that way," Brad said. "All the superpowers are blaming the other superpowers for the disappearances. There are leaders in our country who are pushing for an immediate strike against Russia. And the Russians aren't any too happy with us."

"Either way, it would set off a global chain of events unlike any we've ever seen. Who could want that?"

"Nobody."

"Exactly." Marcus looked Brad straight in the eyes. "I don't think you and I can afford to wait and see what happens next. I think we need a plan."

Brad nodded. "Okay, I can meet you tonight. You pick the time and place."

"My home is in Georgetown." Marcus slipped him a business card with his home address and telephone number. "Why don't you meet me there at nine?"

Brad slid the card into the breast pocket of his shirt. "I'll be there."

Marcus glanced over his shoulder. "I don't have to tell you that this isn't going to be a popular point of view. For now, I'd like you to keep this just between us."

No more than I would, Brad thought. He'd lose his job for sure if anyone knew he was battening down in fear of the Antichrist. With the White House consumed now with news about Carpathia, Brad was certain that any speculation against the Romanian president would be met with one of two reactions: he'd either be ridiculed or fired. Swelder and Fitzhugh were smart enough to know that if they didn't capitalize on Carpathia's meteoric popularity, Max Arnold would. That was sufficient motivation to have the White House scrambling to make sure Fitzhugh was in Carpathia's good graces.

For the first time in recent memory, Brad didn't think it was out of the question for the president to offer the loan of *Air Force One* as a goodwill gesture if that would facilitate Carpathia's trip to Washington. Probably, Brad conceded, the offer wouldn't be made so readily if Fitzhugh hadn't learned on his trip to Seattle that the new *Air Force One* was nearing completion, but nevertheless, Brad couldn't imagine that the joint chiefs were very enthused about their commander's apparent willingness to loan the nation's top military aircraft to a foreign dignitary.

Indeed, there was no reason for anyone at the White House to know that he had his doubts about Carpathia. At least not yet. Brad looked at Marcus and nodded. "Consider it done."

15

Some days it felt like it didn't pay to get out of bed. Despite all she had accomplished with the barge convoy, the last two hours had left Mariette feeling beaten. She and Randal were in the back of the military aircraft, finally on their way home. Security at the landing strip had been extra tight given the Romanian president's widely publicized presence in New York. As if his sideshow hadn't been enough to snarl up the already beleaguered traffic, international financiers and the world banking community had already begun arriving in New York for the upcoming international currency conference.

Despite their military escort and inch-thick sheaf of authorization papers, Mariette and Randal had spent an hour and a half trying to negotiate through the security phases at the airport.

Finally, aboard the plane and in the air, Mariette leaned back in her seat with a heavy sigh of relief. The food and supply shortages were finally on their way to being over. There was still a significant amount of cleanup to be done, and the East Coast supply barges were on their way north. Though a problem of this magnitude would hardly be solved by today's shipments alone, they would buy her and her team enough time that they could perhaps take a couple of days to regroup and get their bearings.

But the country's problems weren't the only ones she faced.

The plane's rear wheels had barely left the ground when Randal reached for his backpack and produced his grandmother's Bible. "Okay, Mom, this is it. We've got to talk."

She knew she couldn't put it off any longer. "What's bothering you, Randal?"

He flipped open the worn leather Bible. "It's like I told you. When Gram died and I took this Bible, I didn't dive into it for a really long time. I just wanted it because it was a part of Gram, you know, not because I wanted to read it."

"I understand." Mariette had a large cameo necklace she'd never worn but that she cherished because Estelle had loved it so much.

"So while everything was happening the night of the disappearances, and people were sort of falling to pieces around me, it was like I felt Gram telling me to pick up her Bible and read it." He looked at her warily. "I don't want you to think I'm some kind of freak, Mom."

Her hands were trembling, so Mariette clasped them in her lap. "I don't."

He took a deep breath. "I didn't have a lot of time. I wanted to get in the car and get moving, or I had no idea how long it would take me to get home. I just read what I could where she'd marked some stuff."

That brought a bittersweet smile to Mariette's lips. "Your grandmother was a Bible marker. I imagine if you looked at her notes, there was plenty to absorb."

"Yeah, and, I mean, it's not like God spoke to me out of a gray cloud or something. It wasn't like that. It's just—" he swallowed—"I started reading, and that's when I came across this." Randal handed her a yellowed piece of paper, dog-eared and worn.

"What is it?"

"Something Gram wrote before she died, I think."

Mariette's hands trembled as she opened the paper. In her mother's elegant handwriting, which had remained careful and precise until the end of her life, were these words:

If you are reading this, it means that I have gone home to be with my beloved Lord. I hope you aren't grieving. I hope you aren't missing me. I hope you know that I am safe in the arms of my Savior. I leave you these thoughts for times when you may wonder how I am.

If you could see me now, you'd never believe
I'm in this beautiful place
You'd never want me to leave.
Where once I was weak,
Now I am strong;
Where once my feet stumbled,
I now dance along
On streets made of gold
singing this song.
I am free here at last
From sorrow and pain,
From the nights filled with suffering and sin's guilty stain.
I have nothing to dread, nothing to fear
For I'm living with Jesus;
He's holding me near.
In the summers of my youth, I sang of His promises.
In the winters of my life, He proved them to me.
If only you could see me now,
You'd know it was true,
And why I prayed every day of your life that you
Would surrender to grace and give your life to Him.
For this is my story, and this is my song,
Praising my Savior, all the day long.

Mariette's eyes misted. "It sounds like Gram."

Randal placed his hand on hers. "It's okay, Mom." His voice dropped to a whisper. "I cried too the first time I read it." His smile was a little sheepish. "And then all I had to do was picture Gram dancing and singing, and I just started laughing because I knew that for the first time in her life, she could actually carry a tune."

That made Mariette laugh. Her mother had loved to sing. She couldn't sing on key, but she had loved to try. She had belted out every hymn and every chorus with a fervent heart and a tone-deaf ear. The image of her mother singing in a heavenly choir was both sweet and heartrending. "I miss her so much."

"I know. Me, too." Randal scooted as close to her as his seat belt would allow. "But here's the thing: I've been reading a lot while I was waiting on you."

She'd noticed that. Randal had had his nose buried in that Bible almost from the moment he'd ridden to the FEMA office with her. He'd stopped to eat or to answer questions or to help her with something, but at every available moment, he'd been back in a corner, reading, studying, absorbing.

"I know how we can see her again." Randal had begun to warm to the topic. A flush of excitement stained his cheeks. "I finally know what Gram was always talking about when she said you have to give your life to Jesus."

Surprised, Mariette folded the letter and slipped it back between the pages of the Bible. "Honey—"

"No, Mom. I'm serious. I *know*." He flipped open the book to a passage he'd marked. "This was one of the first things I read the other night when I was so scared at what was happening. I read it just before I got in the car to come home." He found the verse he wanted with his finger. "Gram had marked it and written my name in the margin." He edged the book toward her. "See?"

Mariette saw the underlined passage with her son's name next to it. Randal read it to her, following the text with his finger.

> "But, beloved, be not ignorant of this one thing, that one day is with the Lord as a thousand years, and a thousand years as one day. The Lord is not slack concerning His promise, as some men count slackness; but is longsuffering to us-ward, not willing that any should perish, but that all should

come to repentance. But the day of the Lord will come as a
thief in the night; in the which the heavens shall pass away
with a great noise, and the elements shall melt with fervent
heat, the earth also and the works that are therein shall be
burned up."

Randal flipped the book shut. "Don't you see, Mom? That's exactly what happened. We have lived through the Day of the Lord, or
the beginning of it."

She shook her head. How many times had she had this same argument with her mother? How was she supposed to believe that the
God her mother claimed was good and kind and loving would simply wipe out life on this planet? "So there's no hope for any of us?
I'm sorry, Randal. I—"

"No. I don't believe that. I don't believe there's no hope."

"But you just said—"

"I've read more. Other passages Gram marked. I believe that
Jesus is still willing to receive us if we're willing to receive Him." He
gave her an earnest look. "I did it, Mom. I received Jesus just like
Gram always said I could."

"Are you trying to tell me—?"

"That I've given my life to Christ?" His eyes took on a determined expression. "Yes. It felt good. It felt good to say that. I hadn't
told anyone but you, not yet anyway."

"Randal—"

"I'm a Christian." His voice held a firm note of authority that
seemed incongruous to her. He was so young, yet he sounded so
wise. "I wouldn't count myself half a man if I didn't tell you that I
honestly believe the only hope for your soul is for you to accept
Jesus as well." He paused. "I don't know what's going to happen
next. I have no idea what the future holds, but I know that I don't
want to face the next few days or months or whatever time we have
left without Christ in my life. And I don't want to be in heaven without you, Mom."

Mariette's heart twisted as she looked into the eyes of this wise, earnest young man she loved so much. Had there ever been a time, she wondered, when the world had been so black-and-white to her? Had she missed the window of opportunity when she could fall easily into grace and find trusting Jesus such a logical and simple step? "Randal—"

"You don't have to say anything," he told her. "If you're not ready or you don't want to, it's okay, but I'm not going to tell you that I won't try and change your mind. I'm going to keep badgering you because I have to."

She hesitated, remembering her conversation with Marcus Dumont. Hadn't his words rung true to her? She still remembered times in her childhood when God had seemed so worthy of her trust. Had He really been the one to turn His back on her—or had she drifted slowly away from Him, too proud and determined to let anyone rule her heart? "I'm glad for you. I know it's a big step."

"You can take it, too, Mom," he urged.

"I think it's too late for me."

"No. No, it isn't. Don't you remember what Gram always said? 'There's always room for one more sinner at God's table.'" His expression turned pleading. "Don't you remember in the car when we talked about Dad, and you told me that you'd discovered that you had to put the past behind you?"

"Yes."

"That's what Jesus does for you," he insisted. "He puts your past behind you. You get to start fresh. The Bible calls it being born again. New life. Gram used to sing that song about being washed in the blood. I never got it before. I couldn't understand how you could be washed clean by blood, but now I see it so clearly. Jesus paid the price for my sin with His blood. He died on the cross so that I can live."

Suddenly, it made sense. Every lesson she'd learned from her mother, every Sunday school teacher's fervent explanation of the love of God had somehow gotten lost amid the barrage of sermons and lectures about God's judgment and wrath. Mariette had spent so long fearing God's judgment that she'd failed to see the truth Randal now showed her. What was it Marcus had said that night on the phone? *"God's justice demanded his soul, but God's mercy took his place."*

Wasn't it the same for her? Her heart raced as she realized this was the truth she'd been hiding from all these years. This was the same still, small voice that had whispered in her heart as a child. Then, she'd ignored it, turned her back on it, but now, with her only child pleading with her to heed it, Mariette found she no longer wanted to resist.

Tears began to flow down her cheeks as she accepted the truth of what Randal was saying. God had loved her. Even when her mother had died and her husband had betrayed her, God had loved her. He loved her still, and she could no longer deny Him His rightful place in her life.

"Mom?" Randal prompted.

"You're right," she said softly.

"Right about what?" His voice held a note of hope.

"About all of it. About what Gram taught you. She taught me the same lessons," she said. "I just waited a little longer than you to accept them."

Randal lifted a hand to gently wipe her tears. "I love you so much. You have been the strongest and best influence in my life for as long as I can remember. I couldn't stand the thought of not sharing this with you."

"I'm glad you did." Weary, Mariette dropped her head back against the hard seat. "I've been fighting God for too long. I can see that now."

"Then let Jesus have control," he urged. "You can't imagine what it's like to realize you don't have to worry about stuff anymore. He's going to take care of it."

"You know, this is going to sound strange," she told him. "You'd think after growing up with your grandmother I'd know this, but I have to admit, I'm not exactly sure how a person turns their life over to Christ."

"Me, either," Randal confessed. "I just sort of knew in my heart it was true. I think God took it from there."

"When I was a kid, Mom would send me to vacation Bible school. The preacher would always come in on the last day and talk to us about salvation. I never understood exactly what he meant, but every year, when he'd ask us to walk down the aisle if we wanted Jesus in our hearts, I would. All my friends did, and I figured I should, too. It sounded good—having Jesus in my heart. I just never really understood how that was supposed to happen."

Randal covered her hand with his. "I don't think it matters. I just think that once we acknowledge our need for God and ask Him to forgive us, He will. I read the story of Nicodemus today. That's where Jesus uses the phrase *born again*. I've never been really comfortable with that term. It always seemed kind of kooky. Something the right-wingers used a lot."

"I think the concept got distorted a little in the last two thousand years."

"Definitely. But I get it now. I feel fresh, new, and for the first time in my life, I have a purpose."

Mariette turned her hand so she could lace her fingers through his. "Have I told you how proud I am of you?"

"Will you pray with me, Mom?" he suddenly asked.

Her throat felt tight so Mariette merely nodded.

Randal bowed his head. "God, I'm not exactly sure how to do this, but I know what I want, and I know that You're real and alive and waiting for me. Please, God, You showed me how to become one of Your children. I know it was You talking to me on the way home and these last few hours when I've been reading Your Word. Please show my mom the same thing."

They sat in silence while Mariette fought a bout of tears. Finally, she found the words. "I used to pray over this boy when he was a baby, God. I never imagined that one day he would pray over me. Thank You for my mother, for her wisdom and the lessons she taught us. I know she's in heaven with You. Please let her know how grateful I am for her prayers and her instruction. And thank You for loving me. Show me Your ways and give me Your wisdom."

"Amen," Randal said.

"Amen," Mariette repeated.

Randal hugged her fiercely, harder than he had in years.

That warmed her. "When we get home, there's someone I'd like us to talk to."

His gaze turned wary. "It better not be Dad. I've been praying about that. I really have. I know I have to talk to him and forgive him, but I don't think I'm ready to—"

"Take it easy, Randal," she said. "It's not your father. Although I think the day is coming when we'll have to sit down with him. Don't you want him to know what's going on in your life?"

"Yes," Randal admitted. "But this is all so new to me. I'm afraid he'll ask a bunch of questions I can't answer." He hesitated. "I'm afraid he'll make me feel foolish. And that he'll deride me for falling for this. I don't want to talk to him until I really know what I'm saying."

"I understand. We'll cross that bridge when we get there. The man I want us to see is a minister."

"A minister?" Randal's eyes narrowed. "Then why is he still here?"

"He told me that he preached the truth for years but never accepted it. I talked to him about the relief effort. His ministry has always pitched in during hard times. That's how I know him, and that's how I heard his story after the Rapture."

"And what about now?"

"Now he claims that he's given his life to Christ. When I spoke with him the other night, he urged me to do the same. He's the one who got me thinking about all this, before I even talked to you. I suppose God sent him to prepare my heart for what you had to say tonight," she said.

"I'd like to talk to him," Randal said. "I was afraid that I'd be all alone in this."

"His name is Marcus Dumont."

"That political activist guy?"

"That's the one. The last time I talked to him was the day I testified at your father's hearings."

"Do you think he knows a lot about what's going on? I've been trying to read the Bible, but the words can be really confusing. I don't understand a lot of it."

"I'm sure Marcus can shed some light on this for both of us."

"Then I'd like to meet him." He glanced at his watch. "Do you think he could see us tonight if we don't get in too late?"

"I have his number. I'll call when we're on the ground."

"Great."

Mariette's eyes drifted to the Bible still clutched in Randal's hand. "In the meantime, why don't you show me what you've been learning from Gram's Bible?"

★   ★   ★

Washington, D.C.
Local Time 7:14 P.M.

"Mr. Benton?" said the voice on the other end of Brad's cell phone. "This is Liza Cannley. I'm glad I finally caught you."

"Hello," Brad said. "You got me on the way out of work. Give me a second to find my car." He looked around for his vehicle in the secure White House parking area. His position as chief of staff entitled him to a driver, but Brad had refused one. The idea of spending any more time than he had to with people on Gerald Fitzhugh's payroll had never appealed to him. He'd chosen, instead, to drive his own car to work each day. The Secret Service had balked, arguing that they couldn't offer him adequate protection if he insisted on driving in and parking in the employee lot, but Brad had assured them that neither an assassin nor a kidnapper would consider him a prime target.

In the end, he'd gotten his way. He was never happier that he'd made that decision than on nights like this when the atmosphere inside the White House and the Old Executive Office Building made him feel claustrophobic. Though if he'd used a driver, he wouldn't be standing in a garage full of nearly identical conservative American-made sedans right now, trying to locate his own.

"I'm sorry it's taken me a while to get back to you. I had planned to call you once I got home tonight," he said.

"That's okay. I haven't been able to reach you on your cell phone anyway until just now," Liza answered. "I'm sure with everything going on, you've had a busy day."

"You could say that."

"I suppose you heard about that business in Jerusalem at the Wailing Wall?"

"I did hear something about that," he said. He had just left a meeting where that incident had been discussed. Two men calling themselves Eli and Moishe had begun preaching at the historic Wailing Wall in Jerusalem just before dawn. With their gray hair, beards, and long burlap robes, the men were originally thought to be just two among the many Israelis who had displayed erratic behavior since the disappearances. The whole country was still spooked by the recent Russian attack. The area around the Wailing Wall had been packed with people wanting to say their prayers ever since those events.

But these two men were very different from the usual seekers at the Wall. Once their message became clear, cries of outrage from the Orthodox Jews had commanded the attention of the Israeli government and its allies. The scene was threatening to turn into a diplomatic incident with international consequences.

Brad continued scanning the garage for his car. Stress did this to him, he told himself. He wasn't forgetting where he parked his car because of incipient Alzheimer's or anything like that.

"Are they really preaching that Jesus Christ is the Jewish Messiah? At the *Wailing Wall*?" Liza asked.

"That's what I understand," he said.

"There's got to be more to this story than meets the eye," she insisted.

"I'm sure there is. But I can't believe you don't want to talk to me about Carpathia."

"I want to talk to you about that, too. But I just watched this bit about Jerusalem on CNN. There's something weird about the scenario . . . but I can't put my finger on what the right word for it is."

"Apocalyptic?" Brad probed.

"Yeah. Maybe that's it. I mean, it seems so odd. You expect a different kind of trouble over there. Palestinians throwing rocks, the occasional suicide bomber . . . now, those I can understand, though the Israelis keep the area too well policed for much of it. But the Wailing Wall is the central symbol of Orthodox Judaism. I can think of only two reasons why anyone would choose to desecrate it like that, by preaching Christianity. Either these guys are part of some weird new terrorist organization that's trying to demoralize the Israelis, or they're for real and they're on what they think is a mission from God."

"Personally, I'd go with the latter," he assured her. *Aha!* He spotted his car right where he'd parked it and walked toward it.

"Maybe it's not so hard to believe after what happened when the Russians attacked Israel. I mean, before that, it would have seemed ridiculous, but now? Who knows?"

Brad pressed the security button for his car. The alarm beeped off as the doors and trunk unlocked. Brad tossed his briefcase into the trunk, then propped one hip against the driver's-side door. "That's true enough. Lately, it seems anything could happen. And has . . ."

"Hmm . . . yeah."

"So what else did you want to talk to me about?"

"Two things, actually."

"You want to know what I think about Nicolae Carpathia, for one."

"Of course. My boss is hot on my case for the administration's response to Carpathia. I told him I thought I had a lead."

Brad thought about his conversation with Marcus. The man had warned him to keep any suspicions he had about Carpathia to himself until they had a chance to discuss the consequences and devise a plan. Carefully, he said, "As you can imagine, we're taking a wait-and-see attitude. The president supports some of what Carpathia has proposed, but he is having trouble getting behind the idea of voluntary nuclear disarmament. It doesn't seem practical for the country."

"What about the single world currency?"

"The U.S. has always supported monetary changes that positively impact the American dollar, and we believe this one will, yes."

"And relocating the UN?"

Brad sighed. "Generally, I'd have to say we don't have a strong opinion on that. Having the UN in New York is practical. Access is easy; we have the transportation network and the security to handle the demands. There aren't a lot of cities that can claim that."

"Including Babylon?"

"The idea of putting it in Iraq is foolish. The country's been way too volatile for years. The infrastructure is in a shambles, the communications system is terrible, and security is a nightmare. The president understands Carpathia's point about the historical significance of Babylon, but no, we're not going to support the idea of relocating the UN there. If he wants to discuss London or Paris, maybe that's another matter."

"Hmm." Liza made a clicking sound with her tongue. "So is Carpathia going to come to Washington for an official visit?"

"It's not on the schedule as of today," Brad told her. "It could change tomorrow."

"Is the White House trying to make it happen?"

"We've talked to Carpathia's people. He's on a fairly tight schedule."

She laughed. "But it's not too tight to sit for a photo shoot after being chosen as *People* magazine's Sexiest Man Alive. That's got to chafe Fitzhugh. The guy's got time to pose for the cover of *People*, but he can't hop an hour flight to D.C.?"

Brad didn't respond.

Liza seized on his silence. "He didn't actually *refuse* to see the president, did he?"

"No," Brad said. "He didn't."

"But he was asked?"

"The president always welcomes foreign dignitaries."

"Come on," Liza said. "You owe me this. Did the president specifically invite Carpathia to Washington?"

Brad hesitated, remembering Marcus's warning. He couldn't see how giving Liza this piece of information would violate his promise. "Yes, he did."

"And Carpathia said no."

"He indicated that he would prefer the president go to him."

Liza let out a low whistle. "Fitz must be livid. I knew I liked Carpathia for a reason."

The remark made Brad wary. He glanced at his watch. "You said there was something else? I'm on my way to an appointment."

"Yeah. George Ramiro."

Brad went still. "Did you learn something?"

"That's just it. I can't reach anyone outside the White House who knows him, anyone who used to know him, or anyone who has any idea where he might be. Everyone has the same story: he resigned for personal reasons, but nobody knows where he is—and they haven't heard from him since well before the disappearances. I tried contacting people in his hometown. Nobody's heard from him. Like you said, it's really suspicious. I just wondered if you'd heard anything else."

"No," he said. "I haven't had much time to look into it. Were you able to reach his family?"

"No," she said. "The general consensus among their friends is that the family's among the missing. The coworkers who hadn't heard the White House's announcement that he resigned just figured he was another one of the casualties. So nobody's even been asking questions."

"I see."

"Are you sure the White House didn't just say he resigned because it seemed easier than explaining to the press that he vanished?"

"Does that make sense to you?"

"Well, no, but if that's not the case, then it's beginning to look like something sinister happened."

That agreed with Brad's suspicions. "Then I'd keep looking if I were you. There's a story in there somewhere."

"If you're right, it might be a bigger story than Carpathia's speech at the UN. I'll be in touch."

Brad told her good-bye, clicked off his cell phone, and dropped it in his pocket. He was reaching for his car door when he saw Jane Lyons, George Ramiro's former assistant, carrying a heavy box across the garage. When Forrest Tetherton had replaced Ramiro as White House press secretary, he'd fired Jane. In Brad's opinion, it was a colossal mistake. As he'd told the president, Tetherton, and Charley Swelder that day on *Air Force One*, Jane was a much better choice than Forrest would ever be.

Brad sprinted across the parking deck to take the box from her. "Jane, let me help you with that."

"Oh, thank you, Mr. Benton. I'm parked over here."

He followed her to her car. "I'm sorry about Tetherton. You deserved better than this."

She shrugged as she unlocked the trunk. "I have to confess, I'm not all that torn up about it. I had already told Mr. Ramiro that I didn't plan to stay through the summer. The campaign season is always more than I can really handle." She gave Brad a thoughtful look. "Although I have to say I was surprised when I got the news about George's resignation. He hadn't given me any indication that he was considering moving on."

"You didn't speak to him personally about it?" He lowered the box into her trunk. "When I saw you the night of the disappearances, I didn't have a chance to ask you."

"I was so upset. Everything was so chaotic. But, no, I never actually spoke to him. Mr. Swelder told me about his resignation, which was weird. George was a very communicative boss. We always knew where we stood with him and what was going on."

"So Charley told you?" Brad pressed. "What did he say?"

"Nothing. I got a copy of a memo from Charley Swelder announcing that George had resigned and that you would handle the questions at the first morning's briefings."

She seemed stung by that, Brad noted. "That wasn't my idea."

Jane shrugged. "Mr. Benton, I know I wasn't very high profile in the White House, but I think I'd proven I was capable of filling in for George when he was covering other areas."

"You had."

"When the Syrians attacked Turkey, George let me handle those announcements to increase my recognition with the press corps."

"George and I discussed that. He was grooming you."

"And then I wasn't asked to handle the press briefing after the disappearances. I have to admit, I was a little surprised. Between that and Forrest's promotion, it was all I needed to see the writing on the wall. Forrest didn't waste any time cleaning house."

"What are your plans?"

"My father lives in Kentucky. I'm going to head home for a while, then decide from there." She gave him a slight smile as she reached into her purse and produced a business card. "I don't have any hard feelings, I assure you. I really enjoyed my time here."

"I'm glad to hear that."

"George always spoke very highly of you, Mr. Benton."

"I had a lot of respect for him," Brad admitted. "He was great at his job."

Jane handed him the card. "The numbers are all changing, but the e-mail's the same. If you know anyone who needs a media specialist—"

"I'll keep you in mind." Brad slipped the card into his breast pocket.

Jane removed a large framed picture from the box before she closed the trunk. "If you don't mind, would you help me get this in the backseat? When I brought it from home, I couldn't believe how hard it was to maneuver into my car. I had to get my roommate to help me."

"Sure." Brad pulled open the door of the sports car. "If you had four doors, it'd be easier."

"Maybe." She laughed lightly. "But I wouldn't look as good."

"Spoken like a true media mogul," he said.

He angled the picture and was sliding it behind the front seat when Brad heard his name from across the parking garage. His assistant, Emma Pettit, was entering the garage from the White House security exit. "Mr. Benton?" she called. "Mr. Benton!"

Brad waved to her across the parking lot. Emma held up a sheaf of papers. "I'm glad I caught you. These are the reports you wanted on Carpathia. I just got everything together."

"Thanks, Emma." Brad indicated his car with a wave of his hand. "The car's unlocked. Toss them on the front seat, will you?"

"Of course." Emma glanced at Jane. "Hello, Jane. I'm sorry about the way things turned out. You didn't deserve this."

Jane smiled. "That's what your boss just said."

"He's plenty smart that way." Emma headed for Brad's late-model sedan.

Brad turned his attention back to the picture. He had just managed to maneuver it through the sports car's door when the unmistakable sound of a gunshot ricocheted off the concrete walls. It was followed by two more loud bangs, shattering glass, and then the sound of squealing tires. To Brad's horror, he saw Emma Pettit lying in a widening pool of blood near his car.

"Emma," he cried as he took off across the parking deck to her. "Emma!"

Jane was right behind him. "Oh no, oh *no*. What was that?"

Brad reached Emma. She held out her hand to him and he took it. She was still conscious but bleeding badly from what looked like a gunshot wound in her chest. He reached for his cell phone with his free hand and thrust it at Jane. "Call 911. Then call Security." He pulled off his coat, bundled it up, and slipped it under Emma's head. "Stay with me, Emma. Please stay with me."

Emma's breathing was shallow and ragged. Brad closed his eyes in horror when he saw torn flesh just below her collarbone and sent up a silent prayer. *Lord,* he thought. *Dear Lord, why?*

The sound of the shots had brought Security and White House personnel running to the scene. Brad heard the ensuing chaos with a sense of disbelief and stunned detachment. His heart was pounding so hard that his limbs felt weak from the spike in his blood pressure and the adrenaline rush.

Beside him, he felt Jane pressing his cell phone into his hand. "I called," she said, her voice shaken. "An ambulance is on its way."

Never taking his eyes off Emma, Brad stuffed the phone into his pocket. "Come on, Emma." Her eyes had shut. "Fight it. Just fight it."

Her eyes fluttered open as her fingers tightened on his hand. "Brad?" she managed to whisper.

He heard sirens in the distance. "Help's coming, Emma. Save your strength."

She shook her head. "No. Today. What you said about hope and God. I've been thinking . . ."

Brad swallowed hard. "Just trust Him, Emma. All you have to do is trust Him to save you."

"I don't want to die like this."

"You don't have to." He smoothed her hair from her face. "Hang on. For me."

"I was going to talk to you tomorrow." Her eyes closed again. "Tomorrow."

Brad's throat clenched. He wanted to press her for details, but the paramedics had arrived. They were pulling him away from her so they could lift her onto a stretcher.

"I've got to talk to her," Brad insisted. "You don't understand."

"I'm sorry, sir. We've got to get her to a hospital. Now."

Another paramedic looked at him. "Does she have any identification?"

"Emma," Brad said, watching as they put the oxygen mask to her face. "Her name's Emma Pettit. She's my personal assistant."

"Is there a next of kin we should call?"

"She is not going to die," Brad said defiantly.

"We'll need to get some information, sir; that's all I'm saying."

Brad leaned over to scoop up Emma's purse from the pavement. "Her insurance and personal information will be in here. I'll go with you to the hospital."

A White House security guard had joined the growing circle around the ambulance. "Mr. Benton? Are you all right?"

"No," Brad growled.

"I mean, were you shot, sir?"

"Do I look shot? Did you catch who did this?"

"We don't know that yet, sir. We're checking." The guard looked at him. "Do you have any idea who might have been after Ms. Pettit?"

"No. Nobody." Brad took a deep breath, trying for control.

Jane gave the guard a hard look. "What kind of question is that? She's a sweet old lady. What do you think this is? Some kind of botched mob hit?"

"We have to consider all the possibilities."

"The real question," Jane insisted, "is where White House security was when some psycho was setting up an assassination attempt in the parking garage."

The guard looked visibly upset.

Brad held up his hand. "Everyone's nerves are a little thin." He watched as the paramedics got ready to lift Emma into the ambulance, then turned to the guard. "I'm sorry; I have no idea who might have done this. I have to go. We can talk later."

"The lady was near your car," the guard pointed out. "Is there any chance that you might have been the target?"

A chill tripped down Brad's spine as he thought of his conversation with Liza Cannley just moments before the shooting. Had something sinister happened to George Ramiro? something like this, perhaps? Brad had suspected it from the start. Were his suspicions the reason that this had happened? Had Liza's probing touched a nerve somewhere that had resulted in this shooting? And if that was so, had he endangered Liza with what he'd revealed tonight? And were they after him?

Brad shuddered as his feet crunched on the broken glass where a bullet had shattered one of his car windows.

"Mr. Benton?" the guard probed.

"I'm not sure what happened," Brad said. "I didn't see it. Right now I've got to get to the hospital with Emma. Talk to Jane—she had a better view than I did."

The paramedics were still working to get Emma into the ambulance. The guard turned to question Jane and the other bystanders. White House Security and the Secret Service were now descending en masse. They had the parking area sealed off and secured in seconds and had ordered a lockdown of the White House.

Brad knew from experience that this could prove to be a very long night. Lockdowns happened when the Secret Service felt that the president's security had been potentially compromised. As long as the Secret Service felt it was necessary to keep the White House locked down, no one left or entered the building until cleared. The night of the disappearances no White House employees on-site had been able to go home until more than sixteen hours after the event.

His hands trembling, Brad reached into his pocket and pulled out his cell phone. He punched Marcus's number.

When the other man answered, Brad asked him to turn on the local news. Nothing happened at the White House, he knew, that didn't end up on the local news within minutes. "I'm all right," he told Marcus. "I can't talk now, but pray for my friend. Her name is Emma."

"Brad—"

"I've got to run. I'll see you as soon as I can." Brad shoved his phone into his pocket when he felt a hand clamp onto his elbow.

"Mr. Benton?" A Secret Service agent stood to his left. "I need to know if you're all right, sir."

"I'm fine," Brad said.

The agent radioed in the report. He indicated the security office across the parking lot. "If you'll come with me, sir? I'm going to put you in a secure place while we look into this."

Brad resisted. "I've got to go with Emma to the hospital."

The agent shook his head. "I'm sorry, sir. I'll finish up with you as soon as I can, but we can't let anyone out while we're in lockdown. You know that."

Brad wanted to rebel but knew it would be futile. He let out a frustrated breath and handed Emma's purse to one of the paramedics. "I've got an appointment," he told the Secret Service agent. "Will it be all right if I make a call to cancel it?"

The agent began steering Brad through the gathering swarm of security personnel. He used his shoulder to clear a path while his eyes darted constantly among the spectators. Brad recognized the technique as something the Service referred to as "moving the man." They were highly trained in negotiating a clear path to safety for the president through the most hostile of environments.

As soon as they cleared the crowd, the agent pulled open the door of the security office. "You'll be safe in here. You can call inside the White House from here."

Brad stuck his hand in his pocket for his cell phone. "I've got—"

"No, sir," the agent told him. He pointed to the black phone on the desk. "I'm sorry. I can't let you use an unsecured outside line right now. You can call inside, but not out. I'll let you know as soon as we've cleared it."

Brad was glad he'd reached Marcus, no matter how briefly. "I understand," he said, then dropped into a battered leather chair. "I'll wait. But who's going to take care of Emma? She's going to need someone at the hospital with her."

"Don't worry. We'll inform the proper authorities," the agent said.

Brad put his head into his hands in despair and wondered who the proper authorities were for that. He could think of only one at the moment.

He began to pray.

16

Washington, D.C.
Georgetown
Local Time 10:15 P.M.

Marcus pulled open his door to find a very shaken Brad standing there. "Are you sure you're okay? The news report looked bad."

Brad nodded. As soon as the Secret Service had released him, he'd gone to the hospital. Emma was taken into surgery, so the hospital had not allowed him to see her. As he handled the necessary paperwork for his friend, he was told it would be many hours before he could see Emma—if then. Her chances weren't good.

Brad knew he couldn't help Emma by slowly going mad in the hospital waiting room. The most useful thing he could think of to do was to call on God for help . . . and to ask others to join in his prayers. He knew where he could find a friend to pray with him.

Brad left his cell phone number at the nurses' station along with instructions that he be called if there was any change at all in Emma's condition, or as soon as she was in the recovery room. Then he left to hail a cab and told the driver to take him to Marcus's place. During the cab ride, he had called the minister and filled him in on what had happened.

"I may have to go at any minute," he said as he followed Marcus down the hall. "I'm tired, but I'm here. I'm sorry I'm so late."

"It's all right," Marcus assured him. "I'm glad you could make it at all. I would have been up waiting to hear from you. How's Emma?"

"When I left, there'd been no change," Brad said wearily. "The hospital is going to call me if there's any shift in her status. She's in surgery now."

Marcus shook his head. "I've been praying for her. Please come with me." He led Brad into his living room.

Looking for a distraction from his fears and pain, Brad examined his surroundings. Marcus's home was elegant and formal, undoubtedly a professional decorator's work. Brad remembered Marcus telling him that he'd lost his wife several years before. Brad mentally compared the look of Marcus's Georgetown house with his own home in California. Though the deep burgundy walls and towering oak bookshelves here were impressive and masculine, the room looked sterile and impersonal, more like a photo background than a living space.

By comparison, every room in the home he'd shared with Christine had possessed a welcoming quality that seemed to invite people to enter and find rest. He could use that rest right now, swamped as he was with exhaustion and emotional overload. He missed his wife. He wanted to call her and tell her about Emma. Talking with his wife had always helped with the pain. Had he ever really appreciated all that Christine had done for him? But it was too late now to make amends to her. It might even be too late to make amends to Emma.

Marcus's living room was so big and impressive that Brad did not immediately notice Mariette Arnold and a young man seated on the sofa. When he saw them, he looked at Marcus, surprised.

"Brad," Marcus said, "I believe you know Ms. Arnold."

"Of course," Brad said. "I know you undertook a herculean task today, Ms. Arnold. You're probably as tired as I am."

"I doubt it. I wasn't on the evening news. You were. Was it as bad as it looked?"

"It was bad," Brad assured her.

"The reporter didn't say if anyone had been killed," Marcus said. "Was anyone hurt besides your assistant?"

"No," Brad said. "Did they mention her name on the news?"

"No."

"Good. I hope they keep it under wraps until they reach her family."

Mariette gave him a sympathetic look. "I'm so sorry."

Brad wiped a hand over his face. He was so tired it hurt just to breathe. "Me, too."

"Do you have any idea who was behind the shooting?" the young man asked. "How could something like that have happened in the White House garage? Aren't you guys ringed in metal detectors and guards and stuff?"

Mariette indicated the young man with a wave of her hand. "This is my son, Randal," she told Brad. "He's home from college. As you can see, he's not shy. And he's still working on tact."

Randal shot his mother a dry look as he rose to extend his hand to Brad. "Mr. Benton. Nice to meet you."

"You, too, Randal."

"Tact may not be my strong suit, but I still want to know," Randal said. "How could it have happened?"

"I don't know. If I had to guess, I'd imagine that the guards were shorthanded. We lost a lot of our security people in the disappearances. I'd guess somebody spotted that weakness and took advantage of it." Brad glanced at Marcus. "As far as who is behind the shooting, I'm not sure."

Marcus gave him a steady look. "Do you think they might have been after you?"

"I don't know," Brad said. "It's possible. Or I might not actually be the target."

"But the lady was next to your car," Randal insisted. "That's what the news said. She was your assistant."

"They released that?" Brad frowned. "I hope Emma's sister didn't hear it. Anyway, this may not have been personal. My car was parked in the White House secure lot. Someone might have been after publicity and not after any one person in particular."

Marcus seemed to consider that. "Brad, if there's something you feel you shouldn't tell us . . ."

"I can talk about some of it. I can admit the shot might have been aimed at me. I've been asking some questions lately," he said simply. "Unpopular questions. I'm not sure yet what the answers to those questions might be, but until I know them, I'd rather not discuss those things."

"I understand," Marcus said. "Given the nature of your position, I'm sure there will be plenty of times in the future when there's information you'll have to withhold."

"It's not that I don't trust you, Marcus. National security and all that."

Marcus held up a hand. "No explanation necessary. I assure you." He indicated a leather wing chair to Brad. "Why don't you have a seat and we'll talk about something else. Mariette and Randal share some of our interest in the Bible and prophecy."

"Oh? It would be a relief to talk about anything but the shooting." Brad managed a slight smile. "Let's just say that the Secret Service likes extremely detailed reports when there's an incident near the White House, and the hospital admissions department wasn't much better."

"I can imagine. Can I get you something to eat or drink?"

Brad shook his head as he shucked off his topcoat. It was still spattered with Emma's blood from where he'd propped her head on it. "I'm not sure I could hold anything down right now. I would appreciate it if we could pray for Emma."

Marcus sat in the other wing chair while Brad took the seat he'd indicated. When Brad was settled, Marcus bowed his head and prayed, "Lord, our blessings are many tonight. I want to thank You for protecting one friend from harm. Thank You for reaching out Your hand to another friend who needed Your salvation. Thank You for using this young man to speak Your truth. Thank You for Your wisdom and Your grace. Tonight we selfishly ask that You would lay Your healing hand on Brad's friend Emma. Lord, You alone know the number of our days, but we entreat You now to protect and watch over this woman. Keep her close, Lord. If it be Your will, then please hasten her recovery. I know she is precious to my friend. I know he is hurting for her even now. Whatever happens, please give us all the strength to deal with it as You would wish us to. Please give us discernment and open minds and hearts that we might better fulfill Your will for our lives. Amen."

"Amen," Brad said simultaneously with Mariette and Randal.

When they all raised their heads, Marcus reached for the Bible on his coffee table. "Are you up to hearing what I've discovered about the Antichrist?"

Brad nodded.

Marcus opened the Bible to the book of Revelation and began to read a passage about the being the prophet referred to as "the beast." When he was done, he raised his head and looked at each of them in turn. "I feel I must warn you all that what I am about to say is unpleasant and frightening." He turned to Brad. "If I'm right, then what happened to you tonight may be just the beginning of what we'll face in the future."

"Marcus—"

"The Bible makes it very clear," Marcus said, "that the beast will do whatever necessary to seize power, will stoop to any level to stop the men who oppose him."

Brad frowned. "I don't think you can relate tonight's events to that."

"I don't have great influence," Marcus told him, "but you do." He set the Bible on the coffee table. "I've studied those Scriptures for years. I knew exactly what the Bible said about the end times and the Antichrist. But I never imagined it would be like this."

Marcus looked at Mariette and Randal. "This afternoon, I told Brad that I believe Nicolae Carpathia is the man the Bible calls the beast."

Mariette's mouth dropped open. "You're kidding."

Randal frowned. "That Romanian guy? The one at the UN?"

"Yes," Marcus said. "He fits the Bible's description exactly."

Randal shook his head. "But didn't he just make this really big deal about global peace and nuclear disarmament? I heard on the radio on the way here that everyone went wild over the guy."

"The Bible clearly states," Marcus said, "that the Antichrist will be evil and a great deceiver. He will deliberately turn people's eyes from the truth."

"I know," Randal said. "That's why I'm confused. I mean, this guy is so mild mannered. The press is always talking about how humble he is. What he wants to do is pretty utopian. I've got a professor who thinks Carpathia has all the answers to the world's problems."

"He certainly appears to," Marcus said. "His ideas seem peaceful and reasonable, at least on the surface."

Mariette sighed. "But you don't trust him."

"No, I don't. And with good cause." Marcus reached for the Bible again. He read several passages that described the Antichrist's prophesied strategy. When he set the book down, he looked at Brad. "Think of Carpathia's goals. The single world currency, 'the mark of the beast,' is clearly prophesied in the text."

"But that one world religion deal," Randal protested. "Nobody's going to go for that, no matter how much they like the guy. I mean, can you see the Muslims and the Jews agreeing on one religion? They'd shrivel up and die first."

"I admit I can't picture it," Marcus said. "But then I wouldn't have imagined that all the world's religious leaders would be willing to meet in New York for a conference this week, either. And Carpathia's going to be there, right in the middle of it. Evidently, the Orthodox Jews are eager to forge ahead with their plans to rebuild the temple, and they're willing to make some fairly major concessions to the Islamic leaders in order to make it happen."

"But still—," Randal said.

Marcus went on. "Then there's Carpathia's suggestion to relocate the UN to Babylon."

"And nuclear disarmament," Mariette added quietly.

"I think the fact that people are listening carefully to these things is the strongest proof that Carpathia's the Antichrist," Marcus said. "His goals are those of the biblical Antichrist, and his ideas are being taken seriously. I believe that if he were merely a normal man, he'd have been laughed out of the UN and New York. And that didn't happen."

Randal looked at all of them wide-eyed. "What if you're right?"

"I think I am," Marcus said. "And I think that when I told Brad my suspicions about Carpathia I may have put him in jeopardy."

"No one knew about our conversation," Brad said. "And that's not the only rock I've been turning over lately that may have raised some eyebrows."

"But it's one of them?" Marcus pressed.

Brad didn't respond.

Marcus looked around the small group. "Whether Carpathia is the Antichrist or not, and whatever the future holds, I believe God has put us together here for a reason, with a purpose and a plan." He glanced at Mariette. "I've had a burden for you since the night you called me looking for answers. I've been praying for you ever since."

"I don't know what to say," Mariette said.

Marcus shook his head. "You don't have to say anything. You have no idea what it's like for me to have someone to pray for and mean it. For years I've promised to pray for people. I never kept those promises. That was just one more of my failures."

Brad reached out and laid a hand on Marcus's arm. Brad wondered if he would have found the physical contact so natural even a week or so ago. He'd given his testimony in church on Sunday morning, and though he'd not yet told Marcus, the simple baptism service they'd shared had left Brad with the feeling that they'd stood on holy ground together.

"We've all been there," Brad told him quietly.

Marcus nodded. "Still, I'm grateful that God gave me another chance. That night we spoke, Mariette—" he shook his head slightly—"I can't explain it. It's as if I felt God telling me you needed intercession. You needed someone to pray for you. I've done it daily ever since."

Tears ran down Mariette's face. "I had no idea. Thank you." Randal reached over and took her hand.

"When you called and asked to see me tonight, I prayed that God would give me one more opportunity to reach you with the truth."

He glanced at Randal. "I had no idea that God had already sent a messenger, and he'd had enough courage to talk to you."

"Thanks," Randal said.

"My son would have done that." Brad wiped a hand over his face. "He used to do that. Brad Jr. was a fine young man." He was struck by the incongruity of the situation—the young college student and the White House chief of staff sharing a moment of grief and spiritual renewal.

"You lost your family," Randal said.

"Yes," Brad said, his face a mask of grief. "My wife. Three kids." Brad took a determined breath. "It's hard. I miss them. I get up in the morning. I brush my teeth. I put on my shoes. And then I want to take a minute and shake my fist at God and tell Him He had no right to do this to me." He buried his face in his hands. "And that's when I remember that I did this to myself."

"Man," Randal said softly, "I can't imagine."

Brad raised his head to look at Randal. "I wish I'd had your courage."

"I was scared to death," Randal admitted. "It was so unreal—the whole thing, I mean. I think the reason I picked up my grandmother's Bible is because the last time I remember feeling that scared was during the summers I spent on her farm. These huge thunderstorms would come through, sometimes even tornadoes. I'd get really freaked-out, and Gram and I would sit down and she'd read the Bible to me. The disappearances felt just like that. So out of control."

Mariette wrapped her arm around her son's shoulders.

Marcus pushed the Bible to the center of the coffee table and drew their attention to it once more. "I wish I could tell you it's going to get better, but I don't think it will."

"I don't either," Randal said. "I've been reading Gram's Bible. I don't understand a lot of it, but it's pretty heavy. All that stuff about horsemen and plagues . . ."

"Trouble is coming," Marcus assured them. "We are in the time the Bible refers to as the Great Tribulation."

"What's going to happen?" Mariette asked.

"I don't know exactly," Marcus said, "but I have studied the Scriptures for years. As Randal said, the language can be difficult to interpret into modern terms, but some of it is crystal clear. The Bible says a devastating famine is on the way. It predicts natural disasters, global war, destruction, and a variety of plagues."

"What are we supposed to do?" Brad asked. "What *can* we do?"

"As I said in my sermon on Sunday," Marcus said, "the Scriptures predict that some people will accept the Lord after the events of the Rapture. There will be a remnant of the Jews who are brought to safety. Those who seek to serve God during this time will face untold persecution. Some will live through to the end to see the Glorious Appearing of Christ, but many will die a martyr's death. By taking you all into my confidence tonight, I know I'm asking you for a potentially horrific sacrifice."

"I'm ready to make it," Randal said emphatically.

His mother glanced at him. "Randal—"

"No, Mom. I am. It's like I have this fire in me all of a sudden. I've never felt like this. I've never had this urge to *do* something, to *be* something." He looked at Marcus. "I was always just Senator Arnold's kid. Anything I did was a reflection on my father. I never had a purpose like this before. It's like I'm really alive for the first time in my life. I have no idea what God might ask of me, but I'm ready to follow Him."

Brad's heart twisted. The young man reminded him in so many ways of his own son. Brad Jr. had possessed the same zeal, the same courage, the same verve to share in the suffering of Christ. Brad felt ashamed that he'd never told his son how much he admired him. "My son used to call it a desire to share in the suffering of Christ."

"Yes," Marcus said. He picked up the Bible again and opened it. "The apostle Paul says it this way in Philippians: 'I can really know Christ and experience the mighty power that raised Him from the dead. I can learn what it means to suffer with Him, sharing in His death.'"

"That's it," Randal insisted. "That's exactly what it feels like. I have this burning need to know Him better, and I know that I can't really do that until I suffer with Him and for Him."

"But you're saying that there's no hope," Mariette said bleakly. "There's nothing we can do to stop this."

Marcus looked at her gently. "We can't stop it, no, but there *is* hope. We have eternal hope. We can share it."

She took a shuddering breath. "I don't know—"

"It'll be okay, Mom," Randal said.

Marcus nodded. "It's frightening. Your mother has every right to be afraid."

"I'm not really afraid for me," Mariette said. "It's Randal." She looked at Marcus and Brad. "My son is here with me. You two don't have as much to lose now."

"Mom—"

"She's your mother," Brad said. "She's got a moral right to be worried sick about you. Goes with the territory."

Mariette laid her hand on Randal's cheek. "Whatever we're facing, I'm glad we'll go through it together."

Randal nodded.

Marcus hesitated. "I've told you all what I think the risks are. If you want to walk away from this right now, that's your choice. I'd never condemn you for that."

No one moved.

"Go ahead, Marcus," Brad finally said. "We're listening."

Marcus looked at him closely. "Brad, I think God has brought you into this circle for several reasons. If you choose, you can wield heavy influence on global events."

"I don't have that much power at the White House," he said. "You know my situation."

"But you're there. Every day. Right in the center of where decisions get made. You'll know things, hear things. You'll have a rare inside glimpse at how the politics of all this unfolds."

"That's true," Brad said. "If Fitz and Swelder don't get rid of me."

"I agree. I think that puts you in the most significant danger," Marcus told him. "If Carpathia is who I think he is, it's only a matter of time before he begins to counsel with and persuade world leaders. You'll probably have to come face-to-face with him sooner or later."

Brad nodded. "I'm sure I will."

"I don't know what it'll be like," Marcus continued, "when you have to look into the face of that much evil."

"I do," Randal said. He picked up his grandmother's Bible and flipped it open to a bookmarked passage. "I found this the other day. I didn't get it then, but it makes sense now." He ran his finger down the page until he found what he sought. "Here it is. God says, 'And when I passed by and saw you again, you were old enough to be married. So I wrapped my cloak around you to cover your nakedness and declared My marriage vows. I made a covenant with you, says the Sovereign Lord, and you became mine.'"

Randal looked up. "Gram used to say that the prophecies of the end times in the Old Testament were just as relevant as the ones in the New Testament. That's why I started looking there. When I came across this, it just seemed sort of poetical, you know." He looked at Brad. "But I think it's exactly what we're talking about. We're all new, like naked infants before the Lord. We're totally exposed and helpless to the evil in the world. But He promises to cover us with His cloak and keep us safe until He's ready to take us to heaven." He glanced at Marcus. "Right?"

Marcus nodded. "I think so. Yes."

Randal said, "So when the time comes and you have to face off with Carpathia, it'll be kind of like those Christians in Rome who had to face the lions. God will give you everything you need for that moment. Even if it's supernatural protection or strength."

"That's very wise, Randal," Marcus told him.

Randal shut the Bible with a slight shrug. "I had a good teacher. I wish I'd listened to her better. Now it's like I can't get enough. I can't read enough. I want to know everything there is to know."

"Keep reading, Randal." Marcus turned his attention to Mariette. "You have a role, too. I've been thinking about the famines and plagues and natural disasters that are on the way. You will have incredible responsibilities in the days to come. The more the world needs assistance and relief efforts, the more your influence will grow. I can certainly understand why God would want you on this team."

"Team?" Randal prompted.

"Yes," Marcus said. "Since this morning, I've felt a need to talk to Brad about forming an alliance—a small, intimate circle of believers who work together to reach lost souls and fight evil as best we can in these difficult days. The Bible promises that God does triumph in the end of this struggle, but throughout time, God has called on faithful men and women to carry out His work here on earth. He doesn't *need* us," Marcus clarified, "to get His work done now any more than He did when He gave Adam dominion over the earth. God can do what He will all on His own. But I believe that He trusts us with His work for our benefit and our communion with Him. I think He's doing that now, and He's asking us to pledge our lives to Him and to one another."

Several moments of silence passed as they all considered what Marcus had said. Randal moved first. He placed his hand on top of Marcus's Bible and stated, "I'm ready."

Brad, moved by the young man's courage, covered Randal's hand with his own and said, "I am, too."

Mariette laid her hand on top of Brad's. "So am I."

With tears in his eyes, Marcus covered their joined hands with both of his. "Thank you, friends," he said quietly.

They sat in silence for several seconds. Marcus stood first. "If you'll all wait here a moment, there's something I think we should share."

He headed quickly toward the kitchen, found what he wanted, and returned to the living room with a can of soda, four paper cups, and some crackers. "I have to apologize," he told the group. "Since my wife died several years ago, I never keep much in the kitchen. I usually eat at the office. I should be able to do better than this—" he shrugged—"but I don't think God will mind if you don't."

He handed them each a cup, then set the soda and the package of crackers down on the table. Reaching for the Bible, he flipped it open and read: "'Then at the proper time Jesus and the twelve apostles sat down together at the table. Jesus said, "I have looked forward to this hour with deep longing, anxious to eat this Passover meal with you before My suffering begins. For I tell you now that I won't eat it again until it comes to fulfillment in the Kingdom of God."'" Marcus reached for the soda and popped open the top.

Lifting the can, he continued to read, "'Then He took a cup of wine, and when He had given thanks for it, He said, "Take this and share it among yourselves. For I will not drink wine again until the Kingdom of God has come."'" Marcus bowed his head. "Thank You, Lord," he prayed quietly, "that You are a God of infinite mercy and grace. That even those of us who rejected and despised You can still come into Your presence and seek Your forgiveness. Thank You for loving us so much."

He poured some of the soda into each of the four cups. Then he set the can down and reached for the package of crackers. He removed four crackers from the wrapper and held them lightly in one hand. Looking at the Bible again, he read, "'Then He took a loaf of bread; and when He had thanked God for it, He broke it in pieces and gave it to the disciples, saying, "This is My body, given for you. Do this in remembrance of Me."'"

Solemnly, Marcus handed each of them one of the crackers. "This is the only way that Jesus commanded us to remember Him. I believe this is what sharing in the fellowship and communion of His suffering means." He bowed his head again. "Lord, thank You for Your sacrifice. Thank You for the incredible gift of Your love. We remember You tonight with this symbol of Your body, bruised and afflicted for us. Amen."

"Amen," the other three echoed.

Marcus ate his cracker in silence while the others followed suit. He raised his cup, then read from the Bible again: "'After supper He took another cup of wine and said, "This wine is the token of God's new covenant to save you—an agreement sealed with the blood I will pour out for you."'"

Marcus looked at the group again. "The cup represents the blood of Jesus that was spilled so that we might be saved. By partaking of it, we are acknowledging not only His lordship but our willingness to remember His suffering and to enter into this covenant with Him." Marcus studied the contents of his cup, then drank it. Brad, Randal, and Mariette did the same.

Long moments of silence passed before Brad placed his now-empty cup on the table. When he looked at Marcus, there were tears in his eyes. "I've taken the Lord's Supper more times than I can count, and it never meant as much as it did right now."

Marcus nodded. "I know the feeling. I've administered it in some of the most beautiful churches in the world to some of the world's most influential leaders, but I'll remember this forever."

Randal leaned forward and braced his elbows on his knees. "So what do we do now?"

Marcus held out his hands to the group. "We pray. And we don't stop."

17

Washington, D.C.
George Washington Hospital
Local Time 8:00 A.M.

Brad sat next to Emma's bed and listened to the beeps and pings of the medical machinery. He'd asked for a call as soon as Emma was out of surgery. He'd stayed up most of the night waiting for it, but the call hadn't come until a half hour ago. Emma's doctors were cautious but encouraged.

She looked still and pale lying in the hospital bed. She'd hate for Brad to see her like this, he knew. Emma was a woman of great dignity and pride. She wouldn't like knowing that he'd seen her with her eyes blackened from loss of blood and her face papery and drained of color.

A shaft of light spilled across the bed when the duty nurse cracked open the door to check on her patient. "Mr. Benton," she said quietly.

He glanced at her. "Yes?"

"Just a few more minutes, okay?"

Brad nodded. "Sure."

The door shut and he looked at Emma again. His heart twisted when he pictured her lying against the bloodstained concrete, her gaze pleading, her voice ragged, asking him for a thread of hope, something to hold on to. With a heavy sigh, Brad reached for her hand. He'd spent his morning jog asking Marcus whether or not

he'd done the right thing the other day when he'd wanted so desperately to talk to Emma about Jesus and he'd decided to wait.
Had he failed her? Had he thrown away the only opportunity
God was going to give him to reach this woman who had been
such a vital part of his family? The thought had him sending up
an anguished prayer for another chance—just one more—to set
things right.

"Emma, I don't know if you can hear me," he whispered.
Maybe he imagined the slight tightening of her fingers; he
wasn't sure. "What you asked me last night in the parking lot . . .
what you asked about hope and about God. I shouldn't have put
this off. I should have told you as soon as I saw you Monday
morning."

Brad scooted his chair a little closer to the side of her bed.
"There *is* hope. I didn't think so either, not after Christine and the
kids—" He struggled for a minute with a fresh rush of tears. Tears
were one of the many things that came easier to him these days.
"But now I know better. Marcus Dumont showed me. People like
you and me, we may have missed God's message of salvation the
first time, but He is still holding out His hand to us. All we have to
do is believe. And if you can't believe, ask Him to help you believe.
If He could love me, if He could *forgive* me, after the way I've lied
about my faith to my friends and my family, then He will forgive
anyone."

Brad clasped her hand in both of his. "Jesus loves you, Emma.
That's all you need to know to realize there's hope. He loves you so
much."

Only the steady drone of medical technology met his impassioned plea, so Brad dipped his head and prayed for his friend's recovery. "Please, Lord, please don't take her from me until I know
she's all right with You. Please."

The slight grip on his hand seemed to loosen. Her expression
looked peaceful, so Brad gently laid her hand on the covers and
slipped from the room. He'd done all he could for the moment. The
rest was in God's hands.

★   ★   ★

Washington, D.C.
The White House
Local Time 9:30 A.M.

"Who shot at you?"

"I have no idea," Brad said. He looked closely at Charley Swelder. He tried not to shift uncomfortably in his chair as the prickly feeling he'd had since entering the room now made his flesh crawl and his heart quicken. The feeling was similar to what he'd experienced Sunday morning in the park when Marcus had spoken with him about the love of God. Marcus had put a name on the oppressive sensation. He'd told Brad he'd been sitting in the presence of evil. Had Brad doubted it even a bit, this morning's meeting would have convinced him that his new friend was right. There was something decidedly sinister about this meeting . . . and about Charley Swelder.

A few weeks ago, Brad would have branded Marcus a kook, or at best a religious fanatic, for predicting that he'd begin to sense evil in the world around him. But the uneasy feeling he'd had since he'd entered this meeting was twisting his gut. With an insight born of his newfound faith, Brad knew exactly what was causing it.

"You're telling me that a sniper tried to take a shot at you, and you have no idea who it was?"

Brad leaned back in the chair in Swelder's office. "Security doesn't know for sure that I was the target."

Swelder regarded him through narrowed eyes. "I seriously doubt it was Emma Pettit."

"Perhaps not." Brad shrugged. "I don't know what to tell you, Charley. If I knew why that happened, I'd have reported it to Security by now. Emma's not just my assistant, she's like a part of my family. Don't you think I want to get to the bottom of this as much as you do?"

Charley tried a new tack. "I met with Lawton this morning," he said, citing an upper-level investigator in the Secret Service. "The Service is convinced the guy was after you. The trajectory of the bullet suggests it was aimed at you but went over your head while you were loading that picture. If you hadn't stooped at the last second, it would have splintered your skull."

"Oh." Brad felt a chill move over him.

"So what I want to know," Charley said, picking up a pen and twirling it between his fingers, "is why you."

"Maybe because I'm the only upper-level official who drives his own car to work?"

"Which stops as of today. I'm assigning you a driver."

"I don't want a driver."

Swelder gave him a chilling look. "Did I offer you a choice? It's a security issue. Regardless of how I may or may not feel about your contribution to this administration, your life has been threatened. That means the president's life has been threatened. I'm assigning you a driver."

Brad thought about protesting. He didn't like the idea of having one of Charley's pawns watching his every move. Then in a moment of divine insight, something occurred to him . . . a solution for a myriad of problems. "I'd rather you didn't, but I'm willing to accept it with one request."

Charley's raised eyebrows suggested that, in his opinion, Brad had little choice in the matter. "Which is?"

"I'd like to select my own driver. As long as you don't object."

Swelder considered the proposition. Brad waited anxiously through seconds of silence. He'd spent too many years in politics not to know the fine points of power brokering and negotiation. Despite Charley's bluster, he couldn't really force Brad to accept a driver. By offering to take one and providing a candidate that Charley approved, Brad had neatly trapped him. The trick now was not to let Charley know he'd pushed him into a corner.

Charley finally broke the silence. "You have someone in mind?"

"Yes."

"Someone already on staff?"

"New kid. Needs a job. Friend of the family."

"He'd have to clear security."

"Not a problem. He's Max Arnold's son."

Swelder's eyes widened a little. "Really?"

"Yes. He's home from college. Good kid." Brad shrugged. "I don't know, but I'm guessing the driver pool is just as short staffed as everyone else following the disappearances."

"Probably," Charley acknowledged.

"Then they probably don't have a driver to spare. I can't see the Secret Service objecting to Senator Arnold's son driving my car, can you?"

"I wonder how Max Arnold would feel about it."

Brad played the card Charley had just dealt him. "He'd probably be really unhappy, which is exactly why the kid would want to do it. Frankly, that's exactly why I thought you'd like the idea."

Charley's smile looked more malicious than amused. "The idea of making Arnold squirm a little is satisfying. I'll admit that much."

"I can't think of a better way to accomplish that than hiring his kid to work in the Fitzhugh White House."

Charley laughed. "You got that straight. Arnold's likely to have a stroke."

"I'm sure you'll be heartbroken. I'll call the kid now." Brad stood. "I assume you're leading the investigation into the shooting."

"I've told the director of the Service to consider this a top priority. I'll let you know when we hear something."

"Fine." Brad got up and turned to leave.

"Benton," Swelder said.

"Yes?"

Swelder reached for a newspaper on his desk. Brad saw it was the *Los Angeles Times.* "There's an article here by your reporter friend out on the West Coast—Cannley. The one you met with in California."

"Like I told Tetherton, I didn't meet with her. She gave me a lift home. I've known Liza Cannley for years. I consider her a friend."

"People who work at the White House in upper-level positions don't have friends in the press corps. You should know that by now."

"I know the rules," Brad assured him.

Swelder's eyes dropped to the article. "She quotes an unnamed source close to the situation who says that President Fitzhugh is attempting to meet with Carpathia but that the Romanian president is refusing to make a trip to Washington." He glanced up. "Any idea who her unnamed source might be?"

He made a mental note to thank Liza for not calling him an unnamed source at the White House. That would have been more difficult to explain away. "Doesn't every member of the press corps have an 'unnamed source close to the situation'?"

"There weren't that many people here who knew about your conversation with Carpathia's people," Swelder insisted.

"Perhaps. But we have no idea how many of his people knew. She could have talked to anybody. She's good at what she does."

"I hope I don't have to tell you how delicate this situation is, Benton."

"Of course not."

The other man seemed satisfied. He nodded and indicated the door of his office with a dismissing wave of his hand. "Go make your call, then. That Arnold kid will have to come in for processing and security clearance."

Brad looked over his shoulder as he exited the White House and walked the short distance to the Ellipse. There didn't appear to be any snipers gunning for him this morning. He was a clear enough target right now that he'd be history if there was one out there.

He'd awakened today with a strange sense of foreboding. He'd stopped at a local dealer to get a new cell phone. He'd decided then that he would make no personal calls from his office at the White House. While he would maintain his original cell phone for any business-related activity, he'd given Marcus, Mariette, and Randal his new private cell number. He punched Marcus's number as he walked.

The day had turned warm. Crowds of tourists clustered around a chunk of airplane debris that had slammed into the once manicured expanse of green lawn. Brad made his way around them and headed for a bench near the sidewalk. For the first time since the disappearances, tourists had begun to crowd into the city. Though the spring was usually a busy time of year, the Park Service was already predicting record numbers of visitors. People seemed to have a need to see the seat of their government and assure themselves that life was continuing despite the devastation of the last few days.

Brad reached the bench and hit the dial button on his phone. Marcus picked up on the second ring. "Hi," Brad said. "It's me."

"I was hoping you'd call. How's Emma?"

"A tiny bit better," Brad told him. "Out of surgery. Still critical. I visited with her this morning for as long as they'd let me stay."

"Is she conscious?"

"Not yet."

"I'll keep praying," Marcus assured him. "Any news about your sniper?"

"Yeah. I'm certain he was aiming at me. The Service is investigating. I'm not really expecting them to find anything."

"Do you think something like this could happen again?"

"I'm not sure yet. Maybe. Depends on who gets upset about the questions I'm asking."

Marcus sighed. "I just wish we knew who you could trust there."

"Well, Charley Swelder has decided I need a driver. They don't want me to use a private vehicle until they have this settled."

"I don't know, Brad. I don't know if I like the idea of you running around town with a Swelder clone driving you."

"I didn't either, until it occurred to me that I could pick my own driver. Fortunately, Randal is Max Arnold's son. Swelder loved the idea of having an Arnold working at the White House, if for no other reason than the reaction it would get from the senator. He's ready to bring Randal on board as soon as he fills out his paperwork. I don't think his security clearance will take long."

Marcus chuckled. "Brilliant. I have to hand it to you. That was a good one."

"I don't want to put the kid in any danger, though," Brad said. "That's my only concern."

"I can understand why you'd feel that way, but you have to remember that all of us are in God's hands. I'll feel better, and I think Mariette will too, if the two of you are looking out for each other. Randal could be invaluable to you."

"I know that. The drivers talk. They hear things from each other. I think he's mature enough to handle it."

"So do I."

Brad looked at the milling crowd of tourists. "I'm going to call Mariette and ask her about it before I talk to Randal."

"That's probably wise. She's in the office today."

"I'll call her there," Brad said.

"Any news from our friend in New York?" Marcus prompted. By mutual consent, the four of them avoided mentioning Carpathia's name over the phone.

"Nothing new yet," Brad said, "but I think we can expect an announcement this afternoon."

"I think so, too. I'm praying for you, Brad."

"I know. Thanks."

Brad hung up and dialed Mariette's number. She answered immediately. As Brad suspected, she was concerned for Randal's safety but clearly saw the advantages to her son, to Brad, and to their joint purpose. She made Brad promise to look out for Randal but agreed that the situation seemed ideal for both of them. After one more phone call, this one to Randal, Brad headed back to his office.

The word at the White House was that the current secretary-general of the UN and the president of Botswana, Mwangati Ngumo, was going to announce his resignation today. Rosenzweig had offered to give him his now coveted formula for agricultural abundance in desert climates. Ngumo was expected to announce that the opportunity to bring desperately needed famine relief to his people was more than enough to lure him back to his country and away from New York.

No one doubted that the UN would immediately turn to Carpathia to take the top job. Brad wondered what Rosenzweig's connection to Carpathia was and why he seemed intent on seeing the man installed at the UN. To his knowledge, the Israeli scientist had never played a great role in world politics. He'd always chosen to bury himself in his research. Yet he seemed to have pitched his tent early and securely in Carpathia's camp. Brad wondered if the scientist had any inkling about the demonic forces surrounding Carpathia.

Brad reached the security entrance to the White House, flashed his badge, and started to walk through the gate.

"Just a minute, Mr. Benton," the guard called. "I've got a package for you."

"For me?"

"Yes. A courier dropped it at the gate. I was going to send it up, but since you're here—"

Brad smiled and accepted the thick envelope. "Thanks."

"Sure. Have a nice day."

Brad studied the envelope as he headed up the walk and toward the entrance of the building. It had no markings, no return address, only his name typed on a label. On impulse, he turned when he entered the building and, instead of going to his office, walked toward the security office in the east wing of the building.

He found the chief of security at his cluttered desk. "Hi, Conner."

The man looked up from the stack of reports he was reading. "Mr. Benton, hi."

"I know you're busy. I'm not going to tie you up."

"It's okay." He waved the report in his direction. "I'm just looking into the initial report about the shooting. For the life of me, I can't figure how somebody could have gotten through Security with that rifle unless it was an inside job. We've been so tight since the disappearances."

"Any theories?"

The chief shook his head. "Not yet. How's Emma?"

"Still in critical condition," Brad said, "but so far she's holding her own."

"I'm glad to hear it. She didn't deserve this."

"Who does?" Brad took the seat across from the desk. "Have we been able to reach her sister yet?"

"I believe the public affairs office is trying to find her, but you know how it is these days. Even if we do have the FBI at our disposal, it's almost impossible to locate anybody."

"I know. Keep me informed, though, will you? Emma's like part of my family. I don't feel right about not talking to her sister myself. I want to call her as soon as she's been officially notified."

"No problem, sir."

"And you don't have any leads on the shooting yet?"

"Nothing. Since you hadn't been threatened or harassed, it might take a while. Could have just been some kook, you know. I was never comfortable with the idea of you driving your own car."

Brad managed a slight smile. "I got that message this morning from Swelder. I'm hiring a driver."

"Good."

"He'll be coming in this afternoon to fill out his security forms."

"His clearance could take a while."

"I don't think so. He's Max Arnold's son."

The chief laughed, the political subtlety obviously not lost on him. "You sure know how to pick 'em, Mr. Benton."

Brad nodded, then handed the chief the package. "I just entered through the east gate. The guard on duty gave me this. Said it was dropped off by courier."

The chief took the envelope and studied it. "You weren't expecting anything?"

"No. I get several reports and briefings a week from various agencies, and some are couriered over. It's not unusual, but given the timing and the circumstances, I thought maybe you'd better check it out."

The chief nodded. "Wise choice. I'll put it through Security, and once it's clear we'll get it right up to you."

"Thanks, Conner." Brad rose to go. "I'll be in my office. I'd appreciate it if you'd let me know when Randal Arnold gets here."

"Sure thing."

★ ★ ★

Crystal City, Virginia
New Covenant Evangelical Ministries
Local Time 10:27 A.M.

"Marcus?" Isack Moore entered Marcus's office with a legal-sized envelope in his hand. "This was just delivered for you."

Marcus glanced up from his Bible. "Thanks." He indicated the chair across from his desk. "I've been so busy the last couple of days, I haven't taken the time to ask you how you're doing, Isack. I'm sorry."

Isack shrugged and dropped into the chair. "It's hard. I finally managed to reach one of my aunts. She's the only family I have left."

"I know you're hurting, Isack. I wish I could tell you something that would ease your pain."

"I know they're in heaven. That's what matters."

"Yes." Marcus considered the younger man for a moment. "What about you?"

"What about me?"

"That first night, we talked about this. Have you come to terms with God, Isack?"

"Have I converted, you mean?"

Marcus stifled a sigh. Isack's tone made it clear that he was no closer to accepting the truth than he had been before. One of the things God was teaching Marcus was how much patience a man had to have when the evangelistic message mattered to him. "I wonder if you've come to terms with God's grace."

The young man's laugh was bitter. "Grace? You call this grace? Marcus, do you even know what it's like out there?" He waved a hand toward the enormous glass windows that overlooked the city. "Have you seen what's going on?"

"Yes," Marcus said, "I know."

Isack shook his head. "Sometimes I think you're so insulated up here in this . . . this . . . ivory tower—"

Marcus accepted the remark without comment.

Isack shifted in his chair and continued, "Before all this, you used to talk about God's judgment and righteous anger, about how God condemns sinners and pours out His wrath on the wicked. Where do you find grace in all that?"

Marcus realized that people like Isack, people who had depended on him for wisdom and leadership, had every right to question him now. He'd allowed his own bitterness with God to taint his message. "No one deserves grace, Isack. That's what makes it grace. God *is* a God of righteousness and purity and holiness. There's no one on earth who can meet His expectations. Only through the blood of Christ can we hope to be clean enough to have fellowship with a holy God."

Isack held up his hands. "I'm sorry, Marcus. I just don't see how you can say that about a God who'd put us all through this."

"God didn't put us through this. We put ourselves through it. If I'd ask one thing of you, it's that you'd try to look past all the ways you saw me fail and see that God is holding out hope to you. He didn't fail you, Isack. I did."

Isack rose to leave. "I'll think about it." He paused. "If you want me to quit my job, I will. I'd understand, if—"

Marcus shook his head. "No. You have a job here as long as you want one."

The organization's entire focus had changed in the last few days. Isack had been instrumental in piecing together whatever shreds of the former leadership still remained. Marcus had been praying about what direction he should take the ministry in now that the Tribulation was upon them. The evangelical message seemed more important than ever, but so did the vast global contacts his organization maintained. Once, he would have pompously stated that he

couldn't have a man working on his staff who didn't espouse the beliefs and mission statement of the organization. Now, however, he
realized that his evangelical message must begin here in his tightest,
most personal circle of influence.

"As long as the money holds out, you mean? We lost most of our
donor base."

"I know that."

"Fund-raising is way down."

"I know that, too."

"You have a plan?" Isack gave him a narrow look. "I mean, a
plan other than 'God will provide'?"

"Yes," Marcus said, having only recently come to terms with the
question himself. He'd struggled with his conscience over this, had
poured out his doubts to his three new prayer partners, and together
they'd come to a consensus. "We spent a lot of years encouraging
our donors to invest in the future by naming us as beneficiaries in
their wills. At the time, I admit, they were giving to us under false
pretenses. They were giving to a ministry they thought was headed
by a man of God. It was their will that their money would support
and continue the work of a ministry they had no idea was a sham. I
was pretending to be someone I'm not."

Isack frowned. "I don't understand."

"I've been considering what I should do about that money now
that so many of our donors are gone. As the beneficiary of their
wills, we stand to receive a significant financial influx as the insurance companies and investment firms settle estate claims from the
disappearances."

"And you're going to keep the money?" Isack sounded incredulous.

"At first I didn't plan to. I felt conflicted about it, knowing that
what we stood for wasn't what they believed. But then some friends
helped me realize that while I may not have been honest when that
money was designated for us, those people left that money because
they wanted us to continue the work of this ministry. That's their
legacy. And I intend to make sure their wishes are honored."

"I see."

Isack's expression remained neutral. Marcus had no idea whether the young man approved or not, but he was at peace with the decision, having accepted Brad's and Mariette's insight that God had provided for their mission through the faithful gifts of His people—seed planters.

"Several lawsuits have already been filed," Marcus explained. "Some insurance companies are claiming that this falls under the 'acts of God' clause and that they won't have to pay out the life insurance policies."

"I can see why. It'll cost millions."

"It will, but I'm confident it'll be resolved. The government will get involved. There are too many people in need of the aid. The economy needs the boost the cash will provide. The administration and Congress won't allow this to linger forever. We'll be fine, Isack. God *will* provide."

"Yeah, sure." He turned to leave. "I was just curious."

"Isack?"

"Yes?"

"I'm always available to you, you know. If there's anything you need—"

"I'm fine," the young man said. "Really, but thanks." He exited the office and shut the large mahogany door.

Marcus prayed that God would give him wisdom and patience to deal with Isack's bitterness and fears, then reached for the legal-sized envelope. It bore only his name, no return address, no other markings. Frowning, he tore it open.

Inside were legal papers from Theopolus Carter. He was representing several families among Marcus's top donors. The heirs were contesting the ministry's right to the bequests, and Theo was using the argument that Marcus had cultivated the donors under false pretenses, misrepresenting himself and his mission. He shook his head and set the papers aside. He'd have to find a new lawyer, he realized, and finding one he could trust was going to be a difficult task in this climate.

He buried his face in his hands and allowed hot tears to flow through his fingers. More and more these days, he found himself overwhelmed by the sadness of the world around him. Once, he'd have thought himself weak for these bursts of emotion, but now he was discovering this same emotional side of the Savior as he poured over the Scriptures with new eyes and a new hunger. Jesus, too, wept over the sorrow around Him. The Savior wept with compassion and empathy when His friends were grieving. He'd cried out His heart to the Father the night of His arrest. Jesus was a man of deep passions.

Marcus no longer felt the need to apologize for tears. Which was just as well. He had many reasons to shed them now.

18

"Hey, Mr. Benton." Randal walked into Brad's office carrying a manila envelope and wearing his temporary badge. He still felt a bit overwhelmed by all this—this sudden kinship with men like Brad Benton and Marcus Dumont, men who seemed so much larger than life. He felt he'd grown more and learned more in the last few days than in the previous twenty years of his life. "I'm approved."

Brad looked up from his desk and smiled at Randal. "That didn't take long."

"I guess there are some benefits to being Max Arnold's kid." Randal handed him the manila envelope. "The guy in Security sent this to you. Said it checked out fine."

Brad indicated the two chairs in front of his desk. "Sit, sit. I'm glad you could come today. I wasn't relishing the thought of a driver out of the pool."

"Yeah, Mom and I talked about that." Randal dropped into one of the chairs. "She's nervous about the sniper thing."

"I can imagine." Brad got up and took the other chair, crossing his long legs in front of him. He placed the envelope on his desk. "She'll be okay with this, right?"

"Sure." Randal fiddled with his tie. "She figures you'll look out for me."

"I was kind of thinking it would be the other way around," Brad said.

"I guess I am younger and quicker," Randal said.

"Younger, anyway," Brad told him.

Randal laughed and glanced around the office. He hoped he didn't look as impressed as he felt by the whole situation. The only adult male role model he'd had for most of his life had been his father—not exactly the sort of man Randal wanted to pattern his life after. The more he got to know Brad and Marcus, the more he saw how distorted his view of the world had really been. "You know, I gotta tell you, I kind of figured you'd have nicer digs than this. I mean, I think my dad's office is maybe twice this size."

"Your dad is one of the highest ranking members of the U.S. Senate. I, on the other hand, am low man on the totem pole here."

"Well, I just want you to know I really appreciate this. It's a great opportunity . . . I mean, for what we're trying to do and all."

"Yes." Brad studied him a moment. "Your mom says you decided not to go back to college."

"Not right now, anyway. If Reverend Dumont is right and we only have seven years to go on earth, college seems kind of pointless, don't you think?"

"Randal—"

"I mean, I'd rather spend the time learning everything I can about the Bible, not about some professor's analysis of the global implications of midterm elections." He and his mom had discussed that decision yesterday over breakfast. She wasn't entirely comfortable with it, but she was coming around. "I told Mom I might consider taking some classes at George Washington . . . later. It just depends on how things go."

"Fair enough," Brad conceded.

"I didn't see any point in making a hasty decision. Classes were canceled till the end of the semester anyway. I don't know what Penn State's going to do about credits, but I'm guessing they'll just credit everyone with whatever hours they were taking, and let that be it." He shrugged. "That means I'll have all summer to decide what to do."

"Just promise me you won't rule anything out until you've spoken to your mother. Or me . . ."

"Sure." Randal gave him a lopsided grin. "I figure that, as bad as traffic is around here, I'll have all the time in the world to bend your ear."

"I'll enjoy that," Brad assured him. "The commute was beginning to feel a little lonely."

"So are you going to show me around? I've never seen the Oval Office."

Brad reached for the envelope on his desk. "Sure. Just let me check this first. Oh, and there's something else your mother and I talked about." Brad tore open the seal and pulled the contents from the envelope. He started flipping through what appeared to be a stack of black-and-white photographs. Randal couldn't make out the images from his vantage point. "Your father—"

Randal interrupted him. "I'm not sure I like this arrangement with you and Mom being friends and all. It's kind of like having your fourth-grade teacher date your dad. . . ." From Brad's expression, Randal sensed he had misspoken. Perhaps the comment reminded Brad too much of his wife and had opened a fresh wound. The way Brad spoke about his wife was another dynamic Randal was adjusting to. He never remembered either of his parents speaking about each other in those same warm tones Brad used when he discussed Christine. "I'm sorry. I didn't mean that the way it came out."

Brad shook his head and took a shuddering breath. He slid the contents back into the envelope. "No. No, sorry."

Randal frowned. "Then it was those pictures, wasn't it? You're upset."

Brad closed his eyes. "Those questions I told you all the other night that I'd been asking—"

"The ones you think may have made you a target in the parking garage?"

"Yes." Brad opened his eyes again. "I just received some of the answers."

"Oh." Randal sat quietly, wondering what he should do.

Finally, Brad rose and rounded his desk to fetch a padded envelope from one of the drawers. He dropped the manila envelope into it and sealed it. Grabbing his pen from the desk set, he scrawled a name on it, then looked at Randal. "I feel I need to discuss this with Marcus, but I promise I'll fill you and your mother in after Marcus and I have consulted."

"Sure. Okay."

Brad tucked the envelope under his arm. "Come on. I'll show you the Oval Office."

On their way out the door, Brad handed the envelope to his new temporary assistant and asked her to send it overnight to Liza Cannley at the *Los Angeles Times*. "Her address is in my index," he told the young woman from the clerical pool.

"Sure thing, Mr. Benton." The girl glanced at Randal with a shy smile. "Good luck," she told Randal.

"Thanks." Randal fell into step behind his new employer and friend and sent up a silent prayer that whatever had been in that envelope would not reach them with its evil. He was certain that's what it was . . . something evil. Brad wouldn't have reacted as he had otherwise. Randal suddenly realized that driving Brad around wasn't really the job God had chosen for him. Watching Brad's back and praying for his safety were his tasks. He shouldered them both willingly and eagerly.

★   ★   ★

Washington, D.C.
Rock Creek Park
Local Time 6:15 A.M.

"You didn't make Randal get up this early and drive you here, did you?" Marcus asked.

Brad fell into step with him as they began their daily run. "No way. I drove the car in and parked it on Calvert. Randal's meeting me there after you and I are done jogging. He'll take me to the office."

"Wise choice. I can't see a college student appreciating hours like this."

"When my son went to college, my wife and I used to swear he'd come home and sleep twenty-three hours a day."

Marcus laughed. "I don't remember having Randal's energy level even when I was twenty years old."

"Me either."

"He came by yesterday afternoon looking for some reading material."

"The boy's got a lot of questions, and I told him he'd probably have a lot of time on his hands while he waited for me. I'm glad he stopped by."

"Me, too. Any word on Emma?"

"I stopped by the hospital last night. They think she improved some. She looked a bit better to me."

"Praise God."

Brad nodded. "I'm going by to see her on my way to the office. I hope she'll be awake."

"I do, too. I know it'll take a load off your mind when she regains consciousness."

"I feel like this is all my fault somehow." Brad frowned. "And I'm worried that we haven't been able to reach her sister yet. I'd really like to talk to her."

"You have no idea where she might be?"

"No, she might have been raptured, but Emma didn't mention her disappearance. She could have gone on a trip and Emma might not have told me. We were close, but it was one of those relationships where she knew a lot about my family, and I didn't know much about hers."

"Maybe that'll change now."

"You bet it will. I'm through being only casually involved in the lives of the people I care about. I've lost one family already. I'm not going to lose another."

"So, you want to tell me about the envelope?"

"Randal told you," Brad guessed.

"Yes. He was concerned. He said you were upset."

They ran in silence for several moments. When they reached a bend in the path, Brad checked over his shoulder before looking at Marcus again. "The envelope held photographs." He brought Marcus up to speed about his suspicions about George Ramiro's fate and Liza Cannley's investigation into George's disappearance. "As far as I know, no one but Liza knows I suspect anything. I haven't discussed it with anyone else."

Marcus nodded, thoughtful. "And you think the questions Liza's been asking may have raised enough suspicion that someone knows you're inquiring?"

"I wasn't sure until yesterday. The sniper—" he paused—"it wasn't necessarily related."

"But the pictures," Marcus guessed. "They had something to do with this?"

Brad dropped his voice so low Marcus had to strain to hear him. "They were pictures of George's body. He was dead . . . at least, he looked dead to me. He had been shot in the head."

"Brad. Oh my . . ."

Brad nodded. "Someone killed George, but I don't know why. Whoever killed him knows I didn't buy the story of his resignation and that I'm looking for answers."

"Was there anything in the envelope besides the pictures?"

"Only a blank sheet of paper as a cover sheet."

"So you don't know if the person who sent them wanted to warn you about digging further or to assist you with information."

"Right. The envelope was unmarked."

"Did anyone else have access to the envelope?"

"Security," Brad told him. "At the gate and in the security office. Since it was unmarked, I had them inspect it for me." He glanced at Marcus. "But it was sealed when Randal delivered it. I don't think anyone opened it."

"I see."

"I promised Randal I'd tell him what this was all about after I had a chance to confer with you about it."

Marcus considered that. Randal would be the closest one to Brad over the next few months. For Randal's protection—and for Brad's—it seemed imperative that the young man be informed of the potential threat. "I think you have to tell him what you saw. He needs to know what's going on if he's going to be around you."

"That's what I thought," Brad said, "but I wanted your perspective first."

Marcus looked down the path. They were nearing the bench where he and Brad had stopped on their first run and he'd shared the gospel with his new friend. He would always consider the spot holy ground, a place where one day he planned to place an Ebenezer, a marker, as a reminder that there they'd experienced the awesome and overwhelming grace of God. Lately they didn't stop there on their runs but continued on to the footbridge, then doubled back to Calvert Street. Today, Marcus needed the comfort of the bench. "I think we should stop and pray," he told Brad. "A little guidance would be very welcome about now."

Brad nodded and headed for the bench, evidently recognizing its unique place in their spiritual journey. He, too, seemed to consider it a tabernacle.

And they both needed the comfort of prayer.

19

Washington, D.C.
George Washington Hospital
Local Time 7:35 A.M.

Brad slipped quietly into Emma's room. Though she was still hooked up to a myriad of monitors and tubes, the nurse at the duty station had assured him this morning that she had made some improvements during the night. According to the nurse, she'd even been awake—off and on at least. Though still weak from the trauma and loss of blood, she appeared to be stabilizing. The nurses were betting that Emma would make it.

Brad felt a rush of relief. On his way to the hospital, his temporary assistant had called to tell him the public affairs office had finally managed to reach Emma's sister. She'd been on her way via train to pay her sister a surprise visit in Washington. The disappearances had given her a deep longing to reconnect with Emma.

Brad hastened to the side of Emma's bed, where he lifted her hand. "I've got good news, Emma. Can you hear me?"

Emma's eyes drifted open slowly. He waited while she tried to focus on his face. The oxygen mask still pressed to her mouth kept her from responding, so Brad placed one hand on her shoulder. "Don't try to talk," he told her, pulling a chair close to the bed and sitting down. "Just listen. I spoke to your sister, Pearl, today. I've been trying to reach her since this happened to let her know what was going on."

Emma's forehead creased.

"I know," Brad said. "I was worried, too, that she wasn't answering her phone or returning messages. But we found her. She's actually on her way here to see you. She should get here late this afternoon."

Emma's body seemed to relax. Brad smiled at her. "The nurse tells me you're doing better. I'm glad. I'm so sorry this happened to you."

At her questioning look, he shook his head. "No, we don't have any leads yet on who did it. But the Secret Service is digging. Don't worry. You're in good hands here." Her frown deepened and Brad laughed. "Don't worry about me either. I can take care of myself. You'll be happy to know they hired me a driver. I'm going to be wrapped up in cotton until the Secret Service figures this one out."

That appeared to satisfy her. Brad scooted his chair a bit closer and leaned toward her. "Emma, I know you're tired, and this can wait if you don't want to hear it, but the other night, when you asked me about my faith in Jesus—"

This time, it was her fingers that tightened. Her gaze went urgently to his, so Brad quieted her by holding her hand in both of his. "It's okay. I've been asking God for two days to give me one more chance to talk to you about this. Just relax and let me tell you what I know."

Brad propped his feet on the metal railing under the bed and began to relate what he supposed would be called his personal testimony. He'd heard that term bandied about before but had never really paid much attention to what it meant, but now, telling someone he cared about who Jesus was, and more importantly, about the miracle Jesus had worked in his life, came as naturally as breathing. Brad poured out his heart, explaining his years of doubt, his rebellion against his mother's beliefs, his pride, his rejection of Christine's consistent witness, and the way God had moved over him in the park when Marcus had told him that salvation was a step away.

"I've been saved now. Emma, all you have to do is recognize your need for the Lord and ask Him to save you, too. Jesus takes it from there."

She searched his face for long seconds.

Brad went on, "I'm not saying it's easy, or that it doesn't cost you anything. If Marcus is to be believed, and I think he is, then the next few years are going to bring all kinds of horrors. Those of us who decide now to accept the Lord are facing everything from persecution to possible martyrdom. But I can't imagine facing any of that without the Lord in my life. Surrendering control to Him set me free, Emma."

He leaned forward and placed his hand on her shoulder again. "You've known me a long time—and you know it's really not like me to talk about something like this—but I wouldn't be half the man Christine believed me to be or half the man God wants me to be if I let another second slip by without telling you that I pray every day that you'll meet Jesus and accept Him." He studied her for a moment. "Christine and the kids are going to want to see you in heaven. And so am I."

Emma held his gaze a few seconds longer; then her eyes drifted slowly shut. Brad saw a peaceful look settle on her face that gave him hope. He tucked her hand back beneath the covers and told her to get some rest. He prayed over her, thanking God for sparing his friend and asking for her continued recovery, then slipped from the room.

That was one less worry on his mind.

But he knew he had a whole new load of worries arriving.

Today was going to be a watershed day in his life. Today was the day Nicolae Carpathia planned to announce his strategy for the UN. Today Carpathia and his allies would begin forming ironclad allegiances to further their agenda.

Brad had no idea how the Fitzhugh administration would receive the Romanian's radical ideas, but he had a feeling that his own position at the White House was about to take a sharp and irrevocable turn. Today was the day he would begin to prove that he could stand for God's truth and God's will in the face of hostility and potentially lethal consequences.

Today was the day he finally began to keep his promises.

★　★　★

Crystal City, Virginia
New Covenant Evangelical Ministries
Local Time 10:14 A.M.

Brad and Randal rode the elevator up to Marcus's suite of offices. The news had broken early about the UN's invitation to Carpathia to serve as secretary-general and about Carpathia's bizarre and far-reaching demands for unilateral disarmament, relocation of the UN headquarters, and a new, permanent Security Council he would handpick. Even stranger was the General Assembly's shocking but unanimous consent to his demands. A week ago, Brad wouldn't have believed it could happen. The White House was scrambling to formulate new policy language and get a handle on the rapidly developing situation.

Marcus had phoned Brad while he was on his way to his office from the hospital and asked Brad to meet him at the ministry's office to watch Carpathia's press conference. Randal had been waiting for him when he finished at the White House, so the two men had made their way across town and over Roosevelt Bridge to the Crystal City office complex.

Randal, Brad knew, was very familiar with Marcus's office suite by now. With his rapacious appetite for knowledge of the Bible, he had browsed through and selected reference books on end-times prophecies from Marcus's private library.

Brad was finding Randal to be exceptionally astute for his age, and he thoroughly enjoyed the times he could talk to the young man about all that he was learning. Randal's energy and his black-and-white way of seeing the world reminded Brad of his own son. Brad had told Mariette on the phone yesterday that he felt he and Randal were developing a keen rapport.

At Mariette's request, Brad was encouraging Randal to make peace with his father, but thus far the young man had refused. Brad expected Randal to budge soon. The kid was already showing signs of caving on the issue, but he just wasn't ready to let go of the anger he'd harbored for so long. Only God could convince him to do that.

Brad glanced at him now as they rode the elevator. "I talked to your mother yesterday. She seems swamped."

"Pretty much. Musselman is more or less useless, so if anything gets done around there, it's because Mom makes it happen." Randal pulled on his tie. "She's kind of worried about her assistant, though."

"David Liu?" Mariette had requested prayer for David several times in their recent conversations.

"Yeah. She says he's sort of coming apart at the seams. I just wish . . ."

"He'd listen to her about Christ?"

"Yeah." He glanced at Brad. "That's the hardest part, you know, waiting for people to come around."

Brad nodded solemnly. "My son used to say that. I don't think I really understood what he meant until Emma was shot."

"How is she?" Randal asked. "I forgot to ask you this morning."

"Doing better. Physically and spiritually. I was able to talk to her for a long time this morning. I think she was receptive."

"Praise God."

Brad nodded. "I'm not sure I could have ever forgiven myself for missing the opportunity to talk to her the other day if it had been my last chance."

"You know what Marcus says," Randal pointed out. "That's in God's hands."

"Just like David Liu."

Randal said, "Yeah, I know. But the thing that's really bugging me is that I can't get Mom to understand why I feel I should just go to her office and talk to him. He's closer to my age than hers. I think he'd listen to me."

"Then we'll pray that God will give you the opportunity."

"Sometimes I think Mom has trouble remembering I'm twenty and not twelve."

"That's perfectly natural." Brad thought of his own mother and the way she used to fuss over him. "She always will. It's not all bad."

Randal shot him a teasing glance. "Granted, at least I still get cookies out of the deal."

The elevator continued to quietly ring at each floor. "Then bring some to work, will you? I haven't had homemade cookies since—" Brad stopped, a sudden image of the green glass bowl on his kitchen counter surging up to haunt him. He rubbed the tears out of his eyes.

Randal's expression turned serious. "I'm sorry. I didn't mean to hit a nerve."

Brad shook his head. "It's okay. It hurts to remember my family, but I'd rather hurt than forget how important they were to me."

"I understand." The elevator stopped at their floor, and the doors slid open.

Brad and Randal walked down the hall in silence to Marcus's suite. They found him in his office, one hip propped against his desk, watching the television.

"Marcus," Brad greeted him and looked swiftly at his watch. He didn't think they were late. "It hasn't started yet, has it?"

Marcus indicated the TV with a wave of the remote. "Not yet. Have you heard about this?"

"What?" Randal hurried across the room. "What's going on?"

"It's Israel," Marcus said. He glanced at Brad. "Interesting development."

Marcus had the set tuned to CNN. Dan Bennett, one of the network's prominent journalists, was reporting live from Jerusalem. Evidently, the two witnesses who had appeared at the Wailing Wall just after the Rapture were now at the center of a shocking conflict.

Brad watched the report with a growing feeling of dread. "It was an ugly and dangerous confrontation for what many here are calling the two heretical prophets, known only as Moishe and Eli," Bennett said. "We know these names only because they have referred to each other thus, but we have been unable to locate anyone who knows any more about them. We know of no last names, no cities of origin, no families or friends. They have been taking turns speaking—

preaching, if you will—for hours and continuing to claim that Jesus Christ is the Messiah. They have proclaimed over and over that the great worldwide disappearances last week, including many here in Israel, evidenced Christ's rapture of his church."

Brad looked at Marcus. "This is the prophecy, isn't it?"

Marcus nodded. "Two witnesses. Two prophets. It's exactly what the Bible states."

On the television, Bennett continued. "Surrounded by zealots most of the day, the preachers were finally attacked just moments ago by two men in their midtwenties. Watch the tape as our cameras caught the action. You can see the two at the back of the crowd, working their way to the front. Both are wearing long, hooded robes and are bearded. You can see that they produce weapons as they emerge from the crowd.

"One has an Uzi automatic weapon and the other a bayonet-type knife that appears to have come from an Israeli-issue military rifle. The one wielding the knife surges forward first, displaying his weapon to Moishe, who had been speaking. Eli, behind him, immediately falls to his knees, his face toward the sky. Moishe stops speaking and merely looks at the man, who appears to trip. He sprawls while the man with the Uzi points the weapon at the preachers and appears to pull the trigger.

"There is no sound of gunfire as the Uzi apparently jams, and the attacker seems to trip over his partner and both wind up on the ground. The group of onlookers has backed away and run for cover, but watch again closely as we rerun this. The one with the gun seems to fall of his own accord.

"As we speak, both attackers lie at the feet of the preachers, who continue to preach. Angry onlookers demand help for the attackers, and Moishe is speaking in Hebrew. Let's listen and we'll translate as we go.

"Moishe is speaking again: 'Carry off your dead, but do not come nigh to us, says the Lord God of Hosts!' This he has said with such volume and authority that the soldiers quickly have checked pulses and carried off the men. We will report any word we receive on the two who attempted to attack the preachers here at the Wailing Wall in Jerusalem. At this moment, the preachers have continued their shouting, proclaiming, 'Jesus of Nazareth, born in Bethlehem, King of the Jews, the chosen one, ruler of all nations.'"

Randal let out a low whistle.

Marcus switched off the television. "The eleventh chapter of Revelation. That's exactly what it predicts."

"I know," Randal said. "I caught your sermon last Sunday."

"You know what this means?" Marcus probed. He looked at Brad. "You realize what's happening?"

"Not entirely, but so far you've been dead-on."

"I knew the events of the Tribulation were coming. We all knew. But I didn't know how long—" He broke off. "I wasn't certain we'd have to face everything so soon."

"It's here," Randal said. "And we're right in the middle of it."

"Yes," Marcus agreed. "This is another sign that everything the Bible predicts is coming our way even faster than I imagined. If Carpathia's next step is to announce UN protection for Israel, we'll know for sure that the clock of the Tribulation has started ticking."

"I think so, too," Brad said. "That's one of the reasons I'm interested in watching Carpathia's announcement today. There's a lot of speculation about whether or not he'll release the names of his new permanent council."

"The delegates are already arriving in New York," Randal said.

"We know some of the players but not all of them," Brad told them.

Randal glanced at Marcus. "I told Brad yesterday that I was talking to one of the other White House drivers. He drives the Pentagon brass a lot. According to them, the president is scrambling to discredit the guy Carpathia picked from the U.S."

Brad had told Marcus that Carpathia, upon the acceptance of his demands by the UN, had moved quickly to appoint his own so-called permanent Security Council. Carpathia was scheduled to meet with the nominees before his official acceptance of his new position as secretary-general. Gerald Fitzhugh and Charley Swelder, still chafing over Carpathia's refusal to fly to Washington, had been furious when Carpathia had flatly rejected their nominee for the new permanent council of the UN.

"I'm not surprised," Marcus said. "I'm sure President Fitzhugh isn't thrilled with the idea that one of his political adversaries is about to hold a permanent seat on Carpathia's Security Council."

Brad shook his head. "He's not. Swelder and Tetherton are lobbying hard to get Carpathia to change his mind, but I don't think he will." He looked at the clock on the wall. "We should know what's going on when he holds his press conference."

"We've got thirty minutes," Randal said. "I think we ought to pray."

"I think that's an excellent idea," Marcus said. He motioned to the side door of his office. Randal and Brad both knew from previous visits that a small prayer chapel was located there. "I've used this chapel more in the past week than in the entire nine years I've occupied the office suite. But I never needed it like we do today."

They bowed their heads.

★ ★ ★

Washington, D.C.
The White House
Local Time 10:05 A.M.

So Carpathia had done it.

Brad began to experience the same clawing feeling he'd first felt that morning in the park, that presence-of-evil feeling, and he was not surprised. This morning on their run he and Marcus had discussed how it was going to feel to watch Nicolae Carpathia being installed as the new secretary-general of the UN. Brad had learned yesterday afternoon that Fitzhugh had finally agreed to Carpathia's terms and had no intention of blocking or objecting to his installation.

The tensest moment of yesterday afternoon had come when Fitzhugh had offered to travel to New York for the ceremony.

Carpathia had declined. He didn't feel the president was an appropriate witness. Carpathia had then announced that he'd already chosen the man from the U.S. he intended to install to his new, permanent Security Council.

The president had not been at all pleased with Carpathia's choice, an up-and-coming senator from Connecticut from a politically powerful family who had publicly criticized the Fitzhugh administration in the past. Still, realizing that the world's apparent love affair with Carpathia made it politically unwise to challenge him at the moment, the president had not pushed the issue. Though he'd fumed loudly enough about it in the privacy of the White House. Brad had listened to Fitzhugh for hours.

Instead, the president had demanded a satellite link to Carpathia's meeting with the Security Council. The meeting was to precede the official press conference announcing the new members of the UN inner circle. Brad had spent most of his afternoon and evening negotiating with Carpathia's people to make the satellite feed possible.

At first, they'd soundly rejected the idea, but after several hours of negotiations, they had finally agreed that as long as they were enjoying U.S. hospitality and visiting the UN on American soil, they needed to give a little. The entire cabinet, the Joint Chiefs of Staff, the national security advisor, and the inner circle White House staff were now present to watch Carpathia's first meeting with his newly assembled advisors.

Brad's palms had been damp and his pulse erratic from the moment he'd walked into the room and seen the picture from the satellite feed. Carpathia looked supremely confident, competent, humble, and harmless. It was difficult to picture him as a prince of evil, but Brad now knew better than to trust that surface image. Brad's head had started to throb as he took his seat at the long table.

The group in the White House conference room indulged in idle chatter while they waited for the meeting to begin. Charley Swelder abruptly commanded their attention by seizing the remote control. "All right, people, here we go."

Everyone took their seats and watched as Carpathia rose to begin introducing the members of his council to one another and to lay out his plan for the future. The only concession Carpathia's people had been willing to make about the satellite feed was that it consisted of one camera positioned at the back of the room, focused only on Carpathia. Brad and the other members of the cabinet and White House staff were not able to see the council members as Carpathia introduced them.

One by one, Carpathia went around the table and named each man. Several members of the White House staff exchanged curious looks when he apparently and uncharacteristically misspoke and introduced two men as the single British representative. One was Carpathia's longtime friend and former head of the London Exchange, Joshua Todd-Cothran, and the other was a lesser-known member of Parliament.

Brad began to feel the presence of evil acutely as he watched the events unfolding before him. The international financier Jonathan Stonagal, one of Carpathia's most ardent and well-known supporters, was also present in the meeting. Though Brad couldn't see the multibillionaire when Carpathia introduced him, there was something in the way the secretary-general looked at the other man that made Brad shudder. He glanced around at the other occupants of the White House conference room, but though everyone seemed attentive to the broadcast, no one looked distressed or particularly concerned. Brad, on the other hand, was gripping the arms of his chair so tightly his wrists had begun to ache. He had an inexplicable and unshakable feeling that something disastrous was about to happen.

Brad was on the verge of coming out of his seat to demand why no one else in the room seemed to notice that things weren't right, when a flurry of activity on the screen had the White House audience gasping in horror. Carpathia had summoned a security guard to his side, asked him for his weapon, and then turned the weapon on Stonagal and Todd-Cothran. He forced one man to kneel in front of the other, calmly instructed his assistant to move back from the scene, and fired a single shot through one man's brain and into the other's heart.

An unnatural silence gripped the occupants of the White House conference room. Brad felt his heartbeat accelerate. He prayed for help. The overwhelming presence of evil in the room frightened him. He felt it closing in on him, pressing down on him like the weight of the world, and he fervently prayed for courage. "'Be strong and courageous,'" Marcus had quoted to him that morning from the book of Joshua. Brad repeated it now like a mantra.

Carpathia turned and faced the camera. His face registered no emotion, no reflection of the horror that he had just brought about. In a gentle voice that seemed intent on lulling his listeners into security, he began to explain that he was sorry they had all witnessed this horrible tragedy.

"What compelled Mr. Stonagal to rush the guard, disarm him, take his own life and that of his British colleague, I do not know and may never fully understand," Nicolae said. He had no idea, he continued, that his good friend Jonathan Stonagal was suicidal. He had no idea that the man could turn violent. He claimed to be badly shaken by the incident and slowly went around the room asking each person what he had seen.

Through the satellite broadcast, the assembled members of the White House staff and cabinet heard person after person attest that Carpathia's account was correct: Stonagal had overpowered the security guard, seized his weapon, murdered Joshua Todd-Cothran, and then killed himself. Though they'd witnessed the murder firsthand, Nicolae Carpathia had somehow managed to erase it from their memories.

Brad scanned his colleagues' faces. He was stunned to realize that they, too, seemed to be buying into the story. The cabinet members, the president's top advisors, the joint chiefs, and the other occupants were all nodding at Carpathia's words.

Only one person present among the new UN ambassadors failed to answer Carpathia's questions, a reporter from *Global Weekly*. Brad recognized the man's name. He'd done a favorable piece on

Fitzhugh a year or so before. For reasons Brad could not understand, Carpathia took the reporter's nonresponse as affirmation and moved on.

Dear God, Brad prayed, *what am I supposed to do? What am I going to do?*

As the Romanian president finished expressing his grief over the loss of his two friends, the satellite feed went dark.

Charley Swelder switched off the large TV and turned to the assembled staff. "Well," he said blandly, "that's it, I guess. He'll be officially installed in a few hours. Looks like we're stuck with Carpathia's nominee. Anybody got any questions?"

Secretary of Defense Ed Leyton tapped his fountain pen on his notepad. "I don't suppose this is going to affect us much. The UN has never had a serious influence on our policy decisions."

"If we get too irritated with him," said General Marsden of the joint chiefs, "we'll just kick 'em out of New York. He seems to want to leave anyway."

That won a collective laugh as people began gathering their belongings. President Fitzhugh gave the group a look. "All right, team. Enough lazing around. Let's get back to work."

Dear God, what just happened?

Brad sat for minutes after the room had cleared, trying to regain his equilibrium. His knees felt too weak to stand, and his head pounded. His pulse rate slowly returned to normal. Could it be that he was the only person in this room who actually remembered what they'd all witnessed? Was Carpathia's power so immense that he was able to brainwash not only a roomful of people in New York, but even the eyewitnesses on the other end of a satellite feed?

The idea had Brad shuddering as he reached for his personal cell phone. He felt soiled, tainted, by what he had just experienced. The concept of Carpathia's enormous power frightened and appalled him, and he desperately needed his brothers and sisters in Christ to help him gain perspective.

Marcus picked up on the other end. "How did it go?" he asked.

"You'll never believe it," Brad said. "Can I meet you in a half hour?"

★   ★   ★

Alexandria, Virginia
Local Time 11:55 P.M.

Bone-tired, Brad got out of the car, double-checked the locks on the White House government-issue sedan, and headed for his apartment.

After the shocking events of the morning, Randal had driven Brad to Marcus's Crystal City offices. Together, the three men had waited, prayed, and fellowshipped until Mariette had been able to join them shortly after three that afternoon. Brad had relayed his story about Carpathia's brutal murder of Stonagal and Todd-Cothran to the other three members of his small inner circle. They had discussed the incident, then spent the rest of the afternoon and evening in prayer and Bible study.

Brad, at least, had needed the cleansing power of God's Word desperately.

Brad was grateful that his friends had so readily realized he needed a break before he could fully process what he'd seen that day. No one had pressed him for details after he'd told them what he'd witnessed.

The conversation had not turned back to Carpathia until after dinner, when Mariette had asked Marcus if Brad might be in any danger because of his knowledge of what had happened in Carpathia's council meeting.

"I don't know," Marcus had said. "It seems possible."

Randal agreed. "If Nicolae Carpathia is powerful enough to erase the memories of all the people in that room and all the people at the White House, then it stands to reason that he probably knows if someone's not fooled. He has to be aware of it any other way."

Mariette frowned. "But why was Brad spared?"

"Spiritual warfare," Brad had said, shocked at how easily the explanation had come to him. The few times in the past he'd heard the phrase, he'd silently mocked it as the ranting of the religious fringe. "I felt the presence of evil in that room. God armored me against it. I can't explain it."

"I can," Randal said. He'd glanced at his mom. "I didn't tell you this before because I didn't want to scare you, but one of the reasons I was in such a hurry to get out of State College the night of the Rapture was because there was something going on that weirded me out. I told you I felt God telling me to pick Gram's Bible up and read it." He looked earnestly at the three adults. "What I didn't tell you was that I felt this presence, like a ghost or something, in the room trying to prevent me from doing it. The more I tried to read, the more invasive it got. Finally, I was just so freaked I knew I had to get out of there."

"Randal." Mariette laid her hand on his arm. "Honey—"

"I experienced the same thing," Brad said, casting a look at Marcus. "You remember. That day in the park."

Marcus had nodded, then grabbed the Bible on his desk. "I told you then, Brad, that I believed you were under attack from the forces of darkness. It makes sense that when God gathered His faithful from the earth, the demons gained more freedom to perpetrate their deception and lies. I believe there will continue to be times that as Christians we know we are in the presence of evil."

"How are we supposed to combat that?" Randal had asked. The young man was so like Brad Jr., always ready for a fight, always zealous and devout to what he believed.

Marcus had opened his Bible. "In one of his letters to the Corinthians, Paul says, 'You cannot drink from the cup of the Lord and from the cup of demons, too. You cannot eat at the Lord's Table and at the table of demons, too.' I believe that even though Paul's intent in the letter was to chasten the Corinthians to put aside their old practice of demon worship, we can apply this passage another way as well."

"I see," Mariette said. "If we dwell on the things of God and in the way of God, then the demons will have no power over us."

Randal looked at the minister. "You think that's it, Marcus?"

Marcus set the Bible aside and looked at the small group. "I do not think the Bible promises us that we won't face persecution or possible harm, but it does say that we do not have to fall victim to the forces of Satan. I believe that's what happened to you today, Brad. You were dwelling in the Lord. We'd had prayer that morning."

"And we prayed together after his visit with Emma," Randal chimed in.

Marcus added, "I think that your awareness of and communion with the Lord are what protected you from what happened today."

Exhausted, Brad had let out a long sigh. "I believe you're right. I also believe life is only going to get more difficult from here."

The four friends were convinced that the events of the Tribulation had truly begun, and they all agreed that they needed each other's prayers and support as they planned for whatever lay ahead.

So their conversation had lasted into the night, and by the time they'd finally separated a few minutes ago, Brad encouraged Randal to go home with his mom. Brad drove the car to his apartment, which was just a few miles from Marcus's offices. Before he left, he told Randal not to bother coming into work the next day until he rode into the city with his mom. Brad would meet Marcus to run in the morning, then drive the government car to the White House. It wasn't what Charley Swelder had intended, but Brad figured that no one would ever know.

Brad trudged up the stairs to his apartment, his coat slung over his shoulder, feeling weary and worn. It was hard to believe that not even a week had passed since the events that had irrevocably changed his life and his world. With the horror of today still so fresh in his mind, he sorely wished he could call Christine tonight. She had a way of always making him see things in a new light. She'd always comforted him, encouraged him, helped him face the challenges that lay ahead.

He was glad now that he'd been to California and picked up a few personal items. Tonight the loneliness of his apartment seemed intolerable. At least he would have the pictures and books and the precious copy of Christine's Bible with its notes and references to ward off the chill in his soul.

Brad unlocked the door of the first-floor apartment he had rented in a colonial brownstone. He hadn't been spending much time here lately. He'd chosen the place for its proximity to the White House, but Christine had liked its charm.

He'd never been so grateful for all the ways she had sought to take care of him. "Thank you, Lord," he whispered as he turned the key in the dead bolt, "for giving me such a wonderful partner."

He found hope in the knowledge that he would see her again. Christ was with him, and one day he would join her in heaven. Brad fumbled with his keys until he found the knob key. He turned the lock. Just as he began to push the door open, he realized he had not fetched the mail. He almost decided to wait until morning, but then he remembered that his daughter Megan had told him when he spoke with her the evening before the Rapture that she'd mailed him a letter. Brad had been looking for it eagerly, but the mail, as with most other services, was still recovering. Things were slow.

He couldn't resist the urge to check the mailbox in case Megan's letter awaited him.

Brad pushed open the door a bit with his foot and set his briefcase down to keep it open, then ran down the front steps to the mailbox. He was pulling open the cast-iron door of the box when an earthshaking explosion nearly sent him flying.

He felt the heat at his back before he saw it. Reflected in the windows of the car, he saw the ball of fire that now engulfed his building. Immediately, lights popped on in the adjacent houses. Neighbors came running. Brad stared at the flames consuming his apartment with a strange sense of dread.

"Somebody call 911," a man called as he raced to join Brad on the sidewalk. "Hey, buddy. You okay?"

Brad didn't respond. He simply stared at the fire and replayed in his mind the sight he'd witnessed on the satellite feed today. Marcus had told him he might still be in danger. If Carpathia was powerful enough to brainwash all his witnesses, he could easily be aware that Brad had not been fooled.

Was that why this had happened? Or did it have something to do with those telling pictures of George Ramiro he'd received and forwarded to Liza? Or was Fitzhugh doing a little housecleaning, starting with his least favorite employee? Somebody wanted him dead—and his enemies were too numerous to even guess who it was. The possibilities made his head spin.

The man shook his arm. "Buddy, you all right? You hurt?"

Brad took a deep breath and managed to shake his head. "No. I'm fine. Fine."

"You live here?" the man asked.

Brad looked at the man for the first time and realized that he had not seen him before. With the hours he kept and the demands of his job and his travel schedule, he'd had little time to acquaint himself with the neighbors. Except for the woman who lived in the next-door apartment whom he sometimes saw walking her dog, Brad realized that he knew none of his other neighbors well enough to speak to. But he at least knew most of them by sight.

Had any of those unknown people died simply because he lived near them?

He heard the wail of a siren in the distance, drowning out the shouts of people and barking of dogs startled by the explosion. Brad looked closely at the stranger. "No," he said. "No, I don't live here. I was visiting someone."

The man nodded, apparently satisfied. "Well, we're going to have to clear the street." A fire truck turned down the street and headed for the inferno. Neighbors were pouring out of the doors to observe the chaos. "You'll need to leave. Head out that way." A bulge that looked suspiciously like a gun in a shoulder harness strained against the man's jacket as he pointed down the street.

"I understand," Brad told the man. He thrust the handful of mail into his jacket pocket and turned to head up the street, now convinced that the sniper's bullet that had nearly claimed Emma's life had been meant for him. Whoever wanted him dead had just stepped up their efforts.

There must have been a bomb in his apartment. His opening the door must have started the timer. His trip to the mailbox and divine intervention had been all that had saved his life. Suddenly, as the shock of the explosion ebbed and reason began to return, Brad had a horrible realization. He stopped in his tracks and turned to watch the inferno. Somewhere in that blaze were the items he'd brought with him from California. His family's clothes. His wife's wedding ring. Christine's Bible.

Brad choked as a wave of anger washed over him. *How dare they?* he thought bitterly. How dare anyone take that from him? There was nothing else in there he cared a whit about, but losing those . . . he contemplated going back. There was a chance that the clothes and other things had survived since they were in the back bedroom. He scanned the burning building trying to figure out how far into the apartment the fire had burned, but he couldn't tell from his vantage point on the street.

Christine's Bible had been in his briefcase. The case was White House issue, so it was both fire- and waterproof. Surely that would have survived. If he'd lost everything else, at least he'd have his wife's Bible. He took two steps toward the blaze as three more police cars sped down the street. The sound of their sirens halted him. "O God," he whispered. "O God, please help."

The street was swarming with emergency personnel and curious bystanders. Already, the firemen were roping off the area, pushing the pedestrians to a safe distance. They'd never let him back in now, no matter what he told them he'd lost.

Devastated, Brad accepted that, for tonight anyway, he couldn't go back. It sickened him to think of leaving that precious possession in the burning building, but he had no choice. With someone intent on killing him, all he could do now was flee and pray that God would somehow miraculously protect his treasure and allow Brad to retrieve it someday. He hesitated a moment longer, then glanced over his shoulder as he started to walk again. No one seemed to notice him, so he thrust his hands in his pockets and hurried toward the corner. Behind him, he heard the clamor as more trucks arrived and the emergency crews began evacuating the neighboring houses. He slipped around the corner to a pay phone by the park and hurriedly dropped some coins into the slot.

Marcus answered on the second ring.

"It's me," Brad said. "They're trying to kill me." He glanced over his shoulder again.

"I was afraid of that," Marcus said. "Can you get out of there?"

"I can get a cab."

"Meet me at the church in fifteen minutes. I know a place where you can stay the night. We'll figure something out."

"I don't want to put anyone in danger," Brad responded. "A hotel—"

"Is out of the question. We're family," Marcus insisted. "And we look out for each other."

Brad hesitated, but as another line of police cars headed down his street, he pulled the collar of his jacket around his face. "I'll be there as quick as I can."

"We'll be waiting for you," Marcus said. "And praying. You can count on that."

And Brad was. He slipped his hand into his jacket pocket, and his fingers closed around the mail. He pulled out an envelope and saw it was the letter from Megan. It had finally come. Like a ray of hope in the darkness, God had allowed it to be delivered today, when Brad most needed it. With his distress at losing Christine's Bible so acute, the letter felt like a lifeline—a promise that God had not forgotten or ignored his grief.

He whispered his thanks, then turned and disappeared into the darkness and the anonymity of the city. Behind him, the fire continued to rage, fed, no doubt, by the gas lines that supplied heat and energy to the apartment building. The din of sirens and emergency personnel shattered the otherwise still night. As Brad walked—his heart pounding, his legs aching, and his spirit grieving—he realized that even though he faced what was becoming the darkest and most difficult time of his life, he had hope.

Last night one of the marked passages in Christine's Bible he'd studied before going to bed had been the final words of Jesus in the last chapter of Matthew: "Be sure of this: I am with you always, even to the end of the age."

Brad pulled a memory from his childhood: his mother was getting ready for church, tucking a flower into her hat, straightening her dress until everything was just so, and humming, always humming, usually a hymn. In this particular memory, she was singing to a young Brad who sat next to her dresser and watched as she tied a complicated knot into her scarf.

Though he hadn't heard the hymn in years, the words came back to him now in a divinely inspired moment of encouragement:

> Standing on the promises that cannot fail,
> When the howling storms of doubt and fear assail,
> By the living Word of God I shall prevail,
> Standing on the promises of God.

Brad tapped his fingers on the surface of Megan's letter and thought about the meaning of those words. What better promise, he wondered, and what better time, than to hold fast to the truth that Jesus had promised to be with him, even to the end of the world. With each step, the weight and anxiety of the day began to drop away. Brad talked quietly to the Lord as he headed for one of the major cross streets, where he knew he could hail a cab. The lights of the downtown area loomed ahead, and he headed up the cobbled street and quietly began to whistle the hymn that God had put into his heart.

No matter what the future held, he would always have God's promises. That, he knew for sure.

Just as he would have evil's challenges.

Holding God's Word close in his heart, Brad Benton walked off into the night.

ABRIDGED AUDIO   Available on three CDs or two cassettes for each title. (Books 1–9 read by Frank Muller, one of the most talented readers of audio books today.)

AN EXPERIENCE IN SOUND AND DRAMA   Dramatic broadcast performances of the best-selling Left Behind series. Twelve half-hour episodes on four CDs or three cassettes for each title.

GRAPHIC NOVELS   Created by a leader in the graphic novel market, the series is now available in this exciting new format.

LEFT BEHIND®: THE KIDS   Four teens are left behind after the Rapture and band together to fight Satan's forces in this series for ten- to fourteen-year-olds.

LEFT BEHIND® > THE KIDS < LIVE-ACTION AUDIO   Feel the reality, listen as the drama unfolds. . . . Twelve action-packed episodes available on four CDs or three cassettes.

CALENDARS, DEVOTIONALS, GIFT BOOKS . . .